Copyright

Other Books

Cyrus Cooper Series:

Book One: Dangerous Minds

Book Two: Rogue Faction Part 1

Book Three: Rogue Faction Part 2

Book Four: Halon Seven

Book Six: Surviving Origin Part 2

Black Rock Series:

Black Rock: The Rising - Death Curse

For more information, please visit:

www.XanderWeaver.com

Prologue - Lost Civilization

Eastern Express Train Line

13 years ago

The door smashed open along its track, and the boy was shoved into the compartment. His father's hand was pressed to his shoulder. Roe knew they were being pursued, but they'd lost the tail. The way it had been explained to him, they would be safe if they made it to the train. Now, the boy wasn't so sure. His father ducked ahead one last time into the corridor before gliding the door shut and throwing the feeble lock that doubled as a latch.

"Have a seat," his father said. "Get comfortable. This is the express—it won't make another stop for almost three hours."

Nyland was average-looking and nondescript in almost every regard. Standing about six feet tall and of modest build, he was neither large nor small. His face was clean-shaven and decidedly unassuming. Everything about him was average and middle of the road. Only the set of his eyes spoke of something special. Anyone taking the time to consider his gaze soon realized the man was calculating and intelligent. His eyes continually soaked in all of his surroundings and missed nothing.

The boy moved to the far side of the small cabin and dropped to the shallow bench at the base of the leftmost wall. The messenger bag he'd been carrying was shoved between his feet, and he began rifling through its contents. "You're losing too much blood," he said without looking up. "Let me have a look before you bleed out."

Only ten years old, Roe had experience that exceeded that of most three times his age. Five feet tall, he sported a mop of shaggy brown hair. It hung over his ears and stopped just short of his eyes. Fixing his father with a serious expression, he motioned him to the seat with a single brisk wave of his hand.

Nyland slid the strap of his rucksack from his shoulder and winced through tearing eyes. He wore a flannel shirt unbuttoned almost to his belt. The palm of his right hand was hidden inside the flap of the open shirt. He withdrew it to reveal a balled-up rag mashed in a fist equally soaked in blood.

"Damnit," Roe snapped. "Why didn't you tell me it was this bad?"

He knelt and tore away the last few buttons on Nyland's shirt. His father gasped when Roe pulled the material from the ribs on Nyland's left side.

Roe groaned and gnashed his teeth at the sight. There was blood, and there was a lot of it.

"You said it was just a scratch," Roe muttered. He was already dumping hydrogen peroxide across a sterile pad.

Nyland slipped his left arm from the flannel and began to work his undershirt away from the knife wound as carefully as possible. Coagulated blood had mixed with cotton fibers from the shirt. Roe could see the pain in Nyland's eyes as he carefully separated flesh from the saturated fabric.

2

Roe had the antiseptic pad ready, but Nyland still hadn't fully separated his shirt from the bloody gash in his side. An exhausted sigh, then Nyland glared at Roe. "Are you ready?"

The boy only nodded wordlessly. Both expected this to be a mess.

Nyland ripped the shirt from the wound, and blood spilled from rended flesh. The gash was wider than Roe expected. It must've been deeper, too, considering the rate at which blood continued to flow. Roe hoped to clean and bandage the cut, even applying sutures if required—but this was too severe. The bleeding wouldn't stop.

Roe clamped the peroxide-soaked pad over the gash and pressed hard. The pressure was solid and consistent despite the shudder and sob it brought to Nyland's sweat-soaked visage. Thankfully, the flow of blood stopped instantly. Taking a breath, Roe looked up at his father.

Blinking through a curtain of unrestrained tears, Nyland returned the silent stare. "It was a lucky swing," the older man offered through clenched teeth.

They both knew it was bad. There was a chance Nyland would make it if they could get him to a trauma center soon. While they'd made it onboard the train without drawing the attention of their attackers, if they visited a hospital, they were as good as caught.

This was all for nothing.

Digging to the bottom of his bag once more, Roe retrieved a package of Quick Clot. Tearing the end from the envelope, he was relieved to find it was a clotting pad rather than the powdered form he'd used in the past. The pad was ideal for this type of injury.

He readied a pair of ACE bandage wraps and prepared to swap the peroxide pad for Quick Clot compress. When Roe gave the word, Nyland pulled the pad away. Blood instantly gushed from the four-inch long jagged tear. Understanding the exact dimensions of the cut fully for the first time, Roe shoved the Quick Clot pad through the torrent of blood and slapped it to Nyland's side with the palm of his small hand.

Sweat beaded and tumbled across Nyland's face, and a dull look began to settle in his eyes. Roe recognized the signs. His father was losing far too much blood. "Stay with me," he urged. "We're almost there. We get this thing secured, then I can get you help."

His words seemed to center Nyland. Focus returned to his expression, and a proud smile tugged at the corners of his mouth. He looked down at Roe, clarity and resolve once more a part of his gaze.

"Trade places with me?" Roe said. They did so, Nyland's hand taking responsibility for the Quick Clot bandage while Roe prepared a role of ACE bandages. Though it sucked the breath from his lungs, Nyland clamped both hands over the bandage to maintain pressure on his wound.

Roe was relieved to see the blood flow had finally stopped. By the time he secured the second of the ACE wraps around his father's torso, they both had free hands for the first time. Nyland sagged into the seat and took a few slow, deep breaths. Roe stayed on the floor and simply leaned against the wall. Exhaustion overtook them both, and they sat silently, covered in blood to their elbows.

"Why didn't you tell me it was this bad?" Roe asked and finally broke the silence.

Nyland didn't open his eyes. He slumped with his head tipped against the wall and looked every bit as exhausted as he probably was. "It was a matter of priorities," he said finally. "If we didn't lose Verhoeven's people, it wouldn't matter." He thought for a moment. "I just can't figure out how they found us this time."

Roe let the matter drop. Arguing about it wouldn't help,

and he was more concerned about getting his father to a medical facility. They'd managed to stem the blood flow for the moment, but safety was nowhere in sight. They had no way of knowing if the knife had injured any of his father's internal organs. The cut—or stab—Roe wasn't entirely sure how to think of it, was deeper than he would've thought possible. Though they'd patched each other up plenty of times, neither had ever suffered an injury like this.

This was far more serious.

Roe considered the obvious. Verhoeven was now willing to take their differences to an entirely new level.

Nyland fell asleep where he sat. Roe turned him around to recline on the bench where he would be more comfortable. The effort didn't even bring his father to the edge of consciousness. Not even when Roe shoved his half-emptied pack under Nyland's head for use as a crude pillow.

Roe cleaned himself up in the small sink in the corner of the small cabin. Sooner or later, the conductor would come to collect their tickets. Answering the door covered in blood would only bring a new kind of trouble. Quiet, anonymous travel was the key to their survival; anything they did that drew attention was a potentially fatal mistake.

Nearly two hours had passed when Roe heard a noise outside the cabin. He'd been passing the time watching the verdant greens of the countryside rush by the large window that occupied nearly the entire outer wall of their room. His gaze shot toward the hallway door, and he listened intently. The sound hadn't been much, but it had been enough to focus his awareness.

Roe slid from his seat and knelt beside Nyland. "Dad," he whispered. "Dad—wake up."

Nyland's eyes snapped instantly open. He didn't move a muscle, but his gaze scanned the room. Roe immediately understood that Nyland had no idea where he was. He was groggy from sleep and with blood loss. "It's alright," Roe whispered. "We're on a train. We've got our own cabin. I think someone is in the hall."

Trying to sit upright, Nyland failed. He wheezed, and beads of sweat sprang from his brow. Roe scowled and considered Nyland's ghostly pale complexion and bloodshot eyes. Roe helped his father, tipping him upright on the bench and then bracing him until he was steady enough to sit alone.

"You're a mess," Roe said. "We need to find an emergency facility." He looked slowly around the cabin while considering how few options they had. "Even if it means stopping the train."

Nyland shook his head. "If we stop this train, we're as good as dead. You know better. I'll make it till we reach our stop. Then we'll see what we can do."

Roe glared at his father. "That's not entirely true. You know Verhoeven can't kill you. He wants the codes. He *needs* them. That's not possible if you're dead."

Taking a long look at him with tired eyes, Nyland shook his head. "He'll do anything to get them. That means you're in more danger than me. He'll hurt you to get the information from me. *You know that.*"

"And when you bleed to death, where does that leave me?" It was a selfish question, but Roe knew it would prove his point. They were in the same predicament either way. Nyland needed help, and he needed it soon. While he had hoped that a little sleep would do his father good, he now regretted letting the time pass.

Nyland was looking worse by the minute.

There was another low, hollow noise in the corridor. A new sense of concern widened Nyland's eyes. He looked quickly around the room, then snatched up his discarded flannel shirt. He shoved one arm into a sleeve but stopped short when he couldn't do the same with the other. The stab wound and the bandages had limited his mobility too much.

"Help me with this," he whispered.

Puzzled, Roe helped his father with the remaining sleeve. He pulled at the collar, guided the shirt over Nyland's shoulders, and then folded it back. Nyland sat back and swallowed hard, as if pushing the pain physically away. He was visibly winded.

More noise came from the hallway. It sounded like multiple people were moving around carefully in a confined space. Three so far, if Roe estimated the noises correctly. That they were trying to keep quiet at all was a bad sign. One look at his father, and Roe knew Nyland was thinking the same.

"They're here?" Roe said. It was a question as much as a statement.

Disaster.

They were cornered on a moving train with nowhere to run. Nyland was injured, mortally, Roe feared, and they couldn't fall back to safety.

Not this time.

Nyland ground his teeth and began picking at the breast pocket of his flannel shirt. He undid the button and fished out a small, thin, handheld device. Roe was surprised to see it. The device was what Verhoeven had sent his people to retrieve. Nyland usually kept in a secret, secure location. Life as they knew it was over if they were caught with it now.

Nyland took a long look at the device in his hand and made a crucial decision. There was no question Verhoeven's people had found them. The idea he'd lost the group before doubling back to retrieve Roe was nothing more than wishful thinking. The train was their best escape, and now they were cornered. Worse than anything, Nyland didn't have any fight left in him. He was running on empty, with no energy reserve to protect the device and no way to save his son.

And then there was the book. Nyland fished it from the pack with a trembling hand. The small journal was almost an inch thick. The cover was rich dark leather that looked almost red in the cabin's light. The natural texture of the leather had worn thin over the years. It was nearly as important to Nyland as the device and Roe.

"Here," he said, sliding the book into the wide hip pocket of Roe's heavy flannel over-shirt. "Best keep it close. You could separate from the bag—we mustn't lose the book."

The hallway door rattled gently on its track for a long second before falling eerily silent. A moment later the door shook again, this time violently. The sad excuse for the lock quickly gave way, and the door slid open with a crash. A tall, broad-shouldered man stepped into the room. He had short dark hair and beady, hooded eyes set deep beneath eyebrows that bridged both eyes without a gap. Nyland recognized him instantly. Even if the face wasn't familiar, the long-bladed weapon in his hand was a dead giveaway. Nyland's hand went to the wound at his side reflexively as he stepped backward. His back hit the cabin window. There was nowhere to run.

The blade in Unibrow's hand was a massive Kukri knife. It had a six-inch grip with a fourteen-inch long, wide, flat blade extending at a thirty-degree angle. A vicious weapon, it was razor sharp. It had split Nyland's flesh earlier in the morning, blood having been spilled before Nyland noticed the weapon. He'd since seen the man use the knife to slash through chainlink with a single blow. The fence that should have offered Nyland time to escape hadn't even slowed the assassin. The miscalculation had nearly cost him his life.

It still might.

8

A petite woman stepped through the doorway next. She had short blond hair and wore a dark sweater and jeans. Though she looked to be in her early thirties, Nyland knew better. She fixed him with a penetrating stare and stood beside the much larger figure of Unibrow.

"You almost got away again," she said. Her voice carried a British accent, though Nyland also knew that to be misleading. For a brief moment, he wondered if she even noticed her own accent after all these years. She'd been using it for so long that he sincerely doubted it. "I almost didn't check the train. It seemed too obvious. At least the game of cat and mouse is finally over."

The bear of a man adjusted his grip on his blade only slightly. The weapon was threatening enough by itself, and Roe stepped forward to block the man's access to his father. Nyland was surprised. Though he didn't want to see Roe hurt, he knew they shared a fate no matter what happened next. The end was only a matter of time.

The woman laughed at the ten-year-old boy's aggressive posture. "This one seems young for a bodyguard," she smirked.

The moment of truth had arrived. Though he'd always feared being cornered in such a way, somehow Nyland never let himself believe he would be outmaneuvered. Confident, apparently overly so, that he could prove his theory before they caught up to them. If he could only demonstrate what he believed in his heart, it would mean there was still hope for his people—and it could keep billions of innocents from experiencing senseless tragedy.

Nyland looked at the device in his hand. If he turned it over to Sasha, she would take it to Verhoeven, and the fool's efforts would once more be back on track. That was unacceptable. It was better to destroy the device. Without it, Verhoeven could do nothing with the codes, even if he could somehow acquire them. Unfortunately, no matter what happened next, Nyland knew he and Roe wouldn't leave the train alive. If he destroyed the device, Sasha would kill them both. She'd never had the self-control to suffer such a defeat with a sense of dignity or grace.

"You've got guts, kid," Sasha chided. "Get out of the way before my friend hands them to you."

Nyland was staring at the device in his hand, a desperate idea taking form. It was thwarted when he heard a quiet gasp slip from Sasha's lips. He looked up and found her staring at Roe.

"What have you done, Nyland?" she muttered. Her voice was quiet; the statement perhaps made to herself. Her eyes bounced back and forth from Roe to Nyland, where he stood occluded behind Roe's right shoulder.

"What have you done?" she repeated. This time anger touched her incredulous tone.

It was the eyes, Nyland knew. They gave it away. His mop of long hair masked many of Roe's features, and thankfully, he'd received most of his facial features from his mother. The boy's strong jaw and wide cheeks offered no resemblance to Nyland.

But the eyes did.

Not only were they an exact match for color, but there was no masking the penetrating stare or the sharp, calculating intelligence behind them. The eyes marked Roe as obviously as any brand. One only needed to take the time to look.

"Just like I said," Nyland countered. "It's possible. And it's the best solution. *Verhoeven is wrong!*"

If anything, Sasha became more outraged by the statement. Wrath flared in her gaze.

"You've become too close to the experiment, doctor," she snapped. "You've jeopardized everything! And for *this*?"

The writing was on the wall—they weren't leaving here

alive. Nyland was now sure he had no choice. His mind snapped back to his previous plan. It wouldn't work without high-level tachyon bombardment. The necessary levels were only ever common during the most dramatic solar storms, and even then, such levels were only possible on the sun's surface. There was no way to predict such a storm or initiate such an event.

Then he remembered reading about a little publicized experiment conducted at CERN in Switzerland. Scientists had been studying tachyon emissions for over a decade, but they had only recently started experimenting with tachyon emitters. If those emitters were active, they could be manipulated... an active burst used here and now. What Nyland considered would likely derail the CERN experiment—it might even undo everything mankind thought it knew about faster-than-light tachyon particles. Nonetheless, how it would interact with the zero-point energy source in his handheld would be critical.

Nyland tapped the screen of his device with speed and precision. He had to override several safety protocols to create the feedback wave in its power core. Perhaps just as critically, he had only seconds to accomplish the complex procedure. If Sasha got her hands on the device, more than just he and Roe were lost. If he and Roe were taken prisoner, it would be only a matter of time before he'd be forced to give up the code. Verhoeven and his people would stop at nothing. And now that they had Roe and knew of their connection, it was information that would undoubtedly be leveraged.

"What are you doing?" Sasha demanded.

Shit!

His time was at an end. Nyland tapped the last confirmation override into the device and swiped a bloody finger across the screen to dim the display. He leaned forward and whispered to Roe, "They must never possess this." Unseen by Sasha or her henchman, he slipped the thin device into the back pocket of Roe's jeans.

The man with the knife raised the blade high and stepped toward Roe. The blade flashed in the light as it arced downward. There was a jarring, keening scream that lasted a second at most. Unibrow shrieked and dropped to the floor in a huddled heap. Nyland felt his mouth go dry. He'd seen the event clearly, though he couldn't believe his eyes. Unibrow had swung the wide blade in a diagonal slash set to cleave Roe in two. But Roe had reached out with one hand and grabbed the wrist in a white-knuckled fist to hold the handle of the hooked Kukri. He stopped the swing in mid-air. He must've driven a thumb into the nerves at the base of the brute's wrist because when Roe slapped the broad flat of the blade with the palm of his free hand, the knife dropped from Unibrow's grip. Roe had snatched the falling blade from the air as it fell and brought it back across his attacker's arm in a powerful backward swing. The razor-sharp edge had lopped Unibrow's hand off with no apparent resistance. In the span of a single heartbeat, the hand had fallen away and struck the floor.

Nyland was aghast. He'd never seen anything like it—certainly not from the likes of Roe. For his part, Roe simply pointed the blade at Sasha in a silent warning. Unibrow lay quivering on the floor in the fetal position. He cupped the bloody stump that was his right arm and made a fruitless effort to stem the arterial flow.

Sasha's eyes were the size of silver dollars. She stepped backward and struck the doorframe before coming to a jarring halt. Her hand dug into the waistband of her jeans and extracted a small semiautomatic pistol. She swung it and aimed at Roe's chest.

"That was impressive." She tried to look confident, but her voice's cracking undermined the effort. She seemed short of breath. "No one has ever gotten the drop on that big dumb fool. I guess he's paying the price." She briefly looked at her associate, bleeding all over the floor.

"Stop this, now!" Nyland shouted. He touched Roe's shoulder and pulled him to his side. There was a real chance Roe would move against Sasha and the gun. It was a mistake he wouldn't survive.

"Give me the codes and you can go," Sasha said. She moved the gun and pointed it squarely at Nyland. "I only want the codes."

It was a lie, Nyland knew. Particularly given the revelation that Roe was his son. Their people couldn't nurture children. She wouldn't let them leave, now knowing what he'd accomplished.

The device in Roe's back pocket beeped once. A second later, it chimed again. This time it was a long, shrill tone. A smile crossed Nyland's face. A tachyon emission had been detected. The device would attract the particles. Since they traveled faster than the speed of light and could move through solid matter—even through the planet itself—it would be a matter of seconds before the zero-point power source of the handheld went critical. Once that started, the feedback loop would become catastrophic.

Roe shot a desperate glance at Nyland. It was starting. The boy could already sense the disturbance; he was standing at the event horizon. Suddenly, Nyland felt it, too. Something akin to a static charge in the air. First, it made his lips tingle. His fingertips and toes quickly followed.

A desperate look crossed Sasha's face. Her gun shifted quickly between Nyland and Roe. She wasn't sure what was happening, but she knew Nyland had done something. A lightheaded sensation struck Nyland, the idea that Sasha was just crazy enough to shoot first and sort out the rest later. Sure enough, her nervous finger tightened on the gun's trigger.

The cabin floor flexed beneath their feet as the sheet metal under the carpeting buckled. Sasha's eyes went wide again as the walls flexed outward as if the pressure inside the room had suddenly increased exponentially. When Nyland's eyes found Roe again, he saw the boy's feet floating several inches above the floor. He was suspended in mid-air. It seemed that even Roe wasn't aware of it happening. The boy seemed more concerned with the grinding and grating noises coming from the walls, the floor, and the ceiling as they were pushed outward by inches and then feet. It was like some invisible bubble was being inflated inside the cabin. It wasn't affecting the people present, but the room seemed ready to come apart at its seams.

Roe's long hair stood out from his head in every direction. The gun spun from Sasha's hand and clung to the ceiling as if stuck to an electromagnet.

Sasha's voice resorted to the native tongue of their people. "Nyland, you fool! What have you done?"

What started as a sense of static in the air was quickly escalating. Nyland's flesh tingled from head to toe. There was a palpable sensation of electricity flowing all around them. An oblong energy bubble had formed around Roe's body, and it was spreading outward. He was suspended inside a translucent blue bubble as it expanded slowly with him at the center.

The train car rocked as the wheels beneath it began to shriek. It was the unmistakable sound of metal binding against metal. In this case, the train trucks were locked against the rails. No, that wasn't right, Nyland realized when the car rocked violently again. It was as if the car's mass had suddenly grown by orders of magnitude. The car was crushing the wheel and brake system on which it rode. The body of the car was becoming more dense by the second. A gravitational force surrounding the bubble where Roe was suspended drove the train into the earth, even as it sailed along the rails.

The effects would only intensify as the event horizon expanded. Roe was riding the edge of it, so he would be safe.

14

But Nyland knew that his own time had come to an end. Once the chain reaction had begun, there was no stopping it. The entire car rocked violently once more, and the intense shriek of rending steel intensified. Sasha read the situation for what it was. Nyland saw the conclusion of the analysis tally in her eyes as she struggled to remain upright in the twisting cabin doorway. She offered a contemptuous stare, but the scream of scorn was lost to the sound of crushing wood, plastic, and steel.

Nyland smiled. He had defeated her in the end. Verhoeven would never regain his prize, and Sasha had missed her chance to communicate what she'd learned about Roe's existence. If Roe survived the eminent cataclysm, he would be safe from Verhoeven and the rest of their people.

His eyes shifting to fall on Roe, Nyland saw utter confusion on his son's features. Roe had no idea what was happening. His expression seemed frozen in time. That could very well be the case for all he knew, Nyland decided. While he knew more than most about the physics of this world, the chain reaction he'd started by interfacing the zero-point energy cell with the tachyon particles had been unheard of since the dawn of this world's creation. While Nyland knew the bubble containing Roe sat upon the event horizon of the chain reaction, thereby making him safe from all that was taking place, he had no idea what kind of ancillary effects this anomaly would have on his son. Furthermore, Nyland was sure this desperate move had sentenced every other soul on the train to certain death.

Sasha eyed her gun, still stuck to the ceiling of the room. Her head turned, and her gaze fell upon the unmoving form of Roe in the center of the bubble. She must have recognized the bubble as safety because she took a hasty step forward...and then another, moving for the bubble's threshold.

The moment her body touched the expanding threshold, her entire body was turned to ashes in a flash of light. She was vaporized like a winged insect flying headlong into a bug zapper powered by a nuclear reactor. There was a blinding flash, and then only a cloud of charred dust was left to hang in the air where she had just been.

It was fitting, Nyland thought with a smile. She'd been the one to doom them, after all. Suddenly feeling increasingly weak, he sank to the bench, which was still somewhat intact at the edge of the room. He could see the energy field expanding. It would be on him in less than a minute by his calculations. That didn't matter. The wound in his side had been as much of a death sentence as the energy field. Bleeding out being a slower and more painful way to go, by his estimation.

He watched Roe's unmoving form and silently wished his young son luck in whatever came next. The boy had never asked to be thrown into this life, but Nyland considered him his most significant achievement in every possible way. Nyland's only honest regret was that Roe's mother had never lived to see what her boy had become. She'd died during childbirth. Still, she'd given her life so the boy could live.

Now Nyland would too.

Roe was the key to the fate of an entire people, but Nyland had never tried to explain that. He always believed they would have more time.

There was more screeching of metal and then what sounded like steel being torn apart. A small explosion reverberated from under the train car. It was followed a second later by another and then another. The car rocked hard to one side and threw Nyland violently against the windows. The floor dropped away as the car's undercarriage disintegrated entirely.

The wall behind Nyland flexed outward, and he saw the same expansion across the ceiling. The world began to spin. The train had derailed, Nyland knew. Hundreds of tons of additional train cars collided with the back of his sleeper car as it launched from the tracks. Forty cars left the tracks one after the other in a cascading pile of carnage.

The last thing Nyland saw, half a second before his head struck the ceiling, was his son still suspended in the growing energy bubble. Roe's face betrayed no knowledge of what was happening outside the energy field. Nyland offered his silent son a brief smile as a goodbye, and then he was gone...along with more than 400 other passengers of the southbound express train.

---

6 miles south of Lusk, Wyoming

2 months ago

The helicopter circled several shattered acres of land in the middle of the open Wyoming plain. Randall Graham leaned to the plexiglass window and studied the bustle of men and equipment below. He estimated more than two dozen pieces of heavy excavating equipment and what had to be over a hundred workmen. The primary dig site was small by comparison, a circle of hard-packed earth perhaps fifty yards in diameter, the clay scarred by machinery and months of physical labor. A rigid tower of steel girders and a massive spool of braided cable marked the dig site. The tower stood just shy of 150 feet, according to the briefing material he'd been provided.

Graham shook his head and considered the countless man-hours already gone into this project. The numbers and associated stress fueled the burning of an ulcer in his gut that had to be growing. At least, for once, the American taxpayers weren't footing the bill for the folly. That fact failed to make the endeavor any less embarrassing. News of the dig had been kept under wraps so far, but there was no question the project was working on borrowed time. Word would spread...it always did.

The airframe shuddered and Graham was flung against the four-point harness of his seatbelt. Bile rose in the back of his throat as the chopper turned and made a second attempt to descend. He clamped his fists and fought a rising fear, temper, and emotional reaction to the flight and was ordered to observe the final stage of the dig.

Why are the bosses taking this project seriously to begin with?

Randall Graham was from the Office of Strategic Planning. His department had had boots on the ground since the project's groundbreaking. Every moment had been overseen without fail. Charlatans, Graham had called the group when they first proposed the dig. A waste of time and money was his evaluation. He had no patience for the Neo-modern cult, calling itself the Order of Origin. It was a mystery how they'd gotten Washington to take them seriously enough to allow the dig.

In fairness, though he knew little of the cult, what he'd put together in recent months suggested it was unlike conventional religious groups. Then again, traditional wasn't the best description of the organization. Other groups preached either creationism or evolutionism in one form or another. The Order of Origin espoused something closer to intelligent design, claiming that life and our universe wasn't God's work but that of other men. To Graham, it was circular logic. He had no patience for any of it.

One of the group's more outrageous claims was that Homo Sapiens were not the first sentient life to inhabit the planet. Outrageously, they said that another race came before man, only to have every trace of their existence wiped from the earth roughly 900 million years ago.

It was an audacious claim but no more outrageous than their purported willingness to prove it. Without going into details, the group's leader, Radley Verhoeven, had provided the coordinates for the dig site and created a privately funded foundation to organize the excavation.

18

The next thing Graham knew, his federally funded team was tasked with oversight of the circus. And while he was supposed to be the ringmaster, he felt more like the guy responsible for keeping the clown car running.

The chopper touched down, and a man dressed in grimy coveralls and wearing a hardhat rushed forward to throw the side door open. "Welcome to the dig," he hollered over the sound of still-spinning rotors. "I'm Bob Caplan."

Graham stepped to the muddy ground and shook an offered hand. Bob passed over a hard hat before moving away from the still-quieting chopper. Giving Graham a quick once over, Bob pointed to a long trailer that appeared to function as the operations office. "We better get you a set of coveralls and boots." His grin was good-natured, but Graham could tell the man found his jacket and tie amusing.

Looking down at his already ruined leather shoes, Graham grumbled a response and fought back a curse. His eyes moved up his own form and he considered the rest of his suit. If there was any chance of it surviving the trip, it was best to take Bob up on the offer.

Bob was still grinning when Graham followed him up the steps and into the trailer.

Passing a set of clean coveralls, Bob grabbed a soiled wingtip from the floor and raised it in a showman-like comparison to one of the steel-toed work boots. "You didn't come prepared, did you?" he said. "You'll break your neck wearing shoes like this around here. It's slippery. Have you ever been to a dig like this?"

"You mean a complete waste of time?" Graham mumbled. He didn't want to take his issues out on the foreman, but he hadn't much restraint left after looking at the wreckage of his four hundred-dollar shoes.

Bob stopped comparing the shoe to the boots and shot Graham a confused look. "For the longest time, I thought that too." He studied Graham as if he were trying to come to a decision. "Wait," he said. "You don't know, do you?"

"Know what?"

Bob's eyes suddenly lit with the kind of excitement that was impossible to fake. "We did a sounding when the bore came up this morning. I don't know what it is, but there's something down there."

Leaning back on the old folding chair, Graham just stared. Bob nodded, then tossed away the shoe before passing over the set of boots. Graham blinked several times, his mind taking long seconds to process the words before finally accepting the footwear. "What's your depth?" he finally asked.

"We just passed 21,000 feet. We should reach the object just before 22,000. We've slowed our decent in preparation. We're taking soundings every fifteen minutes."

"Jesus," Graham muttered, his words low and incredulous. "There's really something down there? You're sure?"

"Absolutely. According to the readings, it's big. 20 by 30 by 30."

"Inches?" It was a dumb question, but Graham wanted to be absolutely sure they were on the same page.

A slow shake of the head from Bob. "Feet," he said in a deadly serious tone. "And it's right where the hippies said it would be—give or take half a meter. What did they claim it would be in it, anyway? No one ever said."

Acid roiled anew in Graham's gut. The Order of Origin. All of this effort came back to them and their outrageous claims. The only thing worse than them wasting his time was for them actually to be proven right.

He'd never even considered the possibility. Not once.

Hippies? That was amusing, now that he considered it.

They were about as far away from hippies as any group could be. They believed a far more advanced version of the human race once inhabited the earth. Their rise and fall had come before that of modern man. The Order of Origin, like the supposed lost civilization, believed in technology and science above all else. If they were somehow proven right…

Graham shook the thought away. Whatever was down there was larger than expected. The numbers rattled around in his head. 20x30x30 would mean 18,000 cubic feet, depending on the wall's thickness. If the object had remained intact under millions of tons of rock and had been in place for hundreds of millions of years, as Verhoeven claimed, the walls must be thick.

Still…

What the hell is down there?

"Is…" Graham stumbled for words. "Whatever it is…is it still intact?"

"We can't be certain until we reach it, but the imaging suggests it is. According to the readings, the dimensions of the container are precise, and the surfaces are true. The edges are square, showing no signs of damage or distortion. That suggests it maintained integrity. Whatever it is, it's stood up to all the pushing, pulling, and grinding the planet has thrown at it.

"And there's no chance this cult put this…*thing*…down there recently?"

Bob shook his head. "Listen, bud," he said. "Suit up, and don't forget your hard hat. I've got to get back out there. We're in the home stretch, and I need to keep an eye on my guys. We've been working for three and a half months on this project and are about to break through. We're not cutting as deep as the Soviets but making a much wider hole. I'll see you out there."

Graham watched as Bob ducked out the door at a speed that belied his age. He looked like a kid on Christmas. It was hard to blame him. The Russian Federation's dig he referred to held the world record for depth, but it was a different beast entirely. A nine-inch diameter hole was drilled in the Soviet tundra between 1970 and 1995. When the project was finally abandoned, it had reached a depth of 28,143 feet, or 5.33 miles. In contrast, this project had gone three quarters that depth in a little over three months, thanks partly to what was learned during the Soviet-Russian effort. The rest had to do with technological advances—and Radley Verhoeven's seemingly bottomless bank account.

Graham pulled the coveralls over his shoulders. He laced the bulky work boots and was still working the zipper on the front of the jumpsuit as he headed out the door.

Bob's excitement was contagious.

Chapter 1 - Specialized Load

Bangkok Thailand

11:06 pm

Beneath the shadows of a rundown building, Cyrus watched the dilapidated structure across the street. He'd been surveying the defunct two-story warehouse for more than an hour. Almost a dozen people had moved up and down the wide trash-filled street, but no one had approached the building in question. The noise of the surrounding city was constant. He was in a rundown industrial zone near the edge of the city limits. Few streetlights functioned, and the area seemed to grow more desolate with each passing moment. It must've been why his contact had chosen the location for the meeting. It was just after 11 p.m., and this portion of the city was just about deserted.

Bangkok had a population of more than 6 million. Light from more gentrified parts of the city could be seen in the distance to the west. Traffic and faint sounds of pedestrian nightlife carried in the air if he listened hard. Cyrus knew it would be a dozen blocks, maybe more, before he could lose himself in a crowd if things went south here. Still, there wasn't yet reason for concern. He was meeting Kastor, a contact from his time with the Coalition. Kastor had always been dependable, and as far as he knew, Cyrus was still with law enforcement. It would be a simple exchange, and then Cyrus could head home.

The sound of a revving motor echoed in the distance. Cyrus slid more deeply into the shadows of his perch on the rickety second-floor fire escape. An old Jeep rolled into view and stopped in the street between him and the warehouse he'd been watching. The vehicle sat motionless, at least two silhouettes visible in the cab. After a few seconds, the driver accelerated aggressively to close the distance between him and the front of the warehouse. The Jeep stopped directly before the wide double doors at the facade's center.

This was a problem. Kastor was supposed to be alone.

A man jumped from the back of the Jeep and heaved at one of two massive sliding warehouse doors. Cyrus scowled. The Jeep was an unwelcome intrusion, and seeing the man wrestling uselessly on the door only reinforced his opinion that the new arrival meant trouble. Kastor had chosen this location. He knew the site inside and out. He would've known that the massive rotting front doors hung on rails far too rusted to operate.

These men weren't with Kastor.

Cyrus checked his watch. It was 11:14 p.m. The meeting was set to take place in less than a minute. If Kastor knew their location had been compromised, he would move to the fallback location. If he didn't, he would be inside the warehouse right now...and trapped.

Cyrus watched as two more men climbed from the jeep and rounded the right side of the building. They were heading for a service door and would be inside in less than a minute. A flash of light from the alley on the building's left told him that the men from the Jeep were not alone. Another team was moving around the rear of the building.

Clearly, they didn't know the building well. Still, they appeared confident in their mission.

There was no question the meeting had been compromised.

Cyrus moved silently and traced the path of the three men. He checked the Jeep as he passed, confirming that no one had remained behind. He followed the group's path through the service entrance and stepped into the darkness of a dilapidated hallway.

Ahead, the corridor opened into a small office. The rear wall of the space had mostly collapsed, likely due to exposure to the elements. The expansive warehouse was visible beyond. Windows high on the tall two-story walls had broken out, and roof sections were missing at random intervals. Pale moonlight showed through and illuminated the indecipherable wreckage covering the structure's floor. The air smelled of mold and rot.

Three men with automatic rifles had spread out across the room. They were taking their time and advancing through the massive space with care and precision. Cyrus was dealing with skilled soldiers, that much was clear. They were moving through a debris field of broken and decaying refuse—plus parts of the collapsed roof—and doing it silently.

Two rapid gunshots boomed from somewhere beyond the long room's far wall. A man yelled and something large crashed. Twenty seconds later, a man was shoved into the warehouse at gunpoint. He had his hands on his head and was struggling to stay on his feet.

The three soldiers Cyrus had followed quickly moved to surround the clumsy man. Two additional soldiers moved in from their positions in the wings while another at the center kept his rifle trained on the newcomer. They were skilled in their teamwork, Cyrus observed once again. Now that he was closer, he could make out their features. Though they were in casual dress, they were unmistakably Chinese military.

Here for the same reason as me.

"Keep your hands on your head," the soldier in the center ordered. His words were Chinese, even though they were in Thailand. One of the wingmen moved in to frisk the prisoner. Cyrus could see him clearly now. It was Kastor. They patted him down and bound his hands behind his back with flex cuffs.

Two men exchanged hushed words in Chinese. Cyrus had a working knowledge of the language. He could understand most of it, though he wouldn't dare attempt to speak it. It could've been worse. They were in Thailand, and he didn't even possess a working knowledge of Thai.

A pair of additional men moved through the doorway behind Kastor. They were also Chinese, and both were armed with H&K automatic rifles.

The fact that the Chinese had crossed into Thailand to retrieve what Kastor had stolen spoke to how seriously they were taking the data breach. That was odd. It was mostly satellite telemetry, nothing of substantial value. Certainly nothing worthy of this kind of response.

Now, Kastor was in trouble for what should've been a relatively small favor. Cyrus continued to observe the room. He was concealed at the edge of a large section of wrecked roof about thirty yards from the men surrounding Kastor.

It was six against one. Well, technically six against two. Kastor could be handy in a fight. He had a slight build, but he was wiry and fast. Unfortunately, he was almost useless with his hands bound behind his back.

"The thumb drive," the man in charge ordered. "Where is

it?"

Kastor looked confused. He said something in what must've been Thai because Cyrus couldn't understand it.

The soldier grunted. "English? How about English?"

That brought a nod from Kastor. "I speak English. Some of my best friends are American," he smiled.

Kastor spoke Chinese too, Cyrus knew. That comment had been for his benefit. Kastor was letting Cyrus know he was aware of his presence.

The soldier motioned to one of the two men bracketing Kastor. The guard slammed the stock of his rifle into Kastor's side. He spiraled in the fall, hitting the floor with a baleful whimper likely caused by the ubiquitous rubble.

Cyrus smiled. The odds had just improved. It was about to be two against six again. There was a reason he'd been willing to work with Kastor. The man was resourceful.

The lead soldier lowered his rifle and swung an arm at the men near the back of the room. "Search the building," he ordered. "He was meeting someone. Find him and retrieve the drive."

Two men disappeared in different directions. A third headed back in the direction where they'd found Kastor. That would take him to the front offices.

Only a few safe paths were available for traversing the wreckage covering the warehouse floor. The soldier moved quickly to his left, which put him on direct course for Cyrus's position. Cyrus slipped a few inches further into the shadowy concealment of his improvised hide and slowed his breathing. The soldier passed within arms reach of him but never noticed. He was rushing to reach the front of the building to fulfill orders.

Three against two, Cyrus thought. If he moved quickly, he could take out the commander and the pair of guards before the others returned to report their fruitless search. Two on three—he would take those odds any day, but he still had one major disadvantage.

These soldiers were just doing their job. They were trying to recover data that had been stolen from their country. Killing them wasn't an option in this situation. Cyrus was only using the data to prove a theory, and China was just reacting to a perceived threat to its interests. Cyrus had killed in self-defense and never lost sleep over it, but this wasn't sanctioned. It would be in cold blood.

Killing these men was a line he wasn't willing to cross.

———————

Cyrus selected two chunks of crumbling concrete from the refuse at his feet. Both were twice the size of his fist, but while one was solid and rocky, the other was ready to disintegrate into dust in his grip. He swung the crumbing chunk, pitching it high into the rafters at the opposite end of the room. It streaked unseen through two shafts of moonlight glowing through holes in the collapsed ceiling before striking the far wall and vaporizing. The strike took the form of gravel bounding as it stuck different obstructions, the echo challenging to place in the space. Loose material continued to clatter as it bounced from higher surfaces to the floor. The single throw made far more noise than Cyrus could've hoped for.

Already in motion, he bolted from his position of cover. He overhanded the second chunk of concrete like a fastball and caught the soldier to Kastor's right fully in the face. The man's feet spun through a shaft of moonlight as he tumbled head over heels. Kastor didn't miss a beat. The flex cuffs fell from his wrists, cut free using whatever jagged debris he'd palmed after being knocked to the ground by the man with the rifle. He spun to the guard to his left, jamming his palm hard beneath the man's chin and kicking his feet out from under him. The guard went down hard and didn't move.

By the time Cyrus halved the distance between him and the soldier in charge, the figure was already shaking off the blow from the thrown litter. His rifle was coming up, and his eyes flashed quickly around the room. Cyrus vaulted a pile of rubble, grabbing a three-foot length of inch thick rebar as he passed. His boots struck the ground, and he brought the steel rod down across the top of the man's automatic rifle. There was a whump as the solid steel of the bar won out over the hollow metal barrel of the assault weapon.

The gun tumbled from the guard's hands. Cyrus turned at the hips and hit him with everything he had. The soldier was a smaller man. The uppercut caught him beneath the jaw and lifted him from the ground. He dropped into a pile amidst the rubble two feet away. Though he was breathing, he certainly wasn't conscious.

"Took you long enough," Kastor scoffed. "For a minute, I thought you would let the bastards take me."

Retrieving the rifle from the floor, Cyrus examined it. It was an H&K MP5. Not exactly standard issue for the Chinese army, but then it wasn't normal for them to operate in Thailand either. He looked at the short barrel of the compact rifle. It was creased and crooked, with a gouge midway across the mounted rail atop the barrel. Firing the weapon might result in it exploding in his face. He ejected the magazine and slipped it into his back pocket.

"Made a mess of that one?" Kastor said with a grin. He was holding a pair of matching weapons. He tossed one to Cyrus. "Why didn't you just shoot them?" he asked.

They'd taken the three men down relatively quietly. There were three more soldiers in the building. Then Cyrus noticed another leg lying among the junk.

Make that two more.

Either could return at any time. "We can't kill them," Cyrus whispered.

Kastor looked at him like a pair of wings had just grown from the sides of his head. "What the hell are you talking about?"

"It's a long story," Cyrus said. "We take them down, but without fatalities." His tone left no room to argue.

Kastor appeared incredulous. He glanced at the unconscious men at his feet. "What if they don't feel the same way?"

Cyrus smiled. He motioned for Kastor to follow and then ducked back to the pile of rubble where he'd previously been hiding. He didn't want to be out in the open when the two remaining soldiers returned.

"I don't get it," Kastor whispered. They were kneeling behind a pile of collapsed ceiling wreckage. Kastor was eyeing the rear of the room while Cyrus watched the front. "All of this over some useless telemetry? It isn't even classified. Well, not highly classified. What's the big deal? They don't want us to know they've got birds pointed in that direction?"

Cyrus debated how much he should share. "It's not the data they're worried about. I've got similar data from Russian satellites. For a change, everyone has their best hardware pointed out into space. They're worried about something else and overreacting in response."

"Pointed into space? What the hell are they looking for?"

The question made Cyrus smile. Things had already gotten out of hand. "That's the billion-dollar question. I'm just trying to prove—or disprove—a theory. I'm not entirely sure what has everyone so worked up. This is just the fastest way to stir the pot. It should've been a cakewalk. I'm sorry to get you into trouble over it."

Kastor shrugged. A look that said, *hey, it's what I do*. He didn't seem very concerned about it. If anything, he seemed more troubled by Cyrus's no-casualties requirement. There was a lot a man like Kastor could, and likely would, read into that. Foremost of which was that Cyrus wasn't here on Coalition orders.

"Now what?" Kastor asked.

"Do you have the data?"

Pulling up his pants leg, Kastor reached into the side of his sock. He fished out a small USB flash drive and held it in the pale light. The drive was about as wide as Cyrus's thumb and half as long. It had a rigid steel case with a sturdy cap screwed over the USB port. "I still don't know what good it'll do you," he whispered.

Cyrus shrugged. His fingers were still crossed on that very question. With the way his trip to Thailand was shaping up, he was becoming more heavily invested in a wild theory with every passing minute. It was supposed to be a simple transaction. Meet with Kastor, buy the drive, then exfiltrate back to base.

Holding up the drive, Kastor glared at Cyrus. "My money?" he asked.

"Already transferred and in your account."

Kastor's brows arched. "Transferred *before* the meet?" He was suspicious.

"I transferred payment right before the Chinese showed up," he explained. "You've always been good for it. I knew there wouldn't be a problem."

Kastor still looked unsure.

Cyrus fished his phone from his pocket and held it up. "You can check it yourself if you don't believe me."

That brought a smile from Kastor. "Oh, I believe you," he grinned. "That's why it's funny. Only you would do something like that on *faith*." He made the last word sound like an expletive.

Cyrus grinned. "You've never steered me wrong. That's good enough for me."

In truth, Cyrus was more concerned with the two remaining guards just then. They were still out there, and the opposition did not share his reluctance to kill. The sooner they escaped, the better.

Kastor swiped his finger across the end of the flash drive. Cyrus saw a light flash green and knew the drive's encryption had been disabled. His friend passed the device over. "It's been a pleasure doing business with—"

A scuffing sound drew their attention back to the warehouse floor. One of the guards had returned from a search of the offices. They saw the man become more alert when he walked closer to the room's center and found himself alone.

That wasn't going to make things easier, Cyrus decided.

A voice called from the front of the room. The other soldier was also back. He looked equally confused by the missing personnel. He was speaking to his compatriot, calling across the open space. Distress was apparent in his tone. They didn't have much time, Cyrus knew. The pair were closing on the area where their fallen comrades lay.

Cyrus slipped the magazine from the MP5 and examined the round on top. His eyes widened, and he pushed the top round free using his thumb. He held the strange bullet up to the light. It was a specialized load from a company called G2 Research. He'd read about the ammunition but never seen it firsthand. The slug in each round was precision machined from copper. The center was milled from each slug, similar to hollow point rounds but more extreme. With these slugs, the remaining outer jacket was cut down its length. This created what looked like 9 vicious copper teeth that extended nearly the entire length of the slug. If the round spun fast enough, it looked like it would become a miniature saw blade. In truth, its effects were far more devastating. While a hollow-point round was designed to flatten or mushroom upon impact with the target to inflict more significant harm, the round from G2 was designed so those 9 copper teeth would splay outward like fingers opening from a closed fist. They were designed to tear tissue and organs apart with utmost efficiency. It was a devastating round. This bullet would create a small hole entering the human body, but the damage it did after piercing human flesh would be catastrophic every time.

These boys came to play.

Cyrus tossed the round to Kastor and watched his friend's eyes bulge with comprehension. "Those bastards," he muttered.

Cyrus nodded. He thought about the man he'd hit with the rebar and how Kastor had gone for the head and neck of the man nearest him. "Were they all wearing body armor?" he asked.

Kastor nodded. "It wasn't obvious at first. I only noticed it when that prick took a poke at me."

Cyrus smiled and slipped the magazine back into his rifle. He adjusted the folding stock for close-quarters operation, then eyed Kastor. As nasty as the copper rounds were, they didn't hold up against body armor. They were hell on soft tissue but much less effective than normal rounds when impacting a flack jacket. "Solid hits to center mass," Cyrus instructed. "We make sure they catch everything in the vest."

Kastor looked confused at first, but understanding quickly spread across his face. He nodded. They peered around opposite sides of their rubble pile. The soldiers were converging on the center of the floor. They moved in and out of streaks of moonshine as they went.

Cyrus waited until the men drew within view of their downed friends. When the first man's posture stiffened, Cyrus tipped himself out of concealment and lowered to

33

one knee. "Hey!" he called. "Over here!"

Both men turned at the same time. Spinning in a startled response, their rifles rose and swept for a target. Cyrus and Kastor opened fire at the same time. They both loosed rapid shots, three rounds each, as fast as they could squeeze the trigger. Their targets caught every slug center of their vests. Both men were knocked from their feet by the onslaught.

Cyrus rushed his target. He jumped a small pile of jagged metal and juked past what looked like a crushed winch assembly. He jumped on his target just as the supine man tried to push himself onto elbows. Cyrus hit him with a pile-driving right cross. The man's head cracked back and bounced off the floor before lolling to the side on a rubbery neck. He was out cold.

Jumping to his feet, Cyrus found Kastor standing over the unconscious form of the last soldier. Presumably, he'd performed in similar action.

"It was good to see you again," Kastor said without pause. "Let me know the next time you're in the market for Chinese intel."

Cyrus shook Kastor's offered hand and they parted ways without pause. Kastor headed for the rear of the warehouse. Cyrus watched until Kastor stepped through a doorway and disappeared into the night. Only one task remained. After searching each unconscious man, Cyrus wasn't surprised by what he found—or in this case, didn't find. None carried identification, though each had a standard issue QX-04 semi-automatic and a set of flex-cuffs.

The cuffs came in handy.

The first three men he and Kastor had taken down were in a neat little group, not more than a dozen paces from each other near the center of the room. Cyrus collected a set of handcuffs from each man and set about shackling them to one another. Perhaps adding insult to injury, he had a little fun with the process. He cuffed the ankle of one man to the wrist of the next. Then, the wrist of that man to the ankle of his associate. It was a tangle of unconscious limbs. Cyrus wished he could be there to see them sort it out once they started waking up.

The remaining two men were more fortunate. They were too far apart for Cyrus to have any fun. He cuffed the one closer to the rear wall to a bulky, rusted drill press. The one ended up shackled to the back half of an ancient Volkswagen.

Cyrus headed for the building's front entrance. He'd dealt with the six-man team; it was unlikely that more men were in the area, but he wouldn't linger and risk detection.

It turned out that there were more Chinese in the area. The five-man team inside the warehouse had not been alone. Cyrus stepped into the decrepit city street and instantly felt eyes upon him. Turning right, he headed south. He maintained a brisk pace but one that wouldn't betray his anxiety. There was always a risk that his watchers might shoot him where he stood. In theory, they still wanted to retrieve their data, but as far as they were concerned, he'd stolen state secrets. The idea was laughable. There was no tangible value to the data on the drive in his pocket. Things were quickly escalating out of control. A six-man team sent to retrieve the data was a bad sign, but it was reasonable and justified. More men on the street spoke of a larger operation. Nothing hinted at capture and interrogation being part of the design.

This op is much bigger than I expected.

The reaction was way out of balance for the crime. Thinking again, Cyrus considered the ammunition the Chinese had used in their rifles. It was nasty stuff. No one used that type of ammo if they were interested in taking prisoners.

The hairs on the back of his neck stood at full alert. Given the region's humidity, it was no small trick, and he reacted instantly. Stepping to his left, he prepared to dart across the street. He made it almost a full step when a shot rang out from behind. The damp pavement three feet in front of him and a half foot to his right sparked as a round ricocheted into the night. The sound of the shot and the location of its strike were telling. It was a rifle round fired by a sniper high and to his rear. Since the buildings in the immediate area maxed out at three stories, it meant the shooter was close.

Cyrus bolted for cover. The darkness would help conceal his position, but his decision to move to the far side of the street meant he had thirty-five feet of open ground to cover before reaching the safety of the shadows at the far curb. Pivoting on his right foot, he took a gamble and zigged to the left. It made his destination another three paces further away, but running in a straight line while in a sniper's sights was essentially assisted suicide. Another shot rang out. He felt the heat from the slug as it passed over his shoulder.

Too damn close!

He poured on the speed and dove for the darkness as soon as it was within reach. The rough patch of crushed asphalt that broke his fall was a welcomed sensation. It was preferable to a bullet, even if it hurt like hell.

A second later, Cyrus was on his feet, keeping to the shadows and moving quickly. He watched for any opening in the wrecked old buildings to his left: an open doorway, a half-boarded-up window. He wasn't picky. Getting off the street was priority one. But for as oppressed as the area was, someone had done a fantastic job boarding up the unsafe old structures.

Cyrus was stuck on the street and couldn't do anything about it.

An engine sparked to life somewhere in the near distance. Cyrus recognized it immediately—a motorcycle of some kind. It was a two-stroke—the high pitch whine was unmistakable. Street legal bikes were four-strokes, quiet and tame in their exhaust note by comparison. Two strokes were used for off-roading. They excelled at high RPMs and were made to take a beating. They sounded more like chainsaws or leafblowers than motorcycles.

Things just became more complicated.

A second engine coughed to life. Cyrus heard the pair whine as the riders revved them before pulling away. He looked over his shoulder and searched the darkness down the street. Nothing moved, but he knew they were out there—somewhere to his right and advancing. He sprinted south, sticking to the shadows and searching for any opportunity to escape the street.

He heard the squeal of tires as he reached the end of the block. Ducking around the corner brought a degree of safety. It meant he'd evaded the sniper, at least for the time being. The first of the motorcycles blasted into view. The rider missed the turn and locked up his brakes. He skidded to the far side of the intersection. The second bike took the cue and slowed in time to make the corner. The rider braked hard, revved the engine, and popped the clutch. Cyrus had a forty-yard lead, but it wouldn't last long.

Cyrus ran, his eyes searching for anything he could use as a weapon or someplace to take cover. He still had his sidearm but remained reluctant to use it against a team of men only doing their jobs. Still, the sniper taking potshots had him reconsidering the rules of engagement. Snipers had a way of doing that. Cyrus was all for the moral high ground, but getting killed would ruin his day.

Just when he thought he'd have to make the tough call, the building on his left opened up. It looked like an old showroom, maybe some kind of boutique firebombed long ago. The expansive front windows had disintegrated long ago, and the French doors at the entrance had been smashed off their hinges.

Cyrus ducked through the doorway and into the inky blackness within.

The motorcycle rider brought the bike into a skid in the street before the store. He was joined seconds later by the second rider. Their headlights blazed across the ruins of the showroom and cast massive shifting shadows along the walls. Cyrus watched them form a covered position near the back wall. The riders were waiting for something. One of them held a hand to his right ear, obviously receiving instructions via radio.

The bikes were big black off-road models. Their makes were not stamped on the gas tanks—military issue, Cyrus guessed. Judging by their throaty-pitched growl, he put them at 1000cc, maybe 1500cc. They were light, fast, and could take a beating. He'd been eyeing the nearby staircase and thinking about leading his pursuers higher into the building. But with bikes like these, the men could easily follow him deep into the structure, up the staircase, and with a speed he couldn't match on foot. Plus, as his eyes adjusted, it became apparent that the plan wouldn't work. Whatever fire claimed the showroom had also consumed most of the stairs. What little remained was unlikely to support his weight. If the riders didn't kill him, falling through the jagged debris likely would.

That was alright. The more he thought about it, the more he liked the motorcycles. One of them could get him to his destination in record time. If he could get his hands on one of the bikes, it would also complicate life for the snipers. Once he was clear of the neighborhood, he could lose himself in the city and make his way to the exfiltration point at his leisure.

He watched the two men on the bikes. With his hand to his ear, the rider motioned to the broken-out windows fronting the street. Both riders flicked their headlights on high and gunned their engines. They charged for the double-wide entrance, single file.

When the first bike hit the empty showroom floor, Cyrus was ready. He had his gun raised and a round chambered. The first rider caught him fully in the beam of the headlight. The shock of looking down the wrong end of a gun must have been intimidating because he locked up both the front and back brakes before laying the motorcycle on its side. He went sliding out of control through the loose debris.

Cyrus stepped forward and stopped the violent slide of the oncoming bike with his foot. The impact almost knocked him off his feet.

The second bike came into view as soon as the first rider went down. Cyrus fired a shot and shattered its headlight. The second rider panicked worse than the first, managing only to use the front brake. His tire struck the first fallen bike, and inertia took over. The motorcycle bucked and the rider vaulted over the handlebars.

Surprised by his good fortune, Cyrus was almost struck by the flailing form of the airborne second rider. He stepped aside in time to miss the slow-moving human missile. The first rider was struggling to gain his feet when Cyrus slapped him across the side of the head with the grip of his gun. He toppled without so much as a sound, out cold.

Before the second rider could right himself, Cyrus delivered a similar blow to the head. Skipping the search for handcuffs this time, Cyrus opted to put a single round through the gas tank of the machine with the wrecked headlight. There was no fiery explosion. He didn't expect one. That sort of thing only happened in the movies. The point was to disable the redundant bike and the pair of riders.

Holstering his gun, Cyrus stood the remaining bike upright. It was entirely undamaged by its slide through the trash and rubble. The engine had died when the machine was dumped. Since the key was still in the 'on' position, he simply thumbed the electric start. The two-stroke engine buzzed to life, and he feathered the throttle. The exhaust crackled with untapped, aggressive horsepower. Shifting into first, he popped the clutch and the rear wheel spun as the bike took off. Three seconds later, he launched the machine from the building's entrance and returned to the street.

Cyrus could see the glow of the more prominent portion of the city to the east. He pointed the bike in that direction and twisted the throttle. There was no sense of eyes following him. He breathed easier for the first time in what seemed like hours. His quick trip to Bangkok proved to be more complicated than he would've ever thought possible.

The Port of Bangkok

11:52 pm

The Port of Bangkok was Cyrus's exfiltration point. It was a sprawling coastal facility occupying over 900 acres. He reached it just before midnight. With thousands of massive containers loaded and unloaded from oceangoing vessels daily, the port operated 24 hours a day. His fight had happened on the other end of the city, and Cyrus was in a hurry to reach the port. It was one of several places someone in his situation might head to slip out of the country. The port, as well as Bangkok's international airport, was sure to be under surveillance. He needed to complete his escape before the Chinese could reacquire him. They'd already proven more motivated and better equipped than anticipated.

The Port's sprawling footprint would work in Cyrus's favor. There was simply too much acreage to secure. The port had its own police force, but the Chinese wouldn't want to involve them any more than Cyrus did. The Chinese would've likely piggybacked on the port's closed-circuit camera network to watch for him—at least that's what he would do in their situation. Luckily, he'd put a great deal of time into researching the camera layout across the installation.

If he could stay out of sight, he would be alright.

He took At Narong Road south along the Port, riding for blocks without seeing a hint of security or surveillance. It was late and the roads were virtually deserted. He'd made good time and done nothing to draw attention to himself.

The port itself had numerous street-level entrances. The one that interested him was east of the main facility. It led to a smaller container yard, still vast in its own right, but one very close to freighter berths and, therefore, saw higher container turnover. Cyrus slowed the bike and buzzed smoothly past the closed steel gate marking the entrance to this end of the facility. A twelve-foot-tall concrete wall bordered the shipping yard. Conveniently, the public road ran this stretch of the facility. There was no sidewalk between the road and the wall. Nature had claimed the few intervening feet and grass, small shrubs and saplings had flourished thanks to neglect. Metal posts projected from the top of the wall. They added four feet to the wall and had spools of razor wire looped between them. Moreover, thirty feet over the gated entrance stood a wide guard tower. Though it offered a sweeping view of the fence line, it was next to useless at night, sitting empty and dark.

Cyrus continued about two hundred yards past the gated entrance. He pulled in the clutch and killed the engine. The bike coasted for a hundred feet before he angled it into a thick patch of overgrowth at the base of the wall. Lowering the bike to its side, he listened to the sounds of the distant dock work and watched for movement on the street around him. No one was visible, and only the green overgrowth swayed in the humid breeze. The bike's exhaust ticked quietly at his feet as it cooled.

Ducking behind a large sapling that had sprouted between the base of the wall and the blacktop of the road, Cyrus retrieved a black nylon rope that was draped over the wall. Seconds later, he'd scaled it and reached the barrier's top.

Two loops of razor wire were his last obstacle. One spooled high and the other low. He unhooked the end of the lower strand, freeing it from where it attached to the nearest of the stanchions set into the wall at regular intervals. He didn't know who was responsible for this particular glitch in perimeter security but was happy with the oversight. He crawled through the gap, careful not to snag himself on the razor-sharp barbs of the higher wire loop. Once on the other side, he rehooked the wire on the small catch drilled in the iron post.

It was a twelve-foot drop to the base of the wall on the opposite side. He landed and was swallowed by the shadow it cast. Those few seconds atop the barricade were the most dangerous part of the infiltration. He'd been visible to all the world, and he could do nothing about it. Now, inside the perimeter, he was breathing easier.

The port was massive. Thousands of train car-sized freight containers were scattered across the dock, most times stacked two high. They were segregated into seemingly unspecified zones with no apparent designation for each arrangement. How they could be sorted was beyond Cyrus.

That was why Cyrus was here—he was looking for *his container*. He knew where it was, but anyone trying to follow him wouldn't stand a chance. It was security through obscurity. His container was stashed among tens of thousands just like it.

Moving through the grounds was the real trick. Security at the port was pretty impressive. For an operation of its size, one with so much ground to cover, the people guarding the port had their work cut out. First of all, the scope of the operation and its round-the-clock shifts meant that old-fashioned practices were not viable. There were no guard dogs to contend with, for example. Also, while there were roving security patrols, the staff guarding the grounds was smaller than it might have been ten or twenty years earlier. Now, the facility was monitored by dozens of cameras—hundreds, actually. They were spread across hundreds of surfaces with haphazard abandon. They were tireless, ever-present sentinels that recorded everything.

Technology was a beautiful thing, Cyrus mused as he moved through the darkness. The moon was casting everything with a pale glow. In turn, the towering freight containers generated endless expanses of shadowy concealment. The cameras offered a false sense of security. After breaching the perimeter wall, he'd stuck to a blind spot between the two closest cameras. He'd retrieved a pair of blue coveralls and a matching baseball cap stashed for him earlier in the day by a dock worker looking for a generous donation to his family's vacation fund. Dressed in the coveralls and with a hat over his brow, Cyrus was effectively invisible to every security camera on the grounds…so long as he kept to himself. He was dressed like a hundred other dock and warehouse laborers, a disguise that worked well only from a distance. But get too close to a camera or a security guard and that disguise disintegrated instantly. There was no hiding his light skin or his taller, wider build.

If he could reach his container, he'd be home free. Prior planning had made him aware of every camera position. Guards and dock workers were easy enough to see coming. In five minutes, he would have the entire crazy night behind him.

A Klaxon alarm began to wail. Dozens of floodlights placed atop light poles scattered across the grounds came to life instantly, and every comforting shadow in sight seemed to disappear in the blink of an eye. Cyrus stood motionless as night became day, and unseen speakers throughout the facility began to blare with alarm.

Walking to the end of the row of containers, Cyrus kept

the bill of his cap low and tried to look like he belonged. Other bodies were materializing in the distance: two men stepped from the large open door of a warehouse; an old man looked up from where he'd been securing straps on a pile of pallets; another man a dozen rows away stepped from an aisle just like the one where Cyrus stood. They'd all been at work on their own tasks and looked equally confused by the sudden disruption of light and sound.

It was a security alert, that much was obvious. But judging by the reactions of the people around him, it wasn't a common occurrence. This clearly wasn't a drill. The dock workers seemed to have no idea what was happening, let alone what they should do. But if the alert was for him, Cyrus wondered, why hadn't security moved against him already?

Gunshots rang out in the distance. It was automatic fire, and it wasn't far away. The shots had come from the direction of the front gate—the entrance he'd passed before ditching the bike and crossing the wall.

Who is shooting…and what were they shooting at?

More bursts of automatic fire came, this time more rapidly. The barrage was answered by another burst of fire from a different caliber of gun. The fire quickly became more intense. There had to be at least half a dozen shooters exchanging shots with two very different types of weapons. One set sounded extraordinarily rapid and precise, while the other was louder, more savage, and a little slower. One was a larger caliber with a lower cyclic rate.

Cyrus didn't think the Chinese would be crazy enough to attack the port outright—not for a crack at him. The port area was a notorious hotbed for illegal activity. Smuggling, theft—hell, half the containers within sight probably contained illegal contraband of some kind. Still, he didn't like coincidences. This entire trip had already snowballed out of control.

Now the snowball felt more like an avalanche.

Cyrus ducked into an alley between rows of containers stacked two and three high. The shooting was taking place in the distance and wasn't slowing down. It sounded like the opposing forces were spreading through the facility. He didn't know what was happening, but his exfiltration was close at hand. Turning left at the next intersection, he felt his adrenaline surge and his heartbeat quicken.

That was troubling on its own. He'd always been calm under pressure, cold as ice, his old mentor had described it more than once. When his pulse quickened like this, it was usually in response to some intangible cue—almost a sixth sense warning of imminent jeopardy. He'd felt the same thing on the street on the other side of the city a half second before the sniper shot nearly took off the top of his head.

Shit!

Cyrus jerked to a stop. Ducking low, he rolled to his right. It was a frantic, aggressive tumble. Even as he made the move, he wasn't sure why he'd chosen it. A man in a dark windbreaker stepped from the corner twenty feet away. The MP5 flashed in his hands and sprayed led in a fully automatic burst.

The rounds stitched the spot Cyrus had been standing only a second before. Given the ammunition he knew the men to be using, the small 9mm loads would've torn him in half. Cyrus had ducked and rolled in a way that no rational person would've had cause or inclination to attempt. The shooter was surprised and released the trigger. He would cease fire only long enough to reacquire the target, then fire the last third of his magazine to complete the intended job.

Cyrus never allowed him to aim. The shooter ceased fire long enough to regain control of his weapon. Cyrus had pulled his Springfield from his appendix holster inside the coveralls. His hardwired instinct was to go for the kill shot—to drop the shooter where he stood. There could be more hitters, and he needed to react decisively. Still, he checked his shot before squeezing off a kill shot to the man's head. The rational part of his mind reminded him who these men were and why they were there. He reigned in the reflexive, motor memory firing off two quick shots... one into each of the man's legs. He spared the guy's life, but there would be a hell of a lot of rehab in his future.

The shooter crumpled to the ground. Cyrus spun in the dirt and kicked the MP5 from the hands of the toppled man. The shooter rolled in the powdery dirt, clamping both palms over one of the gushing wounds. Cyrus retrieved the automatic, clicked the safety on, released the near-empty magazine, and threw it away into the distance. Without taking his eyes off the shooter, he tossed the rifle to the top of the nearest twelve-foot-tall container. It would be safe there.

He looked at the blood seeping between the shooter's clamped fingers. There was a fair amount, but he wouldn't bleed out. Cyrus knew he'd missed the femoral artery. The shooter was so focused on the blood and pain that he seemed to have forgotten about Cyrus.

"Use your belt," Cyrus said. "Tie it off. Your guys should be along any—"

Another Asian in a dark windbreaker darted around the end of the container and nearly ran headlong into Cyrus. The man's eyes went big and round—Cyrus saw his hands tighten on the automatic slung across his chest. The man stumbled back half a step in an attempt to raise the weapon. Cyrus put his left hand out, shoving the auto down and away. He brought a thundering right cross to the center of the smaller man's face. Everything he had went into the impromptu swing. Cyrus had a full windup and twisted at the hips when he followed through on the delivery. The height advantage Cyrus had on his opponent meant more of his body weight was behind the blow when it landed.

The second gunman tipped away from Cyrus's fist like a

lumberjack felling an oak. He didn't crumple and fall away at the knees; he just toppled and hit the dirt all at once. He was out cold. Cyrus was surprised by the results of his hardwired reaction. He looked down at his left hand and found the man's MP5 still locked in his grip…like a parting gift.

A smile crossed Cyrus's face. It had been months since he'd hit someone. After the night he'd had so far, it felt good. Shaking off the grin, he scanned his surroundings. If there were two of these guys out there, more would follow. Shots still echoed in the distance, though it was more sporadic now. Likely the gate guards still putting up some kind of defense.

How many of the Chinese had followed Kastor to Bangkok? It didn't make sense. There was no real value to the information Cyrus was here to acquire. For the Chinese to pull out all the stops like this was out of proportion for the data involved.

Cyrus shelved the question; he would sort it out later. There were answers, but they wouldn't be found here.

He made his way through the next two dozen aisles without incident. The Chinese had attacked the facility because of him. If they managed to overrun the guards, they would take control of the closed-circuit camera system as soon as possible. Cyrus had a distinct advantage—it would take an army to find him on the grounds without the benefit of the camera system. The pair of gunmen who had found him had either been lucky or they'd been pointed in his direction by dock workers. While wearing the uniform, he was invisible, but that only worked when no one was looking for him…he would blend in. He stood out once someone started watching, either the Chinese or Port Security. His clothes couldn't hide that.

Reaching a dark corner of the grounds, Cyrus found the container he was searching for. It wasn't marked in a way that made it distinct. As far as he could tell, it looked like every other container. They varied in color, and sometimes, the steel panels of the massive rectangular boxes looked a little different—maybe some were stronger with more reinforcement because they were newer—but ultimately, they were all the same. The same height, length, and width. They all opened at both ends via massive steel doors hinged along the edges, locking with heavy, complicated latches. Cyrus only knew his container by its location. He would have been out of luck if it had been somehow misplaced earlier in the day.

The container Cyrus was interested in was the bottom of two stacked in its row. The other massive steel box sat neatly atop Cyrus's, proving he would be going nowhere fast. He looked at the second container high above and smiled. That had just been luck. He could've just as easily been on top. If that had been the case, reaching it would've been time-consuming and complicated. He made a mental note to ask Reese if she'd specified that their container needed to be on the ground when she arranged delivery to the Port.

The end of Cyrus's container was just like all of the others. The massive steel doors met in the middle and were latched by a series of sturdy iron cross-members that pivoted on giant pins to lock huge bolts into the floor and ceiling of the container. The latches were secured with three separate oversized padlocks.

Cyrus slid his hand up and behind one of the wide crossmember arms of the door latch. He fished around until he found four small dimpled impressions—one for each fingertip. He tapped different fingers ten times, following a specific sequence. Though the depressions didn't move like buttons on a keypad, they reacted like them. A second after his last tap came a heavy metal thunk followed by the gentle hiss of gas releasing from an actuator. Rather than the doors parting in the middle of the container and swinging out and away from each other, the entire end of the container cracked open. Grabbing hold of the sturdy steel, he pulled and swung the end of the container open on hinges hidden in the rightmost wall. The conventional doors were left entirely in place, along with their latches and locks. Once the trick door was closed again, no one would even suspect the container had been opened.

Swinging the immense door open only far enough to fit himself through, Cyrus stepped inside and quickly pulled it shut behind himself. He pulled on the inside of the door, holding it closed for three seconds until he heard the loud metal thunk reverberate through the enclosure and lock it from external access.

The trick door was held in place with an electromagnetic seal and a pair of massive steel restraining pins.

The container's interior came to life with light as soon as the electromagnetic lock engaged. LED lights lined the perimeter of the ceiling. They bathed the space with a comfortable, pale glow. The long, narrow crate held two vehicles. One was a jet-black diesel Hummer on massive beefy tires. It was so wide that Cyrus had trouble sliding past it on the way to the center of the space. On the far end was a Tesla Roadster, also all black inside and out. Both vehicles were strapped in place with thick canvas restraints.

A massive workbench bisected the space. It stopped just short of the left wall, leaving enough room to step past. The bench was about six feet deep, creating a usable work area from the Hummer's side or the Tesla's. Beneath the bench were a series of heavy stainless steel tool drawers. They varied in height but spanned the entire width of the bench.

Stepping up to the workbench, Cyrus ran his fingers along the underside of the work surface's rounded edge. He located the four dimpled impressions by feel and tapped out a different ten-button sequence, similar to the one used to enter the container. After his last tap, a quiet beep chimed. He bent over and pulled the lowest drawer from beneath the workbench. The drawer glided effortlessly on whisper-smooth rails. When it reached its full extension, Cyrus pulled again. It resisted for the first two seconds but began to extend further, this time under its own power. Cyrus stepped back and out of the way.

As the bottom drawer extended even further, the drawer above it also began to extend. Once the second drawer reached its full extension—about 18 inches short of the drawer below it—it paused. Then the bottom two drawers began to move in tandem; this time, the third drawer slid along with the other two. This continued until all four drawers protruded from the workbench in an ascending, stair-stepped order. Once the fourth and last step reached its full extension of only 18 inches, the center of the workbench separated. Both halves of the bench top tipped down into the space where the bench had been. A large circular platform began rising from the middle of the open space. The platform came level with the surface of the original bench and was soon followed by the original bench top when it rose once again to fill in the open space to the left and right of the circular platform. The open tool drawers had become a short staircase leading to the platform, a transparent acrylic tread topping each and the tools within visible.

Cyrus freed his arms from the coveralls and retrieved his mobile phone from his pants pocket. He tied the sleeves of the coveralls around his waist and walked quickly up the stairs to step on the platform. After tapping the required activation sequence into the phone, he checked once more to be sure he was at the middle of the platform. A gentle rumble emanated from beneath his feet, and the taste of ozone was added to the stagnant air inside the container. There was a flash of light, and then he was gone.

Five seconds after Cyrus disappeared, the silent transformation of the workbench was reversed. The top of the table separated, and the circular platform lowered. The bench top rose back in its place, and the sides of the bench narrowed together once more. One by one, the staircase drawers retracted. Once the process was complete, the LED lights at the perimeter of the ceiling went dark.

It was as if Cyrus had never been there.

Chapter 2 - Kastor Set You Up

Undisclosed location, Australia

Tuesday, 2:09 am local time

When Cyrus arrived on the destination platform of the facility in Australia, the single overhead bulb lighting the small concrete-walled room was noisily blinking to life. It had been wired into the platform's circuitry, but the old overhead fixture was still original to the underground facility's construction many decades earlier. It was slow to warm, flickering and buzzing for the first twenty seconds.

Pulling the heavy door open on silent hinges, he headed down the hallway. The underground facility was a warren of cold crisscrossing double-wide passages linking dozens of rooms. Constructed by the Australian government near the start of the Cold War, it was never used and had long been forgotten. Its loss from the record books was reinforced after Hondo discovered it and claimed it for their team. They had since erased every trace of the facility from bureaucratic records. Buried two hundred feet beneath the Australian outback, it was as safe and anonymous of a location as anyone could ask for. And, thanks to the teleportation platforms, the team could come and go without showing themselves on the surface.

It was the middle of the night, but even as he approached the massive steel doors to the main corridor, Cyrus could see that the lights were on. Incandescent light spilled from under the doors, and disruptions in the illumination told him that he wasn't the only one still awake.

He pushed through the doors to find Sanjay Patel and Dennis Driscoll seated at the first of the massive wooden tables scattered throughout the room. They faced each other, hunched over laptops with tired, bloodshot eyes. The pile of small serving-sized potato chip bags sitting discarded beside Dennis hinted at another of his marathon number-crunching sessions. Likewise, the small collection of spent Red Bull cans near Sanjay suggested he had likely participated this time.

They're onto something.

Dennis was in his early thirties. He was overweight but had shed some of his 225 pounds over the last year. His curly dark hair and bushy pork chop sideburns framed a warm, friendly face. Dennis only hit the chips when he was *in the zone*, as he called it. Though he specialized in quantum encryption, the group's latest project was the commercial deployment of their Quantum Datalink technology, QDL for short.

News of the technology made headlines all over the world. Several telecoms were already working on first-stage deployments. It was a technology that would revolutionize how the world communicated, and it was happening almost overnight. Everyone wanted in on the ground floor: telecoms, cable networks, and, of course, governments and governmental agencies.

Cyrus had seen that coming from day one. Every administration on the planet would want the technology for the security it represented. QDL-based communication essentially did away with phone lines and satellite links. It was a point-to-point communication. A tiny chipset in one device could link directly with another device over any distance. There was absolutely no chance of interference and no opportunity for surveillance. Quantum entanglement linked one device to the next. This meant there was no bandwidth limitation and no latency. It was the Holy Grail of communications technology.

If Sanjay had decided to participate in Dennis's marathon session, they were close to solving one of the technology's few remaining problems. Though Sanjay's usually sour disposition had softened in recent months, he wasn't generally prone to the same stalwart work ethic as Dennis. Sanjay was cold and sometimes challenging to get along with, but he was a brilliant mathematician when he was inspired.

Sanjay always had a bit of a Napoleon complex. At five foot six and 140 pounds, he did his best to look physically imposing. Cyrus always considered him a Chihuahua trying to act like a Great Dane. He'd recently turned 28, and the team had thrown him a private but lavish birthday party. More than anything that seemed to have smoothed Sanjay's rough edges. It was as if the spectacle had finally made him feel like a genuine team member, respected and accepted. He'd been easier to get along with since then. Though, Cyrus feared Sanjay would always be Sanjay.

Dennis looked up from his screen, seeming surprised to see Cyrus. "You're alright," he said. There was awe in his voice.

Sanjay just looked at Cyrus. He seemed equally impressed to see him, but he didn't speak.

"I'm fine. Why wouldn't I be?" Cyrus asked and slapped Dennis on the shoulder as he walked by.

Cyrus had been away for the last week to deal with an operation in Russia and set up the deal in Bangkok. It was natural to assume they'd been concerned, but even as he walked past their table, something about their responses didn't entirely fit. Their expressions seemed somehow off.

It didn't matter to Cyrus at that moment. He just wanted to find Reese. It had been a week, and he missed her more than anyone in a very long time. They'd been together for ten months, but it seemed like a lifetime in many ways. She made his old life easy to forget. Well, maybe not forget, but easier to finally put it in the rearview mirror.

That was saying a lot.

The main hall was filled with a half dozen massive wooden tables just like the one used by Dennis and Sanjay. This was the facility's central communal space. They ate, worked, and socialized here. If there was one thing the underground facility wasn't lacking, it was space. The team numbered seven, with hundreds of thousands of square feet at their disposal. The structure had an additional two levels, all underground. There were still parts of the structure they had yet to explore. It hadn't been a priority, and there hadn't been time. Things moved at a frenetic pace once Tracy Clark disappeared.

Tracy was the eighth member of the team. She specialized in computer science and was the team's most technologically adept engineer. She'd done much of the initial hardware design on the first-generation QDL boards and chips. Cyrus still wished they had Tracy onboard. She was brilliant, and they could develop new, related technology more quickly if she were still a part of the team.

Tracy was good, no question about it. But she wasn't at all who she seemed. She appeared to be in her mid-twenties. The team's founder, Walter Meade, certainly hadn't questioned her credentials. Maybe if he had, things would've ended up differently. If he had, maybe Meade would still be alive, and Cyrus would never have become a part of the group. It was hard to say because Cyrus had nothing but questions. Though he'd been searching for months, he hadn't found a trace of the woman. Not since the day he discovered the photos linking her to something he couldn't explain.

After Meade died, Cyrus became responsible for Meade's team of scientists. It was a posthumous request from the old man that changed Cyrus's life in a way he'd never seen coming. While sorting through the historical records of the project Meade's team was working on, Cyrus discovered that the origin of the project dated back to the start of the 20th century. The work began under the supervision of Rumsfeld Pellagrin in 1902. Pellagrin discovered a new element that later came to be known as Halon-Seven. It was used as a revolutionary power source that Pellagrin believed could power a teleportation technology he'd been devising.

When Pellagrin died in 1957, the technology was far from perfected. He turned the work over to Walter Meade, who worked on it until his death last year. Before his death, Meade had built functional teleportation platforms and refined them greatly. Unfortunately, the successful operation of the prototype platforms required a supply of a rare element known as Halon-Seven. And, by that time, all known sources of it had been acquired. The project reached a standstill well before being brought to market and deployed worldwide. Pellagrin and Meade's lifelong dream of a worldwide system of teleportation platforms had stalled with no plausible means of reaching fruition.

While sorting through the pieces of the mess that was left to him, Cyrus reviewed all records relating to the project. His fresh perspective brought new insight and a shocking realization. A single face was common in photos taken since the start of the project—photos dating back to the early 1900's. Though her hairstyle changed along with her name over the decades, the young woman Cyrus knew as Tracy Clark had been in more than a half dozen photos. The first snapshot he had of her dated back to sometime around 1910. Since that time, she hadn't aged a day.

Cyrus shared the realization with Reese and Hondo, and together, they'd gone to confront Tracy. At the time, the team was sequestered at the underground facility beneath the Australian Outback. Only Cyrus, Hondo, and Reese had the teleportation codes required to leave the base. Still, when they arrived to confront her, Tracy was gone.

That was the last they'd seen of her. Cyrus and Hondo had reached out to contacts in the intelligence community. But they hadn't turned up a trace of the young woman in the last ten months. They had nothing but questions. Tracy had infiltrated a project with world-changing ramifications. But why? And how? How was it possible that she hadn't aged?

So many questions and not a single answer. As close as Cyrus could estimate, Tracy hadn't hindered the project. Nothing indicated the program had been unduly hampered over the decades. Peripheral technologies needed to be developed for Pellagrin's vision to become a reality—things like the modern transistor, microchips, and lasers. Even modern capacitors and superconductors weren't up to the challenge. That's why the discovery of Halon-Seven was crucial to the success of the technology today. Even the current understanding of quantum physics was crude, as explained to Cyrus. Every year, the scientific community gained new insights that changed how we looked at the universe and what we considered the laws of nature themselves.

Reese's laptop sat open on a table near the back of the room, but she was nowhere to be seen. Cyrus walked over and saw that the screen was still on. A pair of headphones sat on the table beside it. The machine hadn't gone to sleep, so she must still be up and about.

He heard a chair scraping across the floor behind him and turned. Reese had just walked into the room; she held an open file folder in her hands. She was reading it while she stepped through the array of haphazardly placed tables and chairs.

Reese must have felt his eyes on her because she stopped moving mid-step. Her eyes rose. The moment they touched his, a brilliant smile spanned her face. She hopped once at the sight of him and bolted in his direction.

As Reese slammed into his arms, Cyrus lifted her and spun her around once. His smile was wider than he would've thought possible. He was exhausted, but the effects of the last week hadn't fully set in until just then. Now, with her in his arms, he finally felt safe. He finally felt like he was home.

She kissed him. A quick peck at first, but a slow, passionate kiss immediately followed. She looked up at him with bright eyes. Her cheeks were pink. "I was worried," she said in a breathless voice. "I didn't know what to do."

Cyrus was confused. "Worried about what?"

"Hondo called. He had me load a radio feed over the web. It was Thai communications chatter about an attack on the Port. It sounded bad. I was sure you were stuck in the middle of it."

Cyrus put her down. "Yeah," he said. He shrugged, unsure how things had gone so sideways. "A Chinese security team must've followed Kastor to the meet. They tried to spring a trap. It was a mess."

"Are you hurt?"

He shook his head.

"Kastor set you up? I thought you trusted him."

"I did," Cyrus said. "I do. It wasn't him. He's good at what he does. Whatever the Chinese are upset about, the data on this drive can't be the root of it. There's something bigger going on." He passed her the USB flash drive and watched her eyes darken.

"I don't understand," she said. "You got the drive? I thought you said it was a trap."

He nodded. "It was. But Kastor is a professional. He knew what he was doing. He got us through."

She scowled. He knew she was questioning his accounting of events. "I'm wrecked," he said. "Why don't you look at the drive in the morning?"

Her eyes brightened. She placed the file folder beside her laptop and shut the lid. Pocketing the memory stick, she grabbed his hand and started for the door. "Not so fast," she said over her shoulder. "You've been gone for a week. First, I get some quality time…then you tell me what *really* happened out there."

Chapter 3 - *You're Kidding, Right?*

Woodstock, Illinois, United States

Cyrus and Reese had never even made it back to their room. Halfway there, Cyrus's phone buzzed with an urgent message from a contact attempting to data mine obscure government servers as part of a related research project. A lead had finally surfaced, and Cyrus wouldn't risk missing the opportunity to follow up. Plans for relaxation were put on hold. He teleported to a platform stashed at a self-storage facility several blocks from Chicago's O'Hare International Airport. Rather than board a plane, he hopped the northwest train for a destination one stop short of the line's end: a small town in Northern Illinois.

Thanks to the grueling international time zone shift, night had become day in the time it had taken him to teleport. Cyrus stepped off the train at 3:01 p.m. at the Woodstock, Illinois, station. The depot was a small, brick building that would've offered travelers a welcome break from the cold midwest weather in winter months. He bypassed the building entirely, skirting its exterior and circling the edge of a large, packed parking lot on the west side. The small town's city square could be seen a few dozen yards away to his left across the road.

A single yellow taxi sat idling at the curb. He offered it only a glance before the driver dropped the car in gear and rolled to his aid. The man behind the wheel mashed a cigarette in an overflowing ashtray and smiled through the open window. "Where you headed?"

Cyrus passed a small fold of paper through the window. The driver flipped it open and frowned. "You're kidding, right?" he said.

"I take it you don't take many fares out there?" Cyrus asked. He pulled the release on the car's rear door and slid onto the cracked and patched vinyl bench seat.

The driver eyed Cyrus in the rearview and shook his head. "You sure the place is still open? I've worked this town for fifteen years—lived here my whole life, in fact. I've never taken *anyone* out there. I'm not sure I've ever met someone who's been there, now that I think about it. I thought the place was condemned years ago."

Cyrus grimaced. That didn't make the lead encouraging. Still, Nathan was never wrong. He'd admitted there had been surprisingly little information regarding their guy, but this lead needed to be checked out.

"One way or another," Cyrus said, "I guess I'm going to find out."

The cab slipped from the curb, signaled, and pulled onto the street. There was no traffic to speak of. At least no traffic by any standard Cyrus would use to measure. The driver seemed to sense this was Cyrus's first time in town. He turned left up Main Street and onto what constituted the town square. The city center was like a wide frame of one-way streets surrounding a verdant park. The streets on each side were paved with century-old bricks. Hundred-year-old two and three-story buildings stood shoulder to shoulder, forming the square's perimeter. Most were fronted with old-fashioned recreations of turn-of-the-century signs for whatever business now called the building home. A massive ornate opera house stood on one corner, facing both the inside and outside of the square's perimeter. The cab passed it, exiting what must have constituted the small town's downtown. The vibrating pulse beneath the cab's wheels quieted as the street transitioned from brick pavers to modern pavement.

"I thought you might enjoy the view," the driver said with a glance in the mirror.

Cyrus smiled. It was a quiet town, and he wished he could've shown it to Reese. That hope faded when his mind returned, once more, to the reason for the trip. He wasn't sure what he would learn at his destination, but he sensed it would be important.

Chapter 4 - Beta Testing

Brown University, Providence, Rhode Island

Alec Barnabe was irritated by the last-minute summons from his colleague, Tommy Wilks. Wilks liked to pretend he called the shots, but they were partners. Truth be told, Wilks never pulled his weight in the partnership and it was all Barnabe could do to keep from shoving the fact in his so-called friend's face. Their project was too important to risk a falling out now. They were beta-testing the latest software build and had a customer paying them a lot of money to put the software through its paces in its first field trial. As much as Barnabe hated it, he took a deep breath and redoubled his effort to be patient with his partner.

They were meeting at the Small Point Cafe, a compact but trendy coffee shop. It was downtown, a couple of blocks west of the Providence River, on Westminster Street. Wilks loved the place. He had a crush on a girl working at the bookstore next door, so he spent much time at the coffee shop on the quiet one-way street.

Barnabe turned the corner and stepped onto Westminster Street. It was quiet, even on a Monday night. But as he drew within sight of the Small Point Cafe, he could see that all of the outdoor tables were occupied. He rolled his eyes and quickened his pace. Frustration ratcheted two notches higher. They would be stuck at an indoor table, not Barnabe's first choice.

As he pushed through the front door of the small cafe, Barnabe saw Wilks at a small two-top just past the register in the back. Less than half the tables were occupied, but Wilks had selected a small spot with no elbow room. Barnabe ground his teeth and threaded his way across the floor.

Wilks was working on his laptop. He didn't look up as Barnabe dropped his messenger bag roughly on the floor, shoved it against the wall, and slumped into the empty seat across the table. Barnabe let out a resigned huff for good measure. Still, Wilks didn't look up from his computer. His eyes remained fixed and unblinking as he stared at the screen.

"What's the big emergency?" Barnabe asked with irritation when Wilks failed to acknowledge him.

Wilks refused to meet his eye...or even blink. His gaze remained fixed on the laptop, his eyes wide and unmoving.

"Hey—I'm talking to you!" Barnabe snapped. He smacked an open hand on the surface of the table as his blood began to boil.

Wilks didn't shift his expression in the slightest. He offered no reaction at all.

"Knock it off, asshole," Barnabe said. His voice was low and filled with menace.

Still no movement from Wilks.

Barnabe glared and kicked Wilks under the table. He felt his toe connect with Wilks' shin. It felt like he'd just kicked a table leg. Wilks's knee was solid and unyielding.

Barnabe's skin began to crawl.

Pushing back against the table, he slid his chair backward several inches. He didn't know what was happening, but something felt desperately wrong. When he pushed away from the table, it shifted and slid closer to Wilks. When it did, two things happened. First, Barnabe saw the power-saver on the laptop screen kick in. The screen went dark, and the glare dropped from Wilks' face. There was no change in his expression. Then the table bumped his chest, only just slightly. Wilks's head rocked forward, tipping slowly at first before dropping harder and stopping only when his chin reached his chest. The rest of his body remained entirely stationary.

Shooting from his seat, Barnabe stumbled. His chair topped and crashed to the tile floor. All eyes in the cafe turned at the same instant. Barnabe had the wherewithal to snatch his messenger bag from the floor before turning and darting for the door. He got within 10 feet of it, but unused chairs spun out from adjacent tables to block his path—two from the left and two from the right. They caught him unprepared, and he plowed headlong into them.

Stumbling through the tangle of empty chairs, Barnabe's vision spun. He struggled to stay on his feet. It didn't make any sense. The chairs had come out of nowhere—closing in on him as if of their own accord. No one was standing or even seated nearby. No one could have pushed them in his direction.

Barnabe shook off what he'd seen. It had to be confusion brought on by what was most certainly a panic attack. He twisted on one foot, stumbled on the last remaining chair, and threw it aside. As the chair back left his grip, his eyes shifted aside and fell on a face that sent an icy chill down his spine. A small man was seated at a table at the far wall. The man was watching him—his attention so intensely focused that it seemed somehow unnatural. The man was minute and frail, with a bald head and only the thinnest traces of eyebrows. He had a button nose and a tiny mouth that pulled wide into a flat, flesh-freezing smile the instant their eyes met.

Barnabe bolted through the doorway and onto the wide sidewalk fronting the one way street. His eyes went left, and he saw two men step away from the rear of a black windowless van parked at the curb thirty yards away. They were big and broad-shouldered, with close-cropped hair. Everything about them resonated with menace.

Barnabe spun to his right and bolted down the walkway. He reached the street corner and turned right without hesitation. Pulling the strap of his computer bag over his head so he wouldn't lose it, he ran with everything he had. The sound of footsteps slapped at the ground somewhere behind.

The two men were giving chase, and Barnabe turned at the next intersection. He somehow managed to pour on additional speed. He didn't know who had killed Tommy Wilks, but he was determined to make sure the same didn't happen to him. If there was one thing Alec Barnabe was good at, it was looking out for number one.

Chapter 5 - A Mountain of Raw Data

Plains, Montana, United States

Radley Verhoeven stepped from the elevator and onto the 15th floor of the Heidelberg Building. The Order of Origin controlled floors 15 through 20, though the general public was restricted to the 20th. An eight-digit PIN code and ocular biometric scan were required before the elevator would stop at floors 15 through 19. Automated facial recognition via security cameras inside the lift inventoried those present before the doors were ever allowed to open.

A dozen computer stations were arrayed across the room before Verhoeven. Six rows of tidy, clutter-free desks were arranged precisely, a wide path separating them into a pair of aisles. A technician occupied each station, everyone sitting silently and working diligently before a large flatscreen display. Every work surface contained a monitor, keyboard, and mouse. There were no phones and no discussion—only the sound of muted keystrokes thrummed in the air.

Walking the aisle slowly, Verhoeven surveyed the work in progress. The screens around him held the personal details of a dozen different applicants. There was no shortage of new prospects. Interest in the Order grew monthly. Their rigorous selection process hinted at the group's exclusivity and made it seem somehow elite. This added to the allure, Verhoeven knew. That appeal, in turn, stoked interest in their ideology.

Every aspect of an applicant's history, psychology, and physiology was analyzed during selection. Some of the technicians were reviewing mundane details such as background checks. Others scrutinized the results of exhaustive personal interviews conducted with either applicants or people integral to the applicant's life: family, teachers, coworkers, and other past associations. Anyone with whom the applicant had regular or meaningful contact.

Verhoeven disregarded those screens. They were the more cursory investigations and of little concern to him. His attention focused on the three technicians working through invasive biological profiles. The three relevant screens displayed blood samples, X-rays and MRI results, and detailed neurological scans. These technicians were profiling the recruits who were truly important to the future of the Order.

A woman entered from the corner of the room. Though she appeared to be in her late twenties or early thirties, Verhoeven knew better. She wore a simple off-white blouse and a knee-length grey skirt. The heels of her shoes clicked quietly across the ceramic tile floor as she approached. Long blond hair framed a flawless pale face with high cheekbones and cornflower blue eyes. She smiled as she drew near but said nothing.

"Good morning, Fiona," Verhoeven said. "What do you think of the latest prospects?"

Fiona Bell smiled again and directed him toward the front of the room. A sizeable flatscreen display was hung on the wall behind a tall mahogany counter. She retrieved a small digital tablet from the bar and the screen on the wall came to life.

"The night shift found something," she said. Her voice was gentle and quiet, accented mildly from her British upbringing. A man's vital statistics appeared on the screen, along with a pair of photos. One was a portrait, while the other showed his face in profile.

"This is Alex Dashell," she went on. "As you can see, he is 26 and displays all appropriate markers. He's everything we would expect. The age is correct, height and weight are bang on, and he was in the foster system as a child. Those records aren't digital so I've sent Hauser to retrieve the hardcopies."

"You think he's one of the missing twelve?" Verhoeven said. There was wonder in his voice, combined with a hint of excitement. "Marvelous. It's about time."

"I think it's a safe bet," Fiona confirmed with a knowing smile.

Verhoeven's gaze returned to the room. The analysts studied the profiles of recent applicants, searching for those ideally suited for the Order's needs. There was no shortage of interest in the Order; it seemed the Order's message was spreading at an accelerating rate. Still, Verhoeven knew that the truly talented people, the ideal resources, weren't likely to come knocking at his door. A lamb could be led to slaughter, while a gazelle had to be hunted and stalked. To that end, another team was at work one floor above. They utilized a cutting-edge artificial intelligence system to scour the world's databanks in search of key prospects—initiates who would help the order complete The Migration.

Verhoeven felt a rush of adrenaline. If Fiona was correct, they had just located one of the lost twelve members of the Arlington Project. That was a thrill, and it couldn't have come at a better time.

Looking down at his frail, liver-spotted hands, Verhoeven

felt an icy chill run the length of his emaciated spine. He was a tall, thin man short of six and a half feet. He'd weighed nearly two hundred pounds two decades earlier, but time had not been kind. He was now down to one forty-five and his skin seemed to hang from a brittle skeleton. Even the veins in his arms and legs were painfully visible, something he'd become all too aware of in recent years. Since then, he'd chosen to hide the unpleasantness behind five-thousand-dollar suits that needed to be tailored far too often. He looked like little more than a walking corpse, and he knew it. A well-dressed corpse, but a corpse nonetheless.

The flesh on Verhoeven's face was tight. It clung to his skull and made his eyes seem bulging and large. The tissue surrounding the muscles and tendons of his jaw was drawn tight in places and hanging loose in others. His sandy brown hair was short and patchy. All in all, he looked like the victim of some sort of wasting disease. His body continued to deteriorate more aggressively with each passing month. When he looked at the photos of Alex Dashell on the display, there came a renewed sense of hope. It was a chance at survival and an opportunity to see his people flourish.

"Spare no effort," Verhoeven said. "Make sure Hauser has whatever resources he requires. I want Dashell here ASAP."

Fiona nodded. Verhoeven smiled, understanding she had already taken the initiative. Resourceful and intelligent, she also knew the lifeline Dashell represented to him personally. Still, the look in her eye meant there was more.

"If Dashell fell into foster care after the loss of Arlington," Fiona explained, "it's possible more of the twelve landed in the same system. He could lead us to others."

Verhoeven nodded. There was no question they needed to step up their efforts. Communication was unreliable, but they knew their people were faltering at an alarming rate. The population of this world held the key to the survival of their race.

He considered what he had to work with. It was estimated that .0025% of the current population was genetically predisposed to their purposes. With a planetary population of 7.125 billion, just over 178,000 candidates were available worldwide. Discard a third of them for being either too old or too young, and they had approximately 118,000 possible candidates. Finding them was like finding the proverbial needle in a haystack. The Arlington experiment had held so much promise but failed spectacularly. Only twelve of the five hundred test subjects had survived. Then, those twelve had been lost the night of the fire, never to be seen again.

Verhoeven shook his head and pushed away the memory of that disappointment. The hope and anticipation practically danced in Fiona's eyes, and he envied her. He felt as worn and frail as he looked, but she was alive and vibrant. They should all be so lucky. He would do whatever was necessary. He'd sworn as much when they first arrived; looking at Fiona now, he renewed that vow. He would not let his people down.

"What's the status of our contractor?" Verhoeven asked. "Has he been located?"

The scowl on Fiona's face was answer enough.

Verhoeven shook his head. "Meeker acted rashly when he killed the boy. Rather than motivate Barnabe, he forced him into hiding. It was a foolish miscalculation —a decision that wasn't his to make. The point was to speed the work on Nyland's journal." She shook her head. "This is intolerable."

His vision began to dim, and Verhoeven realized he was letting his emotions get the better of him. It was yet another side effect of being in this place and something his fragile body couldn't tolerate. He saw concern in Fiona's expression and knew he must look as bad as he felt. Taking a long, slow breath, he worked to renew his calm.

"I'm sorry," he said. "Even after decades here, I still let emotions get to me. Sometimes, it still seems so *new*."

Fiona watched him silently for a moment before finally speaking. "What remains of our people will suffer from the same plight. We need to keep that in mind. It won't be an easy adjustment."

"No," Verhoeven agreed. "But it's worth the discomfort. We're not good with change...but this is a matter of survival."

"In the meantime, we must focus on your short-term viability. We need to make the retrieval of Alex Dashell our number one priority. If he can lead us to the rest of the missing twelve, all the better. Millennia of research will have been for nothing without you to lead us."

Verhoeven found himself grinding his teeth. She was referring to Nyland's experiment, of course. No one had expected it to be the last hope for their people, though it had come to precisely that. Nyland should've been leading the Migration himself. Instead, he'd become too invested in his research, siding with the results of his experiment over the welfare of his race. The results were infuriating—a brilliant mind lost at such a pivotal point in their history.

"Barnabe will decipher the book," Verhoeven said. His voice was calm and reflected no doubt. "We just need to regain control of the Aegis. The book is the key."

"Only if we know where the Aegis has been hidden. You're sure it still exists?" Fiona's tone matched the doubt in her eyes.

Verhoeven offered a withering glance. He stepped past her and headed for the exit. She followed. "Nyland was deluded, but he wasn't insane. I don't believe he destroyed the Aegis. He simply hid it. He put it somewhere he could retrieve it...somewhere he believed was beyond *our* reach."

They walked down a long hallway and turned into a doorless entry. An expansive library spread out before them. The walls were paneled with tall built-in shelves that lined the room's perimeter. The floor space was divided into aisles of matching hand-crafted double-sided oak shelves. Every inch of every shelf was occupied with thick books of every shape and size—all with excessive wear to their bindings, each meticulously indexed in the computer that sat on the desk in the center of the floor.

The desk was a wide, ornate mahogany affair with three 30" displays, a keyboard and mouse, and nothing more. Verhoeven circled it and lowered himself carefully into the chair. Every book in the library's collection had been scanned and cataloged into a digital system that now included millions of volumes collected from around the world. Even with all of that raw data available at his fingertips, he was most interested in the data he had only just acquired.

Verhoeven called a series of topological images to the center of the three displays by tapping a series of commands on the keyboard. Fiona stepped to his shoulder and leaned over the desk for a closer look. The screen was filled with shaded images of an arid, monochrome landscape captured in sharp detail. It seemed to lack vegetation and looked peculiar.

"What am I looking at?" she asked.

Verhoeven tapped the keyboard and the image zoomed out. Another tap, and the screen zoomed back further. Two more taps and the curvature of the terrain came into view. Fiona stepped back with a gasp. "The surface of the moon," Verhoeven said. "As seen from a Chinese spy satellite five days ago."

He turned his chair and looked at Fiona. Her expression went through a rapid succession of changes. First was confusion, he guessed. Then came frustration and, finally, understanding. He recognized the idea when it reached her eye. Her fingers touched her lips and her eyes narrowed on the screen as if seeing the images for the first time.

"That would be an excellent place to hide it," Fiona said.

"And it makes a lot of sense. Nyland would've been concerned about a space agency discovering it sooner or later. I assume we're looking at the dark side of the moon?"

Verhoeven nodded. "We had to commandeer a Chinese satellite to acquire the imagery," he explained. "As you can imagine, they are leaving no stone unturned in an effort to uncover who exploited their system."

Fiona grinned. They both knew the Chinese would never track the incursion back to them. It wasn't even a concern. Each of the so-called super-power nations was combing the space surrounding the Earth for the gravitational anomaly they were expecting. But if Nyland hid the Aegis on the moon, it might be entirely overlooked.

"Did you find it?" Fiona asked. Her voice was filled with a kind of wonder that Verhoeven hadn't heard her express in a long time.

"Unfortunately, no," he said flatly. "We have a mountain of raw data, and it's presenting a unique problem. The equipment we have to work with is too primitive to interpret the data efficiently, and the sensor input from the satellite doesn't allow the type of multispectral imaging that would make this sort of search trivial."

Fiona scowled again. "Where does that leave us?"

Verhoeven levered his frail form and slouched in the chair. He sighed, then pulled himself to his feet. It took a moment to regain his balance. Once done, he looked Fiona squarely in the eye. "I'd hoped to have our young friends apply their algorithm to the search as soon as they'd finished deciphering the journal," he said. "It looks like we'll need to find a new way to motivate Mister Barnabe after the scare Meeker put into him."

Chapter 6 - Room 366

Woodstock, Illinois, United States

The hospital was located several miles outside of town, set in dense woodland at the end of a winding stretch of paved driveway that would be hard-pressed to accommodate a pair of passing vehicles. The surrounding terrain added to the claustrophobic effect as it encroached on the road, pushing thick green tree limbs and overgrowth close to the cab as it passed. Cyrus could see what the driver meant. The facility must not see a lot of traffic. No effort was put into keeping the path open for more than the occasional car.

Rounding a bend, the cab reached a clearing. The drive became a loop, the pinnacle of which was home to a wide set of double doors on an expansive three-story building with a worn brick face. Windows covered the front of the structure at even intervals, each one sealed by a thick steel security screen. The masonry work on the building's face was patched with moss, and barred windows were thick with rust. Despite its rundown appearance, lights could be seen behind many windows across all three floors.

"I'll be damned," the driver said. "It looks like the place *is* open."

The building sat in a clearing spanning several acres—thick woodland surrounding it. Ragged, unkempt grass covered the expanse, maybe four inches tall. It hadn't been mowed in weeks…maybe more than a month. There wasn't a soul in sight; if it weren't for the lighted windows, Cyrus would've sided with the driver and guessed the place had been abandoned.

The cab stopped beneath a portico at the building's entrance; the driver half-turned in his seat. "Are you sure you want out?" he said over his shoulder. "The lights are on, but I'm not sure anyone's home. If the place is open, I have no idea who's running it. I could swear it closed down years back."

Passing his cash through a slot in the plexiglass partition, Cyrus shook his head. "No problem. I'm good."

The driver grimaced. "You want me to wait? It's not like we get much demand for taxis around here anyway. It's no problem."

Cyrus considered it. He had no idea what he might find. He could be finished in ten minutes. Or, by the looks of the building, it could take him an hour just to find someone to speak with.

"That's alright," he said. "I might be a while. I'll call when I'm done here."

The driver passed over a card with his number on it. Cyrus slipped it into his pocket and then climbed out the door. He stood on the front steps and watched the tired old yellow sedan circle the drive and disappear through the narrow gap in the tree line.

The building's front door squeaked as Cyrus pulled it open. Not the usual quiet squeak of the pneumatic closer moving through the motions. The sound was biting and painful. It was metal grating on metal—the sound of a door that hadn't seen maintenance in years. He stepped across the threshold and watched the door bump closed on its own with agonizing slowness, moving across its closing mechanism in fits and spurts until it finished its last two inches of travel with a sudden surge of speed and a metallic bang that echoed through the entryway.

Cyrus rolled his eyes. He felt like he'd reached the end of the earth. If this was a medical institution, there was a reason the townspeople thought it had been shut down. There wasn't even a sign outside to display the facility's name. The place was uninviting through sheer neglect.

Strangely, the building's disrepair seemed to stop at the doorway. Cyrus stood in an expansive marble-tiled lobby with a clean floor that gleamed in the overhead light. An ornate chandelier hung high in the vaulted ceiling. Every bulb lit bright and entirely free of dust. The walls of the lobby were marble that matched the floor. A bench sat against the wall to the left, and the wall to Cyrus's right held a glass case backed in felt with dozens of narrow slits running horizontally across its back. It was the kind of case that typically had a directory with small letters pressed into the felt-lined slots. In this situation, it was likely to display department names or room numbers. The box was empty, holding no letters of any kind.

Similarly, there was an information desk set against the furthest wall. It stood chest high and was paneled in polished oak. The counter was granite and empty; like the chandelier, it was spotless and dust-free.

Walking to the counter, Cyrus considered how the space contradicted the building's exterior. It seemed a great deal of care was given to the interior while almost no attention had been paid to the outside. At least the entry was immaculate, he decided. Given what he'd seen so far, he couldn't guess what the rest of the building might look like.

A man in a white lab coat entered the room from the right end of the counter. He moved swiftly and with confidence, approaching Cyrus with his hand extended. The man's appearance showed no surprise at having a visitor. Cyrus spotted a small camera mounted high on the wall behind the counter and understood why. There were likely more cameras outside the building. He'd been surveilled since his cab turned off the main road.

"I'm Doctor Petridge," the man said with a smile. "Administrator of the facility. How can I help you today?"

Petridge stood shy of six feet and was a little wide in the midsection. He had short, neatly trimmed gray hair and a matching beard. He wore a dark sweater under his lab coat and dark pants. Cyrus was impressed by the man's grip when they shook. When he spoke, he saw a genuine flicker of warmth in the man's eyes.

"Nice to meet you," Cyrus said. "I'm here to visit a patient." He intentionally did not introduce himself and was curious how the doctor would deal with the matter. "His name is Samuel Dabney."

Petridge nodded, clearly familiar with Dabney off the top of his head. "I'm sorry, I didn't catch your name. Are you related to Mister Dabney?"

Here we go.

The less-than-stellar shape of the grounds outside led Cyrus to suspect that the staff might be careless or even unprofessional. If that were the case, getting time alone with Dabney would be easy. But given the polar opposite of the facility's condition, once he stepped through the door, combined with the competent and poised demeanor of the doctor, he now felt less confident.

"I'm sorry," Cyrus said. He pulled a business card from inside his jacket and passed it over. "I'm Jerry Peterson. I'm a stringer for several national papers. I hoped to interview Mister Dabney and get some background for a story I'm developing."

The Peterson persona was legit. He'd used it back when reporting in the years after leaving the Coalition, before meeting Reese and her people. If Petridge looked into it, he would find the profile fully backstopped, with dozens of high-profile stories to Peterson's credit.

A corner of Petridge's mouth turned down. He nodded absently. "I'm afraid you've made the trip for nothing," he said. "Mister Dabney hasn't spoken more than a few words at one time in several years. He's quite uncommunicative and almost entirely unresponsive."

That was disappointing but not entirely a shock to Cyrus. Though Nathan had tracked Dabney to the mental facility, absolutely nothing was known of his mental or physical state. Only that he'd fallen off the grid more than ten years prior. That Nathan had been able to locate Dabney was a testament to his ability to sluice digital archives for even the smallest scraps of data. A single reference to Dabney's once-classified military ID was in an insurance database. According to Nathan, someone had gone to a lot of trouble to expunge any recent record of Dabney from all digital archives. He might never have been found if his ID had not been entered in the incorrect database field when his insurance paperwork was completed.

"That's unfortunate," Cyrus said quietly. "Still, I've come from our Los Angeles office to speak with Mister Dabney. Could I see him? Getting a sense of the man, however limited, will give me more to work with."

The expression on Petridge's face seemed to sour. "I don't think that would be a good idea," he said. "I hope you understand; it's my duty to look out for the wellbeing of my patients. I don't think exposure to the press would be in Samuel's best interest."

His patient?

Cyrus already knew that Samuel Dabney had no next of kin. His parents had both passed, and there were no siblings to grant him access to the man. The doctor needed to sign off on this. Either that, or he had to sneak in to see Dabney himself. That would be...*complicated*.

"I can understand and respect your need to protect your patients," Cyrus offered. "It's commendable. But I have no interest in naming Mister Dabney in my piece. Someone has gone through great trouble to keep his name out of public records. I won't do anything to jeopardize that."

A look of concern flashed in Petridge's eyes. It was quickly replaced by what Cyrus suspected was a sense of near panic. "If you're suggesting some kind of coverup, I can assure you nothing untoward is happening here."

Petridge should've been upset—offended, indignant, maybe even angry, but certainly not frightened. He didn't have a complete sense of Petridge yet, but the man didn't seem to be up to no good.

So what is he up to?

"It's alright, Doc." Cyrus offered his best disarming smile. "Like I said, I have a great deal of respect for privacy. If you let me talk with Mister Dabney, I'll even tell you how I tracked him here. You can clean up that last remaining breadcrumb and sleep better knowing that I'm the last person who will come asking about him."

Petridge might be claiming ignorance of Dabney's situation, but there was no question the offer tempted him. He chewed the inside of his mouth for the two seconds it took him to consider the proposal.

"As I've said, there's no talking with him," Petridge reiterated. "He doesn't speak. I'm sorry to say I haven't progressed with him in that regard."

"Fair enough. Let me see him. Just give me five minutes with him. Then I'll leave and won't bother you or him ever again. And I promise you his name won't appear in anything I write."

It took only another second for Petridge to relent. "This way," he said.

They passed the counter, leaving the same way Petridge had entered the room. They walked around a corner and halfway down a long hall before stopping at a set of elevator doors. Petridge tapped the call button for a car heading up. The elevator doors opened instantly. Cyrus guessed there wasn't a lot of staff on hand, and the elevator hadn't moved since Petridge had made his way to the lobby.

Exiting on the third floor, Petridge led Cyrus down another hall. They stopped outside room 366. Petridge rapped twice on the door before pushing through it without pause. The knock must've been a formality, Cyrus guessed. If Dabney was unresponsive, there was no chance of disrupting him.

Dabney's room was as spotless as every other inch of the hospital's interior. A modern, articulated hospital bed was made with fresh linens. A tall wardrobe stood on the far side of a wide, dirty window with rusting bars outside. The walls were painted in a clean coat of bland institutional off-white, and the tile floors shone with the reflection of the overhead halogen bulbs. Once again, the building's interior starkly contrasted with the exterior.

What stood out in the sterile, institutional room were the ant farms. There were three of the tall, strange structures. They were essentially shallow frames that stood upright. Each was about an inch deep and filled with sandy, earthy material pinched between two glass planes. Ants burrowed in the soil, creating tunnels in the narrow, three-dimensional space. The tunnels were visible through the front pane of glass, thin-bodied ants matching through them with clear intent.

Two of the ant farms were the same size, about 36x24 inches. They sat on tables at opposite corners of the room. The third farm sat in front of the window. This one was larger, perhaps 48x36 inches, and contained thick-bodied black ants. This was unusual, but Cyrus quickly focused on the room's occupant.

A man sat in a high-backed rocking chair beside the bed. He looked in his seventies, though Cyrus knew Dabney to be only 51. His face was creased and wrinkled, presumably with time. Dark half-circles hung under dry silver-gray eyes. His hair was neatly trimmed on the sides but thick and bushy silver on top. It stood up in all sorts of wild directions. Several days' worth of stubble lined the man's jaw. It, too, had gone silver with age.

Everything about the man seemed prematurely old. The man Cyrus was looking at could've easily been Dabney's father rather than Dabney himself. He didn't fit with what Cyrus expected, except, that is, for the light he saw in the man's eyes. He'd seen that same light in several photos Nathan provided with the limited recent information he'd uncovered. The photos were taken two decades earlier when Dabney worked on a classified project at a Paulson, New Jersey laboratory.

"Samuel?" Doctor Petridge asked. "This is Mister Peterson. He would like to ask you some questions. Would that be alright with you?"

Samuel Dabney stared straight ahead. His focus hadn't shifted since they'd entered the room, and he didn't budge now.

"Hello, Samuel," Cyrus said. He stepped into Dabney's eye-line, smiled, and offered an abbreviated wave in an attempt to attract his gaze. "You can call me Jerry if you like. It's nice to meet you."

Dabney remained silent and motionless. His focus never shifted. He would blink once every minute or so, but that was the extent of his movement.

Doctor Petridge looked at Cyrus and shrugged. "Like I said...he's unresponsive. He doesn't talk, he doesn't react. He's here, but he's not." He walked back to the door. "I'm sorry you've wasted your time."

Cyrus studied Dabney. The years had not been kind to him...but what could age a man so drastically? He wanted to know what had led to his placement in the hospital, but he knew Petridge wouldn't give that up. For whatever reason, Petridge was set on sheltering Dabney from the world. Cyrus had gone out on a limb when he guessed that Petridge was somehow involved in the immense work required to scrub Dabney from the public record, but his point had seemed to hit the mark. Whatever their relationship, Petridge was protecting Dabney. Cyrus knew he didn't have anything compelling enough to make Petridge share what he knew.

Still, Cyrus was impressed by the light in the old man's eyes. Despite the years, it was every bit as vibrant as it had been in the old photos. He knelt before Dabney, putting their faces level. The focus of Dabney's pupils shifted with Cyrus's proximity, but he did not react. There was no response of any kind.

"It was nice to meet you, Mister Dabney," Cyrus said. "I wish you well. I'm sorry we don't have more time to talk."

Those words seemed to register with Dabney. The slack look left his face. His dry lips pursed, then began to tremble. His eyes shifted, and he blinked. Once at first, very slowly, then twice more in rapid succession. "My god," he croaked in a dry, raspy voice. "Nyland? Is that you?"

———————

Rocking on his heels, Cyrus shot a look to Doctor Petridge. Petridge's eyebrows were arched, and he was wide-eyed and staring at Dabney. The response was obviously unexpected. But Petridge's lips quickly drew into a tight line. He promptly shoved both hands into the side pockets of his lab coat. Strangely, they were closed fists when they disappeared. According to his posture, Petridge wasn't as surprised that Dabney had spoken...he seemed surprised that he'd spoken to *him*.

"No," Cyrus said to Dabney. "I'm sorry. My name is Jerry, Jerry Peterson."

Dabney's eyes studied Cyrus. He watched them move repeatedly across the features of his face. There was confusion in his stare. Finally, he turned and looked at the doctor.

Shaking his head, Dabney's voice cracked again. "It's alright. You're among friends." He was speaking to Cyrus. "My God...it's been so long."

Cyrus pulled himself upright and glanced at the doctor. Petridge shrugged. He still looked uncomfortable with what was happening, but he seemed less surprised. He stepped forward and looked down at Dabney in the chair.

"I'm sorry, Samuel," Petridge said. "This isn't your friend. This is Mister Peterson. He wants to interview you for a story he's writing for the newspaper."

His gaze shifting slowly between Petridge and Cyrus, Dabney was clearly out of sorts. He sat silently as the look of confusion was replaced by one of concern.

"I don't understand," Dabney said at last.

"This can't be your friend," Petridge said. "It's been two decades, Samuel. He might look like your friend, but it's not possible. Nyland would be much older now."

Petridge looked at Cyrus. "I'm sorry," he said. "As I've said, he doesn't speak often. When he does, he's very confused. Particularly about the date. His sense of time is—" he paused to search for an appropriate word— "jumbled, I suppose you could say."

Dabney shook his head and spoke more clearly for the first time. The traces of confusion were being pushed from his mind with time. "Don't be silly, Doctor," he said. "My friend doesn't age. He looks the same today as he did twenty years ago." He looked at Cyrus. "It's alright. You can tell him...you're among friends. Petridge has been protecting me from *them*."

Cyrus felt his heart race at Dabney's unlikely comment.

My friend doesn't age?

Like Tracy Clark?

Petridge shot Cyrus a grim look that spoke volumes. It said, *see what I mean? And this is what you get!* All in a single glance. Still, Cyrus wasn't writing off the outlandish statement so easily.

"Mister Dabney," Cyrus said. "Could you tell me about your friend? Could you tell me about Nyland? You said we look similar?"

Petridge sighed dramatically and stepped away from Dabney. His frustration was unmistakable, and Cyrus was growing to question the doctor's motivations more and more.

Dabney looked at Cyrus with quizzical eyes. He still seemed dubious of claims that Cyrus was not this man, Nyland. Though Cyrus doubted he could've gained access to the patient using his real name, he suddenly wished he could be less circumspect with Dabney without presenting himself as a reporter. Whatever misidentification occurred, perhaps his real identity would help shed some light on it.

The more Dabney studied Cyrus, the less expressive his face became. His suspicion seemed to wane with further examination. There was calculation behind his eyes. Cyrus could see the wheels turning. Whatever had brought Dabney to the mental institution, he wasn't lost and out of touch the way Doctor Petridge claimed. Whatever was happening, Dabney was becoming more lucid and calculating with each passing minute.

"No," Dabney said at last. "The color of your eyes is wrong. And you don't have a scar next to your nose. Still, the resemblance is uncanny."

Dabney looked to Petridge. "Twenty years, you say?"

Petridge nodded slightly. "Give or take—maybe more. You've never been very clear regarding the timeframe. What I've put together is sketchy at best."

Petridge had been staring at Cyrus for some time. It was a kind of threat analysis, he felt sure of it. The only thing Cyrus didn't know was Petridge's conclusion. When Petridge moved closer to Dabney, Cyrus stepped away, instinctively giving them space. Petridge knelt close at Dabney's side and began to whisper.

"Are you sure about this?" Cyrus heard Petridge say. "You don't know this man. How do you know you can trust him? You understand that he's not Nyland, don't you?"

Dabney sat silent for long seconds with Petridge perched at his ear. Dabney's eyes remained fixed on Cyrus, and Cyrus knew they had reached a critical point. A decision was being made.

"No, he's not Nyland," Dabney said quietly. "But add a couple of decades, and he could be Roe. *He must be.*"

"Roe?" Petridge said more loudly the he intended. He seemed flustered by the mistake. He looked Dabney in the eye. "You've never mentioned that name before."

Dabney smiled for the first time. There was a gleam of satisfaction in his eyes that was unmistakable. "I might not be the man I once was, but I made an oath, and by God, I've kept it."

Chapter 7 - Door-To-Door Bible Salespeople

Wilmington, North Carolina

Tracy Clark flicked on her turn signal and angled into a small parking lot adjacent to the corner convenience store. Only three other vehicles were in the lot: one minivan, a pickup truck, and a bland midsize sedan with a sticker on its bumper identifying it as part of a large nationwide car rental chain. She didn't pull into one of the empty slots. Instead, she rolled to a stop behind the rental car and shifted into park. A woman emerged from the rental, rounded its trunk, and slipped into the passenger seat beside her.

"I'm sorry to bring you all this way on short notice," Tracy said.

The woman shook her head and tugged into the seatbelt. She was older than Tracy, but not by a lot. Like Tracy, she had a slender athletic frame and long hair. But in this case, the newcomer had dark hair that fell well past her shoulders. The newcomer was in her late thirties, while Tracy looked to be in her mid to late twenties. "It's no problem. Nothing is happening at the moment anyway."

"No one will question your absence?" Tracy asked. She

circled the small lot and returned to the low-traffic thoroughfare.

"No. If anything, getting away from time to time is a good idea. They're good people. I'm more likely to draw attention if I don't have personal issues occasionally."

Waiting for the two oncoming cars to pass, Tracy looked at her friend more closely. It had been years since they'd last met face to face. Plenty of calls and even video chats, but seeing her in person was a different matter. "You look good, Gretchen. Island life agrees with you."

Gretchen tapped the button on the door and buzzed her window down. "Island life," she muttered. "You make it sound almost tropical. Do you know what the average temperature is there, year-round?"

Tapping the accelerator, Tracy guided them out into the sparse daytime traffic. "Soak up the sun while you can. If this goes well, we'll get what we need on our first stop."

It took fifteen minutes to cross the sleepy section of town. Though she'd never been there, Tracy had no trouble finding the moderately sized home. It was what architects sometimes called a four-square. Essentially a wide two-story that was as wide as deep, a square. The potentially bland design was accented by a wide wraparound front porch supported by ornate columns and decorated with intricate molding. The windows on the first and second floors had matching molding, and a wide, shallow dormer accented the roof high above. It was tucked on a quiet lane lined with hundred-year-old oaks at the back of a lonely subdivision. The house sat on what might've been a half acre. The neighbors on both sides were close, but not too close. A narrow concrete drive slipped past the house on the left and led to a detached two-stall garage near the back of the property. A massive oak sat dead center in the front yard.

"Not bad," Gretchen said as Tracy glided the car to the

curb. "You said this guy's retired?"

"Retired early, actually," Tracy said. "At the age of thirty-two. Apparently, he came into some money, but I haven't been able to connect the dots on the source of the windfall. It's part of what we're going to sort out. He purchased the house immediately after retiring, but he's been here for going on thirteen years."

They climbed the half-dozen concrete steps on the street and strolled down the short sidewalk to the front porch. Tracy could see Gretchen studying the home from the corner of her eye. The yard was spotless, with freshly cut grass and neatly tended flower beds. The house itself was immaculate. Anthony Elmore clearly took a great deal of pride in his home.

Tracy rang the doorbell while Gretchen remained a few paces back and pretended to admire the property. They were both dressed casually. Tracy wore a caramel-colored lightweight sweater, while Gretchen seemed to relish the seventy-degree weather, wearing a dark button-up blouse over a white tank top. She felt confident they didn't look like door-to-door bible salespeople, but who knew what was common in this neighborhood?

The door opened slowly to reveal a stout man in his mid-forties. He wore jeans and a flannel shirt. He was about five-foot-six, and Tracy had four inches on him. He was a little wide in his midsection but had a thick, dark head of hair and kind eyes. He wiped his hands on a white dishtowel and smiled at the sight of the two of them.

"Mister Elmore," Tracy said. "My name is Tracy Clark—this is Gretchen Gamble. We're with the FBI field office in Atlanta. Would you mind if we asked you a few questions?"

Elmore's expression instantly became more serious. He nodded and stepped aside, gesturing them in. "Anything I can do to help," he said. "But as you probably know, I'm retired. I haven't investigated a derailment in over a decade."

Chapter 8 - Another Ant Farm

Woodstock, Illinois, United States

Doctor Petridge pushed Samuel Dabney down the hallway in a wheelchair. Cyrus followed, close at Petridge's heels. After a brief, though vague, disagreement between Dabney and Petridge, they'd set out on a trip across the hospital. They took the elevator to the 2nd floor, and Petridge led the way down what seemed to be a central hall to an adjoining, somewhat narrower passage. The doctor stopped to swipe a card. He entered on a keypad at a massive steel door, allowing them access to what was obviously a much more secure portion of the building.

"Here we go," Petridge said. He turned the wheelchair to the left and passed through a double-wide entrance where the doors had been removed from their hinges.

Stopping just inside the room, Cyrus moved around Petridge and Dabney. The space was long and rectangular, with a ceiling close to fifteen feet high. Sixteen hospital beds occupied the space, eight with headboards pushed against the far wall and eight more against the nearest. Eleven of the beds were occupied. All of the patients were unconscious;

seven of them were attached to complicated artificial breathing machines that whirred and hissed quietly in the stillness of the room. All the patients were hooked to equipment that monitored their vital signs, and all were attached to at least one intravenous drip hanging from a pole beside each bed.

"What's going on?" Cyrus asked.

"This is my fault," Dabney said quietly in a grim, resigned voice. "All of these people are here because of me."

Petridge mumbled something under his breath, but Cyrus couldn't make it out. Dabney grabbed the wheel of his chair and spun it so he faced the doctor. He focused a penetrating stare. "There's no point in denying it," he said. "I can't help them—I can at least acknowledge responsibility."

Staring at the floor, Petridge shook his head but offered no reply. He shoved his hands in his pockets once more and shuffled his feet. At last, his eyes rose and met with Dabney's. "You're sure this is a good idea?"

Dabney offered a single, sharp nod.

Petridge blew a long breath and looked at Cyrus for an extended moment. "Fine," he said. "I'll make my rounds. Call me if you need me." His gaze shifted back to Dabney. "Good luck, my friend." He patted him on the shoulder as he passed and walked further into the room.

Turning his chair to face the space again, Dabney took time to view every face individually. Cyrus saw his gaze shift slowly from patient to patient, pain clear in his expression.

"What do you know about me?" Dabney asked.

"Embarrassingly little," Cyrus admitted. "I came here on a lark. Your name surfaced in some documents I uncovered. You once worked on a project relating to a group I'm investigating. I'm here to see what you can tell me about them."

"You're investigating the Order?" Dabney asked, offering a curious expression. "If that's the case, you may have bitten off more than you can chew."

"So you're familiar?"

"I wish I never heard of them," he grumbled. "I was experimenting with neural networking and adaptive biologic interfaces when someone approached me from the group. I'd never heard of the Order of Origin at that point. Their organization and theories were entirely unknown to me then, but their money was green, and I needed funding to continue my work. I'm sorry to admit I was a little overconfident in those days—pushing the boundaries of science without sufficient concern for the consequences of my actions. The state of technology was a major limitation at the time. But the Order didn't just offer funding—they provided me with cutting-edge tech beyond anything available anywhere. I figured they had military backing...it was the only explanation for the money and resources at their disposal. I figured the entire cult thing was a front for some kind of CIA research effort. I was happy to use them and had little worry that they were using me."

Cyrus watched the expression on Dabney's face. There was a lot more to the story, that was obvious. "But it wasn't the CIA, was it?" he said. "It wasn't even government."

Dabney's expression was serious—dire even; his eyes were unblinking. He shook his head slowly. "I couldn't have been more wrong. They were a cult, alright. Entirely committed to their beliefs in ways beyond my comprehension. By the time that was clear, I was in too deep. But that wasn't the worst part."

The statement piqued Cyrus's interest, but remained silent and let Dabney continue.

"Do you know what the Order of Origin is all about? What they *really* believe?"

Cyrus shrugged. Everything he knew so far was rumor.

He didn't have any inside intelligence or a source to give him a comprehensive look at the organization. They were zealots, to be sure—but there was a lot of conflicting information regarding the exact nature of the organization's beliefs and intentions. Some of the talk was just too outrageous to be taken seriously.

"They believe in beings from another world...and they are right," Dabney said with a conviction that made it apparent there was no doubt in his mind.

Not sure how to respond to that, Cyrus remained silent. Given what he knew about the Halon, he wouldn't argue against the fact, but supporting it seemed like an equally bad idea. There was more to be learned by simply remaining silent.

"You don't believe me," Dabney said. "Why should you? I didn't buy it either. I figured they were all a bunch of crackpots waiting to lace up their sneakers and chase the next comet into the afterlife. But like I said, their money was good. Their leader, a man named Verhoeven, was willing to fund my research. I was happy to play along. It was the chance of a lifetime and the biggest mistake I ever made."

Cyrus surveyed the room again and wondered how these patients factored into his story. He needed to keep Dabney talking.

"Cults believe all sorts of fringe things," Cyrus said. "If their beliefs were commonly accepted, I guess they wouldn't be considered cults."

Dabney shook his head. "Cults are organizations founded on a religious belief. Beliefs taken on faith that can't be substantiated. What the Order *preaches*, for lack of a better word, isn't based on faith. It's science. It's based on facts, rooted in reality. What they believe can be quantified. That's what makes them so dangerous."

Cyrus found himself scowling. "Forgive me for saying so, but you sound like a proponent of their cause when you take that kind of hardline."

The expression on Dabney's face darkened. "I felt like you at first," he said. "But it's true. I didn't want to believe it, but they proved it. The Order's purpose is to support *our* creators. Real figures rather than mythical beings no one has ever met. I've met them myself—spoken with them. Their existence is indisputable. Believe me...I wish it weren't the case."

"Creators?" Cyrus sputtered, unable to keep the shock from his voice. "As in Gods? You're kidding, right?"

Dabney shook his head. "They're not Gods. Really, they're no different from you and me. They just come from...*somewhere else.*"

Somewhere else. Cyrus ran that through his mind several times before speaking. The key to keeping Dabney talking was to avoid insulting him. Was he saying the Order of Origin was based on members of the Halon race? An alien race making themselves out to be Gods?

"As in, from another planet?" Cyrus offered in an attempt to coax further information from Dabney.

Dabney grinned but shook his head. "Aliens?" He chuckled. "No. Hardly. They come from another universe."

Cyrus found himself unable to reply. The comment caught him entirely unprepared.

Another universe?

"You mean the Order believes these *people* come from another galaxy?" Cyrus said at last.

"Not at all," Dabney said. He pointed to yet another ant farm. Cyrus hadn't noticed it until that moment. It sat on a metal counter near where they stood. It was smaller than the ones upstairs, this one perhaps 24 inches wide and 18 inches tall. There were dozens of pathways burrowed in the dirt with ants working throughout a maze of tunnels. "Another layer of reality," he continued. "Another dimension—one adjacent to our own. Think of the layers of an onion. Peel back one and you find another, and another. Rather a perfect analogy."

Cyrus just stared, first at the ant farm and then at Dabney. There was no question Dabney believed what he was saying. But how seriously should the information be considered? Dabney was a resident in a mental institution, after all. That sort of thing doesn't happen without good reason. Still, Cyrus decided, if he'd told anyone who would listen the things he knew about the Halon, how long would it take him to end up in a place like this?

"This can't be news to you," Dabney said.

Cyrus blinked hard and pulled his stare away from the ant farm. "What?" It was all he could say. He wasn't sure he'd heard him correctly. His mind was drifting with a cascade of potential implications. What Dabney said seemed insane, but that didn't mean he was wrong.

Dabney glanced across the wide room, seeming to take comfort in the fact that Doctor Petridge was now at the far end examining the display of a machine attached to a patient's bed. "Petridge isn't here," he said. "You can level with me about Nyland. I sometimes get mixed up. I know it's been a long time. Is he alright?"

Cyrus was confused and unsure how to respond. "Nyland?" he said.

Grinning, Dabney nodded. He watched Cyrus with genuine interest in his eyes. But after a long silence, the light in his gaze faltered. "You're not faking, are you?" he said. "You have no idea who I'm talking about?"

Cyrus shook his head.

Sitting back in the chair, Dabney puffed out a breath. "Well, I don't get it," he said. "You're the spitting image of him. I don't see how that's—"

Cyrus was looking at the floor when he felt Dabney's eyes lock on him. "What?" he said. The word came out far more defensively than he intended.

"If I didn't know better," Dabney said in a quiet, conspiratorial voice, "I'd bet you were his kid."

"Nyland?" Cyrus said. "You're saying I look enough like your friend to be his son?"

His eyes once more searching the details of Cyrus's face, Dabney nodded. "If I didn't know for a fact it wasn't possible, I'd bet the house on it."

Cyrus clamped his jaw tight and ground his teeth. He fought the urge to roll his eyes. He had no memory of his childhood. By extension, he had no memory of his parents either. His first memories were patchy and scattered but included waking up in the wreckage of a train derailment when he was eight or ten years old. In truth, he had no idea exactly how old he was. The life he knew began the day of that train wreck. But if Dabney was any indication, he might have the first clue leading to the identity of his father. That was if he could take the ramblings of a semi-coherent man who was a long-time resident of a mental hospital.

Fighting his better judgment, Cyrus asked the obvious question. "What do you mean, *if you didn't know for a fact it wasn't possible?*"

Dabney didn't answer; his gaze had shifted. He stared into the middle distance, clearly lost in thought or memory.

"Samuel," Cyrus thundered. He saw the man's eyes focus again as his mind returned to the moment. He repeated the question.

"Nyland can't have children," Dabney said matter-of-factly. "None of the Tangury can. It's why they need us."

"The *Tangury?*" Cyrus said.

Dabney stared. "You really don't know any of this?"

97

Cyrus's frustration was mounting. He was either making progress on his investigation of the Halon, or he was on a world-class snipe hunt. So far, there was no way to be sure. "The Order believes we are being visited by beings from another dimension—a race called the Tangury. They revere these people as Gods and have founded their faith on them. Am I on the right track?"

"No!" Dabney bellowed. "You're not paying attention. I told you—this isn't a matter of faith—it's a matter of *science*. The existence of the Tangury can be scientifically quantified. That's what makes the Order of Origin dangerous. Their members don't operate on blind faith. Everything they believe can be proven. These people are real!"

The outburst caught the attention of Doctor Petridge. He rushed across the room. Cyrus knew his time with Dabney was quickly running out, and he still had countless questions. Far more than he could verbalize at the moment.

"The Tangury are real!" Dabney's voice boarded on screaming. He rocked violently in his chair, his face turning red and the veins in his neck bulging. "They're here and a threat to the entire world." He shook his fist violently toward the ant farm and pointed an accusing finger.

Petridge tried to calm him, but Dabney batted his placating hands away. He glared red-faced at Cyrus and shook a pointing fist in the direction of the ant farm.

"We're nothing to them," Dabney screamed. "Ants trapped under glass—they will use or eradicate us—we are nothing to them. We're a means to an end. Our life—our world—it's nothing more than a science experiment! We're the ants—don't you see? We're the ants!"

Petridge pulled a capped syringe from the pocket of his lab coat. It must've been preloaded for just such a situation because he flicked away the protective cover and plunged the short needle into Dabney's neck. He injected the contents before Dabney could wrestle it away.

Seconds later, every muscle in Dabney's body seemed to turn to mush. His rant stopped mid-sentence, and his swinging arms fell to his sides. His head tipped forward, and his chin slumped to his chest. Petridge grabbed him by the top of the shoulders to keep him from falling face-first from the wheelchair.

Cyrus acted quickly to buckle a seatbelt across Dabney's lap. He held him upright while Petridge pulled a set of shoulder straps from a pocket on the back of the chair and wrapped them around Dabney's lethargic form. Clearly, the chair was outfitted for just this sort of situation. The shoulder straps formed a kind of three-point harness similar to what was used in race cars. The apparatus kept Dabney's limp body upright and relatively comfortable.

Just as Petridge was securing the last buckle of the restraint system, a large orderly came thundering into the room. He was a tall black man with biceps the size of telephone poles. Wide-eyed and out of breath, the man looked like he'd run the length of the building at a full sprint. Cyrus studied the man and wondered if he was here for Dabney or him.

"Thank you, Jordan," Petridge said. "I'm sorry. Samuel just got a little worked up. Everything is fine."

Jordan glared at Cyrus with unabashed accusation before shooting a silent glance back in the doctor's direction.

"That won't be necessary," Petridge said. "Everything is alright. You can go. I'm sorry to trouble you."

Seeming reluctant to do so, Jordan turned and trudged for the hall once more. Cyrus watched him go and considered everything that had just happened.

"I hope you can see," Petridge said, "Mister Dabney is a very special case. All of us are willing to do whatever is necessary to protect him. I need your word—you can't publish what he's told you today."

Cyrus watched Petridge carefully. The man was surprisingly composed, given what just transpired. It wasn't just the outburst that should have rattled him. He must have known what Dabney said.

"Is this the part where you tell me everything I heard was the ramblings of a madman?" Cyrus asked. Skepticism was evident in his tone.

"Far from it, I'm afraid," Petridge said. "Samuel believed everything he told you."

It was an odd statement. Cyrus let it hang in the air for two long seconds while he studied the doctor. "You're not saying he's wrong," he said finally. "You're not claiming that he's nuts."

Petridge grinned. "I'm a psychiatric M.D. If you want my professional opinion, we're all a little *nuts*. But the truth is, I won't dispute anything Samuel told you. I've seen too much to disrespect him like that. He's *proven* too much to me."

Cyrus was momentarily taken aback. "You're saying you believe his claims? That people are visiting us from another dimension?"

Petridge was quiet for a moment. His eyes went briefly back to Dabney before responding. "Samuel Dabney is injured," he said, "but he's not delusional. I can't make you believe what he has said. My advice would be to keep an open mind. It might serve you well."

It was an odd observation coming from a doctor. That, in its way, was concerning on many levels.

"This room," Cyrus said, changing the subject to something he hoped might be more constructive. "Why did you bring us here? You never said."

Placing his hands in his pockets once more, Petridge stood beside Cyrus and faced the ward. "He never made it to that part of the tale?" he asked. "That's a shame. There's a reason Samuel speaks with such conviction. He worked with the

Order for many years. They funded his project. These patients are the result of his work, I'm afraid."

Cyrus's eyes roamed the room once more. Eleven patients, all seemingly comatose. Some were on life-support, others were breathing of their own accord.

"His project did this?" Cyrus asked. His voice was quiet; he was afraid of the answer. "What was he doing?"

"He's a neurobiologist by training," Petridge said. "His dream was to find a way to interface the human brain with computer technology. He was talented. Perhaps a genius...*once.*"

"He said the Order funded his work? What was the project?"

"Experimenting with neuro-digital interfaces," Petridge said simply. "Not my area of expertise, I'm afraid. But you're looking at the unlucky test subjects. The Order pushed him into human trials far ahead of schedule. This is the result."

Cyrus didn't know what to say. He'd come here only to find more questions. Unfortunately, only Dabney would be able to answer them. And looking at the man, he wasn't sure when—or if—that would be possible. Dabney's condition wasn't much better than anyone in this room.

"Holy crap," Cyrus said. "Dabney isn't a patient here, is he?"

Petridge shook his head. "No. He's helping me treat these patients. I'm protecting him—and them—from the Order. They must never know this facility exists."

Chapter 9 - Crackpot Theory

Undisclosed location, Australia

Reese had been up since dawn, not that the sun's position technically affected her two hundred feet below the surface. To help in that regard, the lights in the main hall, primary corridors, and personal living quarters of the underground base had all been replaced with LEDs that automatically adjusted to simulate the ambient light an office building might offer through outward-facing windows. The team sometimes worked for long periods at the underground installation, and simulating natural light was supposed to be more healthy, both mentally and physically. It was something Cyrus had come up with. He said he'd seen a similar setup while working an operation years earlier.

Sipping her coffee, Reese sat once more at her table in the main hall. She wore baggy flannel pajama pants and a half-zipped sweatshirt over a white tank top. She gazed at the screen of her laptop and contemplated the data, just as she had for the last two hours. It was information from the data drive Cyrus had brought back from his operation in Bangkok. If what she saw was worth killing over, she didn't know its secret .

"Your scowl doesn't look encouraging," Hondo said as he carried plated food in each hand across the room. Dropping into a chair opposite her, he placed one platter before himself and slid the other to her.

She looked at breakfast and felt her stomach growl. Until that moment, she hadn't realized how hungry she was. "Thank you," she smiled.

Cyrus had been in Russia and then Bangkok for the last week. Hondo had been away for nearly twice that time. He'd been visiting an old friend who now worked somewhere high in the ranks of British Intelligence. Hondo was trying to pull some strings, hoping to use British MI-6 resources to help locate Tracy Clark. His contact had been reluctant initially but had proven willing in the end. The major caveat was that Hondo had to remain on station to review the surveillance feeds from inside MI-6 headquarters. The English were unwilling to pipe the data to his computer back at their *secret lair*, as his friend called their off-the-grid installation.

Pushing her laptop aside, Reese focused on the plate of eggs and bacon. She grabbed her fork and dug in. She also took a moment to consider what little she'd learned from her morning research.

"Looking at the raw data," she said, "I'm inclined to say that there's literally nothing of value here. Terabytes of gigapixel surface images, sure—but nothing unusual. Nothing unexpected. The telemetry supports that conclusion, one hundred percent. Like the Russians, the Chinese aren't searching surrounding space for a gravitational anomaly. Their sights seem set on the moon's surface if you can believe it. And they aren't content sticking to gravimetric analysis. They are doing photographic analysis as well."

He look surprised. "You mean they're literally photographing the lunar surface?"

She nodded. It was unusual. The United States and the Russians were conducting exhaustive scans of the space surrounding Earth, but those efforts concentrated on non-photographic sensor workups. They were searching for something they didn't expect to locate visually. Everyone seems to believe a gravimetric disruption would point to what they searched for.

If it was even out there, Reese reminded herself.

Hondo watched her. She sensed his eyes on her and was glad he was back. She wished he'd been in Bangkok with Cyrus yesterday. The two of them made an outstanding team. While she knew they had worked together extensively in the past, neither had ever gone into great detail regarding their shared history. But she knew Cyrus trusted Hondo with his life—with all of their lives, in fact. She was also aware Hondo had earned that trust more than once within the last year.

Hondo's real name was Harvey Roberts. No one knew how he'd earned the nickname. It occurred to her that she'd never asked. That was amusing. Everyone just knew him as Hondo. He was tall, a little over six foot, and wide-shouldered. Stark blue eyes showed intelligence, and the dark stubble of a two-day-old beard was always present on his jaw. He was ten years older than Cyrus, though it was hard to tell the age difference by looking at them. Hondo's short dark hair was prematurely patching with grey; his beard had recently begun to follow suit. He had a touch of an Australian accent that sometimes came and went, depending on his mood. It became more prominent with fatigue or stress.

Hondo fixed Reese with an odd expression. She could see he was waiting for some kind of '*but*' to counter her initial conclusion.

Reese shrugged. "It doesn't make sense, does it?" she said. "Chinese Intelligence went after Cyrus like he'd stolen their nuclear launch codes or something. And why are they looking at the moon? Do they know something that no one else does?"

Hondo shoveled another mouthful of eggs and seemed to consider the question. "We pulled comparable data from sources in the US and Russia. The Chinese know other nations are searching the skies. It's a race to see who can find the prize first. Maybe there's nothing special about their data. They just don't want anyone accumulating more information than they have. What's the saying? Knowledge is power? They might not even know what they're afraid of.

"What I heard on the Port's communication band last night didn't make me think the Chinese team was reacting with any kind of restraint. They didn't pull any punches. From the sound of it, a lot of the port guards were hurt or killed."

Reese grimaced. She'd had similar concerns about the Chinese response at the location. His logic for the Chinese effort to stop Cyrus was better than anything she had come up with.

Hondo took a long look at his plate. Reese was pretty sure he wasn't seeing the food. He seemed lost in thought.

"What about you?" he asked after several long seconds. "Do you think there's actually something out there? Everyone's getting worked up on the word of a cult leader. It seems implausible. Why is anyone taking him seriously?"

Cyrus's voice came from the back of the room. "You are out of the loop," he said tiredly. "But that's not your fault. We just have too many questions right now. And not nearly enough answers. If we could find Tracy, I think it would help a lot."

He had a plate piled with eggs and gripped a mug of coffee in his free hand. He walked around the table and took a spot beside Reese. She greeted him with a kiss that brought a smile to his tired face. He sat back in his chair and took a droopy-eyed look at Hondo. "It's good to see you," he said.

"You too," Hondo grinned. "But I've got to say, you've looked better. When's the last time you slept?"

Cyrus shrugged. He hadn't had nearly enough sleep, Reese knew. Though he hadn't said as much, the last week had taken a lot out of him. She knew things hadn't gone smoothly in Thailand, and she suspected his visit to Russia before that hadn't been a picnic either. Then, he'd forgone his first night of sleep in exchange for an impromptu trip to Chicago. He'd had almost nothing to say about visiting the windy city. Whatever he'd seen had troubled him. She wasn't sure why he was reluctant to discuss it. When he'd returned shortly before daybreak, she should've let him sleep, she reasoned. But then she looked at his exhausted but satisfied expression and didn't feel guilty about keeping him up until daybreak. She felt her cheeks warming and caught Cyrus staring at her.

"What?" she spat defensively and looked away. She felt her ears turning red as well. Cyrus laughed and she felt him squeeze her hand.

"The satellite imagery is a long shot at best," Cyrus said with a nod to Hondo. "I didn't expect to stir up a hornet's nest. I still think it's a crackpot theory."

Cyrus turned in his chair. Reese saw him eyeing her laptop. "Have you found anything?" he asked.

She offered a slow shake of her head. "I'm still going through it, but if there's something here, I don't see it. It's beautiful imagery, that's for sure. But I don't see what the fuss is about. If there's something unusual—" she shrugged as if to complete the statement.

Hondo's brow arched at the question. He knew they were looking at satellite imagery, but he had no idea why.

"It's high-def footage of the moon's surface," Cyrus explained.

Reese saw Hondo's confused expression deepen.

"I don't get it," Hondo said. "If you've seen one photo of the moon, you've seen them all."

Cyrus laughed. "You haven't seen these. These are higher resolution than anything before. And, these are shots of the dark side."

Hondo froze with a fork halfway to his mouth. Sitting up straight, he eyed Cyrus, then Reese. He lowered his fork and set it aside, already forgotten. "The dark side of the moon?" he mumbled.

Reese understood what he was thinking. We all go through life taking the moon overhead as a constant. It's always been there, and it always will be. We put men on the moon in 1969 with the Apollo 11 mission. Since then, countless photos and videos of the lunar surface have been taken. What few people ever consider is that the bulk of what we know about the ever-present celestial sentinel is limited to the side that is constantly facing the sun. We knew shockingly little about the opposite half, banished to permanent darkness.

"You're saying we've never taken photos of the dark side before?" Hondo seemed incredulous.

Reese shook her head. "There have been dozens of missions that included lunar orbits. The first was in 1966. Orbital missions persist till today. There are crafts up there right now from many different nations."

"So what's different about the Chinese satellite?" Hondo asked.

Cyrus grinned. "The Chinese satellite doesn't exist—at least not technically. The US partnered with the UK to put a single bird up there. The Russians positioned their own a while back. The Chinese launched their own only recently."

Hondo offered a troubled expression. "What's different about the Chinese satellite that makes it such a secret?"

Reese exchanged a nervous look with Cyrus but left the answer to him.

"Theirs is a next-generation spy bird," Cyrus grinned. "They won't even admit to having the technology that's currently in orbit. What they have up there is beyond top secret."

Hondo laughed. "And they have it pointed at the surface of the moon? You've got to be kidding. What the hell for?"

Pushing his plate away, Cyrus leaned his elbow on the tabletop. "Antarctica is the last unclaimed landmass left on Earth. Every nation wants its resources. It's such a big problem that an accord was signed agreeing that no nation can claim the landmass for itself."

Hondo nodded.

"Think of the moon the same way," Cyrus explained. "It's unclaimed real estate, just ripe for the picking. Everyone wants it, but no one can take it—just like Antarctica. Except the moon might be even more valuable. Where Antarctica sits atop untapped oil and natural gas reserves, the moon is littered with exotic ores, minerals, and metals. It has to be. It's been collecting them since the dawn of time."

Reese rolled her eyes and felt herself smirk. The dawn of time thing was a bit of a stretch. There were many theories regarding the moon's origin. It would take boots on the ground to prove or disprove them to everyone's satisfaction, but there was no question that the moon's surface had been collecting exotic debris for hundreds of millions of years. Maybe even billions. Its pockmarked surface was a testament to the fact.

"Even more appealing," Cyrus continued, "there's no vegetation or natural growth to hamper mining or exploration."

Hondo nodded. "So that's what the satellites are doing? Exploration?"

Cyrus raised a hand in the air and waggled it. "Yes, and no. Officially, yes. That's what each country will claim. They can learn a lot about the moon and the minerals comprising it without ever touching the surface. Much more than they will admit to.

"Those birds are up there as part of a space-based Cold War."

Hondo's expression darkened, but Reese quickly saw understanding touch his eyes. "They want to make sure everyone is playing by the rules," he concluded.

Cyrus nodded.

"That's why the Chinese went apeshit in Bangkok?" Hondo asked.

"It's the dirty little secret no one wants to discuss." Cyrus offered. "Radley Verhoeven's cult, the Order of Origin, has people paying attention for the first time. Verhoeven made some wild claim that there's something out there in space, evidently orbiting the Earth. According to him, it's been there for millions of years, and man didn't create it."

Hondo sat quietly for a few long moments. "Not made by man? And he's being taken seriously?" he asked.

Cyrus shrugged. "Apparently, Verhoeven offered some kind of proof that world leaders found difficult to deny. No one will say what it was, but it must've been compelling. His goofy cult seems to have stoked the fires of the new space race."

"I still don't buy it," Reese said. "What could Verhoeven say or do to get some of the most powerful nations in the world to take him so seriously? Can you imagine the amount of money invested right now? It's inconceivable."

Chapter 10 - I'm Not Stalling

Wilmington, North Carolina

Gretchen studied the house as Anthony Elmore led them to a living room. The house was as spotless inside as it was out. Some of the furnishings were antiques but appeared positioned for accent rather than use. Most of the furniture was contemporary, quality modern pieces that were neither particularly old nor new.

Elmore motioned Tracy and Gretchen to a sofa and sat in a nearby armchair. "Can I offer you something to drink?" he asked.

He was nervous, Gretchen knew. Though he did a good job of disguising it in his physical appearance, his mind had become a live wire, flooded with panic and jumbled thoughts that were too incoherent to follow. They would need to calm him down before she could pull anything useful out of him.

"No, thank you," Tracy said.

Gretchen shook her head to the negative, only partly in silent response to the question. Tracy met her eye simultaneously, allowing her to covey her inability to Read anything useful. It wasn't uncommon for someone to freak right out of the gate. Tracy would know what to do next.

"We would like to discuss your investigation of the Kepler derailment, Mister Elmore," Tracy said.

Elmore exhaled loudly and leaned back in his seat. "Of course you do," he muttered. "You can call me Tony if you like."

"Tony," Tracy said. She produced a sheet of paper that had been folded into quarters. After carefully unfolding it, she passed it to him. "In the course of your investigation, did you locate this device among the train wreckage?"

Spinning the paper right side up, Elmore squinted at the page. It was a sketch done in pencil depicting a digital device of some kind. It was small and very thin, almost like a piece of glass surrounded by a thin opaque bezel. It looked like some kind of futuristic smartphone or a touchscreen remote control.

"I've never seen anything like it," Elmore said. "Nothing this…interesting. Was it recovered from the wreckage? What is it?"

"It's a proprietary computer interface," Tracy said. "One of a kind, unfortunately."

Elmore shook his head. "It looks delicate. Was it made of glass? If it was onboard the train, odds are there wasn't anything left of it. Damage to the passenger compartments was catastrophic. If it was in the luggage car, I'm afraid that didn't fare much better."

Gretchen knew the reply wasn't what Tracy was hoping to hear. Still, she didn't seem surprised and didn't lose a step. She moved right on to the next order of business.

Tracy smiled. "It doesn't surprise you—us coming to discuss the derailment twelve years after the fact?"

He shook his head. "Not really. It's closer to thirteen years now. Do you know how many people have knocked on my door over the last decade? How many people have tracked me down with questions about the wreck? It was my swan song and the one that got away, all rolled into one."

"You never discovered the cause of the derailment," Tracy said. "That can't be a fulfilling way to end your career."

"Tell me about it. Then, to have reporters and law enforcement remind me of it? Ah, no offense…it's just like rubbing salt in the wound."

Tracy let an awkward silence hang in the air. Gretchen smiled politely, unwilling to offer anything to fill the gap. Surprisingly, Elmore didn't fill the silence either.

"Is it unusual to have a wreck that goes unsolved?" Tracy asked.

Elmore shook his head without hesitation. "It was a first for me. The first time that I know of, in fact. But it wasn't your run-of-the-mill train either."

It was an odd statement, and it captured Gretchen's interest. She was getting a clear Read on him now, but so far he wasn't thinking anything he wasn't saying aloud. Nothing helpful, at least.

"How so?" Tracy asked.

"Take your initial question, for example," Elmore explained. "You referred to the case as the Kepler derailment. Most wrecks are referred to by their train number, route, or the location of the incident."

Gretchen noticed how the retired investigator used the word *incident* rather than *accident*. To the average person, the words were often believed to be synonymous—not so with investigators. Something wasn't declared an accident until the cause had been determined—until fault or blame had been assigned.

"In this case," he went on, "the press—and by extension, the public—refer to the case by the contractor who had leased two of the twenty-two cars involved. Why do you suppose that is?"

Tracy didn't comment. Gretchen watched with growing interest.

"The public craves a conspiracy," Elmore said. "And Kepler had several contracts with the Department of Defense. When my team wasn't quick to attribute blame in our investigation, the press began to suppose whatever helped to sell papers."

Gretchen leaned forward, surprised by what she'd just gleaned from his mind. "You were granted a security clearance to investigate DOD involvement. Under order number 7657117-62a, signed by General Whitemoore."

Elmore looked confused, maybe concerned. "Yes," he said and shifted uncomfortably in his seat. "But I was told that information would be redacted. How did you know?"

Tracy forged ahead. She wouldn't let Elmore contemplate that information any longer than was necessary. "So the DOD ordered you to alter the results of your finding," she said. Her voice was calm and matter-of-fact. It was not an accusation but rather a request for confirmation.

"No, of course not," Elmore blurted. "There was no need. There was no evidence suggesting the Kepler cars were related to the wreck in any way." His gaze tightened on Tracy as he continued. "The initiating event happened forward of the Kepler cars. In one of three passenger cars, according to the pattern of the subsequent derailment."

He turned his gaze on her and Gretchen knew they had crossed into dangerous territory. "What office did you say you're with? I didn't see your identification."

Tracy passed over a billfold containing FBI credentials, and Gretchen was surprised. She had no idea where the identification had come from, only that it wasn't authentic.

"But you covered up the results of your investigation," Tracy pushed. Gretchen was impressed by her friend's skill. She wasn't giving Elmore enough time to think. It kept him from second-guessing his decision to speak with them while maintaining pressure on him to help push the necessary information to the forefront of his mind. He didn't need to speak the answers they sought; he just needed to think them. Just like the DOD executive order number and issuing General.

"I did not," Elmore spat. "I think it's time I contacted my attorney."

A long silence followed that statement. Gretchen sensed a calm returning to Elmore. He felt he'd regained footing. He was looking forward to showing them the door. It wasn't a good sign. Though she didn't know what Tracy was after, she was certain she hadn't learned anything of value from the interview.

"I want you to think very hard before involving an attorney," Tracy said. She slid to the edge of the sofa cushion and glared pointedly into his eyes. "If you bring in a lawyer, this stops being a friendly, off the record, conversation."

Elmore scowled and shrugged. A *fine by me* gesture.

"Will your attorney also help you explain how you paid for this home in cash six months after filing your official report?" Tracy pressed.

Elmore stared at her, his gaze unblinking, his stature resolute. Gretchen felt her heart race, knowing she had him right where they wanted him.

God, he has a fantastic poker face!

She sat back and casually crossed her legs. "Yes," she said in answer to an unspoken question. "The paperwork was carefully manipulated. But numbered accounts can be matched to transaction dates when we know where and when to look. And you bought that boat. You're right, that was another big mistake."

The room lapsed into silence. Elmore's face had gone ghostly pale. Tracy seemed content to let him ride the wave of panic for a painfully long time. The source of Elmore's funds had been a mystery, and to Gretchen's knowledge, no one knew about the boat. He had given her that information right there on the spot in a brief flash of paranoid self-doubt.

"I don't care about the crash," Tracy said. "My questions pertain to the recovery effort immediately following the incident. If you level with me about that, no one has to know what we do."

Though he looked like he was going to become physically ill, a pinch of confusion reached Elmore's eyes. "The recovery? I don't understand."

"I don't think you were paid to cover up the cause of the derailment," Tracy said. "But if you did, I couldn't care less. I think someone paid you to omit details from your report. You removed notes and hid details from the press from day one."

Elmore stared at the floor. He breathed long, slow breaths, and the color returned to his cheeks. "Yes," he said finally. "That's true. I was paid to suppress those details. But the fact is, I would've done that anyway. The money was just a lucky break. I didn't see any harm in accepting it because I never could've gone forward with those other details in the first place." He looked Tracy in the eye. "It wouldn't have been right."

Gretchen was confused. It sounded like a bullshit claim, but he was being sincere. *What had he hidden?*

Tracy wasn't any more in the know because she simply watched Elmore. Her eyes remained fixed on him, unyielding and unforgiving.

"I just kept the survivor out of my reports," Elmore said.

"He was just a kid. The press would've eaten him alive. He'd just survived a wreck that had killed 279 passengers. Anything I could do to spare the kid some grief, I—" his voice cracked, and he choked. "I investigated wrecks for a living. I've seen more survivor guilt than I can explain. No kid should have to suffer through what that boy was heading toward."

Gretchen expected shock on Tracy's face—surprise at the very least. But there was none. Tracy did glance in her direction, seemingly to confirm the validity of Elmore's words. Gretchen swallowed hard and offered a slight nod.

"I think you did the right thing," Tracy said. "But I need you to tell me about the boy."

Elmore looked confused. Gretchen was, too, for that matter. How was a young boy relevant to a train wreck thirteen years ago? They hadn't discussed any of this before approaching Elmore, and Gretchen became increasingly concerned.

"He was just a kid," Elmore said. "A boy, maybe ten or twelve years old."

"What was his name?" Tracy asked.

Elmore shrugged. "No one knew. He wasn't on the passenger manifest, so everything about him was a mystery. We had no idea."

Gretchen chimed in before she realized she'd spoken aloud. "What did he say his name was?"

Confusion clouded Elmore's face, and he shook his head. "He didn't know his name. He wasn't even sure how he came to be on that train. He carried no identification, and as far as we could tell, he was traveling alone."

"If he knew his age, he must've known something," Tracy offered. "What did he have to say?"

"He didn't know his age," Elmore countered. "The

doctors decided that. I think they put him at 10 years old, but he could've been a year or two in one direction or the other. Believe me, I was just as frustrated as you are now— even more, maybe. I had a single survivor of a catastrophic derailment that cost 279 lives and resulted in $720 million in damages. His testimony would've made my life a lot easier."

Tracy sat back and crossed her arms. "But you kept the boy out of the report. You removed any mention of him from the records. There are 23,311 pages of notes, memos, and reports of your investigation, and not a trace of the boy in any of it. No government worker exercises that level of competence or efficiency. What aren't you telling me?"

"I had help," Elmore said as if it were a justifiable defense.

Gretchen saw Tracy smile. Now they were getting somewhere.

"The people who paid you?" Tracy asked.

"Presumably," Elmore said.

"You don't know?"

He shrugged again. "I was paid to be thorough. I was paid well, and I did a good job of it. Still...I always suspected someone was helping to hide the paper trail. There would have to be. I could cover my side of things, but there were still other reports that I couldn't cover directly—the eyewitness reports of first responders—that kind of thing. I assumed someone was tying up those loose ends. They would have to. Anyone willing to pay what I was getting would be sure to dot all the I's."

"Who helped you?"

"I have no idea."

Tracy grimaced. She shot a look in Gretchen's direction, but she had nothing to offer. A minuscule turn of her head relayed her regret.

"If you had to guess?" Tracy pressed.

Nothing.

Nothing from Elmore and nothing on his mind. He didn't have a clue. Another fractional negative shake of the head was pointed in Tracy's direction.

Tracy took a moment to ponder the line of questioning. Gretchen guessed she was looking for a new approach, searching for something that might yield information Elmore was holding back. He seemed to be leveling with them now, but it was equally possible he possessed information he wasn't aware of.

"What happened to the boy?" Tracy asked.

A shrug from Elmore. He wasn't a very effusive guy, Gretchen decided.

"Someone took custody of him," she pressed. "You were in charge of the investigation. Certainly, you knew whose care he was placed in?"

Another shrug.

Tracy's disposition was beginning to sour. "You were in the process of covering up his very existence," she offered in a cold, flat tone. "However old he was, he was a minor. Someone had to take responsibility for him. In whose charge did you leave him?"

"It was thirteen years ago," Elmore argued. "I have no idea. It wouldn't be a part of my report, and the kid couldn't help me with the investigation. Once he was in good hands, I didn't give him another thought."

That was a lie. Gretchen didn't need to be a Reader to understand that. It was practically written on his face. Under normal circumstances, Tracy would've been all over it, pressing him for the truth. But this was where she came in, Gretchen knew. She reached out with her senses, grasping the flashes of insight she was receiving from the man. She latched onto them and dug in deeper, seeking a better connection to his mind and deeper access to his thoughts.

Elmore had given a lot of consideration to the plight of the boy. Worried about him, in fact. He'd never questioned that leaving him out of the reports was the right thing to do. Accepting money to do it had seemed wrong—dirty—he thought, but ultimately, he'd gone along with it. He was taking money for something he'd ultimately decided to do even before the old woman had approached him.

Gretchen cleared her throat. "Tell us about the old woman. The one who contacted you about the boy. She asked you to do all of this, didn't she?"

Elmore choked—literally choked at the sound of the question. This spawned a coughing fit that went on until his face was red...and then purple. Gretchen and Tracy followed the man to the kitchen, where he retrieved a glass from a cabinet and filled it from the sink. He drank it down slowly, his asthmatic fit finally coming under control. Gretchen took it for what it was—an opportunity to stall for time. Just the same, the fit had been real. He hadn't expected them to know about the old woman.

"I'm sorry," Elmore wheezed. "Where were we?"

He leaned against the counter. Gretchen was pretty sure he was seeing spots, or stars, from his breakdown. It served him right if he was going to play dumb now.

"The old woman," Tracy said in a flat tone. "I want her contact information now. No more stalling."

Elmore laughed briefly, holding up his hand. "I'm not stalling, I assure you. But I can't give you what I don't have. I have no idea who she was."

Tracy had no patience left. "You turned a 10-year-old boy over to a woman you hadn't vetted? You'll understand if I think you're full of crap."

He nodded. "Perhaps not my finest hour," he admitted. "Bear in mind this was more than a decade ago—"

"And that she paid you 1.5 million dollars," Gretchen countered.

Both Elmore and Tracy turned to her and stared. They both swallowed hard and had surprise showing in their eyes…though for different reasons.

"She clearly had the boy's best interest at heart," Elmore agreed. "She worked for an orphanage, I recall that much. Somewhere up north. I'm sorry—truly—but I don't recall the details."

Tracy shot a glance to Gretchen, question clear in her eyes. She was looking for confirmation. Gretchen nodded and slipped her hands into the hip pockets of her jeans.

Producing a fabricated business card, Tracy passed it to Elmore. "If you recall any relevant details, please contact me night or day." She turned toward the door, doubling back through the house.

Gretchen smiled briefly before following. "You have a lovely home," she said. Her back was to him as her grin turned into a wide smile. He was cursing his decision to take the old woman's money and the foolish ways he'd attempted to hide it.

No words were spoken until they slipped into the car at the curb again. Tracy looked over. "Did you get what we need?"

"Biltmore Home for Boys, Boston, Massachusetts," Gretchen said and fastened her seatbelt. "We're looking for a woman named Eloise Fleischer."

Chapter 11 - Perfect-ish

Miami, Florida

Nathan was already satisfied with the day's work. He'd just dropped a set of papers in the mail for one of his better clients, and it wasn't even time for lunch. A falsified driver's license, social security card, two credit cards, a state ID, a forged vehicle registration, and a letter of credit from Citibank. It was a hell of a morning. Between the accomplishment and the intolerable humidity, he was tempted to take the rest of the day off. The AC in his shop had been running full tilt since sunrise and couldn't keep the heat and humidity at bay.

The quiet rumble of the buzzer beneath his desk sounded. Nathan's eyes moved to the small LCD mounted high on the wall in the corner of his office. His daughter ran the front counter. She hit the chime whenever one of *his customers* walked through the front door of the small boutique electronics shop.

After glancing at the screen, a smile crossed Nathan's face. He shoved up and out of his chair, ducked through the door, and moved quickly along the short hall to the small showroom at the front of the building.

Slipping through a curtain blocking the showroom, Nathan grinned. He patted his eighteen-year-old daughter on the shoulder as he passed.

"Cyrus," he said as he rounded the end of the counter. "How have you been?"

Cyrus shook Nathan's offered hand. "Every day is an adventure," he said.

Nathan fixed him with a penetrating stare. Better than most, he knew Cyrus's penchant for understatement. It made him wonder what was happening. The young man's call late the prior evening had been unexpected and unusual, even for him. More so when he insisted on meeting in person.

"Why don't we step in back," Nathan said. "I can show you what I've come up with."

He motioned Cyrus in the direction of the curtain. Cyrus knew the way. He'd been there many times in the past.

Nathan pulled a chair from the extra work counter along his office wall and spun it for Cyrus's use. The office was fairly large, though every wall was fronted with a functional workspace. A large peninsula added to the work area, splitting the office nearly in two. On one side was a computer with three large flat-screen displays. Several complicated printers surrounded the monitors. The other side of the counter and just about every inch of the remaining workspace was covered with the tools of Nathan's trade. There were rulers, markers, pens, pencils, stamps, stitchers, knives, razors, tweezers, and dozens of other small tools essential for successful document fabrication or duplication. Among other things, Nathan was a master forger.

He was also skilled and very resourceful when it came to procuring hard-to-find weapons and hardware as well as information. His knack for gathering intelligence had brought Cyrus to his door this morning.

Nathan slipped gently into his office chair. He took a moment to adjust the small fan on the corner of his desk. It was a futile attempt to provide them both some much-needed circulation in the stuffy confines of the windowless room.

"I thought I found just what you needed," Nathan said. "Then a bulletin came through about ninety minutes ago. Unfortunately, I think it puts us back at square one. I'm afraid you wasted your time coming out here. It will take me some time to find alternative talent."

Cyrus sat back in the chair but said nothing. The question was evident on his face.

"I found you an egghead—some kid who's done some impressive work with image algorithms," Nathan explained. "I'm told the facial recognition systems used by the CIA, NSA, and British Intelligence use software this kid wrote. He doesn't know that, of course. But I'm told it's cutting-edge, next-generation stuff. Apparently, what this kid wrote blew the doors off anything any agency could cook up in-house."

Cyrus nodded. "He sounds perfect. Just what we need."

Nathan cringed. "Well," he hedged. "Perfect-ish...at best. From what I understand, the kid is a first-class shithead. He was set to get his first Ph.D. from CalTech at fourteen. But he had a major attitude problem. There was talk that he might be expelled over something—I'm still looking for details on the specific issue. He ended up dropping out before he could graduate. He turned up at Brown a year later. He's been there ever since."

"How old is he now?"

"Eighteen," Nathan grumbled.

"So he's working on his PhD there?"

Nathan smirked. "Nope. As best I can tell, he's just farting around. He doesn't seem to be taking school seriously. He's just sort of there. He doesn't seem to have any intent. A genius-level IQ, but he's got a chip on his shoulder. A real bad attitude, I'm told. Keeps undermining himself. He's got the kind of intellect that could take him anywhere, but no one wants to deal with him."

Cyrus seemed to consider that for a moment. Then he shrugged. "I can motivate him. I've worked with some interesting personalities before. Different people just need different kinds of motivation. Besides, I only need the kid's help with a single task. If he can keep his act together long enough, he'll make some good money. What did you say his name was?"

"Barnabe. Alec Barnabe. But it gets worse—that's what I wanted to tell you. It looks like the kid just got into a new kind of trouble."

Cyrus rubbed at the corner of his eyes with his thumb and forefinger. He looked tired. "Do I even want to ask?"

Nathan grabbed a file folder from beside his keyboard and passed it over. "Barnabe partnered with another kid named Wilks on some tech startup. I get the sense that they're running it out of a basement somewhere. Real low rent, but the word is that it has potential. Anyway, that bulletin came through an hour and a half ago. It looks like Barnabe went and killed his partner. Authorities are searching for him as we speak."

Cyrus had just started leafing through the folder. His eyes rose to meet Nathan's. "Murder? No kidding?"

"Happened Monday night," Nathan said. "Kid's been in the wind ever since."

Cyrus put the folder down on the end of the peninsula portion of Nathan's desk. He started with page 1 and methodically leafed through the reports Nathan had compiled since they'd spoken the night before. Nathan watched the process carefully as Cyrus's eyes moved smoothly across the surface of a page of dense text in the span of six or seven seconds. Then he moved on to the next page. Six seconds later, he moved to the next, and so on. Though he'd seen his friend digest information before, he still found the sight disconcerting. He knew Cyrus was reading everything and would be able to recall the details with perfect clarity.

Cyrus sat back in the chair, staring off into the distance. He was processing what he'd learned, Nathan knew. It was another interesting trick he'd seen more than once. He suddenly became increasingly interested in Cyrus's take on the reports in hand.

"As of an hour ago, police consider Barnabe a person of interest," Cyrus said. "But the way this reads, I'm not sure they're looking at him as the killer. He's wanted for questioning."

Nathan nodded. "True, but if you read between the lines…" he hedged.

Cyrus still seemed half-lost in contemplation. His eyes focused once more and landed on Nathan. "Is this kid really as sharp as you say? Are you confident he wrote the facial recognition software? It wasn't his partner?"

"Not the entire solution," Nathan clarified. "He wrote the image processing algorithms. They were faster and more efficient than anything anyone else had. From what I understand, the kid used some open-source code repository for versioning while working on the algorithms. The DOD has backdoors into all the major repositories. They're constantly trolling for useful intellectual property. When they found this kid's work, they hit pay dirt. They've been watching him ever since."

When Cyrus grimaced, Nathan knew Cyrus was sickened by the idea, but he wasn't the least bit surprised.

"Anyway," Nathan said, "I'm sorry for the wasted trip.

I'll contact you as soon as I have another viable candidate. Maybe the next one won't be a psycho asshole."

Shaking his head, Cyrus held up the folder. "No need," he said. "You did good. I can work with him. Something about the timing bothers me. Barnabe's problems could be related to my own. I need to take a closer look. Don't worry about it. I'll transfer payment as soon as I get back to the office."

Nathan was surprised. He didn't see how the kid could be worth the trouble. "Does this have anything to do with the Chinese trouble last week?" he asked.

Cyrus was climbing from his chair but then stopped short. He took a long look at Nathan but said nothing. Nathan wondered if he'd just spoken out of turn. Then Cyrus smiled. "You seriously are tuned in to everything, aren't you."

Nathan sat back, a little relieved. "It was big news in underground information circles. The Chinese don't want to admit losing control of one of their birds, even if only for a few minutes."

The smile faded from Cyrus's face. "Lost control?"

Nathan nodded. "Word is that it wasn't just one satellite either. Supposedly, it was two birds that went dark on them. It was only for three and a half minutes, but both birds were way off course when they restored communications. I guess they don't know who did it or how. Needless to say, Chinese Intelligence is losing its mind right now."

Cyrus sat back and just stared. Somehow, he looked even more tired. After a few long seconds, he took a deep breath and shook his head. "It's a crazy world. I think it's time to find an island somewhere out of the way and tune the rest of the world out. Mankind is coming off the rails."

Cyrus said it as a joke and smiled, but the light failed to reach his eyes. There was a heavy heart there, Nathan thought. It was something he'd recognized in his friend for a while, and he wondered if the comment about tuning out the rest of the world was more tempting than he let on.

Cyrus raised the folder in his hand. "This is good work," he said. "I appreciate it, as always."

"Any time," Nathan said. He shook Cyrus's hand. "Tell Reese and Hondo I said hello."

Chapter 12 - Stay Out of My Head

Biltmore Home for Boys, Boston, Massachusetts

Gretchen stood beneath a massive oak tree and watched the front entrance of the Biltmore Home for Boys. It was a hundred-year-old three-story structure with a wide porch and four thick white pillars supporting a roof with ornate, well-maintained woodwork. Windows checkered the muted red brickwork, and thick shrubs circled all but the wide stairway leading onto the porch. Modest suburban businesses occupied buildings on both sides of the Biltmore Home, those structures easily a hundred years newer in construction while attempts had been made to make their appearance quaint and rustic.

Flipping the newspaper page, Gretchen crossed her legs and eyed the view across the street again. She'd chosen the bench at the permitter of the city park across the street from the Biltmore Home because it provided a clear view of the front entrance and an unimpeded line of sight to the small cafe four buildings down to her left.

She and Tracy had entered the Biltmore Home ten minutes earlier. When they asked to see Eloise Fleischer, the facilities administrator, they'd been told that she'd stepped out but was due to return in a few minutes. When Tracy produced her counterfeit FBI credentials, they'd been shown to Eloise's office to wait for her. The collection of to-go cups in the trash can by her office door had hinted at Eloise's addiction to the small nearby cafe. Tracy had opted to wait for the woman's return while Gretchen had taken up a position across the narrow road. There was a slight concern that someone from the office might alert Eloise to their presence and cause her to avoid returning to the office. Gretchen was in place to ensure that didn't happen. Whatever Eloise's motivation for taking custody of the boy from the train wreck, she'd done it in secret. Who knew what she might do or what protocols she might have in place to maintain that deception?

Gretchen turned the page of her newspaper once more, still peering over the top of the widespread publication. Her patience was rewarded when she saw a short, platinum-haired woman exit the cafe to her extreme left. With her shoulder, the woman pushed the swinging door open, supporting three tall disposable capped cups with practiced ease. She nodded to a passer-by and headed north toward the Biltmore building. Gretchen tracked her progress, noting Eloise's complete lack of situational awareness. The woman didn't scan her surrounding as she moved. She focused on the three coffees and navigating the small amount of suburban foot traffic on her way back to the office.

Folding the paper, Gretchen creased it sharply before dropping it into a municipal trash can. She crossed the quiet two-lane street, heading for the Biltmore Home. She fell into step a few paces behind Eloise Fleischer. They climbed the wide set of stairs and crossed the porch in succession. When Eloise reached the set of double swinging doors at the entrance, Gretchen trotted forward. She held the door for the woman, who responded with a kind smile. Gretchen followed her through the doors and into the lobby.

Eloise placed all three coffees on the reception counter and exchanged words with the receptionist before collecting one of the cups for herself. "Oh," the receptionist said as Eloise headed for the door to the left of the lobby. "Agent Clark from the FBI is waiting in your office," she said as if it were an everyday occurrence.

Eloise's brows arched in response, but she said nothing. She seemed to consider the receptionist's words for a moment, then nodded understanding before disappearing through the doorway. Gretchen had held back after stepping into the lobby, watching the old woman's interaction with the receptionist before drawing attention to herself. She hadn't sensed anything untoward from either Eloise or the receptionist, but she didn't need to be a mind reader to see the concern in Eloise's face at the mention of the FBI.

"I'm sorry," the receptionist said when she looked up to see Gretchen. She must not have noticed her follow Eloise through the door because she said, "You just missed Miss Fleischer. She just went back to her office."

"Thank you," Gretchen said over her shoulder.

When Gretchen entered the small office, Tracy and Eloise shook hands and completed their introductions. "This is my associate," Tracy said without missing a beat, "Gretchen Gamble. We only need a few minutes of your time."

Eloise smiled and circled her desk. "Of course. Please have a seat." She motioned to the pair of chairs opposite her and set her coffee aside. "How can I help you today?"

Tracy smiled and eased herself into the threadbare chair while Gretchen assumed the one beside her. "We're here to follow up on a boy who came into your care about thirteen years ago," Tracy said. "It was following a train derailment down south. The Kepler Derailment, as it was most commonly known."

Her office chair squeaked as Eloise sat back. Her eyes

sought a position somewhere on the room's back wall as she pretended to search her memory. It was all an act, Gretchen knew. The old woman's heart was thundering in response to the mention of the train wreck—or maybe because they had referred to the boy. Either way, though she was playing it cool and betraying nothing visually, her mind was awash with worry. Eloise held out hope that she was being paranoid. She'd known this day would come and dreaded it. Then, a new concern flooded her mind. Gretchen saw a flash of something out of place. A prescription bottle. It was in the top right drawer of the desk. Eloise was feeling short of breath, and there was a numbness in her left arm, yet her gaze betrayed none of this.

Shit.

"A train wreck?" Eloise said, her tone even and controlled. "I'm sure I would remember something like that, no matter how long ago. Are you sure you've got the right orphanage?"

Gretchen realized that the old woman wasn't going to make a move for the prescription bottle. Retrieving her nitroglycerine pill would betray her panic. She was made of sterner stuff.

Tracy was unfazed. "We're in the right place." She had no idea what was happening on the other side of the desk. Whatever her motivations, the old woman would rather experience a heart attack than acknowledge meeting the boy.

Bolting from her chair, Gretchen circled the desk and pulled open the top drawer. Her hands shuffled through the scattered contents and seized a small semitransparent orange bottle wrapped with a faded white label. She popped the childproof lid and dumped two of the small white pills into the palm of her hand. Placing them on the desk before Eloise, she glared. "Take this now," she commanded. "Don't be a fool."

Eloise eyed her from beneath a pinched brow but didn't delay long. She slipped one of the small tablets between her now trembling lips. Understanding crossed Tracy's face. She wiped idly at the corners of her mouth, then crossed and uncrossed her legs. Gretchen rounded back and slipped silently back into her chair.

A long silence followed. Gretchen studied the old woman, astounded by her indecipherable face. All the while, she reached out with her mind. Eloise had impressive mental control as well, she observed. Her thoughts were cohesive and organized—entirely the opposite of what she had come to expect from someone dealing with a life-and-death scare such as this.

Gretchen eased her mind and reached deeper into Eloise's thoughts. Most people were easy to read. Eloise was doing an exceptional job of obfuscating her thoughts. Particularly given what she was going through.

Eloise took a deep breath and placed both palms on the desk before her. Gretchen sensed that the medical danger had just about passed. Still, she couldn't get a clear read on the woman. Eloise eyed Tracy and seemed to study her for a moment. When that same gaze fell upon her, Gretchen knew something was happening behind those eyes—something that was being intentionally muddled and hidden from her. The implications were disturbing. It meant Eloise had experience with Readers and was practiced at—

The old woman slipped her hand into a drawer at her left and produced a nickel-plated, snub-nosed .357 revolver. It was a beefy six-shot that looked like a canon in her small hand. Her eyes focused across the desk's surface as she produced the weapon. There was no emotion in her eyes as she placed the revolver at the center of the blotter before her, producing a loud *thunk* that seemed to fill the small office.

"I don't know who you are," the old woman said. "Maybe you're FBI—maybe you're not. You are certainly one of *them*. Walk away now. I'm only going to ask once." She leveled her gaze at Gretchen. "And stay out of my head, Goddammit!"

Chapter 13 - General Nostalgia

Brown University, Providence, Rhode Island

They had parked on Waterman Street and ventured out on foot. After passing the Catherine Bryan Dill Center and the Performing Arts building, they headed for the lush green park at the corner of Waterman and Prospect. It was called Quiet Green. And it was quiet, Cyrus thought. A small green space in the middle of the city, located on school grounds with sweeping sidewalks, manicured shrubs, and towering trees.

Cyrus held Reese's hand as they walked slowly across the grass. His mind had slipped back to memories from years ago. Not specific memories...more of a general nostalgia. He was struck by how much had changed over the years and how much hadn't. Natasha had been with him the last time he'd visited these grounds. Looking back, life was easier then. Everyone changed—there was no question— but was it natural to come so far and evolve so much in such a short period?

Then again, was it such a short time after all? The question put things in perspective. He'd had 9 amazing months with

Natasha before that part of his life had been ripped apart. Then, 5 years with the Coalition before that, too, ended in tragedy. After that, he'd spent the better part of 4 years pretty much shunning the world. He'd kept everyone and everything at arm's length and hadn't let anyone get close. In that time, a twist of fate had brought Walter Meade into his life. And Meade's death had changed everything for him yet again. His posthumous gift had forced Cyrus from his solitary life and, in a roundabout way, introduced him to Reese.

She was the single most influential person in his world now. When they met, it was as if a new chapter had begun for him. They shared a connection, the sort of bond he'd given up on finding. Unknowingly, it was as if he'd put his heart on a shelf after losing Natasha. It had left a gaping hole deep inside him—a void he never intended to fill. Then he'd met Reese…and everything changed.

"Are you alright?" Reese asked, her voice quiet.

They were still walking slowly. Cyrus realized that he hadn't said a word in some time. It must've seemed strange to her. He stopped suddenly and pulled her into his arms. He didn't know what to say, so he just pulled her close and said nothing.

"This is your first time back," she said. It wasn't a question, just an astute observation. "There are a lot of memories."

He took a deep breath. "Yes, and no. Not like you'd think, I guess. It's strange to be back. More than anything, I'm more shocked by how much the world has changed since my brief time here. Nothing has happened like it was supposed to." He paused for several long seconds. "Does that make any sense?"

She pulled back far enough to look up into his eyes. Her brown eyes glistened and were filled with sadness. "Yes," she said with a slow nod. "Yes, it does."

Cyrus grimaced. She looked upset, though he didn't understand why. More sad than anything, but that didn't make sense either. "What's wrong?"

"I know what this place represented to you," she said. "And I know that everything changed when you left. Your life disintegrated in every conceivable way."

It was the words that she didn't use that hung in the air between them. Cyrus had lost the love of his life not once but twice. First when he left her and later when she died in his arms. He'd also been betrayed by the people he had trusted. She knew it all—every horrible detail. He wasn't the kind to share things, but they'd grown close over the last 10 months. Closer even than he'd ever been with Natasha.

He pushed a furrow of raven-black hair back from the corner of Reese's eye and resisted the urge to tell her exactly how he felt. This wasn't the time, and it certainly wasn't the place. She needed to understand that his feelings were genuine and not the result of some painful trip down memory lane.

"It took time to get here," he said, "but I'm happier than I've ever been. I have you to thank for that."

She smiled, but the sadness clung to her eyes. "I don't know if I could go through it in your place."

Cyrus's eyes scanned the grounds around them. He breathed the scent of freshly cut grass and the blossoms in the nearby flower bed. His memories weren't the only things bothering him since they'd entered the park. A tingling sense alerted him to another presence shortly after entering the park. The sensation had yet to abate. Someone was watching them; he was convinced of it. Where they were, though, remained a mystery. He and Reese had the grounds almost entirely to themselves. No one looked out of the place when it came to the occasional passerby. Still, someone was out there.

Chapter 14 - Without Looking Like a Pervert

Brown University, Providence, Rhode Island

Though he'd kept a discrete eye out, Cyrus still hadn't spotted his observer on the walk back to the rental car. And while he didn't notice anything unusual while driving the dozen or so blocks to the street where the small cafe was located, he still sensed someone out there and watching. It was more troubling since he was good a picking out tails.

Had he become rusty with time? It was a troubling consideration.

Cyrus parked the rented Honda a block and a half away from their destination. They were on a one-way street, headed for the Small Point Cafe. His skills might be rusty, but some things were still hardwired into his psyche. Traffic was almost nonexistent, both on the road and on the sidewalk. Cyrus knew the surroundings would make it impossible to hide if anyone was out there.

Reese cast a curious glance in his direction and let it linger briefly before slightly shaking her head and opening the car door. She'd noticed how short of the destination he'd parked. He smiled—she didn't miss much. She shook her head but finally offered a silent grin. She found it amusing, but she wasn't criticizing. Some would write off his behavior as eccentricity. She, better than most, knew there was a method to everything he did.

Reese rounded the car to meet Cyrus. He stepped away from the car, then pretended he'd forgotten something. He turned back and patted his pockets as if searching for his wallet. While he did it, he watched the reflection in the car windows and glanced over it and into the small shops on the far side of the sidewalk. He'd searched again for his mysterious tail in less than two seconds.

Still seeing nothing, he unlocked the car door using the key fob. Ducking inside, he fished his wallet from a compartment in the console. Turning back to Reese, her eyes met his. The corners of her mouth turned up in an almost imperceptible smile. He led her back around the car and onto the sidewalk. She'd expected to cross the street since the cafe was located across the lane. The unusual move wouldn't be lost on her either, he knew.

Reese's hand slipped into his as they walked. "Since when did you start putting your wallet in the car?" she said in a quiet, accusing voice. She didn't turn to look at him. They just kept walking.

"You're not missing a thing," he said. There was admiration in his tone. Her situational awareness had come a long way since they'd first met.

"Is someone following us?"

"I'm not sure."

She shot him a glance.

He shrugged. "It's not an exact science," he said a bit defensively.

They walked a little further. "Turn in here," Cyrus said suddenly.

He guided her through the doorway on the right, and they stepped into a small lingerie store. Reese shot him a new look, this time a fresh form of amusement in her eyes.

"Go find yourself something...*pretty*," he grinned. "And take your time."

She stepped close and kissed him gently on the cheek. "Don't you want to help?" she whispered.

"Surprise me," he smirked.

Her brows furrowed. She was onto him. Likely happy to play along, she turned on her heel and dashed into the tightly packed maze of racks and shelves stocked with brightly colored and provocatively styled undergarments.

Cyrus moved to the periphery of the front window, not far from the entrance but well out of view from the street. He waited almost five minutes. Long enough to begin worrying. Concerned that his mind was playing tricks. Worried that Reese would find what she was looking for before his target presented itself. Anxious that whoever was out there was really *that good* at the game.

But his patience won out.

After seven minutes of waiting motionless in the corner of the store, Cyrus saw a tall man in a dark windbreaker walk slowly into view of the shop's front window. The man did his best to look like he was wandering the street, perhaps window-shopping. But it was hard for a lone man to linger before a lingerie shop without looking like a pervert.

The man glanced up and down the street. He took a deep breath and swallowed hard, obviously unsure what to do next. Cyrus could see how uncomfortable he was just by how he held himself. Finally, the man turned, stepped closer to the glass, and peered into the shop. He did his best to make the action look natural, but it was impossible. Cyrus saw the man lean to the window. The shop was dim, and the man was having trouble seeing past the glare on the glass from the warm morning sun.

Their stalker had black hair buzzed short and stark blue eyes that pinched against the glare. His gaze washed over the shop's interior in a quick sweep. Cyrus knew what he was seeing. So much merchandise was packed into the small space that it was impossible to make a useful assessment in a brief period.

The stalker seemed to come to the same conclusion. He stepped away from the glass and shoved his hands into his jacket pockets. He grumbled something to himself—evident frustration.

A smile crossed Cyrus' face.

The stalker was tall and broad-shouldered. He wore a button-down shirt beneath the windbreaker, and his pants were some kind of dockers. His shoes seemed a little out of place. They were sneakers, stark white cross trainers that looked like they'd come straight from the shoebox. Cyrus watched as the man appeared to take a moment to steel himself before entering the store. This was making him visibly uncomfortable, Cyrus thought with amusement.

As the tall man stepped through the door, Cyrus made his move. The stalker was frustrated and embarrassed, so his eyes were on the floor as he marched the first three paces. Cyrus was moving just as quickly in the opposite direction but was ready for what was coming.

Cyrus collided with the stalker, and they both stumbled. Cyrus dropped his car keys. The muffled thud of the two bodies impacting was tiny, while the sound of the set of splayed keys impacting on the tile floor seemed to echo through the shop. The stalker's eyes went to Cyrus after the moment of impact before sweeping to the right, and following the sound the keys had made when they hit the floor.

The man's eyes darted back to Cyrus for a second time. There was recognition there. Cyrus was sure of it. The man's sense of embarrassment was forgotten. It had been replaced by alarm—maybe concern. He was certainly upset. More upset than he should've been after such a slight mishap.

"I'm sorry," the man said in a raspy voice. "Excuse me." He turned and ducked through the exit and back onto the street.

Cyrus bent to retrieve his keys and hide his grin from anyone watching. That wasn't a calm or professional response, he thought. He slipped something into the back pocket of his jeans as he rose with the keys. The keys, as it turned out, had been an unnecessary diversion. His target had been so preoccupied that he could've lifted what he wanted from inside his coat without the additional distraction.

Reese's voice came from behind him. "What was that about?"

When Cyrus turned, he first noticed the small bag tucked under her arm. Tiny and black. He was suddenly very interested to see what was inside.

"Focus," she said sharply, tapping her finger on the tip of his nose. "The bag is for later. What just happened?"

He smiled and motioned for the door. "You know me. Just making friends." Taking her hand, they headed for the street.

Chapter 15 - A Really Good Poker Face

Biltmore Home for Boys, Boston, Massachusetts

Tracy eyed the revolver on the desk. The woman was old, but she could still raise the gun and pull the trigger before either of them could take it away. Eloise had remained surprisingly composed since they'd entered her office, and if that pill was what she thought, the lady had kept wits together through a brush with some kind of cardiac episode. While it wasn't apparent to her exactly what had happened, Gretchen was the reason Eloise had taken the medication. Would she really rather die than speak with them about the boy?

"Miss Fleischer," Tracy said. "Do you mind if I call you Eloise?"

There was no reply. Eloise kept her eyes focused on the two of them and the palm of her hand firmly atop the pistol lying on the desk.

"Alright...Eloise. I don't know who you think we are, but I would appreciate your putting the gun away."

The old woman's gaze sharpened. Tracy felt like it was

burrowing into her. It was an odd sensation. The expression was familiar. Glancing at Gretchen, she asked the silent question, *is the old lady a Reader?*

Gretchen offered a slight shake of her head.

Ok. She just has a really good poker face.

"You're with *them*," Eloise said, her voice cold and her throat dry. "So you should know," she paused. "I won't give you anything. By now," she eyed Gretchen, "she realizes I'm harder to manipulate than most."

Tracy shot another glance at Gretchen and received a minimal nod in response.

Impressive.

"By *them*," Tracy began. "I assume you're referring to the Order of Origin? I can assure you we're not part of the group."

An amused smile spread across Eloise's lips and smoothed a few of her wrinkles. There was mirth in her eyes. "You'll forgive me, but saying it doesn't make it so."

"I'm sorry. I'm not sure how to prove that to you. If my—"

"Don't insult my intelligence with that badge," the old woman said. "It takes more than that to play the part, and you haven't got the look."

Despite herself, Tracy smiled. "Fair enough. That wasn't a point in our favor, but we're not looking for trouble. The ID just streamlines the question-and-answer process. I'm sorry I tried to deceive you."

"Call it what it is—a trick, a lie…there's nothing for you here. It's time for you to get up and walk out that door."

The old woman had guts. It was impressive. But they couldn't leave empty-handed. This sort of warm welcome only highlighted the fact that they were finally onto something.

"Please," Tracy said in a soft tone. "Let me ask a couple of questions and we'll be on our way." She reached into her pocket and pulled out the folded slip of paper.

Eloise raised the gun the moment Tracy's hand went into her pocket. The hammer snapped back half a heartbeat later. She didn't offer a word of warning.

"Easy!" Gretchen bellowed. She rocked in her chair, likely not knowing if she should get up or stay down. It was a tough call when someone was pointing a gun at the person next to you.

"It's okay," Tracy whispered through a stifled gasp. She held the paper inches from her pocket, pinched between her index finger and thumb. "I only want to show you this. I don't care about the boy. I just want to find this device. If you can help me with that, we'll leave. You'll never see us again."

The look from Eloise made it clear that she didn't trust either of them. She didn't move for several long seconds. Finally, she motioned the paper forward with her free hand. "Unfold it and hand it over slowly," she said.

Tracy did as she was told. There was a noticeable tremor in the old woman's hand, and she wished she would at least lower the hammer. It would provide them with some level of safety. She had just suffered some kind of cardiac event, after all. She wasn't going to burn any goodwill by voicing the concern or making the request.

The paper was passed over. Tracy swallowed hard and sat back in her chair, trying to remember to breathe from time to time.

Eloise looked at the paper. There was no recognition in her eyes. None at all. She was shrewd, but Tracy felt confident the expression—or lack of one—was genuine.

Laying the paper at the edge of her desk, Eloise sat back.

Her eyes seemed to study them in a way that belayed her position as the superintendent of an orphanage. "What is the device?" she asked.

"I think it's the cause of the train wreck thirteen years ago," Tracy said. "It wasn't among the wreckage recovered at the crash site, so we're going through everything fresh, trying to find it. No one knew it existed until recently."

Eloise remained silent for several long beats. "I can't help you," she said at last.

Tracy nodded slowly with disappointment. She felt Gretchen's eyes upon her. "Then we *will* need your help after all," she said. "We need to speak with the boy. He was the only survivor. We can't close out the case until we talk with him."

"I know the train wreck you're talking about," the old woman said. "It was a long time ago. As I recall, there were no survivors. It was a tragedy. I saw it on the news. No one could've walked away from that wreck."

Offering a slight smile, Tracy shook her head. "Someone walked away from it, and we need to speak with him."

"I can't help you."

Tracy glanced at Gretchen, a signal to go ahead with whatever she had gleaned throughout the conversation.

Gretchen looked confused by whatever she had Read. "You drove over three hundred miles to pick up the boy," she said. Her words were slow as if she was receiving the information as she said it aloud. Maybe she was sorting the facts in her mind as she voiced them, Tracy thought.

"You drove all night, in fact," Gretchen continued. "You heard about the wreck on the radio...how did you know to go there?" Understanding touched Gretchen's eyes. "You knew Nyland? You had an arrangement...if anything happened to him, you would become responsible for the boy. Why? Who was he? Who *is* he?"

Drove all night? She was finally getting something from the old lady. Nyland. That was unexpected.

Eloise shoved the desk with her free hand and rolled her chair backward. She leveled the gun at Tracy once more, the hammer still back and her hand suddenly rock-steady. "If you know Nyland, then you're sure as hell with the Order. Out of here, now. I won't ask you again." She turned the gun on Gretchen. "One more word out of you, and it'll be the last noise you make. I'm not kidding." She was on her feet a half second later.

Tracy's mind spun like a broken top. She didn't know what to make of the armed elderly woman. An unquestionable commitment to protect the boy, that much was clear. And no love for the Order of Origin. She would be an ally rather than an adversary if they could just make their view of the Order clear.

"I need you to believe me." Tracy's tone was pleading. "We're not with the Order. I know Verhoeven personally. I've been working to undermine him for years. There must be some way I can prove it to you. I need to talk with the boy. Finding this device," she glanced at the sheet of paper teetering on the edge of the desk, "is the key to stopping the Order once and for all."

Eloise took a step forward, drawing to the edge of her desk. It and an arm's length separated Tracy from the gun's muzzle. The hole looked gaping from where she sat. Five hollow tip rounds were visible in the cylinder of the weapon.

"The boy," Tracy said, knowing she was pressing her luck. "He must be, what—27? 28 by now? Nyland died on that train. He died to protect this device. He knew how important it was. If we can find it, we can stop the Order— but there isn't much time."

Eloise grumbled something unintelligible under her breath. "Nyland didn't die protecting some gadget," she said. "He was protecting the boy, same as I'm doing."

The statement hit Tracy like an electric shock. The room spun around her as the magnitude of the old woman's words shifted in her mind. If that was true, there was more to the boy than they had guessed. Could he really be more important than the device? More important than the Aegis? She heard Gretchen gasp. It was enough to pry her from her confusion.

Gretchen stared at Eloise, her eyes wide and unblinking. Eloise responded by turning the gun hard on Gretchen, who rocked back in her chair, nearly toppling it in the process.

"Wait!" Tracy yelled. Her hands went up and she slid her body between the gun and Gretchen's trembling form. She wanted to protest but wasn't sure what had just happened. Gretchen had Read something—it was the only explanation.

The old woman's eyes were filled with anger. Her penetrating stare was locked on them both. Tracy knew they had crossed the point of no return. Eloise wasn't going to back down this time. They should've left when they had the chance. Still...there was something in the woman's gaze. She was conflicted.

Eloise grimaced and lowered the gun by a fraction. She took a step backward. Tracy felt the weight of the woman's gaze. Judging, but conflicted. Twisting at the elbow, Eloise turned the gun on herself and placed the muzzle against the side of her head. Tracy's limbs felt like they were made of concrete. She felt rooted in place, unable to comprehend what was happening or why.

Tracy was jolted violently before she knew what was happening. Gretchen launched herself from the chair and dove head-first over the top of the desk. She slammed her outstretched hand into the old woman's arm the moment the gun discharged. The shot sounded like a bomb blast in the confines of the tiny office.

A heartbeat later, Gretchen had disappeared along with

the old woman. Tracy stood shell-shocked. She blinked slowly, then gasped a breath. She blinked again. The room seemed to become somehow brighter, the events seeming to have transpired in slow motion, finally returning to real-time.

Girding herself, Tracy rounded the corner of the desk. Gretchen lay prone atop the old woman, their limbs tangled in a confusing mess. Gretchen stirred and pushed herself up on the palm of her hands before rocking backward to her knees. She came up with the revolver in her hand. She held it awkwardly from the side, the cylinder in her palm with the barrel sticking out from between the fingers of her fist and her thumb wrapped sideways around the side of the hammer.

Eloise groaned and peered up through confused eyes. She was unharmed, at least from the revolver discharge. The fall—the tackle—might be a different story. Tracy glanced up to see a neat hole punched in the crown molding at the perimeter of the room's ceiling.

The office door slammed open and a man and a woman rushed in. Tracy turned to face them. Glancing down, she saw Gretchen tuck the revolver into the back of her waistband before lowering the hem of her sweater over it. She hoisted herself upright.

"Are you alright?" the man exclaimed. "We heard a gunshot." Both he and the woman were out of breath.

Eloise was now sitting on the floor. She eyed the man and the woman over the corner of the desk, then glanced a confused look to Gretchen and then Tracy. "Ah..." she stammered. "A gunshot? Nonsense. I knocked over my chair, that's all. I'm getting clumsy in my old age. This young lady was just helping me up."

Gretchen offered a hand and Eloise was more or less hefted back to her feet. The man and woman stood just inside the door, panting and confused.

"That was a gunshot," the man argued.

"Mark," Eloise countered. "What in the hell would we be doing shooting off guns in here? I'm sorry to startle you. I'm clumsy. Please don't make me feel any worse than I already do."

Mark and the woman looked around the room. They exchanged glances. The woman responded with a shrug. Neither appeared to believe it, but they backed out of the office one after the other. "Do you need me to call an ambulance?" the woman asked. "Did you hit your head?"

"Don't be silly, Julia. But thank you for your concern."

They exited, and Tracy breathed easier. She looked at Gretchen and then Eloise. "Someone better explain what the hell just happened," she said. She made a clumsy effort to circle back to her chair before dropping heavily into the seat.

Gretchen rolled the discarded office chair back into position and gestured for Eloise to sit. Though reluctant, the old woman chose to comply. Gretchen rounded back to her chair and slipped into it.

Eloise stared at Gretchen, the question clearly written in her eyes: *why?*

Tracy shook her head. "You're willing to do whatever it takes to keep your secrets, aren't you?"

Eloise turned her gaze on Tracy. Still, she remained silent.

Tracy looked at Gretchen. "I give up. What the hell just happened?"

"She slipped," Gretchen said. "She thought of the boy. She tried not to. She has discipline—seriously, rare discipline. But she cares too much. She cared about Nyland, and she cares about the boy. She thought about him the last time she saw him. He was sixteen years old at the time. He petitioned the court. He emancipated himself at sixteen and struck out on his own. She was going to pull the trigger because she gave up information she didn't intend to."

Tracy slumped a little. She rubbed her eyes and sighed with frustration. "So she has no idea where he is today."

"She doesn't," Gretchen said. "But I do. I told you about him, in fact. He was a guest at Doctor Voss's place a couple of years ago. His name is Cyrus Cooper."

Tracy felt like all of the air had been suddenly sucked out of the room. She was dizzy… light-headed. She noticed the old woman's confusion and struggled to stay in the moment. She nodded in Eloise's direction. "What?" she said.

It was Gretchen's turn to look confused. "She knew him by a different name. Jonny Webb."

Eloise rocked back in her seat, exhausted and defeated. Tracy couldn't blame her. She could sympathize. Cyrus Cooper. "I've met him too," she said. "Last year. I've been ducking him for the last nine months. He's the one I told you about."

Chapter 16 - His Patience as a Person

Brown University, Providence, Rhode Island

They walked across the single-lane street hand in hand. Cyrus angled them toward the entrance of the Small Point Cafe. Reese sensed something had changed during their brief visit to the lingerie store. She just didn't know what. Cyrus's already cautious demeanor had transformed. He seemed more on edge, but there was something new to his discomfort. If she had to guess, he seemed less decisive, as if he was having second thoughts about their visit to the coffee shop. Maybe he was second-guessing his return to Brown University entirely. It was a reminder of a turbulent time for him.

Cyrus pulled at the shop door and held it for her. He smiled as she passed and then followed her into the building. It was a cozy coffee house, the space narrow but deep. The front was filled with small tables surrounded by wooden chairs. Maybe a dozen tables, half to the left of the door and half to the right. The coffee bar and cash register occupied the leftmost wall. A narrow set of tables lined the right wall, a comfortably wide walkway separating them from the counter and register.

The shop was virtually deserted. Reese wasn't surprised. Most of Westminster Street had been quiet, with nearly every curbside parking space empty. She supposed most of the shop's clientele consisted of school students, most of whom were currently in class.

Cyrus slipped his way past her and headed for the counter. The woman at the register greeted him with a sunny smile. She looked to be in her early forties. Reese figured she was the manager or maybe the owner. "What can I get you?" the woman asked.

"Are you the manager?" Cyrus countered.

"Owner," the woman corrected. "My name's Claire. How can I help you?"

Cyrus often wore two layers of shirts. The bottom layer he kept tucked into his jeans, while the outer layer was always worn loose. Reese knew this had become a habit for him; the outer later hanging free past his belt made it easy to conceal his handgun. He wore only the bottom two or three buttons done up, proving easy access to his sidearm. They'd teleported to their safe house in Manhattan and then rented a car for the three-plus hour drive up 95 to Providence. She thought she was accustomed to all of his tricks by now, so she was surprised when he reached into the back pocket of his jeans and pulled out a fold of leather.

"I'm Special Agent Amstell with the FBI," Cyrus said. He flashed an FBI issue identification from inside a folded flap of leather. "I need to ask you a few questions."

Reese fought to keep her jaw from dropping. She'd never seen this fake ID before and had no idea what he'd planned to do once they reached the coffee shop. She noticed the way he presented the identification. He was careful to keep his finger clenched over the photographic portion of the ID and was even quicker to pocket it before Claire could look too closely.

Just when I thought I knew all the tricks.

The woman blew out a breath and rocked back on her heels. Her sunny disposition disappeared in an instant. "This is about the kid who died?" Claire asked.

Cyrus nodded.

"Haven't the cops asked enough questions?" she complained. "You people are killing my business. I thought they decided the kid died of natural causes. Some kind of heart condition?"

"You've spoken with the local police," Cyrus said. He kept his tone friendly, but he was undeterred by her reluctance to discuss the death of the young man earlier in the week. Ashley wondered how many times Cyrus had done this sort of thing.

"I'm with the FBI," Cyrus continued. "We're conducting a parallel investigation. We look at everything ourselves. You'd be surprised what a fresh set of eyes can bring to an investigation."

Claire fixed Cyrus with a hard gaze. Reese could see wheels turning inside the woman's head. She was anxious to put all the bad publicity behind her and move on.

"What did you say your name was?" Claire asked.

"Agent Amstell," Cyrus said. "But you can call me Peter if you like. "This is Jessica," he said, tipping his head toward Reese. "She's the forensics specialist reviewing the case."

"Forensics—" Claire sputtered. She somehow managed to draw the single word out and make it sound like three, one for each of its syllables. "What exactly are you looking for?"

Cyrus offered a disarming smile. Reese was impressed. He had successfully pulled the wind out of Claire's sails; her tones of indignation seemed to dissipate into the aromatic air surrounding them. "Not a thing," Cyrus said. "But I cover my bases. This way, you only have to see me once. I'll file my report, and Jessica will file hers. The local police are satisfied, so I think it's safe to say we're just completing a formality."

Claire stood silently with her arms across her chest. The frustration in her glare seemed to seep away. Cyrus was saying everything right, and she liked the idea of her life returning to normal.

Cyrus pocketed his identification and produced a small paper pad and a pen. Looking around the shop carefully, he took it in but made no observations. Then he glanced at the clock on the wall and noted the time.

"The boy died Monday evening, sometime between 8 and 9 pm, is that right?" Cyrus asked.

Claire nodded.

"And you were working at that time?"

She nodded again.

"Who else was on shift?" Cyrus asked.

"We were busy on Monday," Claire explained, "so I had Kelly and Mandy in until we closed at eleven."

It was Cyrus's turn to nod. He flipped a few pages in his pad as if to confirm a detail. Reese saw that the page he'd glanced at was blank, but Claire couldn't tell. "Ok," Cyrus went on. "We have their contact information. That's good."

He looked Claire in the eye and waited a moment, likely emphasizing the importance of his next question. "Did you notice anything out of the ordinary Monday night," he asked. "Anything at all?"

Claire didn't answer immediately. To her credit, she leaned a hip against the edge of the counter and considered the question. "I can't say I did," she said after a moment. "Nothing sticks out. We were busy, but it was a typical Monday as far as that goes. I'd planned to have the girls here because it usually takes three of us on a Monday night." She looked around the store. "Things pick up once school is out, believe it or not."

Cyrus smiled. Reese did, too. She couldn't help it. Claire was warming to them; it was a transformation she'd witnessed in a few minutes. Cyrus affected people when he wanted to.

"The boy who died—Thomas Wilks—what do you know about him? Was he a regular?" Cyrus was doing his best to come off as a by-the-book investigator.

Claire pursed her lips. "Tommy," she corrected. "Everyone called him Tommy. I already miss him. He was in here all the time. There were times you would have thought he worked here. I should retire the table he sat at…it was practically reserved for him anyway."

Claire stopped short and began turning red in the cheeks. Cyrus guessed she just realized how insensitive her comment might have sounded. Cyrus grinned. So did Reese; to her, the comment sounded sweet.

"I didn't— I shouldn't—" Claire stammered.

"It's okay," Cyrus offered in a gentle voice. Reese marveled at the way he worked her for information. "It sounds like you thought highly of him."

She nodded. "He was a good kid. I was never too crazy about his choice of friends, but I like to think that spoke to his patience as a person and a good Christian."

Cyrus's eyes narrowed, and his head tipped in response.

"Oh, I mean that friend of his—" Claire explained. "That Barnabe kid. That little tool spent a lot of time here. Tommy's best friend, maybe—a kid named Barnabe. I'm not sure if that was his first or last name. Would've thought they were joined at the hip. I never knew how he could tolerate that little snot."

"You didn't care for Barnabe?"

She shook her head. "No one did. A rude little cuss. He seemed to go out of his way to cause trouble."

Cyrus wrote the name Barnabe in his notebook and nodded. He looked over his shoulder. "I see you've got some cameras." He motioned with the end of his pen, pointing to a tiny camera mounted high on the shop's rear wall. It was positioned in the direction of the front door. He indicated two more; one was behind the counter, aimed at the register, and the other was on the wall over the door, looking backward into the room. The devices were so small that they surprised Reese. She hadn't noticed any of them. "Can I see the recordings from that night?"

Claire scrunched up her nose as if she smelled something foul. After a long second, a hint of mirth touched her eyes, and she smiled. "You FBI guys don't care for the local cops, do you?" she asked. "You won't even get the video from them?"

Cyrus shrugged. "Go directly to the source, I always say."

"Okay," Clair said. "But my security system's all digital—it doesn't use tapes. You'll need a thumb drive if you want a copy of the footage."

Cyrus fished in his hip pocket and produced a short USB memory stick. He waved it in the air, showing her he had it covered. "You can't beat digital," he said simply.

Claire rounded the counter but stopped short. She seemed to think better of it all of a sudden. "The machines in back," she explained. "But I don't like leaving the store unattended." It seemed like a non-issue with only one old man sitting quietly near the front window. He was sipping his coffee while he read the newspaper.

Reese stepped forward. "I can watch the counter for you if you like."

That brought a laugh from Claire. "You're a little over qualified for that, honey. You being a forensic specialist and all."

Reese smiled. "I wouldn't know the first thing about working behind the counter," she admitted. "But if someone tried to make off with anything of yours, I'm more than happy to shoot them. I can hold down the fort."

Cyrus and Claire laughed.

Chapter 17 - A Cold Shiver

Biltmore Home for Boys, Boston, Massachusetts

Gretchen climbed into the car's passenger seat seconds after Tracy slipped behind the wheel opposite her. They sat quietly, gazing across the street at the Biltmore Building and contemplating what they had learned inside. They'd left Eloise Fleischer exhausted and defeated after giving up secrets she had never intended to divulge. Still, after all they had learned, what did they really know?

"Have you ever heard of anyone who couldn't be Read?" Gertrude asked.

Tracy offered a slow, contemplative nod. "Only one. Gertrude found him, apparently entirely by chance. In all of her studies, there was a single person her people couldn't Read or Push. As far as I know, when she died, she still hadn't figured out why he was immune to their abilities."

"It was Cyrus Cooper?"

Tracy met her eye. She offered another slow nod. "How did you know?"

"I tried to read him when he turned up at the Compound

a few years back. I couldn't get a thing off of him. I attributed it to the medication. He'd suffered a gunshot wound before appearing at Doctor Voss's door. He was banged up and in terrible shape. There was a serious infection. I treated him with antibiotics and painkillers. He was unresponsive for days. When he finally came out of it, I tried to Read him. I wanted to know if he was a danger to us inside the Compound. I couldn't get anything out of him. I figured it was due to the physical and mental trauma. He'd suffered a major concussion, so it wasn't out of the realm of possibility."

Tracy seemed to consider this. "Plus, you'd never met anyone you couldn't Read," she added.

Gretchen nodded. "Not without a neural suppressor, anyway. Obviously, I checked him for that."

Tracy's hand went up and touched the flesh behind her left ear. It was a subconscious gesture, Gretchen judged. Her friend wore a neural suppressor. They were friends, but having someone inside your head—even by accident—was unsettling. She could understand Tracy's desire to wear the tiny device.

"Gertrude had the same experience with Cyrus?" Gretchen asked. A cold shiver went through her, remembering Gertrude Waterford. The woman's experimental gene therapy was responsible for her ability to Read others. The procedure had taken place shortly before Gertrude was arrested by federal authorities and later murdered while in their custody. She'd discovered the true depths of Gertrude's insidious nature after she made Tracy's acquaintance. Tracy had explained the invasive and horrible truth behind Gertrude's life's work.

"Yup. It wasn't a head injury that was keeping you out. Gertrude ran into him long before you did. Whatever is different about Cyrus Cooper is far more complicated."

Gretchen shot a glance at her friend behind the wheel.

"But we know Cyrus was on the train with Nyland when he died 13 years ago." She let a brief silence hang. "Cyrus can't be Read, and Nyland knew him. That can't be a coincidence. What was Nyland working on when he died?"

Tracy was grinding her teeth. Gretchen could see it from where she sat. "I have no idea," Tracy admitted. "He'd been out of contact for months before that train wreck. To be honest, I was afraid Verhoeven had gotten to him. Then his body turned up in that derailment."

"If Cyrus was there, maybe he has the Aegis."

The idea didn't appear to excite Tracy. "The way I understand it, he has no childhood memories. Nothing before waking up following that train crash." She slammed her hand on the steering wheel and grumbled something under her breath. "He survived a train wreck as a kid. I can't believe I never put that together!"

Gretchen's look stated the required question.

Tracy elaborated. "Cyrus got cozy with Reese Knoland, the hardware specialist on Meade's teleportation project. What little I know came through her."

While she was up to speed on Walter Meade and the project Tracy had participated in before going into hiding, she was only peripherally aware of the scientists involved in the work. She knew them by name and reputation but had never met them firsthand. Now, Tracy was hiding not only from the Order of Origin but also from Cyrus Cooper and his team.

"Memory loss, and he can't be Read?" Gretchen thought aloud. "Could both be the result of the train wreck?"

Tracy shook her head, then shrugged. She tipped her head back against the seat and grumbled something to herself. She was chewing on an unpleasant thought. "I have no idea," she said at last.

"If Cyrus is looking for you," Gretchen said, "why not talk

to him? If he knows anything about the device, we could save a lot of time."

Tracy squirmed a little in her seat, visibly uncomfortable with the idea. She was in a tough spot with Cyrus Cooper on one side and the Order of Origin on the other.

"Your own people are out to get you," Gretchen urged. "Is there really a downside to talking to Cyrus?"

Tracy stared out the windshield and sat silently with her hands on her legs. Seconds ticked by. Finally, she turned a brief glance to Gretchen. "It's more complicated than that." Her eyes went back to the front, and she sat silently.

There was gravity in that statement, Gretchen knew. She sensed deep conflict in her friend and wondered what Tracy wasn't sharing. For the first time in a long time, she wished her friend wasn't wearing a neural suppressor. The words that weren't being spoken really bothered her.

Chapter 18 - Unpleasant Intent

Brown University, Providence, Rhode Island

Cyrus followed Claire into a small, cramped office beside the bathroom at the back of the store. The desk was pushed against one wall and was stacked high with mounds of loose sheets of paper and thick industry catalogs. If there was a method to her filing system, it involved chaos theory, he guessed. Claire turned to the particleboard cabinet beside the office entrance and slid one of its panels aside. Cyrus was relieved. Inside was a seventeen-inch flatscreen display and a thin, wide digital video recorder. The entire system was controlled with a touchscreen display.

"Very nice," Cyrus said, pulling the lone office chair over to the cabinet. "This is a first-class setup."

"I have my ex-husband to thank for that," Claire said. "I told everyone that he was good for nothing, but that wasn't true. He did a good job setting up the cameras and the recorder. Maybe we'd still be married if he could've gotten a few dishes into the dishwasher."

It sounded like a joke, but Claire didn't look like she found it funny.

"It's pretty straightforward," Claire explained. "You enter the timecode of the footage you want. The recorder stores everything for three months, and then starts recycling the oldest footage first. If you find something interesting, just select it and use the export option. You can save it right to your USB *thingy*."

Cyrus nodded. "Got it. Thank you very much."

Claire returned to the counter after saying something about saving Jessica from expiring from boredom. Cyrus entered the appropriate time code and was instantly greeted by the footage he wanted. The three cameras were displayed on the 17" screen at the same time, each camera holding a quarter of the overall display. The last quarter was a shot of the street out front. From what he could tell, the camera must've been mounted relatively high over the shop entrance. It pointed up Westminster and captured people walking into the store. It also recorded everyone passing on the sidewalk and every car traversing the narrow single-lane road.

The camera over the door inside the shop was mounted at an ideal position for Cyrus. It pointed back across the length of the shop. He could see Tommy Wilks sitting at one of the narrow tables just past the ordering counter. The cameras were high-resolution and captured everything in crisp detail. Tommy was at the table by himself with his laptop open. He had a coffee beside him in a to-go cup. He was typing rapidly on the computer.

Cyrus scrubbed backward through the footage until he saw Wilks first enter the coffee shop at 7:33 p.m. He hit play on the footage and watched in real time. Wilks ordered his drink and waited at the end of the counter until it was ready. He didn't speak to anyone other than to exchange a few words with the cashier. When his drink was ready, he sat at the narrow table along the rightmost wall. He pulled a laptop from his bag, laid it on the table, and flipped open the top. Stickers with odd and brightly colored logos covered the lid. Seconds later, he set to work typing. A few minutes after that, he produced a mobile phone and made a brief call. The camera didn't record audio, but even if it did, Wilks sat too far away from the lens to have any hope of hearing his conversation. The call lasted only twenty-two seconds. After that, he went back to work on the computer.

For the next half hour, Wilks worked without interruption, often pounding away on the keyboard with no obvious awareness of his surroundings. He didn't speak with anyone. He didn't interact with anyone in any way. At 8:09, a small bald man walked past Wilks and headed to the back of the shop. Cyrus knew the restroom was back there. It was likely the man's destination. Scrubbing the footage back several seconds, Cyrus watched more closely as the bald man passed Wilks. The bald guy's head turned as he walked. He seemed to take deliberate notice of Wilks but never touched him.

Cyrus had that camera in full-screen view as he studied Wilks and the bald man. He shrunk it back to quarter screen and switched to the camera at the back of the store. It was pointed in the direction of the front door. Cyrus hadn't paid much attention to that view because Wilks was only slightly visible at the bottom of the frame. The only thing visible was the top of Wilks's head. It was so little of the young man that if Cyrus didn't know it was Wilks sitting there, he could never have identified him. But the angle picked up the small bald man as he threaded his way toward the rear of the store. The bald man walked directly down the center of the shot, moving past Wilks with nothing more than a deliberate passing glance.

Cyrus rewound the footage once more and watched the bald man move from one end of the store to the next. His eyes had been on Wilks the entire time. There was no question about it. Watching the small man move, Cyrus felt a chill. He couldn't decide how to describe what he saw in the bald man's gaze, but it was disconcerting. He seemed fixated on Wilks with some kind of unpleasant intent.

Reese walked into the room; she held a tall to-go cup in

each hand. She handed one to Cyrus. "Nice lady, once you get her talking," she said.

Cyrus took the coffee and set it aside. He scrubbed through the footage once more but couldn't put his finger on exactly what it was about the small man that he found so troubling.

"Are you alright?" Reese asked.

"Yeah," Cyrus said with a tired smile. "Just fine."

Lacking a second chair, Reese knelt on the floor beside him and watched what he was doing. Her position on the floor put her almost at eye level with the screen. Cyrus saw her drink from her cup, and he smiled. He took his cup and sat back in the chair. Taking a deep breath, he sipped the coffee. "Thank you," he said.

She smiled. "Did you find anything?"

"Nothing helpful," he said. He considered telling her about the bald guy but didn't know how to explain his concern. The best he could come up with was how the little guy just seemed out of place. He decided it was better not to say anything.

Cyrus shrunk the footage back to quarter screen and let it play. The little guy was still at the back of the shop, presumably in the restroom. The forward-facing camera showed that the front portion of the store was fairly crowded, but it had cleared out a bit since Wilks had first entered. Wilks continued to sit behind his computer the entire time, his attention fixed on whatever he was doing.

At 8:12, Wilks shifted a little in his seat. His movement seemed unnatural, so Cyrus reversed the footage and brought it to full screen. He let it play again and watched more closely. The timer in the corner of the display turned to 8:12:09. The second it did, Wilks moved. He bobbed forward almost imperceptibly, then flinched hard against the back of his chair. The eyes behind his glasses went big and round, and his jaw waggled in a manner that seemed entirely helpless. Seconds later, his mouth snapped shut and his head tipped back into the pose of a man sitting at a table while displaying perfect posture.

"What just happened?" Reese asked.

Cyrus shook his head. He had no idea. To see Wilks sitting suddenly so rigid and upright was unnatural. He'd spent the better part of the last hour sitting there with abysmal posture, slurping his coffee and oblivious to everything around him.

"He's dead," Cyrus said quietly, tapping his finger on Wilks's upright form. The time code ticked along, and Wilks didn't move. "Whatever *that* was, it was him dying."

"Who dies like that?" Reese asked. "Don't people just sort of slump over when the life leaves them? What makes someone go all upright like that? I would say someone had posed the body if I hadn't witnessed it for myself."

Cyrus nodded. He was thinking the same thing.

The small bald man walked back through the frame a few seconds later. This time, he passed Wilks without the slightest glance.

Cyrus switched camera views to the shot from the front of the room. He watched the bald man walk into the bottom of the frame and move toward the top of the screen as he made his way to the front of the store. When he got there, he turned right. Just as he slipped from view, it looked like he was sitting down.

The bald man had returned to his table at the front of the store, Cyrus reasoned. He wished the camera had a better view of the bald man and the place he'd been sitting, but they were lucky to have what they did. He rewound the footage once more and switched to a full-frame view. He watched once more as the tiny tremors passed through Tommy Wilks, then watched in awe as Wilks suddenly sat more upright.

Cyrus had no doubt that he'd just witnessed the young man's death. He just couldn't understand how it had happened.

Cyrus and Reese stared at the screen. There was more to see, so Cyrus let the footage play. At 8:18, a new character entered the frame. He was young, medium height, and had thick blonde hair. With the full-screen angle they were using, they could only see him from the back. The young man walked briskly into the frame and dropped himself into the chair opposite Wilks's body. The new guy laid his computer bag down at his feet, pushed it against the wall with a foot, and directed his attention to Wilks. He seemed to be speaking the entire time. A moment later, the new guy shoved the table. His chair pushed away from the table, and the table shifted in Wilks's direction. The movement must've put Wilks off balance because his head slumped forward hard, ending with his chin at rest against his chest.

The new guy sprang to his feet. The movement nearly sent his chair flying. He grabbed his bag from the floor and darted for the front of the shop.

Cyrus stopped the footage. He switched to the camera on the wall behind Wilks and let the footage play again. They saw the new guy enter the frame. He was already talking to Wilks as he entered the frame. There was no audio, but the new guy was obviously speaking. It was Alec Barnabe, Cyrus was now certain. He recognized the kid from the reports Nathan gathered. Barnabe dropped into the chair opposite Wilks and slid his computer bag across the floor. He was talking to Wilks the entire time. He looked angry about something. It was only at the last moment that he finally looked at Wilks. Then the table and chair moved, Wilks's head slumped, and Barnabe bolted.

"He never laid a hand on him," Reese said. "I don't get it."

"I don't either," Cyrus admitted. It was a new one for him as well.

He rewound the footage to just before Barnabe's entrance and shrunk the display back to quarter screen so that all four cameras were visible. They watched as everything played out once again.

Barnabe vaulted from his chair and headed for the front of the coffee shop. Cyrus saw Barnabe back in the street view camera as he slammed through the front door, turned right, and ran out of frame.

Reese's hand clamped over his with a vice-like grip. He turned to see her staring at the screen with saucer-shaped eyes. "What's wrong?" he asked. "What did you see?"

"I don't know," she said in a voice that wasn't even a whisper. "Rewind it. I don't even know how to explain it."

Cyrus rewound the footage. "Which camera?" he asked.

It took her a moment to respond. He squeezed her hand back. "Hey," he said. "It's ok. We'll look at it together. Which camera do you want?"

"The one on the back wall."

He switched views and hit play. They watched Barnabe spin from his chair, snatch up his computer bag, and run. Reese leaned closer to the screen and raised a finger. As Barnabe passed the counter's edge and reached the area dedicated to customer seating, chairs swept into his path from the left and right. Barnabe hit the chairs and almost spilled headfirst over them. Somehow, he caught himself. He looked down at the chairs in what seemed like dismay— then he kicked through the mess and ducked out the front door.

Reese turned to Cyrus. "You saw it?"

Cyrus cycled the footage. He wasn't sure what he'd seen. The first time through, he thought the kid just tripped. Now, maybe not. He needed to see it again. When he replayed the footage, he did it at half speed. Barnabe ran past the counter in long, exaggerated steps. When he reached the customer seating area, four chairs converged on him—two from his left and two from his right. They swept in smoothly and crashed together directly in his path. The breathtaking part of what they saw was that no one had been seated at the tables where the chairs had come from. No one was within fifteen feet of the spot, yet the chairs moved to block Barnabe's path, seemingly of their own accord.

Reese sat back on her heels and stared. Her coffee sat on the floor beside her, entirely forgotten. Cyrus ran the footage back again and again. It didn't make any sense. It was shocking and disconcerting, but each time he watched, it felt more and more familiar. Like something from his past was tapping him on the shoulder and daring him to offer it his attention.

On his last pass of the footage, Cyrus noticed two things he'd missed on earlier views. The first was the small bald man at the very edge of the frame. He could only be seen from the forward-facing camera. He'd leaned into the shot right after Barnabe collided with the four chairs. The little man's eyes followed him as he disappeared through the front door. Seconds after Barnabe was gone, the small man turned and surveyed the shop. Presumably, he was observing the reactions of his fellow patrons. But that supposition didn't match the delighted smile playing across his face. If Cyrus had to guess, the small man seemed pleased with what he'd seen.

Cyrus copied the video footage to the flash drive. He offered Reese a hand as she climbed up from the floor. "I think we've got what we came for," he said. "Now we just need to figure out what the hell we saw."

Reese's hand was cold. The strange video had stunned her. Not speechless but entirely at a loss for what to say. Luckily, Cyrus knew what to do next. They needed to find Alec Barnabe. This started because they needed his help.

Now something spooky was happening to Barnabe, and Cyrus felt drawn into whatever was taking place. Though he needed Barnabe, it looked like Barnabe would need his help first.

Chapter 19 - We Are Not a Cult

The Voss Compound, Isle of Kapros

"The birth of the universe," Doctor Alfred Fillmore said. "Our universe? You're referring to the Big Bang?"

"Correct," Radley Verhoeven said with a nod. "The start of everything. The formation of our world. We have the Tangury to thank for it."

Rutger Voss was participating in the discussion using his laptop computer. The video conference included seven other participants logging in from locations worldwide. Seven small boxes lay side by side along the bottom edge of his screen, each displaying a thumbnail-sized live feed from each participant's camera. A large video feed occupied the bulk of the screen above. When any of the conference participants spoke, the software automatically switched their feed to the main, large display.

Leaning back in his chair, Voss studied Radley Verhoeven as he spoke. He recalled the man from a brief encounter more than twenty years prior. When introductions were made at the start of the conference call, Verhoeven had not indicated that he recalled the encounter, so Voss was happy

Surviving Origin Part 1 - Book 5

to leave the experience in his past. Though more than two decades had passed, Verhoeven looked terrible. His face was thin and fleshy, and his skin practically hung from his bones. Time had not been kind to the man, Voss decided.

"This isn't the time for rhetoric," a new voice said. It was one of the spooks Voss knew. Either Kellogg or Parker, he couldn't recall which was which. Both men were in their mid-thirties, clean-shaven, and neatly combed dark hair. Both wore dark suits and matching ties. One was from the NSA and the other from the CIA, but who knew which was which. The only noticeable difference between them was that one had short sideburns. That was Kellogg, Voss guessed once again. "We're not here for a sermon and won't be converted. Stick to the facts," Kellogg warned.

"These are the facts," Verhoeven said. "The Order of Origin offers only facts. Our goal is to disclose the truth. We are not a *cult*." He said the word as if it left an unpleasant taste on his tongue. "The Tangury are real. Their influence on our world is legitimate. Religion asks for leaps of faith. I'm talking about science. I've already offered proof."

A calming voice joined the conversation. "And we thank you for that," Ray Hayfare offered in a warm, supporting tone. "But to be honest, we're not entirely sure what to make of..." he stumbled to find the right words. "The proof you've provided. It's certainly unprecedented. We have experts examining it as we speak. But your claims are just too fantastic."

Hayfare was some kind of special advisor to the President of the United States. He had sandy blond hair, bright blue eyes, and a naturally tanned face. He wore an expensive pinstripe suit with a small American flag on the tie clip. Voss understood why Hayfare had been tapped to chair the meeting. The man had a calming way about him; he seemed a natural-born leader. He was assertive without being demanding and disrespectful, without letting the more caustic personalities at the table walk all over him.

Doctor Seymour Beckworth was his opposite on so many levels. "Fantastic is hardly the appropriate word," he snapped. The video screen changed and was filled with Beckworth's narrow face. His beady eyes and condescending demeanor were accentuated by how he wore his small framed glasses near the tip of his nose. "Your wild theories might work on the small-minded, but you can't expect educated officials to fall for your outrageous claims."

Verhoeven leaned closer to his camera. It was enough to make the auto-switching software pick up the cue and transition him to the main feed. "By now, your specialists will have completed your report on the dig site," he said. "Mister Hayfare, would you please explain the results of that report to Doctor Beckworth? Since he specializes in psychiatry, I'm sure he doesn't fully appreciate the nature of the geologic analysis."

Beckworth bolted forward in the seat at his desk and drew the camera's attention. "I'm a psychologist," he snapped with an angry curl to his lip.

It was hard to tell from the thumbnail view at the bottom of his screen, but Doctor Voss was pretty sure he saw Verhoeven smiling at Beckworth's unprofessional outburst. Voss took a sip of coffee, watched, and listened.

"Soil and core sample analysis were conclusive," Hayfare confirmed. "The closest estimate puts the surrounding strata in the neighborhood of 800 million years. Examination of the vault and surrounding conditions is conclusive. Nothing has been artificially disturbed— certainly not within the last ten thousand years. You can be sure of that."

Voss found himself shifting closer to the screen. Confirmation. He didn't think it would come back positive. The American project was unprecedented. They had dug and drilled over 7 miles to uncover a vault that only Radley Verhoeven knew existed. Geologic analysis confirmed what common sense suggested: that no modern force could have placed the archive at that location. As unlikely as it seemed, it lent credence to Verhoeven's wild claims.

Everyone on the video conference was silent, likely considering the report's implications the same as Voss. He studied the seven small boxes across the screen and then the full-screen feed showing Verhoeven sitting quietly before his own computer.

"What does this mean?" The question came from the other spook. Parker—no sideburns. "Based on this evidence, we're expected to take your word as gospel?" The question seemed to be pointed back at Verhoeven.

"I offer it as proof," Verhoeven said. "I'm certain your people are already examining the vault's contents. What do they tell you?"

That was interesting. Voss perked in his seat at the mention of the vault being opened. No one had explained what had been discovered inside the 18,000 cubic foot enclosure. Until this point, it wasn't even clear if the so-called vault had been brought to the surface, let alone opened.

Doctor Alfred Fillmore and Doctor Seymour Beckworth both leaned closer to their cameras at the mention of the vault, and Voss noticed he wasn't the only one left in the dark. Kellogg, Parker, and Hayfare didn't seem as interested. Apparently, they had already been read in.

The eighth member of the conference call remained motionless and without expression. He hadn't said a word since the call had begun. Hayfare had introduced the man as only James. Strangely, he hadn't indicated if that was the man's given name or his surname. James had only nodded at the introduction, and the conversation had moved on. Something was chilling about the man's stoic demeanor. His age was difficult to determine, particularly since the camera never switched to his feed. He never spoke or moved, so the camera didn't cue on him. The thumbnail-sized video feed was the extent of what Voss had seen. Perhaps in his late thirties or early forties, James had neatly trimmed short dark hair and a trim dark beard. He wore a suit. But beyond that, the details were unclear. The man's purpose here had never been specified, and his affiliation was never provided.

Another spook.

"The contents of the vault have been classified," Ray Hayfare said in a neutral tone.

Voss cleared his throat and spoke for the first time since introductions had been completed. "Then the vault has been raised and the contents examined?" he asked.

"The vault has been raised," Hayfare said. "But I'm afraid that any further information has been classified."

The stonewalling brought a scowl to Voss's face. "Fine," he said. "But surely you can give us information without being specific."

Hayfare shook his head. "I'm afraid that I cannot. I'm very sorry."

Beckworth burst out, "This is absurd. You asked for our professional opinions and fail to provide the information necessary for an informed understanding. I won't tolerate this."

Kellogg and Parker didn't seem surprised with what was happening. Voss couldn't tell if they knew what the vault contained or if they were just accustomed to being frozen out in such a way. For his part, Doctor Fillmore seemed to be at a loss for words.

"How about this," Voss suggested. "Surely, the vault's contents have been carbon-dated by this point. Can you at least tell us if they support the geologic analysis?"

Hayfare paused for a long moment. He took a moment to consult a sheet of notes on the desk beside him before looking once more into the camera. "Carbon dating tests concur with the geologic tests from the dig site," he said at last.

Voss saw surprise register on the faces of everyone on the call. Everyone except James. James continued to remain unreadable and expressionless. Perhaps he was the watchdog, here to ensure no classified data was exposed to the group?

"As I've said," Verhoeven offered with a satisfied expression. "My organization is on the level. You must believe what I've told you."

Beckworth slapped a palm down on his desk and groused at the camera. The bang rattled Voss's speakers as the screen flashed and filled with Beckworth's irritated expression. "You would have us believe that this race created our entire universe," Beckworth snapped. "The Tankarry?"

"The Tangury," Verhoeven said. He offered a patient correction, though it was clear to everyone present that Beckworth wanted to raise the man's ire. "And it's not an entirely unaccepted theory. Doctor Fillmore, would you explain some of the more conventional and unconventional theories?"

Fillmore sat straighter in his chair as his image filled the screen. He seemed surprised to be called upon. He also looked like the prompt had pulled him from mental distraction. Voss could understand. This was all groundbreaking and concerning information. Personally, he was eager to hear what a renowned physicist like Fillmore would think of Verhoeven's claims.

"Well," Fillmore said, his tone unsteady and unsure. "Philosophers have toyed with the idea for generations, of course. And more recently, theoretical physicists have taken a stab at the concept. There is evidence to support Mister Verhoeven's claim of alternative dimensions. Though, life on other planes has never been proven. There's never been a way to quantify the concept."

As Fillmore spoke, the weariness disappeared from his tone, and his voice became more comfortable and rhythmic. He went from a clumsy and uncomfortable improvised speaker and quickly evolved into the skilled orator he had become through countless lectures. Clearly, his mind was rapidly assimilating, even accepting the idea they were discussing.

"There are those in the community," Fillmore went on, "who speculate that our entire universe is a hologram projected in another two-dimensional universe. The concept is embraced primarily by those who try to reconcile the principles of string theory with Einstein's Theory of Relativity. Theoretically speaking, in a lower dimensional universe with no gravity—"

"Hold on a second, Doctor," Hayfare interrupted. "We're recording and transcribing this conversation for the President, his cabinet, and the Joint Chiefs. Let's keep this at a level we can all understand. Is that possible?"

The camera switched back to Fillmore. His cheeks turned pink, and he offered a sheepish nod to the camera. "I'm very sorry. The point is that there are numerous theories in physics postulating extra-dimensional space. Some suggest there are simply more aspects to the world we inhabit— aspects other than the X, Y, and Z—"

"I'm sorry?" Hayfare interrupted once more.

Fillmore looked at a loss for a more simplified way to explain what was, in his mind, already simplified explanation.

"Look at the keyboard in front of you," Voss said. "You see it in three dimensions. It has length, width, and depth. We also perceive a fourth dimension: time. That mouse is on your desk at a specific location at a specific point in time. If you know the time and its location in three-dimensional space, you know exactly where the mouse is."

"Precisely," Fillmore smiled. "Thank you. "But some theories postulate other aspects of our space-time while others suggest entire other planes of existence, either adjacent to our own or entirely unrelated."

Beckworth scowled once more. "Why can't you give a simple answer, man? Is what he's claiming plausible or not?"

Fillmore sat back in his chair and lowered his hands out of frame. "Physics is about developing an understanding of our world. We develop theories and principles to fit our knowledge about the world, not vice versa. Nothing Mister Verhoeven has claimed can be disproven by physics or quantum theory. I can tell you that much. If he is on the level, mankind stands to take a gigantic leap forward in our understanding of the universe. I, for one, hope he's on the level."

Beckworth rolled his eyes. Verhoeven offered a satisfied grin. Kellogg, Parker, and James all sat expressionless.

"So his claims are plausible. Is that what you're saying, Doctor Fillmore?" Hayfare said.

"Yes, plausible," Fillmore acknowledged.

"What about you, Doctor Voss?" Hayfare asked.

"The geologic data is compelling, and the carbon dating is convincing. But if we're to believe another race of beings created our universe, I think the vault's contents are entirely relevant. Doctor Fillmore can testify on a theoretical level, but Doctor Beckworth is correct. You must provide us with all the relevant information if you want our professional opinions."

Hayfare shook his head. "The contents of the vault are irrelevant to our discussion. We're here to decide if Radley Verhoeven's claims—if the Order of Origin's belief—has merit."

"But why?" Voss offered in a calm, collected voice. "Why

the concern? What possible relevance does this have now? Mankind has puzzled over these questions since the dawn of time. What's changed?"

Hayfare looked suddenly very uncomfortable.

Verhoeven moved, drawing the focus of the main camera. "Modern man was not the first intelligent species with dominion over the Earth," he said.

"Verhoeven—" Hayfare warned. He leaned closer to the camera and attempted to do something with his keyboard, but he must have been unsuccessful because he failed to stop Verhoeven.

"The contents of the vault prove that another version of modern man inhabited this planet approximately 800 million years ago," Verhoeven explained. "What they don't want you to know is simple. That extinct race was more technically advanced than we are today. The big secret? Every nation on Earth is currently fighting over the technology recovered from inside that vault."

Chapter 20 - Why Aren't We Dead

Brown University, Providence, Rhode Island

Reese followed Cyrus from the coffee shop. They'd left their drinks behind; neither had an appetite after viewing the strange security footage. She was still pondering what they'd seen and trying to decide if they had learned anything useful when Cyrus suddenly stopped mid-stride. She bounced off his back and staggered backward a step. They were only a pace off the curb and crossing the street. Her first thought was that a car was coming. But Cyrus didn't step back from the street; he remained motionless right where he was.

"Is that any way to greet an old friend?" she heard a voice say.

Reese moved from behind Cyrus and saw a man leaning against the front of a large black Chevy SUV. He was in his late forties, she guessed. His eyes were dark and hooded, and he had short hair that seemed prematurely grey. He was clean-shaven with a pronounced scar across the left side of his jaw. The way his eyes bore into Cyrus was troubling. There was nothing confrontational about how he stood; he was leaning against the four-wheel-drive as if he didn't have a care in the world. The look he gave and his general presence made the encounter threatening.

The man wore a vest over a drab green shirt. It was festooned with dozens of pockets. Each compartment bulged as if it was loaded with hardware. He wore loose canvas pants that had pockets up and down the legs. It was tactical gear, she realized. Her eyes moved instantly up and down the street. As far as she could tell, they were alone.

"That depends on why you're here," Cyrus said. "Are you here as a friend?"

The man nodded. "That was a neat trick you pulled with the FBI ID. I guess you've still got the touch."

Cyrus reached inside his outer shirt and produced the FBI credentials. Reese noticed that his actions were slow and deliberate. Her heart raced and her eyes began scanning the street once more. She expanded her search to the windows of surrounding buildings.

The man laughed. "I'll be damned. You've taught her well. She's scoping for hostiles."

Reese assumed the man was belittling her—but when she looked him in the eye, he seemed sincere.

"She's the brains," Cyrus said. "I just bust heads when the need arises—the same as always. I see you're still using the same number sequences on forged IDs. How does the FBI feel about you masquerading as special agents?" He tossed the stolen fake ID over to the man.

The newcomer shrugged. "What they don't know won't hurt them—you know that. Aren't you going to introduce me to your friend?"

Cyrus seemed to take a long moment to come to a decision. He took a deep breath and motioned Reese to the other side of the street. She fell in beside him as they approached the grey-haired man.

"Reese, this is Luke Reid. Luke, I'm sure you're already familiar with Reese," Cyrus said.

Reid held out his hand in response to the introduction. Reese eyed him suspiciously. Cyrus gave her the slightest nod, and they shook.

"It's nice to finally meet you, Miss Knoland," Reid said. "I've been hoping to make your acquaintance for a while. Seems Cyrus has been trying to keep you all to himself."

Reid's threatening demeanor was replaced by one of warmth and acceptance. It was like seeing the lights turned on in a dark room. The threat of danger was suddenly and completely gone. In the blink of an eye, he seemed relaxed and peaceful.

"Why are you here, Reid?" Cyrus asked. Judging by the tone of his voice, Cyrus wasn't dropping his guard. "Are you looking into this death as well?"

Reid shook his head. "Actually, I'm here for you. Clayton's trying to get ahold of you. He's been turning the place upside down looking for you." He grinned.

"He sent you?" Cyrus seemed suspicious.

Reid shrugged. "He didn't want to. I think he felt he was giving something up by asking me to find you. It meant admitting he couldn't do it on his own."

Cyrus fixed Reid with a hard stare. It was as if he were trying to decide if his words were true. "Clayton finally has control of the Coalition. Since when does he pass on a chance to throw his weight around?"

Reid squirmed uncomfortably. "A lot has changed since you left," he said. "Monica was into some bad stuff. She got us into something nasty, and we didn't even know it. But I suspect you know more about that than I do." Reese read some meaningful intent in the gaze that accompanied the words.

"Once the Red Queen was gone, Clayton cleaned house," Reid went on. "Lots of changes. He shut down all field operations until he was sure he had a handle on every single one of them. There's a bounty on Monica. Clayton says we won't know the full extent of her actions until she's questioned, but he's taken steps to mitigate what he can. For what it's worth, he's been doing a good job. He's still a dick...but he's suited for the gig."

Reese wasn't entirely sure what they were talking about. Cyrus had told her a great deal about the mess he'd uncovered at the Coalition, but the internal politics of the place had never been entirely clear to her. Neither had Cyrus's final days there or the details surrounding his resignation. She only knew he harbored resentment for the organization and had gone out of his way to avoid interacting with anyone from his past who might be linked with it.

"I covered this with Clayton," Cyrus said. "I'm looking into the Order of Origin my way. Why are you *really* here?"

Reid looked suddenly uncomfortable. "You haven't been reporting in," he said. "He doesn't know what's happening and has to answer to people. The Order is making big claims. A lot of people in Washington are concerned. They don't know if they should take Verhoeven seriously or if they're making fools of themselves and killing their political careers when they use taxpayer money to search the skies based on his crazy claims."

"This can't be rushed," Cyrus countered.

"We're dealing with politicians. When did practical matters start factoring into politics?"

"You shouldn't be here," Cyrus said. "I made a deal with Clayton. Charlie is my handler. All communication with the Coalition goes through her. You shouldn't be here unannounced."

Reid defensively raised both palms. "It's okay," he said in

a calming voice. "It's just me. And I'm here off the record. Well," he seemed to reconsider. "Technically, it's me and *Special Agent Amstell*," he said the name with amusement. "Clayton doesn't know I'm here. But I saw you were in town and thought you might like some backup."

Coalition Command worked out of Maryland, a little over 300 miles from where they stood, as the crow flies. It was too geographically convenient for Reid. Cyrus decided his face must have popped on some kind of facial recognition filter and alerted his old teammate to his arrival in town. His proximity to his old home base had been too much for Reid to ignore.

Cyrus's face darkened. "I don't need backup. It was good to see you again, Reid. But tell your people to stop watching me. I don't like having a shadow. It's been bugging me since we pulled into town."

Reese saw confusion in Reid's eyes. It was as if he didn't understand Cyrus's statement. He opened his mouth to speak, but Cyrus interrupted.

"I thought you said it was just you and Amstell," Cyrus said.

The three were standing in front of Reid's Suburban, parked just off the single lane of traffic passing the front of the Small Point Cafe. The road was between them and the storefront; technically, they were standing somewhat in the street, but there'd been no traffic. Cyrus tipped his head toward another Chevy Suburban, this one also all black. It was moving slowly down the lane in their direction. It was a virtual duplicate of Reid's 4x4.

"We are alone," Reid said. "They're not with—"

The rear driver-side door of the oncoming Suburban flew open, and a young man stepped out. He was in his late twenties, Reese guessed. She felt her knees weaken when she saw the short rifle in his hands.

Cyrus grabbed Reese by the arm and yanked. They tumbled behind the front end of Reid's four-wheel-drive. He heard the wheels of the oncoming Suburban squeak as it stopped twenty-five yards up the street. A gun barked. The shots gouged divots in the pavement a few feet away. He landed with Reese in a heap on the sidewalk on the far side of the 4x4.

Coming out of the fall, Cyrus already had his Springfield in hand. He came up over the hood firing. Three rounds stitched the windshield of the assaulting vehicle. Blood splattered the glass, proving he'd scored at least one hit. The man who'd stepped from the rear of the vehicle ducked behind his open door just as Cyrus peppered it with four more rounds.

Reid was unaccounted for. A voice sounded like an alarm clock in the back of Cyrus's mind, and he made his first conscious decision. Until that moment, everything he'd done had been based on instinct. He fired wild shots at the SUV, hoping to keep his adversaries pinned. If Reid hadn't made it to cover, he was in the street.

Cyrus ducked and circled the front of the parked 4x4. Reid's body came into view. He was on his back in the street—entirely in the open. Staying low, Cyrus stepped from the front of the Chevy with his gun high in his right hand. No target was immediately evident, which was helpful. He needed to keep it that way. He fired a series of rounds into the grill of the opposing Chevy as he grabbed the collar of Reid's vest with his left hand. He threw his weight backward and jerked Reid into the cover behind the parked four-wheel-drive. Automatic fire rang out, and rounds sparked off the pavement only inches away. Cyrus didn't stop pulling until they were on the sidewalk behind the truck.

Digging his hands in Reid's hip pocket, Cyrus mumbled something. "Shit!" he snapped and started checking the other pocket. From the corner of his eye, he could see Reese peering over the edge of the door frame, looking through Reid's SUV and assessing.

"They're about to get brave," Reese reported. Shots rang out, and she ducked.

A smile lit Cyrus's face as his hand returned from Reid's pocket with keys for the Suburban. He threw them to Reese. "Get in there," he ordered. "You're driving."

Reese tapped the button on the key fob and unlocked the truck. She pulled the rear passenger side door open before doing the same with the front door but jumping inside to pull the door closed behind her. Cyrus heard the doors lock once again and was glad she'd thought ahead. It would buy them a few more seconds.

Cyrus already had Reid under the arms. He pivoted Reid's body over his right shoulder and shoved him onto the rear bench seat. Skittering through the door, Cyrus yelled, "Go!" The massive vehicle shifted, and the door slammed behind him as they lurched away from the curb.

For as little traffic as Westminster Street saw that day, frustratingly, someone still had parked in front of Reid's Suburban. But Reese wasn't deterred. Cyrus spun in the seat in time to see the front of the truck strike the back of that Mercedes SUV. He heard the sound of shrieking metal. Rounds stuck the side of their truck. It sounded—and felt—like someone hitting the fender with a hammer. Reese dropped the transmission into first and mashed her foot on the accelerator. The entire vehicle bucked. Cyrus heard their beefy all-terrain tires scrape across the pavement, then the sound of bending metal. Then the Suburban bucked and juked once more before jumping hard to the left and taking off. Reese shifted back into drive and accelerated rapidly. More gunshots came. They smacked against the vehicle body and windows, but the windows didn't break, and the body panels didn't puncture.

"Turn right up here," Cyrus ordered. He was frustrated. He'd hoped to lean out and blow the tires of the pursuing vehicle before they pulled away, but the fight with the Mercedes had been unexpected. He turned his attention to Reid.

Reid's eyes were open but rolling listlessly in their sockets. Cyrus unbuttoned the tactical vest. It was the same vest Reid always wore. He was relieved to find a kevlar vest beneath it. Three rounds had stitched the center of his chest. It must've hurt like hell. It had knocked the wind out of him.

"You asshole," Cyrus sputtered and smiled. "I thought you were actually hurt!" He began checking Reid for rounds that were missed by the vest.

Reid had been shot a total of three times, his body armor stopping every slug. While examining the back of his head by feeling alone, Cyrus's hand came away bloody. Probing more thoroughly, he found grit and small chunks of asphalt in the wound. Reid had fallen hard after being shot. The blow to the head was more serious than the shots to the chest. His head strike had nearly knocked him cold. There would be a concussion, there was no question about it. The human brain concusses when it gets slammed around inside the skull. That's just how things work.

"Left or right?" Reese called from the front seat.

"Whatever direction keeps us away from traffic. We're okay as long as we keep moving."

"Okay?" Her tone was incredulous.

"Okay, ish," he admitted.

"Got it. Keep us moving," she responded.

Cyrus set about checking Reid's vitals. Aside from the bump on the head and what little blood it produced, he seemed to be in good shape. It was likely that several ribs were broken. He'd taken three shots at fairly close range, and the slugs lodged in his vest were .45s.

"You're gonna feel that in the morning, buddy," Cyrus whispered.

The sound of screeching tires drew Cyrus's attention. He pivoted in his position hunched over Reid and saw another four-wheel-drive slide around the corner behind them as it took up the chase. Someone leaned from a passenger side window and opened fire. Rounds impacted the rear of their Chevy but failed to do damage. More troubling, Cyrus knew some of the rounds were stray and had failed to reach their mark. The potential for collateral damage was staggering.

He was nearly thrown against the windows as Reese juked around a slow-moving car. Cyrus saw a street sign flash past at the intersection and heard a horn blare. In a perfect world, they could lead the chase out of town. But who knew how many people would be killed by stray gunfire before they reached the city limits.

"Turn right at the next street," Cyrus said. "Then turn right on Washington and head north. There will be stoplights. Do what you can. We have to reach the bridge."

"On it!"

The brakes locked, and Reese put the Suburban into a four-wheeled skid to make the last-minute corner. Somehow, she'd found the traction control override and manipulated the massive vehicle like a professional driver.

Impressive.

"Drive it like you stole it," he offered in a wry tone.

"We did steal it," she said and grinned in the rearview mirror.

Cyrus climbed over Reid's immobile form and tapped the button on the window control. The window dropped, and he leaned out. The trailing SUV rounded the corner close behind. It navigated the intersection far less gracefully than Reese, making it Cyrus's turn to smile. Steadying his shoulder against the window frame, he released half a breath and fired a single round. The hammer fell, the action cycled, and the muzzle flashed. The shot flew true and blew out the front left tire of the pursuing vehicle. The 4x4's front sank toward the pavement in a heartbeat, and sparks began flying from the tire's rim.

Cyrus eyed their pursuers. The gap began to expand. The 4x4 slowed, but it wasn't giving up the chase. The driver continued to manage an aggressive speed on only three good tires.

"Cyrus?" Reese called from the front.

He ducked back inside. Her eyes met his in the rearview mirror.

"Why aren't we dead?" she asked.

He grinned and said, "We have Reid to thank for that. He brought one of the Coalition's tactical vehicles. It's outfitted with armor and bulletproof glass."

Her eyes left the mirror. He saw her sag a little behind the wheel. Her shoulders shook slightly, and he wasn't sure if she was laughing or crying. Back on the street, he'd known they would be safe if they could get into the truck. Now he realized she'd slipped into the driver's seat and started the engine, thinking she was about to get lit up with incoming fire. Even assuming that, she'd moved without question. She'd done it because she didn't have a choice and because all of their lives had been hanging on her ability to get them out of there.

That was true bravery, Cyrus knew. She had more guts than half the guys he'd served with at the Coalition, and she didn't have any of their training.

———

Their lead continued to grow, and Cyrus felt a surge of hope. They were already out of shooting range. Soon, they would lose the tail altogether. He decided they no longer needed the bridge and turned to tell Reese where to drive. Just as his eyes moved forward, another Mercedes four-wheel-drive skidded to a stop in the intersection forty yards ahead. Two men with rifles spilled from the passenger side and took aim.

"Oh, shit!" Reese yelled. She locked the brakes and twisted the wheel to the right, but they were moving too fast. Neither of the gunmen had a chance to fire a round. One dove hard for the outside curb while the other foolishly just dropped his rifle and raised his hands.

Cyrus felt the Suburban slide to the left and braced his shoulder against the headrest of the driver's seat. His free hand clamped the collar of Reid's vest, and he heaved the unconscious body in his direction with every ounce of his strength. Time seemed to slow. Cyrus saw the side of their vehicle approaching the front quarter of the Mercedes and the motionless gunman standing terrified between the two vehicles. He saw Reese crank the steering wheel, turning hand-over-hand into the skid, and he felt her ease off the brake. Just before impact, he heard the engine surge as she feathered the accelerator.

The broadside of the Suburban struck the leading edge of the Mercedes. There was a solid metal-on-metal slap, but it wasn't nearly as loud or as jarring as Cyrus expected. The gunman trapped between the two massive trucks didn't stand a chance. It would be a hell of a mess, Cyrus thought. The Mercedes spun from the impact on its front end, and Cyrus was thrown to his right as the Suburban rebounded. He stuck a shoulder hard against the passenger side seat and struggled to maintain his grip in Reid's collar. Reese spun the wheel hard in the opposite direction and feathered the gas once more. The 4x4 jerked hard as its tires grabbed the pavement and launched it forward like a racehorse leaving the starting gate.

They blasted through another stoplight a second later. Cyrus met Reese's eyes in the mirror again. "You alright?" he asked.

She nodded rapidly, her eyes darting back to the road. Her knuckles were white on the wheel at ten and two. In profile, he could see her swallow hard as she searched for her voice.

"You?" she asked finally.

Cyrus had both hands on Reid. He gripped his limp form hard and pulled on his vest for leverage. Reid's eyes were still drifting, but they were struggling to focus. Cyrus shifted him into position, trying to keep him lying on the seat with his feet in the passenger side footwell.

"Fantastic," Cyrus said. "You're in charge of driving from now on. You never told me you were a professional."

A look through the rear windows confirmed Cyrus's fear. The SUV with the blown tire was still back there and had gained ground. Even worse, the survivors from the second Mercedes had collected themselves and were back in motion. Cyrus thought of the gunman who'd been trapped in the collisions. They needed to end this before someone innocent was in a similar situation.

Cyrus slapped Reid gently on the side of the face. Reid's eyes fluttered and struggled to focus. "Hey," he said. "Reid! Are you with me? Can you hear me?"

Dilated eyes moved and settled on Cyrus. One pupil was contracting to focus while the other remained wide and unreactive. He'd hit his head *hard*. Harder than Cyrus had initially thought.

"Reid!" Cyrus barked. "This transport has a tactical package. What's the code for the locker?"

Reid's vision shifted, and his good eye threatened to close again, but he seemed to fight against his drifting consciousness. His face scrunched, and his good eye returned to focus on Cyrus. "Locker?" he mumbled.

"The locker," Cyrus persisted.

Reese called from the front seat. "Bridge coming up fast. What should I do?"

"Reid!" Cyrus bellowed. "The locker in the back of the truck. What's the combination?"

Reid's eyes pinched shut, and his face pinched with exertion or pain—maybe both. Reid's face was red, and Cyrus thought he was witnessing an aneurysm. It would be a hell of a way for a guy like Reid to go out.

"Oh," Reid grunted through lips that were turning purple. "Eight...one...two...four."

Cyrus turned to the windshield. They were fifty yards from the bridge. "Put us sideways, just past the halfway point," Cyrus ordered. "But make it fast because I have to get out before they get here."

Reese's eyes went to the mirror, wide and confused. But to her credit, she didn't waste time with questions. Cyrus felt her accelerate hard as they cleared the last buildings before reaching the riverfront. They'd caught the green light, so the only car in the area was stopped and waiting on their left. Cyrus saw the driver's eyes go wide as they blasted past, doing close to fifty.

Bracing himself for the move he knew to be coming, Cyrus put his back against the front passenger seat and secured Reid's supine form with both hands. Reese locked the brakes, and their speed bled off with sharp jolts to the brakes. At the last moment, she spun the wheel hard to the left and knifed the SUV sideways to block the bridge.

The bridge was three lanes wide, with an expanse of sidewalk along each side. There was no way to block it entirely using just one truck, but Cyrus had other plans. Pushing out the driver-side rear door, he rounded the back of the Suburban and popped the tailgate. A custom-built drawer system occupied the entire floor of the cargo bed. He entered Reid's code into the numeric keypad and silently hoped Reid had been with it enough to provide the correct numbers.

There was a beep, and a green light flashed behind the keys. Cyrus pulled on the handle, and a vehicle-wide, 10-inch deep lockbox slid on telescoping rails. An array of tactical weaponry was nestled inside the space and packed into recesses of black foam.

The oncoming vehicles were obvious. The first Mercedes was impossible to miss; it thundered toward them on three good tires and one crushed chrome rim rasping, grinding, and protesting with every revolution. The second Mercedes was fifty feet behind. The bodywork around the front right wheel was folded and covered in blood, but it was still functional. Its driver must have been slow to recover from the collision since the Mercedes with the flat was in the lead.

Cyrus discarded his initial plan when he realized the proximity of the two pursuing vehicles. He didn't have the head start he'd hoped for. The first Mercedes was grinding to a halt just beyond the start of the bridge. Two men were already jumping from the back. Cyrus resorted to plan B and grabbed a rifle from the drawer. He'd just ducked around the side of the Suburban when the first incoming shots rang out.

Cyrus stood behind the Suburban's rear tire, looking into the vehicle and out the other side. Both Mercedes had stopped short of the bridge. Five men had taken up positions and were preparing to attack.

Reese popped the passenger side door open a crack and looked at Cyrus. She knew she was safe inside the truck, but he couldn't blame her for not wanting to be on the driver's side when it was closer to the gunfire. Shots sounded, and rounds pounded the opposite side of the truck as if to punctuate the point.

"What now?" Reese asked.

"Put this window down now," Cyrus said, tapping the rear window between them. "Be ready to drop the opposite window when I say."

She closed the door, and he saw her slipping back into the driver's seat. It was the only seat that could control every window in the vehicle. The moment she dropped behind the wheel, bullets peppered the window at her side. She jumped and shuddered visibly with fright, but the rear window beside Cyrus dropped without a second of delay.

She had more guts than anyone had a right to, he thought once again. It was his turn to make her proud.

"Reid?" Cyrus said through the open window. "Can you hear me, buddy?"

"Ah..." he grumbled. "I'm here. Give me a gun. I'm good." His voice sounded anything but ready. He tried to sit up but lacked the physical dexterity to pull it off on the first try.

Cyrus stepped out from behind the wheel and leaned in the rear window. He'd been careful to remain behind the wheels, preventing anyone a shot at his ankles or feet, even from a distance. It would take long odds for one of the guys to hit him under the truck, but if he were in their position, he would skip a few rounds off the pavement under the 4x4. Luck was luck. You never knew when it would pay off.

"Just stay down, buddy," Cyrus said. He touched Reid's shoulder and eased him again onto his back. "I need you to trust me, Reid. Can you do that? I'm going to make some noise. I want you to cover your ears and keep yourself down. Whatever you do, you have to stay down. You got it?"

Reese looked between the seats and met his eyes. She seemed to realize his plan for the first time. He could tell because she looked at him like he was out of his mind.

Reid looked up at Cyrus and met his eye. Cyrus knew he'd been understood.

Looking at Reese, Cyrus said, "As soon as that window

goes down, cover your ears and hit the floor, just to be safe."

She shook her head. "I need to be ready to put the window up again."

Cyrus grinned. "We only get one chance at this. You won't need to put it up again."

Her brows furrowed. Shots rang out, and her window was hammered with more rounds. Cyrus slipped a magazine into the rifle, slammed the bolt, and placed his arm on the bottom of the door's open window frame. As he laid the rifle across his forearm, he was already taking a steadying breath. He could see the figures behind the two SUVs through the far window. They were becoming bolder…they were using the vehicles for cover less and less and getting ready to charge.

Five men. By now, even the slowest among them would understand Reid's truck was armored. They wouldn't expect the window to open. They would anticipate any counterattack to come from around the front or back of the truck. The key would be to hit them before they knew what was happening.

Police sirens sounded in the distance, striking Cyrus as out of place. Not that they were sounding—it was the fact that they were only now sounding. He was standing in the center of a city. He should've had police crawling all over him by now. Though he hadn't missed their presence until now, he suddenly wondered what had delayed them.

Peering through the darkened glass on the far side of the Suburban, Cyrus saw the opposing force react to the alarms. Three of the men let their attention momentarily drift as they tried to find a vector in on the approaching noise.

Cyrus had two objectives. The first was to avoid any non-hostile casualties. The second was to keep any of the gunmen from falling back and taking secondary prisoners. Things would get worse if these men escaped to take hostages, and he had to take the targets down before someone was killed by stray fire.

"Now," Cyrus ordered.

Reese reacted instantly. The window opposite Cyrus buzzed down with alacrity. The instant the glass cleared his scope, he squeezed the trigger. The muzzle of his rifle was two feet inside the Suburban, and he could feel the pressure inside the truck change instantly. The sound of the shot was deafening, but he didn't wait. He fired again and again. Three shots in the span of a second and a half—he didn't wait to confirm the kill; he knew the shots were accurate.

The fourth target ducked to the side and ran for the rear of the furthest SUV. Cyrus was hampered by the window's narrow field of fire. His rifle tracked the man as he moved. He squeezed the trigger, and another shot rang out. It seemed like minutes had passed since his last shot, but it had been only seconds. The Mercedes's rear window shattered and his target toppled.

The last remaining target had been smart. He ducked where he'd stood. If he were even smarter, Cyrus thought, he would put the support pillar between him and the rifle. A structural support pillar was located between the front and rear doors on the 4x4. The steel was thickest there, and it would make the best bullet stop.

Cyrus waited. He saw a shadow move beneath the Mercedes. The target was where he'd expected, tucked between the front and back doors on the opposite side of the truck.

Maybe he could scare him out of there.

Firing two quick shots, Cyrus blew out both tires on the driver's side. As he'd expected, the man panicked and ran for the next truck. Estimating his target's path and speed, Cyrus fired once more. His round blew out the SUV's rear window and struck the door on the far side. A guttural scream told Cyrus he'd judged things correctly. If he was lucky, it hadn't been a kill shot. He wanted this gunman alive for information.

"Close the windows and don't come out until the cops get here," Cyrus said. He grimly smiled at Reese before leaving his cover position for the first time. The truck windows buzzing closed could be heard as he moved away.

As he advanced on the pair of enemy vehicles, Cyrus slung the rifle on its strap over his shoulder and pulled his Springfield. He moved swiftly, circling the pair of wrecked SUVs from the left. Four bodies lay splattered on the asphalt before him. A fifth was thirty feet away and crawling away slowly. He was leaving a thick trail of blood from a ragged hole in his side. A shattered hip, Cyrus realized. It was nasty, but the man would live.

Cyrus moved from one corpse to the next, checking each for a pulse. As he expected, the first four had likely been dead by the time they hit the ground. He moved on to the fifth. The man continued to crawl, his shirt drenched in sweat, his pants soaked in blood.

Cyrus stepped on the end of the man's pant leg and ended the slow, senseless escape attempt. The man slapped a fist on the ground and grumbled something unintelligible. He wheezed as he looked back over his shoulder at Cyrus, defeated mentally and physically.

The sirens were close now and about to become a new kind of danger. Cyrus looked at the man on the ground and shook his head. "Just lay still," he said.

Cyrus stepped away from the man and slipped the rifle off his back. He was just laying it on the pavement when the first of the responding squad cars skidded around the nearest corner, lights flashing and horn blasting. Cyrus ejected the magazine from his Springfield and let it fall to the ground. He pulled the slide back and watched as the chambered round spun up into the air, cartwheeled, and bounced across the pavement. He locked the chamber open and lay the gun gently beside the rifle on the street.

More squad cars came into view. They were converging from every direction. Better late than never, Cyrus decided. He knelt on the ground with his hands raised just as the first car stopped. An officer emerged from the passenger side of the squad car. He waved his pistol wildly and barked orders with anger and authority.

Cyrus put his hands on the pavement and lay on his belly. He placed his hands behind his head. A second later, he felt what must've been an entire professional defensive line descend on his back. There were knees in his kidneys and hands on the back of his head, shoving his face into the asphalt. He didn't resist, but it wasn't easy to follow the shouted commands. Half a dozen people were bellowing at him—each ordering variations on the same instructions.

From the corner of his eye, he caught flashes of paramedics and three men in SWAT uniforms working on the man he'd shot in the hip. The SWAT guys secured the shooter's hands, and paramedics went to work. The SWAT guys were good—never more than a few feet away at any given moment and never taking their eyes off a man they clearly knew to be dangerous.

Two paramedics moved the shooter to a wheeled gurney. They would take him to the hospital first, but Cyrus had little concern. The SWAT guys looked competent. He couldn't see them slipping up and letting the lone survivor escape. Besides, where could he go? The rifle round had shattered his hip. The pain had to be excruciating.

Just before they wheeled the shooter away, the third paramedic came into view. He was a small man, and his uniform hung from his whisper-thin frame. He kept his blue EMT cap low over his brow, but Cyrus recognized him. His pale bald scalp was obvious everywhere the cap didn't cover. The little man adjusted the wheel brake on the gurney and shoved it toward the waiting ambulance. Cyrus watched the small man go. There was nothing he could do and nothing he could say. No one would be willing to listen to him now.

Chapter 21 - Swiss Candies

Providence Public Safety Complex, Providence, Rhode Island

The Providence Public Safety Complex was home to the municipal courts, the fire department, and the police department. Theoretically, it was an efficient arrangement that placed the bulk of the city's governmental oversight under a single roof. The building was a sprawling brick and glass complex located directly across the street from a massive six-story concrete parking garage.

Who knew how many police officers the city employed, but it seemed the morning's events had brought the entire force to high alert. Cyrus had been driven to the police station in handcuffs in the back of a prison transport van. Along the way, he'd lost track of how many squad cars he'd seen prowling the streets of the once-quiet Providence, Rhode Island.

It was almost 7 pm, and Cyrus was alone. Since being deposited there that morning, he'd had a cell entirely to himself. Reluctantly, he'd harbored some hope that Luke Reid would vouch for him—at least once he'd had a chance to receive medical attention.

That hadn't happened.

Cyrus didn't know what would come next, but he knew he could do nothing other than wait for the next shoe to drop. Countless traffic cameras throughout downtown would've captured portions of the morning's events. It would take time for the police to review the footage, examine the evidence, and construct what they believed to be a compelling narrative. They would decide for themselves what had happened before interviewing him. What he had to say would match their beliefs or send the investigation in another direction.

What had happened?

The footage he'd retrieved from the cafe was concerning, but he didn't know how it connected to the attack that had followed minutes later. The attackers might have been after Reid. It didn't seem likely they knew about the footage or were concerned about the cafe's security system. Police detectives had already reviewed it and found nothing. Cyrus had seen something out of the ordinary—something a detective wasn't likely to notice or at least was certain to misinterpret. Even trained investigators often saw only what they expected.

For the moment, all he could do was wait. He passed the hours laying on the bench along the back wall of the 15x20 holding cell. It was a space designed for a dozen prisoners, but Cyrus had it to himself. It was the advantage of being classified as dangerous. After the violence of the morning, the powers that be had opted for solitary confinement.

Cyrus lay with an arm folded over his forehead to keep the harsh fluorescent light from his eyes. The bench was a solid 2x12 bolted to posts buried in the concrete floor. The wood had been worn smooth by years of constant use, and it was the only bed he would see, so he'd made the most of it. Sooner or later, someone would decide what to do with him. Until that time came, he was catching up on shuteye.

A little after 7 pm, Cyrus heard the sound of the heavily bolted latch turning in his cell door. It was enough to wake him, but he chose not to acknowledge the new presence in the cell block. The cell door rattled as it slid along its track, and he heard footsteps for the first time. The footfalls were quiet, but they were in the cell with him. He hadn't heard them approaching and wondered if he'd just been in too deep of sleep or if his visitor had made a conscious effort to approach silently.

The cell door clattered again, and the lock clanked as the bolt dropped back into position. Still, Cyrus didn't move. He sensed a presence nearby and took a slow breath. The smell of leather hung in the air…along with the slightest hint of mint. Both were distinct in the confines, which smelled of many things, none of which included leather or mint.

"How are you doing, Clayton?" Cyrus said without raising his arm from where it lay draped across his eyes. "I was wondering when you would show up."

The man in the room chuckled. "Neat trick," he said. "I didn't even see you look."

"I didn't," Cyrus said. "You haven't shaken your taste for those Swiss candies. They have a distinct, if subtle, odor."

Clayton laughed. "The way it smells here, I'm surprised your olfactory senses haven't driven you mad."

Inclining slowly on the bench, Cyrus turned and squinted against the light. Thomas Clayton was a short man with a full head of gray hair parted at one side. He was a little overweight but not in terrible shape for a man in his late sixties who spent his life behind a desk. Clayton had crossed Cyrus's path only once in recent years. Though he wasn't surprised by his presence here, he wasn't excited to see him either.

Clayton's wardrobe hadn't changed, even if his position inside the Coalition had. Clayton was the number two man, second to Monica Fichtner when Cyrus was still in the outfit. When Monica disappeared under mysterious circumstances, Clayton assumed control. From what Cyrus had heard, Clayton had worked hard to clean up Monica's mess. But that didn't mean he trusted him. He and Clayton had never really seen eye to eye.

Clayton had repeatedly tried to get Cyrus to return to work for the Coalition. Cyrus had flatly refused every overture. That was until he hit a wall in his attempt to locate Tracy Clark. He needed access to Coalition resources, which meant making a deal with Clayton. A deal with the devil…at least, that's how the arrangement felt at the time.

Their arrangement stipulated that Cyrus would have no direct interaction with the Coalition. Charlie Greene was placed at Coalition Command to function as his handler. She was an intermediary, a layer of insulation between him and everyone at the agency. No one there was supposed to know of his affiliation with the agency, let alone contact him directly. Everything went through Charlie—no exceptions. It was why the sudden appearance of Luke Reid was so troubling. Their arrangement wasn't holding up.

"How's Reid?" Cyrus asked. He was angry but in no hurry to escalate the conflict with Clayton.

"A serious concussion, but he's stable," Clayton said. He took a long look at Cyrus but didn't offer anything further. Turning, he strolled to the far end of the cell. His hands were tucked into the pockets of his pants. Cyrus could tell he was chewing on a way to approach what he'd come to say.

"What about Reese?" Cyrus asked. "Is she locked up like me?"

Clayton turned slowly. His gaze drifted across the empty cell. An empty bench at the base of the cement block wall at the rear of the pen, another along the bars at the far wall…there was grime on the floor and a layer of filth on the bars surrounding the cell on two sides. The accommodations were making Clayton more uncomfortable the closer he looked.

"Locked up," Clayton said, "but not like this. She's been confined to an interrogation room. She's being treated well."

Cyrus fixed Clayton with a stare, but he didn't say a word. The look in his eyes spoke volumes: *she'd better be, or there will be hell to pay.*

"You've gotten close to her," Clayton observed.

Cyrus remained silent.

"It's not a criticism," Clayton continued. "I just didn't expect it. I was never sure you had what it takes for a long-term relationship."

"Is that what the company shrinks told you?"

Clayton scowled. "Let's just say I've always seen a bit of myself in you and leave it at that."

The comment surprised Cyrus. Was Clayton reaching out? Was that an attempt to relate on some personal level? He'd never seen this side of him before. Maybe Clayton had a knack for his office after all.

"Why don't we cut to the chase," Cyrus suggested. He wasn't in the mood to play games, and they both knew Clayton was holding the winning hand. "Why did you send Reid?"

Clayton remained at the far end of the cell as if he judged the space between them to be a suitable buffer. It made Cyrus suspicious of what he was about to say. Clayton was about fifteen feet away, still standing with his hands in his hip pockets. "I didn't," he said quietly. "He came here on his own. I didn't know anything about it."

"Yeah, right," Cyrus grunted. "Want to try that again?"

Clayton had been after Cyrus to come back to work for some time. His final attempt had been a step too far. He had stowed away aboard a private flight Cyrus had chartered almost a year ago. It was a desperate attempt to get some uninterrupted face-to-face time, but it had proven the last straw. No one knew more about the Coalition's dirty laundry than Cyrus. He'd been forced to explain as much to Clayton, a veiled threat no longer veiled. Clayton had finally backed down.

Then, the Order of Origin started to make worldwide headlines with an archaeological dig in Wyoming. Something had been discovered miles beneath the surface of the earth. Impossibly deep. Overnight, the little-known cult garnered universal recognition. Though what had been discovered beneath the plains of Wyoming was still not public knowledge, two things were clear. First, it was of interest to the major governments of the world. World leaders had convened to meet with the Order's leader, Radley Verhoeven. Not-so-secret, private talks were held. The Order of Origin had the attention of the world. And second, the cult was using that attention for all it was worth. Their recruitment process was selective, and thanks to the recent publicity, it was now far-reaching. Their meager ranks had begun to swell. When Cyrus agreed to partner with Clayton for a limited time, the Order of Origin was the topic of conversation.

"Reid came here on his own," Clayton said. "He doesn't like the way I'm handling this cult."

Cyrus suddenly felt cold. Reid was a dyed-in-the-wool company man—he never went against orders. Something had happened if he was butting heads with Clayton over the Order.

"What did you do?" Cyrus asked.

"I've made two attempts to put an agent inside the group. Both efforts failed."

Cyrus knew Clayton intended to make the attempt, but he had no idea the operation had been launched. Clayton wanted Cyrus to conduct the infiltration. In his day, he'd been one of the agency's most successful undercover assets. Cyrus wasn't unwilling, but he refused to make his approach without a better understanding of the organization. Previously, little was known about the group, its hierarchy, or even its recruitment practices. Knowledge was power, and Cyrus wouldn't move until he was comfortable with the intelligence. Besides, locating Tracy Clark was his number one priority.

"Who'd you send in?" Cyrus asked.

"Harper was first," Clayton said. "You wouldn't know the second agent. She wasn't around back when you were with us."

Cyrus had a hard time keeping the surprise out of his voice. "Harper's dead?" He was a competent and skilled agent. It would take a real pro to get the drop on someone like him.

"No," Clayton grunted. "Not dead. Neither one was harmed. Neither one made it through the door. Didn't make it through the first interview, actually. They never got that far. It was like the group saw them coming. They just turned them away."

Cyrus took a moment to consider that. Penetrating a hostile organization was the most dangerous part of any undercover assignment. But these agents hadn't been killed.

Glaring at Clayton, Cyrus said, "Care to explain?"

"Both agents had fresh legends," Clayton said with a shrug. He began pacing as he spoke. "Fully backstopped and entirely bulletproof. I'm not kidding; these were the best backgrounds you could imagine. In both cases, we went back and forged support for their identities—back to childhood. There's no way the group could've known they were law enforcement."

If Nathan, Cyrus's forger friend, had made the same boast, he would've believed it without question. Nathan was the best there was. But the Coalition knew what it was doing, too. For legal reasons, the Coalition didn't keep forgers on staff; it contracted with the best in the business, outsourcing the work and maintaining plausible deniability. Given the legally questionable work the Coalition often conducted, the idea always rankled Cyrus. He never understood how document forgery crossed some unforgivable line when wet work was okay.

"Three possibilities," Cyrus offered. He held up one finger. "Either your forger sold you out." His second finger went up, "The forger just isn't as good as you think, or" his third finger rose, "you have a mole in the outfit."

Clayton stopped walking and offered an amused look. "You've never had a problem with Nathan's work in the past," he said.

"Nathan created the legends?"

Clayton nodded.

"He did all of the background work as well?" Cyrus persisted. "No one...*helped*?"

Clayton nodded.

Well, shit.

That idea went right out the window. If Nathan was responsible for the documentation, it was rock solid. If it was leaked, it hadn't been leaked on his end. Nathan would die before compromising his ethics. Cyrus knew that without question; they'd had a *conversation* about it before.

"Then it was someone at the Coalition," Cyrus countered. "You have a mole in your operation."

Clayton strolled to the end of Cyrus's bench without eye contact. He sat down hard. Looking at the floor, he nodded, seemingly to himself. "I thought that was the case after

Harper failed to penetrate the group," he said. "So Mendez was entirely off-book. She wasn't Coalition—she wasn't even law enforcement. Only Nathan and I knew about her. He cooked up her documentation and covered logistics. It didn't matter. She got bounced halfway through the interview. It was like they could tell what she was up to just by looking at her."

That didn't make sense. Harper was one of the best. He could beat the best lie detectors—even cutting-edge biometric ones. The man was a borderline sociopath; Cyrus had worked with him in the past. He was good. He was born to lie. And if Clayton sent someone in after that—whoever this Mendez was—she would've been at least as good, or she wouldn't be worth the effort.

"Tell me about the interview you mentioned," Cyrus said. "How did that work?"

"As you know, the Order of Origin started as a fringe religious group. They were on the radar, but no one knew much about them. But since that discovery in Wyoming, they're worldwide news. Everyone knows the name.

"Before that, they used to recruit the occasional misanthrope here or misfit there. Now, they have people begging to join. From what we can tell, better than 99% are turned down. *They're crazy selective*. There's a class-action lawsuit gearing up in court right now, trying to hit them with discrimination charges. People don't even understand what the cult espouses, but they've become a cultural phenomenon. It's way out of control."

Clayton looked angry and confused at the same time. But more than anything, he looked unsettled.

"There's your answer," Cyrus said. "If they bounce 99% of applicants, then your guys were just part of the background noise. It wasn't a conspiracy. They just weren't part of the 1%."

Clayton huffed out a breath and shook his head. "You

don't understand. I *engineered* their legends based on known members. They literally had perfect profiles. There's no reason my agents should've been bounced."

Chapter 22 - Crazy Theories

Cyrus considered that. He knew the analytical research that went into a cover and what went into building the perfect legend. If Clayton was sincere, he'd worked hard on this set of covers. At least one of the agents should've made it through the door. "Tell me about the interview process," Cyrus said. "Give me specifics."

"First-stage contact is made via the web," Clayton explained. "If that goes favorably, a personal interview is arranged. If the interview goes well, the potential recruit is invited to visit the group's compound in Montana."

"So Harper and Mendez made contact via the web and made it as far as the interview, only to get turned away short of visiting the compound?" Cyrus summarized.

"That's being generous," Clayton scoffed. "They made it to the face-to-face interview, but both were bounced less than five minutes in. I wouldn't even call it an interview…They weren't there long enough. Introductions were barely made."

It was a bad situation, but covert infiltration was tricky even under ideal circumstances. And it was dangerous. Cyrus had run into the Order of Origin tangentially in an operation years earlier. The group was small, and almost nothing was known about them then. It wasn't a surprise that the cult had eventually drawn the attention of the Coalition—even before that media frenzy in Wyoming.

Cyrus watched Clayton, searching his face for any hint of deception. "Why are you here? You were supposed to stay hands-off. I finish my operation, then work your case—That was the deal. All contact goes through Charlie until then."

Clayton looked confused.

"What?" Cyrus asked.

He seemed to be at a loss for words. Clayton shifted uneasily on his seat, and his eyes moved slowly around the room. Finally, he spoke. "The five-man fire team that attacked you...we've ID'd them. They're known members of the Order of Origin. I thought you'd started work on my end of the deal.

"The Order of Origin just tried to kill you."

The video footage from the cafe's security system came to mind. Specifically the way the chairs had slid across the floor to block Alec Barnabe's escape. No one had been there to push them into his way. What he witnessed reminded him of Gertrude Waterford's work and the people she had genetically manipulated. Evidence indicated the Order of Origin had killed her, likely for some as yet unknown transgression.

Maybe there was a connection. But was that enough to explain the cult putting a hit out on him? It occurred to Cyrus how vulnerable he was while sitting in this cell. If the Order had assets like Gertrude's grandchildren...

Cyrus leveled a glare at Clayton. "So what about the mess from today?"

"Taken care of. It's a matter of homeland security. The police chief is sorry things weren't sorted out more quickly. He doesn't know why you didn't identify yourself in the first place." Clayton smirked with the statement and tossed a leather billfold to Cyrus. "He feels badly about the misunderstanding and how long you've been locked up."

Cyrus flipped open the folded leather. Inside was a photo identification with his name and the Department of Homeland Security hologram. He rolled his eyes.

"Homeland? Really?" he muttered.

Clayton stood and faced Cyrus. "It'll provide you the type of cooperation you need from locals. It's fully backstopped so federal support won't be a problem either. Call me directly if you need anything else."

"You're serious about this?" Cyrus clarified.

"Entirely."

"Then we're back to the original plan. Everything goes through Charlie. We don't know who we can trust at Command, but Charlie is on the list. In fact, Charlie *is the list*. Make sure she has any and all resources at her disposal," Cyrus insisted.

"Already done."

"There's more. I want her moved to a private, secure workspace. Level four, biometric security protecting her office and a three-man detail on her at all times."

The corner of Clayton's lip curled. It happened when he was frustrated or irritated. Just then, Cyrus was betting on both. Clayton wasn't accustomed to having terms dictated. "That's more than a little overkill."

"Not if there's even a chance the Order has someone inside the Coalition," Cyrus insisted. "What you know about these people is the tip of a very slippery iceberg. Charlie is my lifeline, and you're hers. Make it happen." There was a hint of threat in his voice.

Clayton's hands went up defensively. Maybe there was

more than just of hint in his voice, Cyrus mused. "You got it," Clayton said.

"In the meantime, I want to talk to the shooter they brought in when they arrested me."

"Can't do that," Clayton said flatly.

Cyrus shot him an irritated look. Was he getting stonewalled already?

"I can't put you in a room with him," Clayton explained. "The hitter died in the ambulance en route to the hospital after being picked up at the crime scene."

Dead?

That didn't seem likely. The shot had been blind luck, but the round caught him in the hip. It was a jacketed rifle slug traveling faster than the speed of sound, but it had broken a car window and passed through a door before striking flesh and bone. A lot of speed had been sapped before impact. It was likely the round broke the guy's hip, but there hadn't been much blood. Since he'd gone directly into an ambulance under the supervision of trained medics, he should've survived.

Cyrus was growing more suspicious by the second. "Cause of death?" he asked. The memory of the small bald medic was triggering alarms in his mind. Though he'd only seen the man for an instant, he'd since matched the face on the recording from the cafe. It wasn't a coincidence.

Clayton shrugged. "Presumably complications from his gunshot wound. I haven't received a full report yet."

"I wouldn't bet on it," Cyrus muttered, mostly to himself.

"Carver's working on him now. I had him on a plane as soon as I knew we had fatalities."

Cyrus shot a suspicious glance at Clayton. Ken Carver was their top forensic pathologist as well as a skilled surgeon. "Why would you do that?"

He shrugged. "Honestly? *Because you're you.* You may have left the Coalition, but trouble follows you. Do you think I didn't know about that blowout in Vegas last year? Or that thing with the murder-for-hire crew in Chicago before that?"

Cyrus grinned. "The Chicago thing was an FBI operation. I was there as a journalist. I don't know anything about a story in Vegas."

His eyes played slowly around the large cell, but Cyrus wasn't seeing the room. He was connecting dots in his mind. It was necessary to look at the investigation with fresh eyes. Carver was intelligent and extremely sharp. In Cyrus's experience, the two were not mutually exclusive.

"When Carver's done with the shooter," Cyrus said, "have him look at the body of Tommy Wilks. He'll be in the local morgue. He was a suspicious death earlier this week— it's still an open investigation. I have a feeling there will be a connection."

Clayton looked confused. Cyrus just glared at him until he nodded understanding. His attention returning to the team of shooters, Cyrus struggled to connect them to his investigation. He'd come to town to enlist the help of Alec Barnabe and ended up in a firefight with Order operatives. Had the hit squad followed him here? It didn't seem likely, considering how he'd traveled to town and given that no one knew he was headed there in the first place. Could the team have been there looking for Barnabe on their own? Barnabe was in hiding, after all. Presumably from the police, but maybe that wasn't the case.

Can he be hiding from the Order?

The more he considered it, Cyrus began to think he'd been attacked because he was searching for Alec Barnabe. It supported the fact that the hit team was also searching for Barnabe.

But why?

The Order of Origin had the most technically capable nations of the world searching space for something that was clearly very difficult to find. It was likely that the Order was searching for whatever it was on its own. If they were, Barnabe's image-searching algorithms would be a powerful tool. One that was already utilized by law enforcement in their facial recognition systems. It was plausible that the Order of Origin intended to apply the same tool for a search of space. But he only knew the Chinese, Russians, and Americans were searching space because of his recently acquired information.

"What aren't you telling me?" Cyrus said. "What did the Order find in Wyoming? Why are world leaders taking them seriously?"

Clayton's disposition soured. "No one's saying what was dug up in Wyoming, but that's putting the cart before the horse anyway. The Order had everyone's attention before that dig. Whatever was found out there just motivated world leaders to take their crackpot theories as more than science fiction."

"What theories?" For all of the headlines surrounding the Order of Origin, Cyrus had yet to hear what they were preaching, for lack of a better word. He knew it wasn't a conventional religion, but he'd heard little. Rumors suggest that it was some derivation of creationism, but that didn't seem logical either.

Shoving his fists into his pockets, Clayton eyed the ceiling. "According to Radley Verhoeven, the group's leader, our world was created by intelligent design. We, the human race, are the result of that *design*."

Intelligent design…creationism…Cyrus wasn't sure how they differed. He'd never been religious, but he'd always expected that someone could be spiritual without being religious. In the history of man, more lives have been taken in the name of religion than any other endeavor. In his mind, spirituality was a kind of faith without hard edges and implacable rigidity. Spirituality was about flexibility, an open mind, and common ground, whereas religion with a capital R—more often than not—was about conformity and specific shared beliefs and understanding. Either way, intelligent design indicated some outside influence or higher power.

"So the Order believes in some kind of God," Cyrus said.

"They claim, no," Clayton offered with a shake of his head. "Not a God or Gods. Intelligent beings, not unlike ourselves, if you can believe that. Just a race that's more technically advanced."

That was more in line with what little Cyrus had heard of the organization. They spoke of technology being the key to the future of man and the way to save our world from itself. These days, no one seemed to dispute that the world was near a tipping point. With the planet's population expanding at an ever-increasing rate and the food supply a finite resource, it seemed likely that technology would hold the key to solving many of the world's most pressing problems.

Is the Order of Origin forcing that issue and trying to form a religion around the concept?

"Crazy people can say anything they want," Cyrus said. "Why is anyone taking Verhoeven seriously?"

"They weren't," Clayton said in a quiet voice. "He made wild claims that were largely ignored. Typically, someone in his position, a cult leader, for example, would shout crazy proclamations from the rooftops. Crazy people, as you say, can't help themselves.

"In Verhoeven's case, he wasn't making his claims publicly. He kept his group small. His claims were made via private correspondence to key members of the House and Senate. He never climbed onto a public soapbox and made himself out to be a crazy person."

"He did that in private?" Cyrus didn't understand. "Letters to the government making wild claims? He can't be the first. What did he say? Why did anyone listen?"

An ashen look had spread across Clayton's face. He seemed unwilling to go into detail. "Radley Verhoeven claims that our world—our universe—was created by another race of beings as an experiment. The event we refer to as the Big Bang was, in fact, the formation of a new dimension of reality, created for the sole purpose of their study."

A grin crossed Cyrus's face. It was a fanciful explanation, impossible to prove, and as grand as anyone could hope for. It was a foundational supposition for a cult. But who would believe something so outrageous?

Clayton glared at Cyrus. "You've already written off the entire idea," he said flatly.

"Of course," Cyrus said in a matter-of-fact tone. His amusement was impossible to hide. "The idea is fantastic and impossible to prove as well as disprove. I'm surprised a cult didn't spring up sooner."

"Then let me elaborate and further your amusement. Our universe was created by a race known as the Tangury. Their people were fighting against their own extinction. According to Verhoeven, the Tangury people were genetically similar to us but could not reproduce. Our world was created similar to how we use computer simulations to test strategies or scenarios. They created us in their image to prototype a solution to their own evolutionary shortcoming."

The entire concept was absurd. Cyrus saw far too many holes in the idea right from the beginning. He didn't even know where to begin. "The Tangury?" he mused, rolling the word around in his mouth as he said it. "Let's start with the obvious question. If the Tangury can't reproduce, how could they survive long enough to evolve into a race capable of mastering whatever is necessary to birth an entirely new dimension."

Clayton shook his head. "Trust me, they have an answer for everything. Apparently, this race comes from a world with physical laws entirely different from our own. A place we couldn't rationalize, though Verhoeven has a grasp on the concepts. The Tangury come from a place that doesn't suffer from the concept of time."

Cyrus turned on his seat and glared at Clayton, his expression one of utter confusion. He rose from the bench and shoved his hands into his own pockets. His stare remained fixed on Clayton. "No concept of time?" What did that even mean? They didn't know what it was, or no time elapsed? Someone once said that the only purpose for time was to keep everything from happening at once. It was nonsensical, of course, but it did foster questions. If other physical dimensions were out there—and some scientists firmly believed there were—might they operate on entirely different physical laws? One of the problems with having an eidetic memory was that Cyrus could recall virtually everything he had ever read. This included a series of scientific papers written by physicists who speculated that the force of gravity in our universe wasn't nearly as powerful as it should be. Experiments suggested that the gravitational constant should be many times greater than what it is. Those same scientists speculated that the actual force we attribute to gravity is some sort of bleed-through influence from a neighboring dimension. It was commonly believed that another dimension was simply a natural extension of reality beyond our perception. But what if it were another plane of existence, set one on top of another like the layers of an onion?

The idea was fantastic and implausible. Interesting, but impossible to prove or disprove. But a plane of existence without time? A place without entropy? Everything we did in life was measured against the ruler of time: hours,

minutes, seconds; days, weeks, years; decades, centuries...
How would life work without time?

Clayton was pacing the cell. "It sort of pickles the brain,
doesn't it? It's an interesting mental exercise if nothing else.
What is time, really?"

One thing kept Cyrus from discrediting the concept
without a second thought. The photographs of Tracy Clark
flashed through his mind. A dozen different images were
taken of the woman over the span of a century. Her hairstyle
had changed from one image to the next, but her age
remained entirely unchanged. In each photo, she looked the
same as the day she disappeared from their underground
base.

*Could the Tangury be the Halon? Could Tracy be one of the
Tangury?*

"What's wrong?" Clayton asked.

Cyrus did his best to hide the growing concern behind his
eyes. If there was any truth to Verhoeven's claims, it meant
he was on the level. He didn't want to believe that. Besides,
it was still too much of a leap.

Shaking his head, Cyrus said, "Why are some of the most
powerful nations spending billions searching the skies?
What are they looking for?"

Clayton's jaw hung slightly agape. "You're surprisingly
well informed," he said after a long moment. "Where did
you get your intelligence?"

"Stop stalling."

"I'm not stalling," Clayton grumbled. "That's just highly
classified information. I only heard about it this morning.
How long have you known?"

"Still stalling."

Clayton frowned. "Another of Verhoeven's wild claims.

Supposedly, the Tangury created our universe, and they've been keeping an eye on Earth ever since."

Cyrus burst out laughing. "What? Ever since? Ever since when?"

Visibly gnashing his teeth, Clayton swallowed hard. It seemed like he was choking on unpleasant words. "Since the planet coalesced. If we were to believe him, there's been a satellite monitoring our planet since before it could even support single-celled life."

Cyrus walked across the cell, amusement on his face. The idea was absurd. "All I see are reasons to write Verhoeven off as a crackpot," he said after a moment. "The Earth is what, two billion years old? He wants us to believe an alien race has had a spy bird up there for *two billion years*?"

"Four and a half."

"What?"

"The Earth," Clayton said. "I'm told the planet is closer to four and a half billion years old."

Cyrus raised his palms, along with his eyebrows. Sort of a *kind of proves my point* gesture. He didn't say a word.

"Like I said, Verhoeven has an answer to everything."

Dropping hard back onto the bench, Cyrus glared at Clayton. He was all ears. "I can't wait to hear how he explains this one."

"Time doesn't pass for the Tangury," Clayton said. "The...satellite, for lack of a better word, doesn't exist fully in our dimension."

"Come again?"

Clayton looked even more frustrated. "I'll send you the technical gist. Honestly, it's beyond me. But our sharpest minds admit that, at least the concept is plausible.

"They say the satellite exists in a sort of bubble in space. It exists in our dimension, but only partially. Something about the technology is unique, allowing the device to exist in our dimension and the Tangury world at the same time."

Cyrus rubbed his eyes. The effort didn't help the headache that was forming. The absurdity of what he was hearing made him think the so-called experts were potheads who had escaped from a Star Trek convention. But his mind kept returning to Tracy Clark and the endless list of unanswered questions surrounding her and her connection to the meteors and the teleportation platforms. It was enough to keep him from walking out the door.

"Let me get this straight," Cyrus said. "Verhoeven claims that there is a satellite out there in space that another race has been using to watch the evolution of life on Earth. It's been there for *billions of years,* and now we have a massive international effort underway to find it?"

Clayton paused, then shrugged and nodded. "Sounds about right."

Cyrus rolled his eyes. "Mankind has been looking at the stars for thousands of years, and no one has noticed something up there looking back at us."

"Oh," Clayton mumbled. "That's because it's invisible."

Shooting the man a look, Cyrus said, "Excuse me?"

"Something to do with the way it's in two dimensions simultaneously," Clayton said. "It's not visible on either side, but apparently it can transmit data across what Verhoeven calls the Threshold."

"Fantastic!" Cyrus said with a laugh. But his grin quickly disappeared, and his eyes grew serious. "Let me guess. They are trying to locate it by searching for a gravitational anomaly." It was a statement rather than a question. He felt his stomach sink along with the realization.

Clayton's expression sagged. "Where in the hell are you

getting your information?" He grimaced. "I was only read-in as of this morning."

While he didn't know what to make of the Order's wild claims, Cyrus was at least certain that Clayton was on the level with the crazy details. There was data from US, Russian, and Chinese sources showing that they were, in fact, searching the heavens for some sort of gravitational anomaly. On top of that, he knew what the Coalition apparently did not. The Chinese had temporarily lost control of multiple satellites for a short period. He was willing to bet that, whatever else was happening, the Order of Origin was searching space for this alien device, and they had coopted the world's nations to help them do it.

"I still don't get it," Cyrus said. "What did Verhoeven say to make world leaders take him seriously?"

Clayton cast a grudging look in Cyrus's direction and studied him. He turned and paced the cell, talking over his shoulder as he moved in the opposite direction and not making eye contact when moving past Cyrus.

"Verhoeven claims we aren't the first Homo sapiens to inhabit this planet," Clayton explained. "He says our kind walked the earth hundreds of millions of years ago, only to be wiped out so the experiment could begin again. Start with a clean slate, he put it."

Cyrus said nothing. What could he say to that?

"Our world was nothing but a simulation to them," Clayton went on. "He claims things didn't go according to plan, so they purged the planet, rebooting the experiment and starting from scratch. A couple of million years later, along comes early man and everything we know about our evolution."

A vision of Samuel Dabney's ant farms came to mind, and what should have been patently absurd wasn't quite as easy to dismiss. Dabney was damaged goods, there was no question about it. But how had he gotten that way? He'd been working for someone on a project. Though he wasn't a betting man, Cyrus was willing to wager that Dabney had worked for or with the Order of Origin. The ideology seemed the same.

"All I hear is one outlandish claim after another," Cyrus said. He wasn't feeling as confident under the surface as his words claimed, but he wouldn't let those concerns show in front of Clayton. "Still no reason for anyone to take the Order seriously."

Clayton met his eye and swallowed hard. "If Verhoeven's right, we should've found some trace of some ancient civilization by now. But he claims the bird the Tangury have out there in space is why we'll never find a trace. That device can trigger a global geologic upheaval that could once more wipe the planet free from every trace of our existence."

Though he wanted to write it off as more fantasy, Cyrus remained silent this time. He watched Clayton. It was obvious that he believed everything he was saying. That didn't mean it was true—it just meant that Verhoeven had made believers of the non-believing.

"How?" Cyrus asked. "How does a crackpot with wild claims convince world leaders to invest in his crazy theories?"

Clayton took a moment to answer. When he did, it was in an uncharacteristically quiet tone that expressed his overwhelming concern. "Whatever they dug up in Wyoming made people believe," he said.

"And you don't know what that is?"

He shook his head. "Not a clue," Clayton muttered. "No one is talking. No guesses—not even rumors. But whatever it was, it made believers of the people at the very top of the food chain."

It was frustrating. Cyrus didn't have answers, only more questions. At the very least, he had an idea of what the

Order of Origin was really preaching. We were the ants in a farm belonging to people from another dimension. If there was any truth to this, it seemed that Tracy Clark was the best place to begin. It all came back to her. For reasons he couldn't explain, she didn't seem to age. If there was any truth to Verhoeven's wild tales, those facts seemed to intersect.

Cyrus took a resigned breath and walked over to Clayton. They stood inches apart. After a tense moment, he put a hand on the cell door. It had been closed, but Cyrus now knew it wasn't locked. He slipped past Clayton, pushed through the door, and headed for the exit sign on the wall. He left without offering another word.

Chapter 23 - You Must Be Clairvoyant

Hilton, Providence, Rhode Island

The Hilton was a monolithic structure in the heart of the small city. It was a tall twelve-floor block-shaped building entirely lacking in architectural grace. Cyrus planned to return to Australia by nightfall, but things had gotten out of control. Matters were resolved to the satisfaction of the local authorities; now, he just wanted to find Alec Barnabe and move ahead with the search for Tracy.

Cyrus sat on a chair and stared out the window. He'd hoped for a room with a balcony. He wanted to look out over the city and plan his moves for the following day. But the Providence Hilton didn't have any rooms with balconies. Not a single one. As such, he sat in a chair at the window, gazing past the glare in the glass and examining what he could see from the 8th floor.

At least the beds were comfortable. Reese snored quietly on the king-size only a few feet away. It was just after 11 pm, and she'd been asleep for hours already. Her time in police custody seemed to have taken more of a toll on her than the car chase and subsequent gunfight. And while Cyrus had slept in his cell, she sat by herself in an interrogation room, terrified about the kind of charges they might face.

Cyrus's cell phone rang. The quiet tone sounded like a riot in the silent stillness of the hotel room, and Reese reacted. She rolled onto an elbow with a start and blinked at him through blurry eyes.

Cyrus held up the phone. "It's Clayton," he said. "I can take it in the hall."

"No. It's okay," she said in a husky, dry voice. "Put it on speaker. I want to hear."

Cyrus glanced at the caller ID once more and accepted the call. He tapped the screen and activated the speakerphone. "What have you got for me?" he asked by way of a greeting.

"You must be clairvoyant," Clayton's voice responded. He sounded tired. "Your hitter's cause of death matched whatever killed that kid from the coffee shop. Damned if I understand how, but Cutter says it was exactly the same symptomology."

"And that was?" Cyrus hoped he wouldn't need to coax every detail out of Clayton and wished he could get this information from Charlie. Once Clayton realized there wasn't an apparent reason for the prisoner's death, he'd been like a dog with a bone. The upshot was that Clayton could hound Carver until the analysis was complete.

"It sure wasn't a rifle round," Clayton grumbled. "You can bet on it. Beyond that? We're not sure what killed them—we just know how they died."

"Fine," Cyrus conceded. "Tell me what you know." He moved from the chair and sat beside Reese on the bed.

Reese grabbed an extra pillow and propped it beneath her head. Covering her mouth, she yawned, now fully awake. She didn't say a word, but Cyrus could read the intrigue in her eyes. How could the death of a hired assassin and that of a kid in a cafe possibly be connected, she was asking herself.

"Massive cardiovascular trauma," Clayton said. "Cutter said he's never seen anything like this. Perimortem bruising on every square inch of the hearts of both victims. It was the sort of thing you would expect to see if the body had been a part of a massive high-speed collision."

Cyrus considered that. Tommy Wilks had been sitting by himself in a cafe when he'd just up and died. It was all right there on camera. There was no one at his table, and there'd been no impact or collision. And the shooter had been in an ambulance when he'd expired. He died in front of three trained medical technicians. Well, two EMTs and the little bald guy. It remained to be seen if he was really an EMT.

"That doesn't make sense," Cyrus said. He felt foolish for stating the obvious, but it seemed the most efficient way to keep Clayton talking.

"Carver said the same thing more than once." Clayton seemed out of his element relaying the information. He was accustomed to having the evidence shown to him. "Carver says the level of bruising isn't consistent with the impact scenario. When that occurs, there's always greater trauma to one side of the heart. If not the left or right, then certainly the front and back. The damage, in this case, was consistent and catastrophic."

"What could do that?" Reese asked.

Clayton took a raspy breath but remained silent for a long moment. Cyrus was about to restate Reese's question, though it irritated him that Clayton was playing favorites.

"He doesn't know," Clayton said at last. Cyrus saw relief in Reese's eyes and knew she had interpreted the silence the same way he had. "He said it was like someone had reached into both men's chests and squeezed their hearts until they stopped beating."

Cyrus nodded absently. The room heater purred quietly

beneath the window a few feet away. Cyrus silently considered the implications of the new information.

"Does that help at all?" Clayton asked.

"Not as much as an interrogation of the shooter," Cyrus said. "But the fact that someone didn't want us talking to him speaks volumes all by itself."

"Which brings us to your third EMT," Clayton said. "There's no record of him. The other two were interviewed but didn't know much about the bald guy. Neither had worked with him before. He arrived right before they deployed, and no one thought anything of it. I guess they get hospital staff shifted into rotations on the Rescue Squad regularly. Right after they reached the hospital, your guy disappeared."

Edward Meeker sat at the end of his queen-sized bed and stared at the television. The screen wasn't tuned to some mindless reality TV program; he was watching something only slightly more interesting. The 50" flat panel was slit down the middle; the left showed a hallway one floor above. The camera lens was fixed on the unmoving closed door to room 843. The right side of the screen was a feed from the elevator. Two elevators serviced the twelve-floor building, but his surveillance kit only included a pair of cameras. Disabling the second elevator had been a simple enough matter. It would be at least a day before hotel maintenance resolved the problem he'd created, and that was if the custodian was good at his job.

Tapping the laptop's keyboard on the dresser beside the television, Meeker triggered the software's motion activation feature and linked it to the facial recognition database. The camera would start capturing footage when there was any movement in the hallway outside room 843 and every time the elevator moved. A tone would sound if Cyrus Cooper appeared on camera, even for an instant.

Circling to the head of the bed, Meeker tapped the power button on the television remote and watched the screen go dark. He was content to let the technology do the heavy lifting for him. Throwing back the blankets, he stripped down to his boxer shorts and crawled under the covers. He tapped the button on the nightstand lamp and lay back on his pillow. The darkness of the room was nearly complete— only the tiny LED built into the frame of his laptop at the end of the bed pulsed from time to time as data was captured to the hard drive.

Exhaustion washed over him, but Meeker found himself unable to fall asleep. He was frustrated with the events of the afternoon. It didn't make sense to send Cruze and his team of thugs after Cooper and the girl. Meeker knew he'd killed the Wilks boy precisely according to plan. He should've also been allowed to dispatch Cyrus Cooper and the girl. Cruze was nothing more than a blunt instrument. With nothing special to offer, how could he possibly expect to rise through the ranks of the Order?

Verhoeven had seen fit to send the moron after Cooper. It wasn't logical. Still, Meeker felt vindicated, given the way things had played out. He'd been asked to dispatch Cruze in the end. Even Verhoeven knew Cruze couldn't be trusted to remain silent.

Cruze had been given his shot and he'd failed. Meeker knew he should feel good about that. But Verhoeven's lack of confidence in him was disconcerting. Though he'd never been a powerful or imposing man in his own right, the Order's work had changed that. Meeker was stronger and more powerful than he'd ever dared to dream. He could snatch the very life from a man without even breaking a sweat.

Meeker smiled as his eyes grew heavy. He wasn't sure why Verhoeven had chosen Cruze over him, but he knew the error had been spectacular. Footage of the car chase and subsequent shootout on the city streets was played over and over on the nightly news. Meeker knew, one way or another, Verhoeven would be forced to recognize his usefulness. The Order of Origin would change everything mankind knew about the world it lived in. Meeker knew with absolute certainty that he would play a pivotal role in what was to come.

Reese rolled over and squinted against the light spilling in the split in the curtains. Cyrus sat at the small table by the window. His laptop was open, and he worked his finger back and forth across the trackpad. It was just past seven in the morning.

"What time did you get up?" Reese said after stifling a yawn. "I didn't notice you getting out of bed."

Cyrus slipped from the chair and crossed the few feet of space that separated them. He dropped to the bed at her side, leaned over her, and kissed her deeply. "I didn't want to wake you," he said. "We had a lot of excitement yesterday. You should sleep while you can. I have a feeling the fun isn't over yet."

The smile disappeared from her face. "Four guys dead, and you think there's more where they came from?"

He shrugged.

She knew he was probably right. The four were a matching set of roided-out thugs. There wasn't a deep thinker among them—hired muscle. Reese shook her head and tried to push the thought aside.

"What is it?" Cyrus asked.

"Just noticing how you've rubbed off on me. I looked at the bodies from yesterday and made a threat assessment. Observations that would've been lost on me a year ago. *Things have changed.*"

Cyrus laughed. "You're telling me." He slid to the edge of the bed and rocked off the mattress's thick padding and onto his feet. He crossed to the table and dropped into the chair behind his laptop. "Your driving for one thing. That was impressive work yesterday—nerves of steel. I know professionals who couldn't handle an SUV like that."

Reese felt her face flushing and rolled her eyes.

"I'm not kidding," Cyrus offered, his tone making that clear. "You did good. And you kept your head when they started peppering your window with rounds."

"You said the glass was bulletproof."

"Knowing that and keeping your shit together are still two different things," Cyrus grinned.

She nodded. "I'll admit it. There were a lot of questions going through my mind at that point." She was tempted to ask what it was that made a window bulletproof. And how much is too much when it comes to fire? There would be a point of failure where the physical glass couldn't stand up to the onslaught any longer. The caliber of the bullet would be a factor, she knew. But there would be others. Like how many strikes over a period of time, perhaps.

She wanted to know how it all worked. She wanted to understand. But seeing Cyrus genuinely impressed with her fortitude was enough. She settled for a shy shrug. In truth, everything had happened very quickly. There had been little time to think, only time to act. Looking back, she had surprised herself.

There was no question—it was an amazing feeling.

———

Cyrus had turned his laptop around so the screen faced the bulk of the hotel room. Reese was just walking out of the bathroom and was towel-drying her hair. She wore an airy yellow sundress that showed off her tan. Hanging from a simple silver chain around her neck was a small Celtic knot with a compact jet-black stone in the middle.

Her raven hair looked obsidian while wet, glistening in the light. She saw him staring and shot him a look. "What?"

Cyrus offered an approving glance at her dress. He'd always been a fan of *the little yellow number*, as he called it. But his eyes motioned toward her feet, and his smile broadened. She wore simple white boat shoes with the dress. They didn't look bad, but they didn't look right either.

Reese shrugged, her eyebrows arching. "If I've learned one thing in my time with you, sensible footwear can mean the difference between life and death. What can I say? I'm prepared to make concessions."

Cyrus laughed. He stepped in, slipped his arms around her waist, and pulled her close. He kissed her gently, and then he kissed her more deeply. "I'm rubbing off on you in the strangest ways," he said quietly.

She grinned, tossed aside the towel, and kissed him in return. There was a growing sense of need in her touch; he could feel the temperature of her skin rising beneath the thin fabric of her dress.

Reese took a step in the direction of the bed, pulling him along. "What other bad habits do you have to share?" she smiled.

Cyrus felt his heart race. They took another clumsy step in the direction of the bed. Then, the laptop chimed with the sound of an incoming call. Cyrus stopped short, and Reese went tumbling to the bed without him.

She looked up, dark hair falling errantly across her face. Propping herself up on her elbows, Reese took a deep breath and blew some of the hair from her brow. Cyrus saw her glaring back with frustrated eyes. "Really?" was all she said.

Cyrus threw his head back and let out an exasperated sigh. "Shit," he muttered. He'd already forgotten about the conference call they'd set up for first thing this morning.

Reese was still straightening the lines of her dress when Cyrus tapped the keyboard and connected the call. The screen of the laptop blinked to life and split down the center. Hondo's face filled the right half while Charlie Green occupied the left.

Hondo was bright-eyed and alert even though he was connecting with them from Australia. It was nearing 10:30 in the evening there. They'd all become accustomed to using the teleportation platforms, so timezones and their resulting offsets were no longer the problem they'd once been. Hondo had a good two days' worth of stubble on his jaw. It stood out against the deep tan of his complexion.

It had been several days since Cyrus had checked in with Charlie. She'd only been a part of their team for two weeks before he and Reese headed for Brown University and found themselves in this mess. Charlie was roughly his age, but he thought she had an old soul. She had a big heart and was one of the few truly genuine people he'd met. Though he hadn't kept in touch with her after leaving the Coalition, he'd looked in on her occasionally. He felt compelled to keep an eye on her after she became entangled in his final operation for the Coalition. She'd gone out on a limb for him and gotten herself into some trouble as a result. Everything was cleared up in the end, but Charlie was distraught when she realized their boss, the head of the Coalition at the time, had been conducting private operations using company staff and resources. While the exact details of the misconduct were highly classified, Charlie's position had exposed her to more dirt than she'd been comfortable sweeping under the rug. She'd resigned over the matter and bounced from one job to the next ever since.

Cyrus felt more than a little responsible for her break with the Coalition. He'd met many people in the quiet years that followed his time in the private sector. He'd pointed a couple of them in her direction anytime they were hiring. For reasons he never understood, she never stayed at any job longer than a few months. She had become nomadic, wandering from position to position but never finding work she was happy with or well-suited for. When the need to interface with the Coalition arose again, she was the first person Cyrus thought of. She was the only person he knew he could trust and the only person who knew the Coalition and its resources inside and out. It was an ideal position for her, at least on paper.

Hondo watched silently from the screen as Cyrus and Reese moved a pair of chairs around in front of the computer. Cyrus saw the look in his friend's eyes as he slipped into the seat and knew what was coming.

"Did we interrupt something?" Hondo asked. He offered a broad, knowing smile.

"Not at all," Cyrus mumbled.

Reese shook her head emphatically, but her cheeks were flush. She made a guilty effort once more to straighten the lines of her dress.

Charlie laughed. Cyrus watched her eyes bouncing left the right. He knew she was enjoying the split screen view on her monitor: Hondo on one side and himself and Reese on the other. "We could come back later," Charlie offered. "I've got nowhere to be and nothing but time."

Reese bowed her head and ducked it behind her upraised hand. Cyrus could see her turning red and knew she was more self-conscious of that reaction. A little ribbing from her friends was nothing to someone with her sense of humor. Then again, he reminded himself that this was her first encounter with Charlie.

"I'm sorry," Cyrus said. He would use the introductions to try and get things back on track. "Charlie Greene, this is Reese Knoland. And I think you've already met Hondo?"

Charlie nodded. She was in her late twenties with dark, shoulder-length hair. She'd cut it since Cyrus had seen her last. It suited her, he instantly decided. She also had warm green eyes that were so bright and distinct that they seemed iridescent against the laptop's LCD screen. "It's nice to meet you, Reese. Hondo has told me so much about you. I've read your papers on digital fiberoptic interfaces for entangled particles. The work you're doing will change everything about how the world communicates."

Reese blinked slowly at the computer screen, dumbstruck. Cyrus didn't think it was possible, but the color of her cheeks reddened further. "Ah..." she stammered. "Thank you?"

Cyrus laughed. Charlie was talking about Reese's work on the Quantum Data Link technology. So far, the team had done an excellent job of staying out of the spotlight. The technology was making waves; every telecommunication company on the planet was already testing some hardware variation. Some were already moving forward with deployment. News had already spread to the end user community, getting coverage in local and major newspapers alike. However, after the danger the team had experienced following the leak surrounding the development of the teleportation platforms, no one on the team was willing to come forward to take credit for the technological breakthrough.

Hondo and Charlie had met about six months prior when Cyrus pulled some strings and set Charlie up with a nonprofit organization organizing emergency aid in different parts of Africa. Hondo had acted as a cutout, meeting with Charlie and setting her up with the charity. To Cyrus's surprise, Charlie had streamlined the organization's logistics and made a quick exit. He had no idea why she decided not to stick around. The charitable organization seemed like a good fit for her.

Nonetheless, Charlie and Hondo had gotten along well. When Cyrus arranged the conference call, he'd need to explain his connection to Hondo. He suspected Charlie had discovered his invisible work behind the scenes of her recent career opportunities. She hadn't said anything, but it would explain why she'd resurfaced to help with this operation.

"It's nice to put a face to the name finally," Reese said. Cyrus could tell she was trying to recover from the tongue-tied response. But there was something more in the way she made the statement. No, that wasn't it. It was more the look in her eyes. Charlie wasn't what she'd pictured when he'd explained how she helped him on the Shadowlight mission.

"You as well," Charlie said. "I don't understand how you, or your team for that matter, have managed to keep your faces out of the news given how your QDL product is catching on."

Cyrus could imagine the icy chill running down Reese's back at that moment. She'd seen firsthand how press and publicity had negative sides. Plenty of corporations were willing to do anything to manipulate the Quantum Data Link technology. Like the teleportation platforms, the technology would change the world, and there were those invested in maintaining the status quo.

"You have Cyrus to thank for that," Reese said. "He showed us that there is such a thing as negative press. Potentially dangerous, *life-threatening press*."

Charlie nodded. The understanding was evident in her eyes. Cyrus was sure she knew the type of threats they were alluding to.

"Has Clayton got you up and running in the new office?" Cyrus asked. "Is he playing by the rules?"

Charlie nodded again. "I'm set up in a secure office with biometric locks. I've got full network and admin-level access to the logistics systems, just like the old days. Tell me what you need, and you'll have it." She thought for a brief moment as if weighing her words. "You must have him over a barrel."

Cyrus grinned. "Clayton came to me and asked for help,

and I came to you. I appreciate you coming back for this. I needed someone I could trust sitting in that chair. It's the only way this will work."

She nodded but didn't say a word. She knew exactly what he meant. Though neither had said as much out loud, it was the reason she'd accepted the job.

"My first request," Cyrus said. "I'll send you a couple of photos after we disconnect. I need you to run a network-wide facial recognition search. MI-6 has already run through the motions," his eyes moved momentarily to Hondo on the opposite side of the screen, then back to Charlie. "They came up dry. I'm hoping we'll have better luck using Coalition resources. Run the photos against everything you have. I need to find this woman as soon as possible."

Reese shot Cyrus a glance. Understanding registered in her eyes, and she quickly looked away. She had put the pieces together. Hondo's face betrayed nothing. He wasn't the least bit surprised by the request. He'd seen it coming all along.

"Anything else?" Charlie asked.

"I want you to take a closer look at Thomas Clayton," Cyrus said. "It goes without saying that he'll be anticipating as much, so you'll have to get creative. Dig where you can, but don't get caught."

Charlie leaned closer to the screen just slightly and lowered her voice, even though there was no need. "Do you know something I don't?"

"Only that we've been burned before. I won't let it happen a second time."

She nodded. "Understood. Anything else?"

"Not at the moment," Cyrus said.

Reese glanced at him. "What about Alec Barnabe?" she

whispered. "Can she help track him down?"

Cyrus shook his head. "Clayton would've already tried that. Reid's still in the hospital, but I bet he's already got someone running down every lead they have. Besides, I think I already know where Barnabe is hiding."

Turning his attention back to the video screen, Cyrus said, "Why don't you do a more exhaustive analysis of the Order of Origin? They've been in the news a lot lately. I'm betting more dirt on them is surfacing as a result. Clayton has already provided a report, but I would feel better knowing that no stone has gone unturned. Remember, as long as you contact us over the QDL connection, our communications are secure."

"Understood," Charlie said. "I'll be in touch."

A moment later, her side of the screen blinked dark, and Hondo's image filled the space. "What have you got for me?" he asked.

"Let's plan for the best," Cyrus said. "Go ahead and contact our friend and arrange for the time we need on the mainframe. With any luck, we'll collect Mister Barnabe and return by nightfall."

"Roger that," Hondo confirmed. "Watch your backs out there."

Hondo signed off, and the laptop screen went dark. Cyrus closed the lid and disconnected the power cord. He packed the small machine in a compact messenger-style bag with a shoulder strap.

"You said you would never go back to the Coalition," Reese said after he'd finished with the computer.

Cyrus turned one of the chairs so it faced where she sat on the edge of the bed. He slipped into the seat and met her eyes but didn't respond.

"You didn't let Clayton pressure you into his operation,"

Reese continued. "You're using him for access to Coalition resources. You wanted access to their facial recognition network."

Offering a half-hearted smile, Cyrus nodded. "I'm not sure it's a fair trade, but I have a feeling the attack on Alec Barnabe and this cult Clayton is getting worked up over is related."

"How could it be? Clayton has been trying to get you to work the cult case for almost a year. We came here looking for Barnabe. Why should that have anything to do with the cult?"

Cyrus thought about how the chairs in the cafe seemed to move of their own accord. Explaining that would be a hard sell to someone scientifically minded like Reese.

"Tommy Wilks and the last surviving shooter from yesterday died the same way, wouldn't you agree?" he asked.

She nodded. "Seems like it. Both suffered extreme cardiovascular trauma. Something unusual and unique."

"Something no one recognizes, by all accounts. Wouldn't you agree?" he coaxed.

She nodded again without hesitation. "According to your buddy Clayton. But it's up to you to judge the validity of his word on that, considering you don't trust him."

It was a fair point, but Clayton didn't have a reason to lie about the details of the two deaths. Even if he did, he knew better than to add a convoluted and easily confirmable detail like that.

"I believe Clayton was on the level regarding the deaths," Cyrus said.

"So what killed them?"

"Not *what*," Cyrus corrected. "We're looking for *who*

killed them."

Reese took a moment to consider the statement. "But if we know what he used, couldn't that lead us to the killer?"

Cyrus smiled. It was sound, practical logic. She was thinking like a conventional investigator. "In this case, I don't think a weapon was used. I think the man who killed them was the weapon."

Chapter 24 - Book Barn

Brown University, Providence, Rhode Island

Cyrus slipped the rental car to the curb and killed the engine. The Small Point Cafe was thirty yards ahead on their left; the street was busy with traffic. Cars moved past them along the one-way street with surprising regularity, and the sidewalks on both sides were congested with foot traffic. There was a large bookstore to the right of the cafe. The name Cheryl's Book Barn was proudly displayed over a pair of glass doors fronting the sidewalk. The storefront was wide and occupied twice as much curb space as the coffee shop. It was also on the corner of the same building, so it fronted an adjacent street. Glancing in the rearview mirror, Cyrus saw the front window of the lingerie shop a few doors behind them. He smiled, recalling the awkward display from Agent Amstell the day before.

Most of the shops were still closed at the early hour. It was almost 8:30 am. The cafe was open, and curiously, so was the bookstore. They were the two staples of student life, Cyrus reasoned. Most of the people passing the car windows were young and likely students. The majority of the traffic was moving to and from the cafe. It was doing an impressive amount of early morning business. The occasional person stepped into the bookstore. Apparently, there was justification for it to be open early.

"We're back to talk to Claire?" Reese asked, glancing in the direction of the cafe.

Cyrus shook his head. "According to the local PD, Barnabe hasn't gone home since the night Wilks died," he said. "He's no longer considered a suspect, but his disappearance was enough for the sheriff to consider him a person of interest. It was enough to warrant a 24-hour watch on the apartment. Since Barnabe hasn't returned home, one of two things are likely."

"Either he went into hiding, or someone has grabbed him," Reese reasoned. "But either way, how does that help us? Why are we here?"

"If someone grabbed him," Cyrus reasoned, "he could be anywhere. He could be alive or dead. But what if he went into hiding?"

"Same problem," Reese responded. "He could be anywhere. He probably skipped town. There's no way of knowing."

Cyrus considered her logic. "Maybe," he conceded. "But you've read Barnabe's file. He would've had a PhD from CalTech at 14 if he could've kept his act together. But on paper, he's described as antagonistic and egotistical. He's got a genius-level IQ, but he's been at Brown making a concerted effort to graduate. He has no degree, and he still has no direction. We're not talking about a kid with many friends, so he's not someone with many options when the going gets tough."

Reese considered the points and nodded. "Okay," she agreed. "Why does that bring us here?"

"Barnabe was meeting with Wilks the night Wilks died. The cafe owner said Wilks was in all the time. She said she was frustrated at how often Barnabe came in with him. The two of them were working on some kind of project, but no one knew what they were up to."

Cyrus pulled out his phone and loaded a copy of the footage from the security cameras at the cafe. He scrubbed through the video and froze on a frame from shortly after Wilks sat down at the cafe table the night he died. He handed the phone to Reese. "What do you see?" he asked.

She looked at the black-and-white image frozen on the screen. It showed Wilks sitting at the small table along the wall with his hand flipping back his laptop screen. He had just placed the computer on the table and opened the lid. Cyrus had chosen this frame specifically.

Cyrus watched as Reese zoomed in on the image. The quality of the photo degraded quickly as it resized, so she stopped and zoomed back, stopping at a medium-level view. Details were still discernible and were now more visible. He was sure her eyes had zeroed in on the collage of stickers plastered across the laptop lid. There were logos for bands he didn't recognize and some that he did. There were logos for software packages by Adobe and PropellerHead.

Reese slid her fingers across the screen and zoomed in more closely. Cyrus saw her eyes tighten, and she looked up. He followed her gaze to the sign over the entrance to the cafe. The cafe's logo was a sticker on the lid of the computer. Reese's head turned fractionally as her sightline shifted to the nearby bookstore. Its logo was a line art cartoon of an open book. It matched another sticker on the lid of the laptop.

"The bookstore?" Reese said.

"I looked it up last night," Cyrus explained. "Social media is an investigator's best friend. Tommy Wilks has been dating the same girl for the last 16 months. She started working at the bookstore two months ago."

Reese nodded. "It explains why he's in the cafe so often."

Raising a cautioning finger, Cyrus smiled. "Yes, and no. Kelly Mills started working at Cheryl's Book Barn only two months ago. But when I returned to Wilks's online photo archive, I found other images that included his laptop."

"So?"

Cyrus paused and took a long look at the Book Barn. "The bookstore's logo has been on his laptop for the better part of the last year," he said.

Reese waited for further elaboration, but none came. "Meaning?" she finally asked.

Looking her in the eye, Cyrus said, "Let's find out."

Chapter 25 - Blend Into a Crowd

Cheryl's Book Barn, Providence, Rhode Island

Reese followed Cyrus through the door of Cheryl's Book Barn. The store was bright and airy, lined on two sides by tall, expansive windows facing the street. Rows of shelves crisscrossed the expansive floor, each meticulously maintained and stacked end to end with books of every shape and size. The shelves themselves weren't as tall as they might have been. At maybe five feet in height, they made it easy to look across the entire store and gave the shop an open, spacious feel despite its narrow aisles.

Reese liked the store immediately.

Cyrus stopped and took a moment to observe the space. Reese could see calculation behind his eyes. "What now?" she asked.

"Now we ask questions," he said, heading across the floor.

The service counter was located near a pair of doors on the adjoining wall. It was a long, high surface with a pair of small space-saving cash registers and a computer probably used to catalog inventory. Reese had spent a short time working at the school bookstore at the start of her freshman year at MIT. She had fond memories of the experience. Walking through the clean, well-manicured shop brought back a sense of nostalgia.

A gray-haired woman in her early fifties was working behind the counter. She had a stack of hardcover books and was moving them from the counter onto a wheeled cart. Cyrus was headed toward her but veered off at the last moment. Turning left, he stepped to the nearest shelf, picked up a book, and pretended to leaf through it.

Reese saw his eyes scanning the rest of the shop and felt the hairs of her arms prickle. "What's wrong?" she whispered.

A door along the back wall had opened. A young woman was negotiating the doorway, pushing a wheeled cart before her. She snagged the cart's edge on the doorknob and had to back up before trying again. She looked frustrated and ready to break into tears by the time she made it through.

"We need to talk with her," Cyrus said quietly. "She was Tommy Wilks's girlfriend."

Reese took another look at the young woman. She was short and pale, with blond hair pulled into a ponytail. It wasn't the door that had her so upset, she realized. There were dark circles under her eyes. She'd been on the verge of tears before her minor disagreement with the narrow opening. She'd probably been on the verge of tears for days. She was obviously having difficulty keeping it together for reasons other than work.

"Grace Mikelson," Reese mumbled. "I almost didn't recognize her."

"I think Wilks spent so much time at the cafe because he spent a lot of time over here, too," Cyrus said. "His girlfriend worked next door."

It made sense, she reasoned. "But how does that help us find Barnabe?"

Cyrus glanced at her. A hint of a smile touched the corners of his mouth. "Their social media accounts fill in the blanks," he said. "According to Grace's account, she's only been working here a couple of months. If Wilks were only coming here to see her, his link to the store would be fairly recent."

Reese nodded, the question still evident in her eyes.

"But Wilks's media account tells a different story," Cyrus said. "Remember all the stickers on the cover of his laptop on the video? I went back through his online photo archive. The stickers for the Small Point Cafe and the Book Barn date back almost a year. He was a fan of the bookstore long before Grace started working here. I think he was spending a lot of time here...maybe that's why Grace took the job in the first place."

Reese followed the logic, but she wasn't sure what it meant. "How does that help us with Barnabe?"

"Based on the conversation with the cafe owner, it sounded like Barnabe kept turning up at the cafe because of Wilks. She said she didn't like Barnabe and was never happy to see him. She didn't seem to feel the same way about Wilks. I got the impression that every time Barnabe showed up, he was with Wilks."

"Okay..." Reese responded. She still wasn't seeing the connection.

"Whatever Barnabe and Wilks were working on, they weren't using a school lab. If they were, we would know about it. Barnabe was paranoid and, by all accounts, a bit of an asshole. For whatever reason, whatever they were working on, they chose to do it in secret."

Reese nodded. It made sense. Barnabe didn't seem interested in pursuing his doctorate or even graduating.

Academically, it was like he was treading water. On paper, he was a genius. Scholastically, he was a wreck. Still, he hadn't given up. It was like he was content to remain a student.

"Whatever Wilks and Barnabe were working on," Cyrus said, "I think they were doing it here."

"Here?" Reese couldn't keep the disbelief from her voice. "In a bookstore? Why would they do that?"

Cyrus grinned. "We can ask Barnabe when we find him."

The grey-haired woman finished loading her cart and exchanged it for the one Grace had wheeled from the backroom. Without a word between them, Grace took the newly loaded cart and headed into the aisles of the showroom floor.

Reese caught the older woman's sympathetic look as the carts were exchanged. Grace was showing classic signs of depression. She failed to meet the older woman's eyes, and her face was drawn and emotionless; she moved with a sluggish gait that implied she was running on autopilot. She had lost someone close to her and was just trying to make it through the day.

"We need to be gentle with her," Reese warned.

Cyrus met her eye. His question was written on his face.

"She's hurting," she clarified. "Keep that in mind. She looks like she might fold with the slightest provocation. We don't want to make a hard time even harder."

Cyrus nodded. He slipped his hand gently over hers, and they walked slowly deeper into the dense confines of the shop.

———

Edward Meeker watched what was happening inside the Book Barn from behind the tinted windows of a white Ford

Econoline van parked at the curb outside. He'd been ready when Cyrus and Reese left the hotel, and he'd followed them. He wasn't entirely surprised when he registered they were heading back to the cafe, though he couldn't guess what follow-up information they hoped to gather.

Meeker knew he'd left no trace evidence leading back to him. But when the couple skipped the cafe and entered the bookstore next door, Meeker's interest was piqued.

He turned in the passenger seat and looked to the back of the van. A pair of men sat on a bench seat that ran the length of the cargo space. Both were dressed in T-shirts and jeans. They were clean-shaven and were supposed to blend into a crowd, but Meeker couldn't imagine them blending in anywhere—no matter how they were dressed. Both were white with short dark hair. They were medium height and medium build, but somehow, they never seemed to blend. It didn't matter where they went. The pair just radiated menace. They had always made Meeker uncomfortable, and now more than ever, he resented their being forced into his part of the operation.

The men were on hand because Jasmine Peng never worked without them. Jasmine was five foot four with porcelain skin and long jet-black hair. She was of Chinese descent, with dark, intense eyes. Meeker had never liked her, and he certainly had not expected her to be inserted into *his* operation. Her arrival this morning raised several troubling questions.

Before leaving the hotel that morning, Meeker had followed protocol and reported the movements of Cooper and the girl. As he'd been ordered the day before, he was supposed to follow them to whoever they were meeting and dispose of the lot. Disappointingly, he found that his orders had changed. Verhoeven had taken an interest in Cyrus Cooper and now wanted to know more about him. Jasmine Peng had been dispatched and had already landed in Providence, Meeker learned. He was to rendezvous with her and then let her interrogate Cooper and the girl.

Meeker didn't trust Jasmine any more than he had Cruze the day before. Cruze was a dangerous and violent thug. He and his men had shot up half the city in their attempt to kill Cooper. And for what? It was senseless mayhem and violence—it lacked grace and elegance. Cruze, of all people, could've done better, but he'd resorted to his old ways rather than using the tools the Order had given him. It was why Meeker had slipped into the ambulance and killed the operative before he could be transported to the hospital. The Order might have been exposed if Cruze had been taken into custody. So he'd acted without orders or approval and disposed of his associate before Cruze realized he was in mortal danger.

He had taken the initiative.

It was for the good of the Order, Meeker reasoned. Certainly, Verhoeven would understand. If he were on site, he would've made the same decision. Still, Jasmine's arrival was disconcerting. If Verhoeven disagreed with his call, he realized Jasmine could just as easily be here for him.

The thought left a bitter taste in his mouth. Meeker swallowed hard and tried to quiet his mind. He didn't need the intrusive bitch putting her nose where it didn't belong. What was between his ears was his own business. Who was she to pry?

Meeker took a deep breath and calmed himself. He turned back to the driver's seat and saw Jasmine staring at him. Her eyes were dark and slightly pinched, but her face was expressionless. She didn't say a word...still, a chill passed through his body.

"Guilty conscience?" Jasmine said. "Something you would like to confess?"

Meeker scowled and returned his attention to the interior of the bookstore. "Can you Read them from here?" he asked.

She turned to the bookstore. "It doesn't work that way," she said quietly.

Meeker smiled. Not as all-powerful as she would like him to believe, he decided.

"When this is over," Jasmine said. "I think we need to have a talk about Mister Cruze."

Meeker's mouth went dry, and he felt his stomach sink. He focused his attention on the store and made every effort to quiet his mind.

God, I hate this bitch.

———

They caught up with Grace Mikelson seven rows into the fiction section. She'd parked the cart and added stock to a shelf about level with Cyrus's shoulder.

"Excuse me," Cyrus said. "Are you Grace?"

She turned, and the question became redundant. Her name was written on the tag she wore on her polo shirt right above the store's logo. "Can I help you find something?" she asked.

"Actually, you can help us find *someone*." Though he presented the suggestion with his best disarming smile, her expression became instantly suspicious. "I'm trying to reach Alec Barnabe."

Grace didn't hesitate at all. "Sorry. I don't know who that is."

She wasn't a very good liar. Her entire body seemed to stiffen, and she avoided his eyes when she spoke. She wasn't just covering for a friend, she was afraid.

"It's alright," Cyrus said and presented the DHS identification provided by Thomas Clayton. "My name is Cyrus. Alec isn't in any trouble. I'm working on a case and need his professional opinion concerning some evidence. I just need a moment of his time."

Grace stared hard at the identification, but she didn't say

a word. Cyrus took the hint and passed the leather sleeve to her. She seemed intent on examining it. That was unusual. Normally, he just flashed a badge or ID, and it was enough to satisfy even the most paranoid of people.

"I understand you were close with Alec's friend, Mister Wilks," Cyrus said. "I'm very sorry for your loss."

The comment snapped her attention away from the ID. Her eyes met his, and she passed the wallet back. "I don't know where Barnabe is," she said in a dry, husky voice.

Her eyes were brimming with tears. Any mention of Wilks would continue to be a delicate topic for some time. Cyrus could understand the sense of loss. He had sympathy.

"I think you know where he is," Cyrus insisted. "I think he's here. I'm fairly sure he's in the building—in the back room right now. I won't cause him any trouble. In fact, I might be able to help him with the trouble he's already in."

The suspicion returned to Grace's eyes. "What do you know about that?"

Cyrus shrugged. "Not nearly enough, I'm afraid. But I'm in a position to help." He raised the wallet containing his identification. "I know someone is after him, but I don't know who...or why."

"I can't help you," Grace insisted.

Cyrus was about to speak when he felt Reese's hand on his arm. At first, he thought it was a warning for restraint, but then he looked up and saw Alec Barnabe ducking his head through the doorway on the back wall. The young man motioned to Cyrus, waving him over. Cyrus saw the small camera on the wall near the door and realized Barnabe must've been watching everything from the back room.

Grace saw Barnabe's gesture and rolled her eyes. "Good luck with that one," she said. Her voice sounded suddenly defeated. "He's not very good with strangers." She thought for a moment. "He's not very good with friends, either."

Cyrus saw a puzzled look cross Reese's face. She didn't understand the warning any better than he did.

Stepping forward, Cyrus placed his hand gently on Grace's, where it rested on the cart's handle. "I really am sorry for your loss," he said quietly. "It's not easy. But I don't think losing the people close to us should be. It's the price we pay for letting someone in." He glanced briefly at Reese and took a breath. He looked back into Grace's eyes and spoke again. "But it's worth it. Remind yourself of that. It might not feel like it right now, but it's worth it. Loss only hurts when it's someone special. Don't close yourself off to the people who care about you. It might save you pain right now, but it hurts more in the long run."

Cyrus didn't like giving advice any more than he liked having unsolicited advice pushed upon him, but he knew Grace was standing on the edge of a very slippery slope. It was one he'd navigated far too recently, and he'd made a mess of it.

The exchange was awkward, and Cyrus felt terribly uncomfortable. He sensed Reese's eyes on him and saw Barnabe still watching from the doorway. Taking a quick step to the left, Cyrus slipped past Grace and the cart before heading for the rear of the store.

Barnabe ducked behind the door as Cyrus drew near. Cyrus turned the doorknob and glanced over his shoulder. He expected Reese to be at his heels, but she was gone. He saw her still back with Grace, locked in a bearhug of an embrace. Tears were rolling down Grace's cheeks. Reese met his eyes and waved him on with a tiny gesture. She would catch up. Cyrus sighed and stepped through the door.

Barnabe was waiting on the other side. The room was large, a warehouse-like overstock space filled with aisles of narrow shelves nearly eight feet tall and stacked with books.

The lights were off, and there were no windows. What little light was from the emergency exit sign on the wall over the door and a single nightlight plugged into a nearby outlet.

"Alec Barnabe?" Cyrus asked. "I'm Cyrus Cooper. I'm working with the Department of Homeland—"

"Yes, yes," Barnabe snapped. "I heard all that." He snatched the identification from Cyrus's hand before he had the wallet open and ready to present. Barnabe stepped closer to the door where the light was better and held the ID close to his nose for examination. His eyes moved back and forth between the ID and Cyrus several times as if he were thoroughly comparing the photo.

"What does DHS want with me?" Barnabe grumbled. He made no effort to return the identification.

"I asked for the best image analysis specialist in the field, and your name came up," Cyrus offered.

Barnabe huffed and threw the ID back at Cyrus. He didn't toss it in his direction. He threw it at his chest. Turning on a heel, Barnabe headed into the darkness. "You mean you heard they stole my facial recognition algorithm," he fumed as he stormed away. "And you want me to write something similar for you."

Cyrus grinned. He suddenly understood Grace's warning and suspected Barnabe wasn't just irritated about how his facial recognition software had been highjacked—she was implying this was his standard operating mode. The cafe owner had also commented on Barnabe's prickly demeanor.

"You know about that?" Cyrus asked. He had a hard time keeping the amusement from his voice. It must not have worked because Barnabe stopped, spun, and glared at him. "What?" Cyrus said. He could see the anger in Barnabe's eyes.

Though he looked like he would verbally unload on him right there, Barnabe said nothing. He turned and continued further into the darkness. They rounded the end of a shelving unit and stepped into a small, dull bubble of light. A three-foot wide table was covered with a pair of large screen flat panel monitors, a keyboard, and a mouse. A smaller, additional LCD screen sat at the very edge of the table. It displayed feeds from the security cameras scattered around the shop. A lone lamp on an articulated arm was bolted to the right side of the table's surface. It was the source of the pale glow. A white cloth lay draped over something to the left of the computer displays. Whatever was under it was small, but Cyrus had no idea what it might be.

Beneath the table was a row of five short computer mini-towers. They stood side by side, shoulder to shoulder, with no gap between them. Small blue LED lights blinked rapidly on their faces in random sequences. A three-inch wide insulated tube ran from the side of the leftmost computer and connected to a small cube-shaped freezer. The freezer was the kind of thing you would see in a school dorm or an office. The five computers were running completely silent; there was no fan noise. The tube carried coolant, Cyrus realized. He was looking at some kind of ad-hoc, over-clocked server farm.

"Tell me what you want," Barnabe said without preamble.

"Like you said, I want your help with some advanced image analysis."

"DHS doesn't have people for that? Or, at least, people who can steal what they need to do that sort of thing?" There was no disguising the venom in Barnabe's tone.

Reese appeared from the darkness and joined Cyrus. He felt considerably better with her back at his side. The sensation caught him off guard, and he wondered what had changed. He'd once been comfortable working entirely by himself. Now, he was most content as part of a team. Reese and Hondo had become a pivotal part of his life.

For the first time since Walter Meade dropped him back into a world of espionage—a world he'd sworn off entirely—Cyrus realized he wasn't the same person he'd been when he worked for the Coalition. The idea felt oddly reassuring. It meant he wasn't betraying himself or his morals by temporarily dealing with Thomas Clayton.

"DHS has its resources," Cyrus said. "I prefer to distance myself from the bureaucracy whenever possible. If we can come to an arrangement on our own, I would rather work with someone outside of government."

Curiosity was evident in Barnabe's eyes. He looked like he had a hundred questions, but Cyrus was starting to understand how the kid's mind worked. He wouldn't bite at the temptation in any obvious way.

"I understand you're in some trouble," Cyrus said. "Why don't you let me help you with that? Then we can discuss my project, and you can decide if you're interested."

Barnabe took a step back and shoved his hands into his pockets. "Trouble? I don't know what you're talking about."

Cyrus tipped his head to the right beyond the illumination of the light bubble. A small cot was pushed up against the wall. It held a pillow and a messy pile of blankets. Barnabe had clearly been sleeping there for some time.

"I know the local cops have been looking for you. They're investigating the death of your friend and consider you a person of interest."

Barnabe looked away but remained silent.

Barnabe was young. Cyrus knew he was 18, but he looked younger. Discounting his rumpled shirt and baggy flannel pants, he had a face that didn't appear to need shaving. His blond hair was styled and thick on haircare product, even if it looked like it hadn't been cared for in days. He was perhaps five-eight and 140 pounds. His face seemed to express every thought that passed through his mind. In the few short minutes Cyrus had spent with him, he'd seen nothing but dark eyes and scowl from the boy. No, he decided, Barnaby's appearance fell short of his age, Cyrus decided. If he didn't know better, he would've pegged the kid as being 16 years old.

"The county coroner has ruled Wilks's death as heart failure," Cyrus continued. Barnabe's glance shot suddenly in his direction. "You're not a suspect." Cyrus watched him closely. Barnabe didn't react. Where there should've been relief or calculation, there was nothing. "But that's not why you're hiding, is it?"

Cyrus followed Barnabe's eyes when they moved away. This time, they fell on the white cloth draped over the end of the table. They remained there for only a moment before shifting to traverse the room. As his gaze moved on, Cyrus saw calculation in the gaze. Barnabe was sharp. He realized he'd let his subconscious give something away and was doing his best to hide it.

Cyrus stepped forward and put his hand on the white cloth. Barnabe reacted instantly, bolting in Cyrus's direction with his arms raised. With a slight flick of his ankle, Cyrus spun the wheeled desk chair in Barnabe's direction. The kid collided with the chair, tripped, and toppled to the concrete floor.

Pulling back the cloth, Cyrus found an old book. It was about an inch thick, with a leather cover long ago cracked with fatigue. He ran his fingers across the unusual surface. The cracks and the texture of the leather had since worn smooth, speaking to years of use. The moment his finger swept across the book's surface, Cyrus felt an odd sensation. It was like a buzzing behind both of his ears. Not so much a sound but a subtle yet distinctive perception. His vision dimmed, and the sounds from the room around him fell away. A gentle, rhythmic clatter seemed to come from somewhere in the distance. The strange sensation seemed to last for long moments, but when his vision brightened again, he was sure that only a second or two had passed. He stared at the book, unsure what to make of the experience. He had the sense that he was recalling an event, but the memory was just outside his reach. It was like glimpsing a portion of a dream that was days old and long forgotten.

He studied the book. Whatever it was, it had been around for a long time. The leather was a little unusual in that it carried a reddish hue. Nothing was written on the cover, but the volume seemed familiar.

"Take it easy," Cyrus said. He looked at Barnabe on the floor. The kid had made no effort to return to his feet. He just glared up at Cyrus with anger in his eyes. "It's just a book," Cyrus said quietly.

Barnabe stared. "You really aren't one of them, are you?" he asked finally.

"One of who?" Cyrus asked.

Climbing to his feet, Barnabe dusted himself off. He glanced briefly at Cyrus before looking away. When he spoke, he refused to make eye contact. "Ever heard of the Order of Origin? It's a cult."

The muscles in Cyrus's neck tightened. He was hoping there had been some kind of coincidence in play. He didn't believe in coincidence as a rule—as an investigator—still; he'd held out hope. "They've been making headlines lately," he said. "You're saying that's who's after you?"

It was a redundant question. The video footage from the cafe had been enough for Cyrus to connect those dots. But it didn't explain why the Order was after some genius kid who couldn't manage to graduate from college.

Barnabe didn't speak. He continued to avoid Cyrus's eye. To Cyrus, that was usually a sign that someone was lying, maybe stalling to buy time so he could fabricate a half-truth. But that didn't seem to be the case with Barnabe. The kid just had a chip on his shoulder. A big, ugly chip. If the cafe owner and Tommy Wilks's girlfriend were to be believed, it was likely just Barnabe's usual, abrasive manner. Cyrus had worked with people like him before.

"Spill it, kid," Cyrus said in a flat voice that touched on anger. "If you want my help, you'd better cut to the chase."

Barnabe glared. "Who said I want your help? You came here asking for *my help*!"

Cyrus shook his head. "If you've got the goon squad from the Order of Origin after you, you need help. And if you know who you're dealing with, then you know police protection isn't going to cut it."

Both Barnabe and Reese turned to Cyrus. Barnabe's glance indicated he knew the Order was more than just a fringe religious group. Reese's glance meant it was time to bring her up to speed on his limited but colorful history with the group.

"They aren't your average religious whack jobs," Cyrus said.

"You're kidding, right?" Barnabe sputtered. "Those people are completely psychotic."

Movement on one of the monitors caught Cyrus's attention. The display sat at an awkward angle, perched on the very edge of Barnaby's improvised and messy desk. The screen showed footage from surveillance cameras located around the bookstore. As had been the case with a similar rig in the next-door cafe, this monitor was split into quadrants. One corner displayed a narrow alleyway with brick walls, while two other quarters contained feeds from the front showroom. It was those views that captured Cyrus's attention. A pair of men had just used the northern entrance simultaneously as another used the western entrance. All four men looked similar—tall with short hair and grave, serious expressions. They moved with purpose.

Not shopping for books.

The video feed showing the brick alley changed. A white panel van backed into the frame. Cyrus heard the squeak of its brakes, and his eyes were drawn to the wide door on the cinderblock wall twenty feet to his left. The door had a massive push bar across it, and a pair of thick steel hasps secured its iron frame. The door could only be opened from the inside, but the van in the alley was blocking their escape. There was no question that the driver coordinated his movements with the men entering through the front.

"You'll want our help," Cyrus heard Reese say. She was continuing to argue the point with Barnabe. Watching the video feed, Cyrus knew no time was left for debate. There was no chance of escape, either.

The surveillance feeds were about to become a problem. The small monitor displaying them was perched precariously on the end of the desk. He was tempted to give it the slightest nudge, sending it to the floor where it would likely become permanently disabled, but the act would draw unwelcome attention. He settled for tugging the power cord from the back of the display. The video feed went dark. Neither Barnabe nor Reese seemed to notice.

Cyrus slipped the phone from his pocket and tapped a ten-digit number not pre-programmed in memory. He didn't wait for the line to be answered—he didn't wait for it to ring, for that matter. The volume control was already turned low. He fingered the button twice more and felt the phone vibrate, telling him it was now silent. Tapping the volume rocker once more put the phone into a completely silent mode—now, not even a vibration would signal an alert. He pressed the speakerphone icon on the touch-screen and then clicked the display dark. Stepping past Reese, he moved just beyond the bubble of light emanating from the lone desk lamp. Feeling the edge of the nearest shelf, he placed the phone face down and angled the bottom toward Barnabe's desk.

When Cyrus turned, Reese was still arguing with Barnabe. Neither of them had noticed his actions.

"You can't help me," Barnabe protested. "The Order has people everywhere. You have no idea what they're capable of!"

A woman's voice rose from the distant darkness. "I don't think you're being fair, Mister Barnabe." She stepped closer, and the bubble of light caught a hint of her features. Her voice carried a trace of some Eastern accent, Chinese or Japanese. It was subtle, and her English was good, so Cyrus couldn't be sure which. "You take our money, then badmouth us to your friends? The Order will change everything you know about this world. You just need to keep an open mind."

Cyrus slipped his hand to the gun holstered in the waistband at the small of his back. He'd only gripped the weapon when a series of laser sights penetrated the gloom and found targets. Two dots appeared on his chest, steady and precise. More troubling were the single dots positioned over the hearts of Reese and Barnabe.

Chapter 26 - *Just Lucky, I Guess*

Cheryl's Book Barn, Providence, Rhode Island

The woman with the slight accent moved a step closer and further into the light. She wasn't tall—maybe five-five or five-six, and she was small. If she were a hundred pounds, Cyrus would've been surprised. There was a feline quality to how she moved, but it was more than that. The attribute seemed to describe her physically as well. Small, sleek, and thin, she had a narrow face with wide, intelligent eyes and narrow red lips. Her hair was dark. It might've been the light or the lack of it. She was standing at the very edge of the bubble from the small desk lamp. Her hair hung well past her shoulders. Though her eyes were likely brown, they looked as black as her hair from where Cyrus stood.

She wore black pants and a leather vest over a form-fitting long-sleeved black top. There was a gun in her left hand—a Glock 26 from the look of it—but she carried it casually, lost in her grip, and pointed at the floor. Even the relatively small Glock seemed large in her petite hand. The four laser sights reaching from the darkness had Cyrus's group covered. She seemed comfortable enough with their support because she didn't bother to raise her pistol.

She hadn't missed the move Cyrus made for his gun. Meeting his eye, she moved forward and slid past him. Her hand slipped behind his back, and he felt her slide the gun from the holster in the back of his jeans. Her eyes stayed on his as she moved past him and placed the gun on a shelf just beyond the perimeter of light. Unknowingly, she'd placed it just inches from where he had stashed the phone.

Seeming satisfied with Cyrus's disarmament, the woman glared at Barnabe. "You've been avoiding me," she said. "You accept our money, and then you hide from us? What sort of impression do you think that makes?"

Barnabe's eyes went wide, and he stopped blinking. "Jasmine? No—hiding? You've got the wrong idea."

Jasmine shook her head and stepped closer. She looked him in the eyes. Barnabe was a foot taller, so he had to look down to meet her gaze—still, there was no question who was in control of the conversation. Jasmine took another step forward, and Barnabe retreated by half a pace. It didn't matter. Jasmine reached around him and retrieved the leather book from the desk behind him. The book in her hand, she backed off two paces.

"You've spent a great deal of time with our book," Jasmine said. The tone of her voice remained conversational, even a bit on the quiet side. Judging by Barnabe's reaction, even her calm tones intimidated. "I hope you have something to show for it."

Cyrus's eyes fell on the book in Jasmine's hand. It seemed she had contracted Barnabe to decipher whatever secrets it held. The way Reese had explained Barnabe's work, the same image analysis could be used to crack codes or break encryption, depending on how it was applied.

Cyrus suddenly found himself interested in the leather-bound tome. Whatever it was, it was valuable to the Order of Origin.

Barnabe motioned to the twin large-screen monitors in the

center of his desk. "The server is still parsing the data," he offered in a weak, awkward voice. "But parts of the manuscript have started to become obvious. Nouns mostly, a couple of proper names—the algorithm adjusts itself using each discovery to uncover the cipher. It's only a matter of time now."

Jasmine's eyes had fallen on Cyrus while Barnabe spoke. The news returned her attention to Barnabe. Cyrus saw the young man wither under her gaze. "Names? What names?" she demanded.

"Ah…" Barnabe wheezed and turned quickly to the desk. The sound of the action being cycled on a rifle emanated from the darkness, and Barnabe froze. He threw both hands in the air. His entire body was shaking with tension. "It's alright!" he whimpered. "I'm just checking my notes."

A satisfied smile crossed Jasmine's face. "Please continue, Mister Barnabe. I suggest you move slowly. Sudden moves make my associates nervous. Trust me—you don't want these men to feel threatened."

Cyrus looked at Reese—her eyes were wide and focused on him. She was hanging in there, but there was tension in her expression.

Jasmine turned to Reese, centering her attention on her fully for the first time. She studied her for a moment before looking at him.

"Your girlfriend is scared," Jasmine said to Cyrus. The amusement she'd had at Barnabe's expense now seemed directed at them. "Right now, she's wondering what Barnabe is doing for me and what he's gotten the two of you involved in."

The stiffness seemed to leave Reese suddenly. Her eyes moved to Jasmine, an unspoken question clear in her expression. Jasmine wasn't looking at Reese when it happened, but her face seemed to brighten as if she sensed Reese's wonder.

"I'm very good at reading people," Jasmine stated in response to whatever question had gone unasked.

Cyrus felt an icy chill in the pit of his stomach. Jasmine wasn't what she seemed. She was a part of the Order, and the Order liked people with *talents*.

"It's curious," Jasmine said. Her eyes moved slowly between Reese and Cyrus. They finally shifted back to Barnabe. Cyrus could see some sort of calculation or analysis in her mind. "It's Cyrus, right?" she asked.

Cyrus nodded but said nothing. No one had used his name since Jasmine and her four friends arrived. It was evidence that further supported his suspicion.

"Reese and Barnabe are scared," she went on. "But not you—not so much. In fact, you don't seem worried at all. Why is that?"

Cyrus shrugged. "I think you hired Barnabe for something," he said. "Whatever that was, he hasn't finished it yet. But he's a smart kid. Whatever you want, you'll soon have it. There's no reason to hurt anyone. I think you'll be content to put a scare into him and then move along. That way, Barnabe is motivated, you get what you want, and no one gets hurt."

Jasmine grinned. "Salient analysis," she said. "Maybe the best way to motivate Mister Barnabe is to hurt you or Miss Knoland. What do you think?"

Cyrus shook his head, but he wasn't any more concerned. "Barnabe's already plenty motivated. He's terrified of you. Hurting us would likely be a detriment to his effectiveness. Plus, you would have police to deal with. And the resulting investigation would become a problem for you and the Order."

The smile spread further across Jasmine's face. Her eyes locked on Cyrus, and he felt the full intensity of her stare. Her gaze bore into him; he felt pressure in his sinuses and the first pangs of a headache forming between his temples.

After several seemingly endless seconds, Jasmine's expression soured. She broke her gaze and stepped backward half a pace. Looking him over head to toe, she seemed confused. Her attention moved to Reese next. Whatever she found there didn't bother her like it had with him. She moved to Barnabe but didn't waste much time examining him.

"What makes you think the authorities would come looking for you?" Jasmine asked.

Cyrus remained silent.

"The identification in your pocket is fabricated," Jasmine continued. "Homeland Security doesn't know who you are. They won't miss someone they never sent."

Cyrus recognized the comment for what it was. She was trying to put a scare into him. He would've been unnerved if he didn't know who—or what—he was dealing with.

Jasmine's head snapped to the right, and her gaze landed on Reese. "The Coalition?" Jasmine mumbled. She glanced back at Cyrus and seemed to take a fresh look at him. "You must be kidding?"

Barnabe looked confused—as if he'd missed an entire portion of the conversation.

Cyrus ignored Jasmine and watched Reese. She stood slack-jawed, staring at Jasmine with unrestrained wonder and terror in her eyes. Her jaw moved as if working silently to form words that wouldn't come.

"Don't let her get to you," Cyrus said. His tone was calm and steady despite the strange, one-sided conversation. "She's messing with your head—a Reader. She's using a parlor trick to try and get under your skin."

Cyrus felt everyone's attention fall on him. Reese, unblinking, looking for an explanation; Barnabe watched him in unrestrained confusion; Jasmine fixed her penetrating stare on him once more and seemed to concentrate with every bit of her considerable focus. No one spoke for what seemed like minutes.

Jasmine was the first to break the silence. *"You know what a Reader is…"* she muttered.

It was Cyrus's turn to fix her with a stare. He remained silent. It seemed the most efficient way to get under the skin of someone accustomed to pulling the thoughts directly from people's minds.

Jasmine raised her Glock and pointed it at Reese's face. "Don't play games with me, Cyrus. Tell me what you know about Readers. Why can I read everyone in the room except for you?"

His heart skipped a beat, and Cyrus knew he'd overplayed his hand. Putting Reese in greater danger wasn't the objective. He raised a placating hand and cleared a throat that had suddenly gone dry.

"I know the Order has an affinity for special members," he said. "Rare, hard to find folks like yourself. Readers, Pushers, and God knows what else. I've crossed paths with a few before."

Jasmine seemed momentarily distracted. She tipped her head slightly with an expression that mimicked a confused dog's look. Then her eyes rolled. Her hand slapped at her left ear, and she dug into its canal with her fingernail. A second later, she lowered her hand. In it was a small metallic device about the size of a single grain of rice. Jasmine slipped the Glock into a holster on her slender hip and picked up the metallic grain, pinching it between the tip of her finger and the pad of her thumb. She applied pressure until the device crunched audibly. Dropping what was left to the floor, she ground it into the concrete with the heel of her boot.

"Too many voices," Jasmine grumbled. "At least that was

one I could do something about."

The tiny device had been a comm unit, Cyrus knew. Miniaturized to the point where it could be slipped into the ear canal, it was virtually invisible to the naked eye. Operatives normally needed a special tool to extract the device once it was in place. The module allowed transparent, two-way communication for the person wearing it. A microphone embedded in the grain-sized transceiver picked up every sound in the room by using the wearer's skeleton as a conductive microphone. And since it was worn in the ear canal, it also functioned as a conventional listening device.

Someone had been listening to everything that was said. That same person had been passing instructions along to Jasmine. It seemed she'd had enough of the voice in her ear and had stopped it.

"I don't suppose you want to share the name of whoever was on the other end of that thing," Cyrus said.

Jasmine glared at him. "I do not," she grumbled. "Sufficed to say, we're all wondering how it is that you're immune to my charms."

Cyrus shrugged. "Just lucky, I guess."

Jasmine took a step forward and pointed her gun at his chest. "That's not good enough. I want an answer now," she demanded. "No one has ever proven immune to my abilities. Not without…"

She lowered her gun and took a step forward. Her position blocked the pair of laser dots on Cyrus's chest; he knew it was an ideal time to move. But the laser dots remained steady and fixed on Reese and Barnabe. He couldn't move against Jasmine without losing both of them.

Cyrus heard nothing but sensed a pair of men moving in the darkness surrounding their meager circle of light. The riflemen were seeking alternate positions to regain their sight lines. He would've done the same in their position. It meant the four men with Jasmine were professionals, not whackjob cult members without skills.

"Are you one of *them*?" Jasmine asked. Equal parts of wonder and concern were evident in her voice.

One of whom?

The question almost spilled from his lips before he could stop it. But keeping Jasmine off balance was more advantageous than an answer.

She grabbed him by the jaw and pushed his chin hard to the left. A moment later, she pushed it hard to the right. She was looking behind his ears, he realized. Looking for a neural dampener.

Cyrus raised an eyebrow and watched her. He let the silence hang for a long moment before finally shrugging in response. "You don't know much about me, but I know a little about you. Gertrude Waterford worked for the Order. She made you. Why did the Order have her killed?"

Jasmine appeared confused by the question. Cyrus didn't know which part of the statement confounded her. Was she unfamiliar with Waterford, or was she surprised that the Order had been behind Waterford's assassination?"

Cyrus had questions of his own, but time had run out. He had more pressing concerns to deal with at the moment. He'd waited long enough. As much as he wanted information from Jasmine, he knew this wasn't the environment for getting answers.

"What did you want from Barnabe?" he asked. "You come in here with four riflemen and leave them hiding in the dark. I can see how that might intimidate someone like Barnabe, but it's still cheap theatrics. For God's sake, he's hiding in the storeroom behind a bookstore. How much of a threat can he be?"

"Hey!" Barnabe bristled.

Cyrus shot him a withering glance and did his best to keep Jasmine's attention off the details Cyrus had just sent out into the ether. If he kept her talking, she had less chance of realizing what was happening. He was just glad she'd removed the communications device. She might have more men stationed outside the store, and he didn't want them warned if things didn't go smoothly.

"Tell me you didn't hurt the clerks out front," Cyrus persisted. He watched Jasmine's eyes for any hint of recognition—any sign she saw through his distraction.

Jasmine shook her head. "The Order is going to remake this world. Personally, I don't have a problem breaking a few heads if it helps get the job done, but we don't kill unless we have no other choice."

"Like Gertrude Waterford?" Cyrus pushed.

Once more, confusion touched Jasmine's eyes.

Cyrus heard nothing from the surrounding darkness but saw the laser marks disappear from Reese and Barnabe at the same instant. If the pair of marks weren't gone from his chest, they soon would be.

"Enough," Jasmine said. She turned to Barnabe. "How long does it take to complete the decryption?"

Barnabe seemed to straighten under her attention. He glanced at the monitor for an update on the progress. Before he could speak, Jasmine raised her gun. Her gaze darted across the three of them, and she muttered something in Chinese. Ducking to the side, she grabbed Reese by the arm and pressed the muzzle of her Glock tight into her back.

Jasmine stepped behind Reese, using her as a human shield. She pulled her close and screwed the gun in tight. It was jammed beneath her lower ribs, angled at an upward trajectory that threatened damage to virtually every vital organ if she fired even a single shot.

"Get them back," Jasmine bellowed.

Three men swept to the perimeter of the lamp's reach. They moved silently with rifles raised. Each was cloaked in black battle fatigues, complete with a tactical helmet and vest. The three stopped at the light's perimeter, and their rifles were raised and pointed at Jasmine and Reese. Unlike Jasmine's unseen men, these men carried rifles that didn't use laser sights. The man closest to Cyrus was Luke Reid, out of the hospital early and ready for action.

Cyrus's last-minute call to Charlie Greene had been a hail Mary. He'd dialed Charlie's number and put the call on speaker only after turning the volume all the way down. Charlie had come through, tracking his position and sending in the cavalry.

"Take it easy, Jasmine," Cyrus warned. "There's no way out of here. Let her go, and no one gets hurt."

Jasmine twisted Reese back and forth, using her for cover. Reese had a small form, but Jasmine was just plain tiny by comparison—more than able to hide behind her. "You're forgetting I'm a Reader," Jasmine bellowed. "I know exactly what they plan to do. Make them back off. You don't need to read minds to know what happens if they don't."

Cyrus searched for a scenario that worked to his advantage. Jasmine was a Reader, and he was the only one immune to her influence. That didn't mean Reid was useless to him. It just meant Reid had to help in a way that even he didn't expect. Anything Reid knew, Jasmine would as well. Cyrus's eyes fell on the wide loading door facing the alley. It was only a few feet away and might solve his problem.

"Is their van still parked in the alley?" Cyrus asked.

Reid hesitated briefly before prying his eyes from the red dot optics of his M4. Cyrus could see the wheels turning as he tried to intuit the correct answer. "Affirmative," he said at last. The reply lacked conviction. Not because it was a lie, Cyrus knew. Reid just didn't know if he was supposed to be honest.

"Good," Cyrus said with relief. "Pull your two guys back and have them wait outside. Jasmine will take the van. She can drive out of here."

Reid looked concerned. "No way. It's not procedure—it's not going to happen."

"It doesn't matter," Jasmine responded. "If he pulls back, his men will be waiting to shoot me down in the street."

"No, they won't," Cyrus countered.

"The hell they won't," Jasmine grumbled. "It was the very first thought to cross his mind."

"No," Cyrus said again. *"They won't.* He's going to have his men sit tight in the bookstore. They won't leave the building. You'll be safe in the alley. We'll let you pull out and clear the area. Just walk away. If no one gets hurt—we can call this a draw.

"You see the monitor behind you—the dark one? Barnabe's going to plug it back in. Once it's back up and running, you'll see Reid's men sitting tight out front in the store. You'll know you can take the van and know you're safe."

Reese was pulled backward an awkward step; she nearly fell. Cyrus knew Jasmine was looking at the small monitor he'd unplugged before she and her henchmen had swarmed the room.

"Have them pull back," Jasmine said. "Do it now."

Cyrus nodded to Reid. "Where are the van keys?"

Reid grimaced but stayed silent. His men didn't move.

Jasmine spoke. "They're in his hip pocket." Her words were laced with venom and distrust. "Tell them to get going. Do it now!"

"You stay," Cyrus said to Reid. "I want your guys standing in the center of the showroom. No one moves; no one takes a shot. I don't want anyone taking action against her. If she holds up her end, we hold up ours."

Reid looked fit to chew nails. His eyes were unblinking, and the muscles at the back of his jaw were drawn and corded. He stared at Jasmine for a long second, then turned that same hateful stare on Cyrus. He wasn't comfortable with the concession. Reid was a by-the-book kind of operative. This deal went against everything in that book.

A slight tip of his head was the only motion Reid made, but his two men responded instantly. Both retreated into the darkness like wraiths. Neither lowered their rifle, and neither made a sound. They just stepped backward and were swallowed by the inky black.

"Ok," Cyrus said. "That's a good start. Barnabe, I want you to move slowly over to the desk. Take the loose power cord from the floor and plug it into the back of the security display."

Barnabe didn't move. He'd been frozen on the scene's periphery as events played out. His eyes remained locked on Jasmine and Reese. Cyrus couldn't tell if he was unresponsive with fright or if he was attempting to make a point.

"Do it, Barnabe. Do it NOW," Jasmine snapped.

Barnabe snapped to attention as if slipping from a trance. His eyes seemed to focus for the first time in recent minutes. He looked quickly between Jasmine and Cyrus.

"Just plug in the monitor," Cyrus said. "No screwing around. Just move smooth and easy. She won't hurt anyone unless we give her a reason."

Barnabe did as he was told. He stepped forward on rubbery legs to pass Reese and Jasmine. He knelt beside the desk and retrieved the fallen power cable. After affixing it to the rear of the small screen, he pressed the power button and retreated to his original position. Jasmine remained hidden behind Reese, but Cyrus could see her splitting attention between him and Barnabe. She was also keeping an eye on Reid. Despite his instructions, Reid would be watching for any opportunity to end the standoff. It was a fact that Jasmine was no doubt entirely aware of since she didn't offer the slightest hint of exposure.

The monitor with the security feed came to life, showing the same split-screen view from earlier. There were two shots of the front showroom, one of the back alley where the van was parked, and the fourth was dark—likely a camera somewhere in the storeroom where it was too dark to record.

"Alright," Cyrus said. "Now Reid will go out and back the van to the door. You can step out the door and directly into the van."

Cyrus saw Jasmine glare at him from behind Reese's shoulder. She twisted the muzzle of the gun tighter into Reese's ribs and made her squirm. "Do you take me for a fool?" Jasmine said. "Your friend has a man on the street and another on the roof across the road. You're walking me into a trap!"

Tipping his head, Cyrus shot Reid a look. "Are you kidding? You've read the reports—I know you have. She's a Reader—you know what that means. Did you seriously think that would work?"

Reid grimaced. He looked like a six-year-old who'd been caught with his hand in the cookie jar. He shrugged and offered, "Sorry," in a meek voice.

"Call them in," Jasmine demanded. "Once I see them in the showroom, I'll take the van and a hostage. After I'm safely away, I'll release your girlfriend."

Cyrus's expression coalesced to stone, and he shot Jasmine a look that was just as withering. "Reid was out of line, but you can't blame him for trying, given the circumstances. You can go, but you're not taking a hostage.

I'm willing to give, but there's a line I won't cross. Reese. Stays. Here." His tone had an icy edge that left no room for argument, but he still hadn't raised his voice.

Jasmine didn't respond immediately. The seconds of silence that followed seemed to last forever. They were at a tipping point, and Cyrus knew it. He couldn't let the negotiations stall now.

"Pull in the street team," Cyrus ordered. "I want them in the store, in front of the cameras, with the rest of your men."

Reid remained motionless.

"Reid," Cyrus barked, raising his voice for the first time. "Pull them in now. That's an order."

Tapping a button on the collar of his uniform, Reid relayed the order to the perimeter team. Truth be told, Cyrus was impressed with Reid's ability to pull together a complete team in such short order. At best, he'd expected his emergency call to Charlie to garner a Sheriff's deputy or two. Reid must've checked himself out of the hospital to lead this operation.

Two minutes later, a pair of plainclothes men walked in the north-facing door of the bookstore. Their arrival was clearly visible on the security feed. Both were carrying M4 rifles and looked confused and concerned with the order to pull back to the Book Barn.

"Satisfied?" Cyrus asked.

Jasmine peeked from behind Reese and met Reid's eye. She stared for a moment before disappearing again. Cyrus saw concern in Reese's gaze. Whatever was coming would happen soon, and she knew it. And if she knew it, Jasmine knew it. But there was confusion, too. Reese had no idea what the plan was. That was good.

"Back the van right up to the door," Cyrus said to Reid. "Leave the motor running and come back inside. I want you up front with your guys. After that, Jasmine walks out and gets in the van. She leaves unmolested, *but Reese stays here."*

Reid looked uncomfortable with the order, but the time for voicing his concerns had passed. Finally, he lowered his rifle and slung it on a strap over his shoulder. He took a long look at Cyrus and then a glance at Jasmine. With exaggerated slowness, he slipped the SIG from the holster on his hip and passed it to Cyrus. Cyrus offered the barest hint of a smile and accepted the weapon. Jasmine looked ready to object but then sensed no profit in pushing back.

Cyrus knew Jasmine would wait for Reid to move the van into position and then fall back into the store before making her move. She would demand, once more, to take a hostage and ensure her escape. But she was savvy. She would wait until Cyrus was alone before pressing the issue again. One-on-one, she would like her odds. Cyrus liked his odds, too. He was the only one in the room who Jasmine couldn't Read.

Reid moved slowly across the room. Jasmine dragged Reese backward, edging to Cyrus's right by two steps while Reid reached the door. Reid passed between Cyrus and the lonely lamp on the desk as he went. Reid's closeness to the room's only light source left a wide shadow that lasted a full second. Cyrus kept his eyes fixed on Reese and Jasmine; specifically, he kept his eyes glued to the gun jammed in the side of Reese's ribs.

Cyrus kept Reid's SIG hanging casually at his side as Reid stepped to the door. His non-threatening stance made it easier for everyone present to keep their attention focused on Reid as he unbolted the door. In addition to the push-bar release, a pair of heavy steel hasps latched the door tight. A long, thick bolt had been dropped through the eye of each hasp. There were no nuts at the ends of the bolts; their presence in the hasps was enough to prevent prying the door open from the outside.

Reid slipped the first bolt free and set it on the small shelf to the right of the door. A moment later, he'd done the same with the second bolt. Bracing himself, he placed a hand against the wide push-bar and shoved it. The moment the door cracked open, blinding daylight spilled into the room.

Cyrus had squinted his eyes against the impending blindness—even still, searing pain stabbed at his brain. But by the time that pain registered, he had closed two-thirds of the distance between himself and Reese. A series of gasps cascaded across the room in response to the blinding flash of light as it flooded the dark room. Focusing on Reading Reid, Jasmine got a double dose of the painful light. The last sound was a shriek from Jasmine as Cyrus wrapped his palm around the action of her gun and twisted it nearly 180 degrees. There was a crack and a snap accompanied by a fresh, agonized scream. It was the bones in her hand and wrist snapping if Cyrus had to guess. The gun discharged with a flash and a report that sounded like a massive explosion in the confined space. Cyrus sensed the round striking the ceiling ten feet past his shoulder. He yanked Jasmine by her crushed wrist and felt her form slip past Reese. A fraction of a second later, she was face down on the concrete with her arm twisted savagely behind her back, and his knee was crushing her even further into the floor.

Reid propped the alley door open using a cinderblock as a doorstop. Cyrus heard him radioing his men even as he passed over a pair of handcuffs. Reid shook his head and grinned. Cyrus climbed from Jasmine's small prone form, and Reid replaced him. He began patting her down and searching for hidden weapons.

Cyrus turned to Reese. "Are you alright?"

Reese looked dazed. She was still blinking her eyes against the light flooding through the exterior door. Thankfully, color was already returning to her face. She straightened the lines of her sundress, took a deep breath, and looked him in the eye. "A Reader?" she said. "You're serious? This bitch can read minds?"

Cyrus grinned. Not so much phased by another violent

display, Reese was more interested in what had been said along the way.

"Can she retrieve any thought—any detail? Or is she limited to what's being processed by the mind at a given point? How does it work? Does she hear thoughts, or does she sense them? I have so many questions!"

Cyrus laughed and took her hand. "Why don't we get some fresh air?" The smell of gunpowder hung strong in the confines of the stagnant storeroom, and the sunshine filling the alley was appealing after so long in the dark. Cyrus noticed Barnabe again. The kid was sitting on his butt along the wall. His knees were pulled tight to his chest, and his eyes were unblinking. His hair was more tousled than before, and he was as pale as any computer geek had a right to be.

"You okay, Barnabe?" Cyrus asked. He offered him a hand.

Barnabe was slow to respond. It was two seconds before he blinked and looked up at Cyrus and Reese. He blinked again and eyed Cyrus's hand as if it were some strange foreign artifact. After taking a long breath, he finally took Cyrus's grip and was hoisted to his feet.

"Are you alright?" Cyrus repeated.

Barnabe blinked and breathed. He took his time but finally nodded. "I think so."

Cyrus noticed the odd way Reese was looking at Barnabe. He took a step back and looked Barnabe over, head to toe. There was a wide wet spot in the crotch of Barnabe's corduroys.

"Oh," Cyrus said quietly. "Yeah…That'll happen."

Barnabe looked down at himself and seemed to realize the wet spot for the first time. He looked up at Reese, who was turning pink in the cheeks, likely embarrassed for having drawn attention to the accident.

"I knew it," Barnabe said with a beaming grin. "Your girl's checking out my package. Don't worry, bud," he slapped Cyrus on the shoulder and headed for the door. "It happens all the time. Don't hold it against her."

Reese's brows arched, and her face blanched. She stared silently as Barnabe strolled through the doorway and out of sight. She sputtered, straining to form words but failing miserably.

"It's ok, dear," Cyrus said. "We both knew you were just using me until something better came along. It was only a matter of time." He kissed her on top of the head.

He watched Reid, who was still dealing with Jasmine, on the floor. Given her newly broken wrist, he seemed to be having trouble cuffing her. Her ability as a Reader meant they would need to take special care in transporting and incarcerating her. They also needed to be careful who she was exposed to while in custody. A prisoner who could pull thoughts from the minds of those around her would be able to learn a lot.

There was another issue. Cyrus searched the floor for the small earbud Jasmine had broken, then crushed after deciding she'd had enough of whoever was squeaking in her ear. A small dark scuff marked the concrete where she'd been standing. He knew it was all that remained of her earpiece.

"Jasmine was in communication with someone," Cyrus said to Reese. "That earbud was cutting-edge tech but had a limited transmission range. Could you check the van outside? I'm betting you'll find an uplink connecting her to whoever was on the other end. See if you can learn anything."

Reese nodded and headed for the door. Her cheeks were still pink.

Cyrus stepped to Reid. Jasmine was still face down on the unforgiving floor. She was pinned beneath Reid's knee while he tried to find a way to position the handcuff on her thin right wrist. The bones were visible beneath her skin, wedged at unnatural angles and poking sharply against the flesh. Every time Reid moved, Jasmine whimpered in pain.

It took a moment to find a clean sheet of paper on the shambles that was Barnabe's desk. Cyrus scribbled the name of a drug on it and knelt beside Reid. "There's a pharmacy down the street," he said. "Get a supply of this and a syringe. We need to keep her doped while she's in custody."

Reid offered a blank look in response.

"She's a Reader," Cyrus explained. "Consider the secrets you don't want her to know. Every thought that crosses your mind is fair game. The same goes for anyone in proximity. She's out of commission while she's in pain, but that won't last forever. If we don't dull her senses, we'll be putting a fox inside the henhouse."

The concern was obvious in Reid's expression. He took the sheet of paper and stepped away from Jasmine. "What about you? Something tells me you have more secrets than any of us."

"She can't read me," Cyrus said.

Reid looked concerned.

"I know," Cyrus said. "Even the Readers don't know why. Seems I'm the only one they've encountered who can't be Read."

"You've met more of these...*people*? I know you had that thing with the Pusher a few years back. But I don't recall anything about a Reader."

Cyrus shrugged and eyed the paper in Reid's hands.

"Alright," Reid relented.

Watching Reid leave, Cyrus considered the report he'd

filed after the Waterford case. Neither it nor his debrief had included particulars relating to Ashley's ability. Though he'd been early in his time with the Coalition, something told him that leaving her mind-reading ability out of the report would be better for her in the long run. It was the correct decision, given everything that had happened with the Coalition since then.

Now he knew Ashley Waterford wasn't the only Reader out there. It opened the door to a range of concerns. If Ashley wasn't the only Reader, did it mean her brother, William, wasn't the only Pusher? And if there were more like them, how many were there? Were they all linked to the Order of Origin? It seemed likely they could all be traced back to Gertrude Waterford's work, but that was only an assumption. How could he confirm it? And maybe most importantly, if Waterford's work had resulted in Readers and Pushers, what other empowered individuals might she have created?

Cyrus ground his teeth.

Why am I the only one immune to the Readers?

Chapter 27 - Tough Luck

Meeker stood across the street from the Book Barn in the mouth of the adjacent alley. Peering from behind a dumpster, he'd seen Luke Reid arrive with the rest of the team. He dropped the handheld radio into a pile of refuse, confused by Jasmine's abrupt termination of communication.

Minutes later, he saw the woman led from the storefront in shackles. She was limping, and her face was scrunched in what must have been substantial pain. Meeker smiled at the woman's devastating defeat and in recognition of what this would do for his position in the Order.

"Your loss, my gain," he whispered as he disappeared deeper into the alley. "Tough luck."

Chapter 28 - Little Tool

Manhattan, New York

The drive back to Manhattan was uneventful. Cyrus piloted the rental while Reese passed the time sitting quietly in the passenger seat. Peacefulness had taken some time to settle over the car, however. Barnabe was in the backseat; he'd been a chatterbox for the first thirty to forty miles. He'd talked non-stop, a reluctant addition to the trip, asking dozens of questions. Reese found his demeanor abrasive and irritating even after he had a chance to calm down following the events at the bookstore. Since they'd left Providence, Cyrus hadn't been talkative. He'd met Barnabe's endless questions with stoic indifference. In fact, he'd offered the young man very few words in reply to direct questions. Barnabe finally took the hint once confronted with Cyrus's withering stare, offered through the rearview mirror. He'd fallen into a sullen, silent state that had lasted the remainder of the journey. Reese knew the questions would return, it was only a matter of time. Once they reached the safe house, dozens of new questions would be added to his unaddressed growing list.

Reese watched Cyrus as the car slowed on the city streets.

His eyes were in constant motion, observing the traffic ahead and around them. She knew he habitually maintained an inventory of the cars in the rearview, watching for any hint of a tail. It was a routine she'd become accustomed to. But they were in the clear. If he'd seen something, she would've read it in his demeanor.

He'd been quiet on the long drive—far quieter than normal. What had happened in Providence had weighed heavily on him. Though she didn't fully understand the meaning of events, she respected that he wouldn't explain it in front of Barnabe.

Barnabe had been an unwelcome surprise, but Cyrus had insisted on bringing him along. She and Barnabe had both bristled at the idea; it was the first thing on which the two had ever agreed. She found any harmony with Barnabe unsettling. Barnabe was unpleasant—as unlikeable of a person as she'd ever met. He seemed to go out of his way to alienate those around him. His personality wasn't just abrasive, it was caustic. She felt on edge just having him near.

The Order had an interest in Barnabe, Cyrus had explained. He wouldn't be safe until they knew the full extent of that interest. It seemed related to the small leather-bound book Barnabe had scanned into his computer. For reasons still unclear, Barnabe had proven reluctant to discuss that matter.

Cyrus had been upfront with Barnabe, explaining that they also needed his help. He clarified they needed his assistance with some maps, but he didn't go into detail. Barnabe seemed interested, but Reese guessed he was more motivated by having something to hold over them than he was in the actual work. She didn't know him well, but it was more like Barnabe to enjoy leverage over others than to be interested in a challenge.

He wasn't that deep or difficult to understand.

They'd faced off shortly before leaving Providence. Reese was still irritated over the brief interaction.

"I don't see what you bring to the table," Barnabe said. He walked around the parked car and made of show of gather his personal effects. "You need my help. *I don't need you.*"

Cyrus stood beside the car, obviously reluctant to speak. Reese could tell he was studying Barnabe, but she didn't know what he was waiting for. They needed Barnabe—at least, his image processing algorithms to parse the lunar images. She didn't understand why Cyrus was choosing to remain silent.

"You don't need us?" Reese countered. She looked at Cyrus. "We should go. They said he was smart—he was supposed to be some kind of genius. If he couldn't tell those people were there for him, he's a fool."

Cyrus nodded. He waited for a beat, then put his hand on the driver-side door handle.

"They wouldn't hurt me," Barnabe said. "They needed me."

Reese glared at him. "There's no question they needed you," she countered. "If you had half a brain, you'd be more concerned about what happened after that. What would they do when they didn't need you anymore? What happens once they have what they want? Did you see how many guns were in that room?"

Barnabe ran his hands through his hair and paced back and forth. He started to speak but stopped short. More pacing followed. "What about you?" he said. "You brought guns, too!"

Reese looked at Cyrus. It was the kind of look that said, *is he kidding?* "Listen to me, you little twerp," she said instead. "At any point, did *either of us* point a gun at you? Did we threaten you in any way?" She was practically yelling now—asking questions but leaving no time for answers.

"Who got you out of that room alive, you little tool?" she grumbled quietly.

Cyrus looked at Barnabe, who met his gaze and offered a look that said, *is she for real?* Cyrus simply shrugged and opened the car door.

"Wait!" Barnabe relented. "Just wait a second."

"You wait a second, you ungrateful twerp," Reese said. She circled to the passenger side door and flipped the release. "We came looking for your help and ended up saving your ass. We're still asking for your help and willing to pay for it. Nothing is worth putting up with your attitude." She looked at Cyrus. "What was the name of the second guy on the list? We were warned about Barnabe— you were right. We should've gone with whats-his-name…"

"Fuller! Not Fuller?" Barnabe griped.

Cyrus snapped his fingers and pointed at Barnabe. "That was it," he said. "Fuller. They said Barnabe wasn't worth the trouble. Fuller would get the job done and without the attitude."

"Lesson learned," Reese said. She shot a scathing look at Barnabe. "Good luck with the thrill-kill-cult. You were made for each other."

Reese slipped into the passenger seat and pulled the door closed with an angry bang. Barnabe was at her window in a heartbeat. Unfortunately, the window had been left open.

"Wait a minute," Barnabe pleaded. "Just wait!"

Cyrus slipped behind the wheel and closed his door. Barnabe leaned against the passenger door and fixed each of them with a pained, helpless expression. "Please wait?" he asked.

Reese stared at him silently. Cyrus said nothing.

"Can you protect me?" Barnabe asked. "I mean, for real.

Can you keep me safe?"

Reese shot Cyrus a look as if seeking his opinion as to whether Barnabe was even worth the effort. Cyrus let the moment hang. Finally, he tipped his head slightly to acknowledge the affirmative.

"Are you sure?" Barnabe insisted.

"He got you out of there alive, didn't he?" Reese countered. "But ask the question again—just once more, I dare you. We'll leave you here to try your luck with the local police. See if they can protect you."

Barnabe held up both hands in a mock defensive gesture, but his face was entirely serious. "If you get me out of this, I'll help you with whatever you need, no charge. Just don't let the Order near me."

That had sealed the deal. For better or worse, Barnabe was their third wheel for the duration.

Reese still harbored the sinking feeling that he would be more trouble than he was worth. She spent the rest of the drive back to Manhattan consoling herself with the fact that she and Cyrus had effectively scammed Barnabe into participating. There had been no second name on their list. Barnabe was the go-to name for finding whatever the Chinese were searching for.

Chapter 29 - Expediency

Plains, Montana, United States

Fiona Bell followed Verhoeven as he stepped from the elevator more than three hundred feet below the surface of their facility outside of Plains, Montana. This was level four; Verhoeven had been spending a great deal of time here recently. He hadn't explained the reason behind his long hours in seclusion. Apparently, he was finally willing to share the results of his most recent endeavor.

Verhoeven led her down the wide, concrete-lined hall before turning right into what she knew was the level's main laboratory. A new reactor had been installed just to power whatever Verhoeven had been constructing. While he'd been working here, she had supervised its installation on Level Eight.

Twelve oblong conditioning pods were arranged in a circle in the center of the room. Each bed was vaguely human-shaped: an elongated oval that was closer to a teardrop in its form. One of the technicians lay on the bed while another worked the array of touchscreen controls built into the unit's frame. The bed, or pod as they called it, was wide at the shoulders and narrowed slowly closer to the occupant's hips and even further at the foot. Similarly, its curved form swept inward above the shoulders, drawing to a curved apex above the head.

The dozen pods were arranged in a circle, like the petals of a flower, the foot of each at the center and the heads fanning out in a pattern that allowed technicians easy access to the controls of each device. Thick wires snaked at the foot of each pod and disappeared into a wide black barrel-shaped tower as tall as a man at the center of the configuration. It was the processing core, Fiona realized. She'd never seen the conditioning pods in this configuration before.

Verhoeven must have read the question on her face because he was smiling when she looked at him. "Impressive, isn't it?" he said.

She nodded. "It looks like we're ready for the Migration," she said. If that was the case, they were ahead of schedule.

"No," Verhoeven said. He pointed to a pair of technicians wheeling another pod across the room. This one was different. It stood upright on the wheeled cart and had a small ledge at the bottom to stand on.

The technicians rolled the new device around the perimeter of the other pods, stopping at what she judged to be the circle's 9 o'clock position. The apparatus was lowered from the cart. This unit remained upright, supported by a sleek silver tubular steel frame. One tech set about stringing a thick cable from the pod's rear. He threaded it across the floor and attached it to the core at the center of the adjacent cluster.

The remaining tech reclined the vertical pod, tipping the head backward and the foot forward by thirty degrees. Whoever used this pod would stand in it, reclined slightly. That was unusual because it suggested that the device's operator would remain conscious. The other pods lay flat like beds because their occupants would be dormant and anesthetized.

Verhoeven must have understood she was searching for meaning in what she saw because a satisfied smile crossed his face once more. "We're preparing for visitors," he said. He pointed to the vast open section of floor to their right. "Another cluster will be assembled there. We have room for another if necessary, though I doubt that will be required."

The pods were used for neural reconditioning, Fiona knew. Two decades of research had gone into their design and development. Now, they worked efficiently, provided the subjects in them matched the appropriate prerequisites. Still, she'd never seen the pods used in this configuration. There was no application calling for them to be networked in such a way—at least not until the Migration. But when that time came, they wouldn't be slaved to a single processing core. Judging by this configuration, it was as if all pods were going to be subjected to the same—

Fiona's eyes went wide as understanding dawned. Verhoeven laughed at her expression. She was unable to conceal the admiration in her eyes. The pods were not initially designed for this…but it was a brilliant idea.

"But why?" she asked before realizing the words had left her lips.

"Expediency," Verhoeven said in a flat, neutral tone. "We're dealing with too many people, and our timetable is short. The latest report shows that the Blight has begun to spread more rapidly. We no longer have the luxury of *time*."

His voice had an undercurrent of disdain when he said the last word. Fiona knew precisely what he meant. Time was a curse upon their race, though she knew Verhoeven had a unique contempt for the foreign concept. His body was weak and growing increasingly frail by the day.

"What about Alex Dashell?" she asked. A level of personal concern was unmistakable in her voice.

"Javier Cruze is currently in Florida," Verhoeven said. Javier was the younger of two brothers loyal to the Order. So loyal that not even the sacrifice of his brother in Rhode Island had phased him. "He will retrieve him. The test results are back; His ratings are off the charts. There's no question he *is* one of the twelve."

She breathed easier, given this new information. "*Finally*. We're lucky any of them survived. Could there be more of them out there?"

Verhoeven began inspecting the upright pod and its connections. He paused and met her eye. "Soon, it won't matter. Thanks to our selection process and the augmentation regimen, the others will be spared what happened to us. Too many of us have died already. We must act decisively if we're to have any future at all."

Fiona watched as Verhoeven tracked the pair of thick cables running from the back of the pod. He followed them to the processing core at the center of the cluster. Watching him stoop beneath the support ring attaching the twelve pods was troubling. His movements were slow and clumsy. He was obviously in a great deal of pain. She could tell that his deterioration was progressing unchecked now. Still, he said nothing, and she pretended not to notice his condition. Once he cleared the minor obstacle of the support ring, it took him only seconds to confirm the configuration of the wires to the array. She could read only satisfaction in his face.

"A set of pods is ready for the second configuration," Verhoeven said, pointing to the empty space near the back of the room. "Everything is waiting on Level 2. Please supervise the technicians and ensure the second array is completed and operational by midnight. I'm going to monitor Cruze's progress with Dashell."

Fiona watched as Verhoeven limped awkwardly from the room. Her thoughts returned to the catastrophic operation in New England. She was relieved when Verhoeven hadn't blamed her for their inability to retrieve the journal. Meeker's failure wasn't a shock. The smug little man had always been wired wrong. Jasmine, on the other hand, was a powerful Reader. She had never failed to complete an assignment.

Now, she never would again. It was a shame.

Somehow, Verhoeven thought his modified pods would solve the mystery of the journal and accelerate the Migration. Apparently, he wasn't in the mood to share his plan—at least not yet. That didn't bother her much. As long as they were accelerating the timetable, she was satisfied. Their people were dying, and time, she lamented, was not on their side.

Chapter 30 - Over the Edge

Sarasota, Florida, United States

Javier Cruze walked down the silent coastal road. Residential buildings lined the street on both sides. According to what he'd read, they were upscale, single-family homes, the least of them worth at least a half million dollars. The Gulf could be seen in the moonlight beyond the yards of the houses to his right. These were people who paid through the nose for the privilege of living right on the water, only to risk having their homes wiped out each time a hurricane moved through the area.

The entire idea of living in such a place irritated Cruze. He'd grown up in a village deep in the heart of Mexico. The place he'd come from was so poor that the town, if it could be called that, didn't even have a name. But the people here weren't even living extravagant lifestyles. Where he stood, homes could easily cost more than a million dollars, but he wasn't looking at mansions or impressive estates. The houses were small, perhaps two thousand square feet at most, and on quarter-acre plots of land. It was their proximity to the coast that made them valuable.

It was a value Cruze couldn't see. He wasn't impressed.

He strolled down the street. The moon was nearly full, and the block was silent. Here and there, a car sat in the occasional driveway, but by and large, most had been sequestered to garages for the duration of the night. The street was deserted. There wasn't a car parked along the street as far as the eye could see. It was the reason he was moving in on foot. Leaving his ride on the road would risk drawing attention in a neighborhood like this.

Cruze passed a dozen mailboxes before he found the house he'd been looking for. He looked left and right to ensure he was still alone, then walked briskly up the short concrete driveway. There were lights on in several of the single-story ranch's front windows. His target didn't live alone, but that wasn't a concern. Stopping at the front door, Cruze pressed the button for the doorbell.

The first response was the bark of a dog. It was the incessant yapping of some small breed that irritated Cruze. He didn't like dogs–he didn't care for cats either. The barking grew more insistent, and he could judge the dog's location. If he was right, the animal was in the backyard. The clatter of its bark rattled through the house and out the open front windows because he could also hear the same sound from outside. The racket reflected off the homes of both nearby neighbors and reached him in the front yard.

At least he wouldn't have to deal with the dog, Cruze was thinking as he heard the sound of footsteps behind the front door. The lock jiggled and the knob turned. A young woman peeked around the edge of the doorway and eyed him.

"Can I help you?" she asked.

She was a teenager. Long hair and freckles. "I'm looking for Alex Dashell," Cruze said. His voice carried a heavy Spanish accent. "Is he home?"

The girl scrunched up her face. It might've been because

of the question. It was also a late hour to receive visitors. Or it could've been because of his accent. He didn't figure the Dashell family received many Mexican visitors. Not unless they were there to clean the pool or mow the lawn. His knuckles creaked as he clenched his fists with irritation.

The girl must have noticed. Her eyes narrowed a moment before the door slammed shut. "Dad!" he heard her yell from beyond the threshold. "Daddy! Help!"

It was all the confirmation Cruze needed. His target was home. He backed up half a step and braced himself as if he were going to kick in the door. His focus narrowed on the doorknob and deadbolt lock, and he lashed out with his mind. Though he never moved a step, the door exploded in splinters along the leading edge. It blasted inward, swinging wildly on its hinges as a shower of fractured wood landed at Cruze's unmoving feet.

Cruze stepped forward. He moved through the door and found the teenage girl ten yards away, sitting on her backside in the hallway. She stared up at him through unblinking eyes. He pulled a silenced semi-automatic from inside his windbreaker and shot her once through the heart. She crumpled to the tile floor without making a sound.

There was a scream, and Cruze turned. A woman was standing in the doorway to his right. The mother, he assumed. She was young to have a teenage daughter, maybe no more than twenty-five herself. The daughter was adopted, he reminded himself. The family details were part of the information packet provided, along with the home address. Cruze hadn't paid much attention to the particulars relating to the family. Retrieving the father was the objective. The rest was white noise as far as he was concerned. He would approach the operation with his normal level of enthusiasm. As long as he took the father unharmed, Verhoeven wouldn't object.

The woman was wearing pajama pants and a T-shirt. Tears were already streaming from her eyes. Cruze silenced her display with a single bullet to her heart.

There was a door banging against its frame somewhere near the back of the house and Cruze heard a man's voice. He couldn't make out the words, but he assumed it must be his target. He stepped over the crumpled form of the teenager and walked further into the house. He arrived in the kitchen just as a man entered the room from the other end. The man held a pump action shotgun in shaky hands. He skidded to a stop at the sight of Cruze, and his eyes went wide.

Cruze smiled at the sight of the shotgun. He never understood what made people think they were good for home defense. Sure, hitting the target with a shot in their general direction might be possible—but that was only if the gun was loaded with the right kind of rounds. In his experience, shotguns were too long and bulky for good home defense.

The man pumped the shotgun. The metal-on-metal ratcheting sound seemed to fill the small kitchen. "Don't move!" the man bellowed. "Don't move, or I'll shoot!"

Cruze studied the man. He was in his mid to late twenties and maybe six feet tall with short, sandy blond hair. He had bright, intelligent eyes that stared at him in a fit of panic. That he hadn't fired already was interesting, Cruze thought. Personally, he would've pulled the trigger by now. He wouldn't have hesitated for a second.

With his gun hanging casually in the grip of his right hand, Cruze took a step forward. The man retreated by a step rather than fire. Cruze knew he would, and his smile grew wide.

"Not another step!" the man yelled. His voice was strained and seemed on the brink of panic.

What would it take to put him over the edge?

"You might as well shoot," Cruze said. His voice was low,

and his accent was thick. "What do you have to lose? Your wife and daughter are dead."

Dashell's eyes narrowed. Cruze expected a momentary delay as the reality of the words crept in, but there was none. The shotgun roared. The muzzle flash lit the dark kitchen, and the gun rocked in Dashell's hands. He hadn't yet raised it to his shoulder, instead shooting from the hip at close range.

The flash of light filled Cruze's eyes and he felt heat from the gun's discharge slap him in the face. He should've taken the brunt of the blast square in the chest—Dashell's aim had been true, and their proximity made the shot a certainty—but Cruze remained standing and unharmed.

Dashell was shocked by Cruze's survival. But to his credit, he had the presence of mind to fire once more. Cruze heard the clank of the shotgun as Dashell attempted to pump the next round into the chamber. The sound was irregular because the pump wouldn't cycle properly. Dashell was making his second attempt when Cruze's vision cleared enough to see him. The muzzle flash had blinded him momentarily in the darkness.

Dashell retreated by two steps and fought with his weapon. The action failed to cycle, so he couldn't prepare it to fire the next round. Cruze saw the light switch on the wall beside Dashell and reached out with his mind. It flipped and the overhead lights blazed, chasing every shadow from the room. Dashell retreated yet another step, his head swiveling frantically as he tried to understand how the lights had come on when Cruze hadn't moved even a step.

Cruze waited patiently. This was the part of the job that made his work fun. Dashell hadn't yet reached the most exciting part of their encounter, so Cruze waited and watched.

It took only a second or two for Dashell's gaze to fall on Cruze. Once it did, the shotgun slipped from his hands and crashed to the floor. Dashell stared with unblinking eyes as he realized how the intruder had survived the shotgun blast. Hanging there in the air between the two of them was a cloud of BB-sized buckshot from his gun. It just floated there, suspended in mid-air, two feet from Cruze's chest.

Cruze studied the buckshot with amusement. At least Dashell had used the proper load for home defense, he mused.

His eyes fell fully on Dashell once more. "This was fun," he said. Then he reached out with his will and Dashell was smashed against the wall, knocking him unconscious.

Slipping a phone from his pocket, Cruze tapped a number from his speed dial. "Bring the van around," he said. "It's done."

Chapter 31 - Social Skills of a Single-Celled Organism

Manhattan, New York

The elevator dinged and the doors parted. Cyrus stepped from the car and proceeded down the long hallway. Barnabe and Reese followed him. "I still think I should've brought my equipment," Barnabe persisted. "My hardware is custom. I have two dozen processors running in parallel with a proprietary liquid cooling system. I'm talking about some hardcore overclocking—not some amateur hack job."

"I told you, I'll set you up on a server cluster that will more than meet your needs." This discussion had already gone on for longer than necessary, as far as Cyrus was concerned. "I promise, everything you need will be provided."

"I realize you *think* that's the case," Barnabe argued. "Substantial resources are required for my algorithms to run with any level of efficacy."

Cyrus grinned and shot a glance over his shoulder. Finally, an argument that would put the kid on his heels. "Are you saying your code isn't optimized?"

"What? My code is tight. Don't be ridiculous!" Barnabe sounded confused, then offended. "I just don't believe you're intelligent enough to understand the scope of resources I require."

Cyrus stopped short. Barnabe was still flustered by his last statement and missed the abrupt halt. He collided with Cyrus, bouncing off him as surely as he'd struck a solid wall.

Cyrus turned slowly and offered a withering glare.

"Ah..." Barnabe stammered. "No offense..."

With a tired shake of his head, Cyrus pulled a key from his pocket and inserted it into the deadbolt lock on the door to his immediate left. After repeating the procedure on a locked doorknob, he pushed through the entry and into the apartment. He held the door, and Reese swept past. A prim, satisfied smile on the corners of her lips. She knew he was egging Barnabe on. The kid was a little asshat with the social skills of a single-celled organism. Where Barnabe seemed to enjoy rubbing people the wrong way, Cyrus was finding amusement where he could and putting him in one awkward situation after another.

When Barnabe passed through the door, he did it at twice the speed of Reese. Proximity to Cyrus seemed to make him increasingly uncomfortable. At least they had that much in common. Cyrus eased the door shut and secured both locks.

Barnabe walked through the small, barren apartment. There was no furniture. Likewise, there was no television or radio. A scowl creased his brow as he ducked down the rear hallway to check the bedrooms and the bathroom. Cyrus knew he would find no dressers, just as there were no beds. There wasn't even toilet paper in the bathroom. A thick layer of dust had collected on the kitchen counter and was obvious on the sills of both living room windows.

"I don't get it," Barnabe said as he returned from the back hall. "This is your idea of a safe house? It's terrible. I can't live like this. No one could live like this. You can't expect me to—"

"Barnabe," Cyrus cut in. "If you stop talking for a minute and relax, everything will make sense."

The kid was getting more excited with every passing second. Cyrus's words had a startling effect, if not a calming one. Barnabe watched him for a moment before finally blinking and taking a breath. His entire body seemed to relax when he took another protracted inhalation. Cyrus saw Barnabe's eyes fall on the wide circular platform in the center of the living room floor.

"What's that?" Barnabe asked.

The platform was about three feet in diameter, raised from the floor by two stairs. Aside from the pair of steps, the perimeter of the platform was plated in a flawless chrome finish. The deck was coated in a non-reflective, nonslip material, completely dust-free. The platform was the only part of the apartment that was immaculate.

"I don't get it," Barnabe persisted. "What's going on."

Reese smiled. "We promised to take you someplace safe." She stepped onto the platform and turned to face Cyrus and Barnabe. "See you on the other side."

Cyrus tapped the last button and completed the sequence on the mobile phone in his hand. A low, quiet growl emanated from deep inside the platform. Three flashes of light came back to back, each brighter than the last. The sequence took less than a second to complete. When the light disappeared, Reese had vanished.

Barnabe stood with his mouth agape and his eyes unblinking. Seconds passed. He didn't speak—he didn't even move.

"What…What just happened?" he said at last. He was still looking straight ahead as if afraid to take his eyes off the platform. Maybe thinking that, if he did, he would miss the rest of the prank.

"She's gone," Cyrus said. "Step up there. You're next."

Turning his head slowly, Barnaby's face was still slack with shock. "Next...for what?"

Cyrus rolled his eyes. "Just get up there. We don't have all day."

To his credit, Barnabe did as instructed. Moving in slow robotic shifts, he shuffled up the pair of steps and took his spot in the middle of the small stage. His eyes were wide as he watched Cyrus.

"Now wha—"

Cyrus tapped the button on his phone and the lights pulsed once more. A half second later, Barnabe was gone. Cyrus smiled and took a deep breath. The silence was blissful. Having the room to himself seemed almost heavenly. How could he have come to dislike someone so much in such a short stretch of time?

The phone in Cyrus's hand began vibrating incessantly. A powerful pulse shook the device with a ferocity well beyond its normal silent ringer. He glanced down to see a red bar across the top edge of the screen, just below the clock. Tapping it, an alert message filled the screen.

What the hell?

He jumped onto the platform and entered the activation sequence once more. The light flashed, and dark, cold concrete slabs replaced the apartment around him.

Chapter 32 - Not a Tracking Signal

Undisclosed location, Australia

Reese was already moving the detection wand over her feet when the stabbing light pulse announced Cyrus's arrival. She glanced up in time to see him retrieve a second wand from the small cabinet bolted to the concrete wall and shove Barnabe to the other side of the small room.

Barnabe stumbled as Cyrus manhandled him. The backpack he'd been holding fell from his hands, spilling some of its contents. "What's going on?" he stammered.

"Anything?" Cyrus said, shooting a glance over his shoulder to Reese.

Reese had the wand up to her shoulders but hadn't yet triggered a reading. She moved it over her head and circled her skull for good measure. "It's not me," she confirmed.

Cyrus was already waving the wand over Barnabe. He started with Barnabe's head before moving down his torso. When he reached his feet, he spun Barnabe 180 degrees and repeated the process, this time sweeping his back. Reese knew the second pass was unnecessary; the scanner could detect signals within 36 inches of the wand. She knelt over Barnabe's bag and played the wand across it for good measure. A shrill beep emanated from the scanning device.

She sensed Cyrus's attention as she set the scanner aside. Losing the cinch scrap at the top of the shoulder duffle, Reese spilled the remaining contents of the bag across the cold floor. Cyrus went to the cabinet and returned with a small handheld device. He passed it to her.

Reese began preparing the spectrum analyzer while Cyrus arranged the contents of Barnabe's bag evenly across the floor. It took her only seconds to put the device in the proper mode. When she looked down, she surveyed the handful of items Barnabe had brought. He had a pair of jeans, two shirts, an extra set of socks, underpants with far more holes than was standard, several pens, a spiral-bound notebook, an asthma inhaler, and the strange leather-bound book.

She shot a look at Cyrus. "That's it?" She was expecting more. A phone, laptop, some clothes… Nothing present should have been giving off a radio transmission.

Cyrus turned Barnabe's bag upside down and shook it. Nothing came out. "Start with the bag," Cyrus suggested. "It would be the easiest to bug."

Reese set the bag aside and extended a short wand-like antenna from the end of the device. She played it slowly over the surface of the backpack. She covered every inch of the front surface without detecting a positive reading. Cyrus flipped the pack face down on the floor. Repeating the process a second time produced the same negative result.

Her brows furrowed, Reese moved on to the remaining contents of the pack. They were several stories underground in a facility that was originally designed to withstand a nuclear strike. They had also retrofitted the base after claiming it for their own. The teleportation room had been further shielded to insulate it for this sort of eventuality, but that didn't mean they were safe. Locating the source of the rogue signal was still critical. Until they identified the source, they couldn't be entirely certain their location hadn't been compromised.

Scanning Barnabe's sundries was a simple matter. The process took only seconds and failed to produce results. The moment Reese placed the scanner near the leather bound journal, a reading registered on the screen in her hand.

Reese's mouth went dry, and her pulse quickened. She passed the device over the book once more, repeating the process far more slowly the second time.

Cyrus was already tapping the screen of his phone. The platform behind them began to hum as power cycled through it. "Give it to me," Cyrus said. "I'll get it out of here."

They'd both been kneeling over the book. Cyrus snatched it from the floor and climbed to his feet. Reese looked up at him through pinched eyes. She raised one finger and shook her head absently to stay his departure.

"No," she finally managed to say. "It's alright. It's not a tracking signal."

Reese rocked back on her heels and sat down on the floor. She folded her legs before her and stared at the small device in her lap. The readings made it clear that it wasn't a radio transmission, but that didn't mean she understood what she was seeing. She considered the screen and the unusual energy signature. It was unlike anything she'd ever seen before. No one had.

Cyrus eyed Barnabe who stood with his back to the cold concrete wall. It was clear he didn't understand what was happening. Barnabe's gaze shifted away from Reese sitting on the floor. He stared at the teleportation platform. His eyes blinked slowly. He was still wrestling with the idea that he'd been teleported to a new location. The wonder of it would keep him distracted for the time being.

Taking a place on the floor beside Reese, Cyrus placed a hand on her knee. "Are you alright? What is it?" he asked.

She shook her head slowly and absently, staring at the book in her grip. A moment later, she seemed to refocus on the present. "It's not a transmission," she confirmed. "It's not strong enough to track us, I can say that for sure."

Cyrus wasn't ready to place confidence in the assessment quite as easily. "Are you sure? Radioactive isotopes emit a slight but unique signature that can be tracked by satellite. Maybe that's what you're seeing."

Reese shook her head. "This isn't radioactive…at least not in any way we're familiar with. It has a strange signature, though. It was enough to trigger the sensor inside the platform, but it's not an explosive and certainly not a transmission. If I didn't know better, I would say it was a power source."

Taking the book, Cyrus rolled it over in his hands and considered every observation with fresh eyes. He ran his fingers across the front and back covers, then down the narrow spine. He didn't feel any unusual bumps or gaps in the texture that hinted at something concealed beneath the material. He flipped it over and fanned the pages. The writing was strange and indecipherable, handwritten in a peculiar, unintelligible script. There was nothing concealed between the pages. Passing the book to Reese, he let her scan it once more.

"Whatever it is, the signature is stable," she said. "I'll need more sensitive tools to narrow down the part of the book generating the signal. As far as I can tell right now, the entire book is encased in a subtle power field. Whatever it is, I've never seen anything like it."

Barnabe knelt beside Cyrus. Saying nothing for a long moment, he stared at the book in Reese's hands. "I might have some insight into that," he said finally. "I don't think that's really a book."

Chapter 33 - Manmade Lightning

Plains, Montana, United States

The numbers over the elevator door moved with agonizing slowness. The car jolted to a stop as it reached Sub-level 4, and a muffled ding sounded from somewhere in the antiquated electronic control system. At last, the door slid open and Fiona Bell pushed past a pair of technicians waiting for the car. She moved quickly down the corridor while fighting the urge to break into a run. Verhoeven had promised to notify her before beginning the procedure. That hadn't happened. Apparently, he had grown impatient. If the security office hadn't called to report the unusual power draw on SL-4, she would still be unaware of the procedure.

Shouldering through a heavy set of doors, Fiona stepped into Lab Number 3. What she saw froze her in her tracks. The lights had been turned down low, but the room pulsed with sharp blue strobes of illumination. A sphere hovered in mid-air, sizzling and sparking as blue foot-long fingers of electricity danced across its surface. The globe was about three feet in diameter and might have been transparent. The glare from the vibrant blue light hurt her eyes and made it impossible to be sure.

The air was thick with static electricity and smelled of ozone. A pair of conditioning pods lay side-by-side beneath the hovering orb. She could see the silhouette of a man on each bed, though their features were impossible to discern, given the constant shifts of light and shadow. She'd seen the procedure before but never like this. She'd never seen the orb this large, and it had never thrown out bolts of blue electricity before. Judging by its current size, it was powered by at least twice as much energy as they'd used on even their most aggressive Transplant. She didn't know how the Vessel could sustain the influx. No wonder Verhoeven hadn't told her what he had planned. If Verhoeven was right and Alex Dashell survived this, Verhoeven's own body would be destroyed.

Still, the procedure had begun, and there was no turning back. Fiona moved to the edge of the room as a stray bolt of static electricity cracked through the air like manmade lightning.

Her heart was in her throat. Maybe it was a mistake to enter the room at all. As if to illustrate the point, another blue bolt of static electricity cracked and leaped beyond what had previously been considered the safe perimeter. It struck a wheeled metal cart and sent it tumbling into the darkness.

Shrieking despite herself, Fiona moved toward the door. She didn't get far. More lightning rang out. This bolt struck the concrete wall less than two feet before her face. Shards of rubble exploded from the surface and struck her upraised arms.

Dropping to the floor, Fiona rolled against the base of the vertical surface. She put every possible inch of distance between herself and the sphere. Her eyes widened as they fell on the source of the lightning once more. The orb had grown at least a foot since she'd entered the room. It hovered perhaps three feet shy of the ceiling. Still centered over the pair of Conditioning pods, the bottom of the ball was now within five feet of the men inside. If it continued to grow, they would never survive. Jacobs Ladders, long crooked fingers of electricity, danced across the surface of both beds. It was as if some kind of invisible field protected the men inside.

In the past, the procedure looked nothing like this.

Eyeing the door, Fiona considered crawling for safety. The air was thick with an electrical charge that seemed to permeate her bones. What the hell was he thinking? He was desperate, to be sure. But there was no way the Vessel would survive this. No human could endure this level of infusion.

All at once, the room went dark and silent. It was so sudden that Fiona moved her hands quickly between her ears and her eyes to be sure she was still conscious. A low rumble sounded from the middle of the room, and a dull orange light danced across the levitating globe. Rocking upright, Fiona put her back against the wall and pulled her knees tight to her chest. The orb began to shrink. Its size reduced slowly at first, but the speed increased as its diameter grew and then shrank. Finally, there was a pop, and the light was gone altogether. The sound hadn't come from the sphere, Fiona realized. The quiet noise had been the sound of her ears popping. The air pressure had changed suddenly at the same moment that the ball of light disappeared for the last time.

The sudden silence seemed deafening. Fiona felt her heart racing. She wanted to stand, but her entire body trembled. She knew it was a weakness resulting from the exposure to the electromagnetic fields.

Lights scattered around the perimeter of the room suddenly engaged. They came to life slowly, beginning as a pale glow. The illumination brightened slowly but steadily until the lab was bathed in about 80% of its normal brightness.

Fiona focused on the pair of pods in the center of the room

once more. A figure sat upright on the rightmost device. His face was expressionless, but he was observing her. Still unable to gain her feet, Fiona couldn't find her voice. She simply stared back at the man. It was Alex Dashell. His body had survived the procedure.

But what of his mind?

Dashell swung his legs over the side of the bed and slid barefoot to the floor. He was shirtless, wearing only a baggy set of pajama-like pants. His hair was a mess, likely because he was at ground zero for the single largest electrical storm Fiona had ever witnessed.

Padding slowly across the floor, Dashell paused to stand over Fiona. She stared up at him. He walked well enough, if a little clumsily. It was like he was getting used to a new pair of legs...and maybe he was.

Dashell leaned forward and offered Fiona a hand. He wobbled a bit as he leaned in her direction. For half a second, she thought he might fall forward and land on top of her. A smile spread across Dashell's face. He seemed to find his own awkwardness entertaining. Reluctantly, Fiona took his hand and was pulled to her feet.

"You look as though you've seen a ghost," Dashell said. His eyes were bright and filled with amusement. They remained fixed on her in a way she found unsettling. "Maybe you don't recognize me."

Fiona's brows arched as she stared into Dashell's eyes. They were bright and young and full of life. In truth, she didn't recognize what she saw or the way they looked at her. "Verhoeven? Is that you?"

"Of course," Dashell laughed. It was a deep murmur that resonated from his chest as well as his mouth. It was hearty and healthy.

"It worked?" she said in a quiet voice. "The light show...I didn't think there was any way you could survive the process. What were you thinking?"

She watched him closely. It was unsettling, even though she knew what to expect from the process. Alex Dashell was no more. His body was now host to Radley Verhoeven.

"It's this body," Verhoeven explained. He turned toward the pods and motioned for her to follow. "As we suspected, Dashell *was* one of the twelve. Gertrude did as we asked. These bodies are much more acceptable. We thought there was something wrong with Dashell when we examined his HGG. His readings were far from what we expected. It turned out that Waterford outdid herself. Dashell's HGG was off the charts. His neural pathways are far more reactive than we believed possible."

They stopped at the foot of the pods. A dark scorch scarred the fabric of where Dashell's body had been. Fiona looked Verhoeven over once more. The skin of his strong, broad shoulders was unmarked. There was no sign of damage from the procedure. She saw a proud grin on his face. He had already come to the same conclusion.

Looking back into the pods, Fiona went weak in the knees. Her eyes had fallen on Verhoeven's previous form. What was left of his old body looked worse than ever. The flesh on its bare chest was cracked with dry flakes as if blasted with a blowtorch. His face was even worse. The front of his skull had collapsed during the procedure. All of his hair had burned away, and thick gelatinous fluid still leaked from his ears and holes that had burned in his neck tissue. Some of the dark fluid had turned hard, crusting into black pools, likely due to the extreme temperatures present during the procedure. The odor of burnt pork hung in the air.

Fiona felt the content of her stomach churn and quickly looked away. She braced herself on the rail at the pod's side even though she was reluctant to touch the device.

Verhoeven laughed at her response. "We always knew I wouldn't get another chance at this," he said. "Dashell's

HGG factor meant I had to go all in. He was too resilient for anything less."

Fighting another wave of nausea, Fiona watched the floor. "We've never had a Transplant do that before."

"It's these bodies," Verhoeven said proudly. "Waterford did well. We need to know if more of the twelve survived."

His eyes moved across her form. She saw a new appreciation there. An interest, perhaps.

"We still don't know why your body accepted *this place*," he said. "Or why mine did not. If we could've made sense of it, the Migration would already be complete. But the mortality rate is far too high. The Migration remains the only hope for our people. Transplantation remains our only viable means. It's a shame we lost Waterford. This body is strong. It will make a more suitable long-term solution."

She was surprised. "You can tell already?"

Verhoeven nodded. "No question about it."

"It's still only a stopgap," Fiona countered. "You may have found a long-term solution, but we suffered a major loss when Waterford was killed. The first round of hosts will last twenty, perhaps twenty-five years at most. Then we're back where we started. We can move to new hosts, but that's only a short-term solution. Your second host lasted eight years—your third, only three."

"Yes, but this will buy us more time," Verhoeven said. "Once the Migration is complete, we will focus all efforts on recreating Waterford's work. Perhaps even building on what Nyland discovered. Once the Migration is complete, time will finally be on our side."

Time, she lamented. It was such a foreign concept where they came from. Here, it meant everything. "Nyland set our cause back by decades," Fiona grumbled. "The delay has already cost millions of lives. We can't wait. If we don't act soon, our race will be lost."

Chapter 34 - Understanding the Real Problem

Undisclosed location, Australia

It was just before 10 a.m., and the entire team was assembled in the dining hall. Cyrus had just finished introducing Barnabe to the group. The kid had made an effort to look unimpressed as each member explained who they were and briefly summarized their specialty area, but by the time introductions had concluded, Cyrus could tell Barnabe was dazzled. The kid would never admit as much, but how he'd remained silent and engaged throughout the process spoke volumes.

Dennis and Sanjay retreated to a table at the room's periphery, where their laptops waited. Barnabe watched them with curious eyes. Alfie was a skeletal-looking wisp of a man of Arab descent with dark skin, dark hair, and sharp features. He offered Barnabe a quiet nod before leaving the dining hall. Chad Brewster was a burly ex-ball player with sandy blond hair and a personality that was the mirror opposite of Alfie. He slapped Barnabe on the shoulder and shook his hand before following Alfie from the room.

"So," Cyrus said. "What do you think?"

Barnabe dropped his backpack into an empty chair nearest the first large wooden table, one of many scattered through the main hall. He pulled out the chair beside it, lowered himself into the seat, and finished by offering a tired expression. "We're in an underground facility at a secret location somewhere under the Australian Outback," he summarized. "You've assembled a team of eggheads...apparently, you head the group, though you don't seem to share their intellect. From what I can tell, everyone on *your team* is much more highly educated. So why are you in charge? How could you lead any of them?"

Cyrus glanced at Reese but said nothing. Barnabe seemed to find an abrasive approach to every situation. He tried to invoke hostility with each breath. There wasn't much to like about him. Based on the look Reese was pointing at the kid, she shared his assessment.

Letting the silence hang, Cyrus took a seat opposite Barnabe. Three feet of table separated them. Reese moved past him, her hand slipping gently across Cyrus's shoulder and the back of his neck. She lowered into a chair at his side. The only other occupants of the central hall were Dennis and Sanjay, but they were working quietly in the distance. Barnabe wasn't causing trouble to attract attention; he was just being himself.

"I'm not in charge," Cyrus said. Reese responded by shooting him a contemplative look. It forced him to take a breath and reconsider the statement.

"You saved their lives, protected the technology, and instituted the plan for deployment," Reese said. "Using the proceeds from the Quantum Data Link deployment to subsidize the eventual release of the teleportation platforms was your idea. It solved a lot of problems within the group at the same time. They look to you as a leader, whether you like it or not."

Though he'd never wanted the responsibility, it had been thrust upon him a year earlier when his friend died, leaving him a mysterious inheritance. That inheritance had led him to his very first meeting with Reese. He had stepped in to defend the project and its researchers. Along the way, he'd become a part of something that would one day reshape the world.

"Alright," Cyrus relented. "For lack of a better phrase, fine. I'm in charge. But you're right. I'm not the brains of the outfit."

"So, what do you bring to the table?" Barnabe grumbled.

Reese leaned across the table and drew Barnabe's eye. "Show some respect. You're alive because of him. Every one of us owes him a similar debt. There's more to this team than accreditations."

Barnabe scowled. "You would say that," he grumbled. "You're screwing him. That doesn't make him—"

Cyrus jammed his palms against the side of the table and sent the massive wooden structure sliding in Barnabe's direction. The leading edge struck him in the chest, forced him against the back of his chair, and sent the chair sliding several inches across the floor with a high-pitched squeal.

"Get your shit," Cyrus snapped. He was on his feet and heading for the door. "I'm taking you back. You can deal with the Order by yourself."

Barnabe stared. He rubbed his chest and coughed air back into his lungs. He did not rise from his chair.

"Move your ass," Cyrus said. His tone was cold, and his voice was low, but he didn't seem angry. All the same, his reaction had a chilling effect on Barnabe. "Stop messing around. If you don't appreciate what we're doing for you, I'll take you back."

"You...you need me!" Barnabe sputtered.

"Plan B," Cyrus countered and motioned for the door. "There's always a plan B. We'll go with that."

"What? Why?" Barnabe warbled.

With his finger raised, Cyrus stalked back toward him, and his brows furrowed. "Because we don't need you nearly as much as you need us. And because I won't tolerate your disrespect—not toward me or anyone around me."

He placed both hands on the table and leaned closer to Barnabe. "In case this morning's events were wasted on you, Jasmine should've made it clear that the Order has it out for you. Whatever deal you had with them is no longer on the table. They're going to take what they want from you. You're so proud of your superior IQ? Want to bet the Order has more people like Jasmine—people entirely capable of tearing what they need right from your mind, whether you like it or not?"

Barnabe looked around the room. His glance fell briefly on Reese—just long enough to see there wouldn't be any sympathy from her. He looked to Sanjay and Dennis next, on the far side of the room. The pair sat watching the loud display. Their faces showed interest but no willingness to intervene.

"You can't send me out there," Barnabe countered. "If the Order catches me, they'll find out about your base. I haven't seen much, but I've seen enough to know you're too invested to give up this location."

Cyrus walked around the table. He scooped Barnabe's bag from the chair and cocked his head in the direction of the door. "Move," he said. His voice left no room for debate.

"You'd risk compromising your base?" Barnabe asked. His voice cracked. The cocksure demeanor was in full collapse. He was gripping his seat with both hands.

"What do you know about this location?" Cyrus asked. Despite the stress of the situation, his tone was brisk but conversational. "You know we're somewhere underneath the Australian Outback. You teleported here from a location in New York. The Manhattan platform can be moved within

316

the hour. The Order can peel you like a banana, and you won't be able to divulge the location of this facility."

Barnabe clamped his jaw tight. His eyes were fixed on the surface of the table. Cyrus wasn't even sure the kid was breathing anymore. The seconds seemed to stretch on endlessly. Cyrus stared at Barnabe, but he didn't move against him physically. He didn't continue the debate either.

"Alright," Barnabe said at last. "What do you want? I'll give you what you want. Just don't let them near me."

Cyrus remained silent, his eyes locked on Barnabe. Finally, he circled the table so it was once more separated them. Reese was again at his side. He pulled a chair out for her, and she took a seat. Her eyes remained fixed on Barnabe.

"I don't want you to *give* me anything," Cyrus said. His voice had softened, and he now stood more casually. "I expect you to treat everyone here with a level of respect. We brought you here for your protection. If you can help us examine the satellite telemetry, that help will be appreciated. Either way, you will have our protection—but only as long as you act with civility."

A pink hue tinted Reese's cheeks. Barnabe had gone pale and was sweating profusely. Cyrus knew Reese was trying not to crack a smile. She'd found the attitude adjustment fiercely satisfying and was fighting any display that might undermine its effectiveness...he was sure of it.

When Barnabe spoke, his voice was quiet and quavering. "I–I'm sorry," he said.

Cyrus watched him for a long moment, then nodded. "Fine," he said as if the matter was settled once and for all.

Reese pushed her chair back from the table and looked up at Cyrus. "Why don't we go for a walk," she said calmly, almost carefree. She slipped her hand into his and guided him toward the double doors.

Just before passing through the exit, Cyrus heard Dennis Driscoll at the table with Barnabe. "And that, my boy, is why Cyrus is in charge," he said thoughtfully. "He treats every one of us like family."

They had the leather-bound journal laid out on one of the eight-foot stretches of stainless steel counter in a lab on level two. Three such labs had been similarly outfitted on this floor of the facility. One of the others was an exact duplicate of this, about thirty feet wide and twenty deep. Steel counters were bolted to most of the walls, except where tall shelves or cabinets housed instruments and equipment stores. A pair of long, free-standing counters occupied the center of the floor. Reese was using one of them for her work.

The book was laid upon a white microfiber mat that was about two feet square. A lamp with a wide, round magnifying lens built-in was attached to an articulated arm bolted to the opposite side of the table. A laser scanner was also housed on the underside of the lamp, ready to capture images and feed them to the laptop on the counter to her right.

Cyrus sat silently off to the side on a tall stool. He'd been watching for more than ten minutes without comment. Reese felt his reassuring presence and was grateful for his patience.

Turning to her right, Reese adjusted the small dials on a short stack of instruments to the right of the book. She lifted a small plastic-handled probe from its cradle and moved it beneath the focus of the lamp. The laptop screen to her left began to change as data poured in from the probe. Watching the readings carefully, she moved the instrument in a circuit around the perimeter of the book. She kept the probe from touching the book and maintained a precise distance until she completed a full circuit.

Setting the device back in the cradle, Reese was already considering the data displayed on the laptop. Her fingernail ticked absently on the polished metal countertop while she pondered the readings. She tapped a few keys before turning to the analog dials of the stacked devices and making nearly a dozen adjustments.

She retrieved the probe once more and paused to take a deep breath. Satisfied with the steadiness of her hand, she moved the small wand very close to the edge of the book. A tone emanated from the laptop. It clicked, more like what she would expect from a Geiger counter. She cocked her head toward Cyrus and saw his nervous expression.

"It's not radiation," she said with a soft smile. "It's just a poorly selected sound effect on the part of the software developer. This thing isn't radioactive; I'm certain of that much. It is, however, giving off an energy signature unlike anything I've ever encountered."

Cyrus moved to the counter and examined the display of shifting numbers and colored bars on the computer. She knew the information meant nothing to him.

"Is the signature similar to Halon-Seven?" he asked.

The question gave Reese pause. She slipped the probe back into its cradle and tapped the keyboard to silence the computer and pause its recording. "That's an interesting question," she said. "Is there any reason to think this book is related to the meteors?"

Halon-Seven, the supercapacitor with previously unheard-of properties, had come to Earth aboard a series of meteorites. Though the substance had been discovered more than a hundred years earlier, the true nature of it was still a mystery. They had only recently discovered that it was not a rare naturally occurring element but rather a manufactured compound entirely beyond the grasp of modern science.

Cyrus cocked his head and seemed to consider his own

question more seriously. "No," he said. "I don't think so. But this isn't the first time something entirely unheard of has crossed our path. You know how I feel about coincidence. It's odd to come across something like this when we're trying to gather lunar telemetry and when we're trying to understand the Halon better."

They knew only a few things for certain regarding Halon-Seven—all of them recent breakthroughs. First, it wasn't naturally occurring. Second, it was exceedingly rare. Third, it had come to Earth aboard meteors that had impacted within the last 150 years. And fourth, the compound wasn't manufactured by any Earthly intelligence. Encoded in the complex structure of the compound had been a message—a signature of sorts—written in seven languages of Earth. That single word had been, Halon. Presumably the race or people who had created the amazing material and sent it to Earth.

As a result, the group had named the compound Halon-Seven. And it had been the key to a century-long quest to master point-to-point teleportation. Halon-Seven functioned as a supercapacitor, among other things. It's ability to absorb, store, and release power had been the key to teleporting matter over any distance.

Cyrus and Reese were leading a group of scientists developing the hardware that would eventually revolutionize how humans traveled the world. A single sticking point was keeping their teleportation platforms from mass production. Each platform required a significant amount of Halon-Seven to operate. And supplies were critically low. Less than two dozen platforms had been built before the world's supply depleted. The problem had stopped the project in its tracks. A worldwide rollout of the technology was required if it was ever to succeed. And with that, the hunt for a new source of Halon-Seven had begun.

"No," Cyrus said. He seemed to have decided for himself right there on the spot. "I don't see how the book can be related. The association just seemed possible given the timing and all that we've seen."

Reese shook her head. "It's a book. There's nothing here that even hints at a power source. These readings make no sense."

A voice came from the other side of the room. "That's because it's not a book," Barnabe said. He walked further into the room. Everything about him spoke of nervousness like he was waiting for one or both of them to chase him off.

Cyrus appeared to consider the comment. He stared at the leather-bound object momentarily before looking back at Barnabe. "It sure looks like a book," he said without a hint of derisive humor.

Taking the comment as an invitation, or at least a sign that he was welcome, Barnabe moved closer. He circled to the back of the steel counter, looked at the array of equipment, and considered the book.

"Jasmine Peng brought this to me," Barnabe explained. "Actually, she brought it to Tommy Wilks, and Tommy got me involved right away. Tommy and I wrote an algorithm for polymorphic pattern matching. It's proven extremely versatile. We can apply it to all kinds of different challenges. The NSA is using it in their next-gen facial recognition software."

Cyrus grinned. "You know about that?"

Barnabe shrugged. "They had some trouble getting it working with their latest generation AI. They went to Tommy and asked him to write a patch. We both did the math, but I did the coding for the project, so he had to level with me about its use before I would help. I may not have what it takes to strap on a gun and take the fight to the bad guys, but I like to think I did my part."

Reese sensed a newfound respect in the way Cyrus looked at Barnabe. She still considered him a despicable little worm, but couldn't help letting the experience alter her perception in a positive way. A very small way.

"Jasmine wanted you to apply the algorithm to the book?" Cyrus asked.

"She said the book was written in some kind of unknown code. She wanted us to use our system to decipher it." Barnabe looked suddenly more pale than usual. "Tommy put our software to work protecting the country, and my contribution was signing a cutthroat cult as a client." He paused. "I got him killed."

"What happened?" Reese asked.

Barnabe was slow to answer. He seemed lost in his thoughts for several long beats. Then he snapped out of it and shook off the discomfort enough to speak. "We dug into the book," he explained. "Scanned everything into the computer and set the software loose on the data. It should've taken a couple of hours—at most—to find the cipher key and translate the entire book. But days passed, and the algorithm turned up nothing. Whatever code was used for that writing, we've never seen anything like it."

"Why was Tommy Wilks killed," Cyrus asked.

Barnabe shook his head as if to ward off the memory. "It was that bitch, Jasmine," he said. "She pressured us for weeks. Finally, Tommy pushed back. When Jasmine started to get out of hand, we looked more closely into her. We found out who she was—we realized she was a member of the Order of Origin. Tommy drew the line. He was going to return their money and give the book back."

"And they killed him," Cyrus concluded.

Barnabe nodded. "Jasmine said it could just as easily have been me. But they looked at our talents and decided that I was the brains behind our team. They killed Tommy to motivate me."

"So you agreed," Reese said.

"I needed to buy time," Barnabe explained. "I didn't have a choice. But I couldn't have given her what she wanted, even if I was willing. That's what she didn't understand. The writing isn't encrypted—at least not in any way I've ever seen."

Cyrus leaned against the counter. They were all staring at the book. "You're saying someone devised an unbreakable form of encryption?" he asked.

Barnabe scowled. "Of course not. Every code can be broken. It's just a matter of using the right algorithm to find the key and having enough processing power at your disposal."

Reese tapped her finger absently on the counter. Though her gaze remained fixed on Barnabe, the book pages passed through her mind. She had an idea and a question but also doubts whether Barnabe would be truthful with his answer. "So, which is the problem here?" she asked. "Is it the software or the processing power?"

Barnabe grinned. "Neither one," he said with a chuckle. "That's why we couldn't break it. You've hit on the answer right here—you just don't see it yet."

Reese and Cyrus exchanged looks, but neither commented.

"Come on," Barnabe persisted. "You're right there. You're half a step from understanding the *real* problem. Why does *the book* have an *energy signature*?"

Cyrus and Reese only stared back at him.

"If you take the probe and scan this, would it have an energy signature?" Barnabe pointed to the laptop set askew at the left edge of Reese's workspace.

"Of course," she said. "It's a computer. It's plugged into the wall. Even if it wasn't, it has a battery. But that doesn't…"

Her voice trailed off. She stared at the book. Nearly thirty seconds passed before she finally blinked again. She glanced briefly at Barnabe before sending a concerned look in Cyrus's direction. Her fingers hit the laptop's keys and she began tapping the trackpad with aggressive swipes of her finger.

"Reese?" Cyrus said. There was concern in his voice.

She looked up at him, her jaw hanging slack. "I don't believe it," she muttered.

"What?" Cyrus insisted.

Reese offered a slow, confused shake of her head. "I don't know what the hell that thing is," she said, "but it sure as hell isn't a book."

When Reese walked through the door, Hondo had just placed the last of three large duffle bags on one of the tables in the center of the main hall. Barnabe followed close at her heels. They were talking quietly about something math-related—a calculation, maybe. Higher math had never been Hondo's thing. The limited trigonometry necessary for a long-range rifle shot was the extent of his interest in calculations. But he had a great deal of respect for the people on Reese's team. They were first-rate, though it didn't mean he understood most of the things they discussed.

Judging by the expression on Reese's face, her conversation with Barnabe wasn't the highlight of her morning. She perked up when her eyes landed on him.

"Hey!" Reese said. She quickened her pace and threaded a course through the tangle of massive unused tables between him and the door. "Hondo, this is Barnabe. He's going to be staying with us for a while."

Hondo offered a hand. Barnabe had a weak grip, which wasn't a surprise. He was in his late teens, and judging by his skin tone, he didn't seem to get much sunlight. The

Australian Outback would fix that in short order. Unfortunately, Hondo also knew Barnabe would never spend any time on the surface while he was in country.

"Glad to meet you," Hondo said. "Heard a lot about you."

Barnabe seemed uncomfortable as he examined Hondo. Hondo wasn't sure if the kid was troubled by the reputation he knew he'd cultivated in the short time he'd been with them—or maybe it was Hondo's appearance. At 6 foot 4, he had wide, bulging shoulders and a sturdy frame. His jaw was thick with several days' worth of stubble that had gone prematurely grey; he was only 39. Piercing blue eyes peered out from hooded lids—the result of countless hours spent in the harsh sun all over the world. He was an American by birth, though he'd been raised in Australia and had retired there after leaving the Army Rangers. He still wore the same floppy bush hat that had been a part of his field gear back in the day.

"I'm Alec," Barnabe said in a weak voice as he shook Hondo's hand. "Most people just call me Barnabe."

Barnabe's eyes were already on the bags surrounding Hondo. Reese looked at them with concern. Hondo tipped his head toward the far end of the room, where Cyrus paced slowly while he talked on his mobile phone. "He's got an idea," Hondo said. "We're heading out. He's making arrangements now."

The surprise on Reese's face told him the decision had been recent and swift. It confused him. He didn't know the plan yet, but it was rare to hear about things before Reese.

Something big is happening.

"I almost forgot," Hondo said. He flipped open a small pocket on his green Camo vest and passed a phone to Barnabe. "I need your old phone."

They traded devices. While Barnabe examined the new smartphone, Hondo gripped Barnabe's device securely between his hands, squeezed, and twisted. The phone shattered into tiny bits.

"What the hell!" Barnabe bellowed. "That was my phone! I had data on it. *Irreplaceable data.*"

Reese smiled. "Don't worry," she said. "It's been duplicated. Your photos, contacts, documents...all of your data is on the new phone." Her expression soured. "Even your porn. It's all been moved to the new device."

Barnabe's cheeks reddened.

Hondo laughed. "This phone can't be tracked using conventional methods. It's encrypted, and it has a direct link to our internal network. If you want us to keep you safe, this is part of what it takes."

Shoving the phone into his pocket, Barnabe eyed the floor. "You guys don't respect a guy's privacy much," he mumbled.

Hondo slapped him on the shoulder and laughed.

Cyrus ended his call and joined the group. "Is that our gear?" he asked.

Hondo nodded. "All set. What's the plan?"

"Charlie's got a hit on facial recognition," Cyrus explained. "We have a lead on Tracy. We're catching a plane out of Heathrow to follow up on it. Even more concerning, facial recognition records link Tracy to members of the Order of Origin."

Cyrus looked unnerved by whatever had been discussed on the call, but it didn't appear he would share those details with the group. Hondo wondered what else had been said or with whom he had spoken.

Barnabe seemed to pale at the mention of the Order. "Heathrow?" he asked. "As in *London?*"

Chapter 35 - *It was Called Shadowlight*

Somewhere over the North Sea

After teleporting to London, Cyrus, Reese, Hondo, and Barnabe had boarded a private jet at London's Heathrow airport. They were now flying northeast and destined for the Isle of Kapros. It would be a short but luxurious flight aboard the Gulfstream G450; Kapros was just off Norway's west coast.

One hand lay on the closed cover of Barnabe's leather-bound book. The same sensation could be felt near his ears each time Cyrus came in contact with the book, but nothing more. He had flipped through it a number of times, hoping to trigger another flash of insight like the one he'd experienced his first time touching it. Nothing had happened since. The sensation he felt in his skull was minimal but present. Whenever he considered describing it to Reese, he fell short of finding words to explain the sensation. Thus far, he had kept the experience to himself.

The strange handwritten scrawl continued to intrigue him. Barnabe thought it was written in code, but the more he studied the pages, Cyrus suspected it was written in some unknown language. Two words on the book's first page seemed to support the idea. Though he didn't know why, Cyrus was sure he recognized them. *Topel* meant *forge*, and he had the sense that *grannel* was synonymous with *crucible*.

Cyrus's thoughts returned to the cabin of the jet and the trip at hand. He had spent a great deal of time on Kapros while on an earlier operation. The contents of his stomach began to churn more violently as they drew closer to their destination. The sensation was foreign to him, but the reaction wasn't entirely unexpected. Though he'd thought endlessly about that mission, he had never seriously considered returning to the Voss Compound or what he would say if he ever faced the people he'd failed so completely. His brief phone call to Voss had been difficult enough, and that had been all business. This visit would be anything but.

He knew his return to the island would be painful. As hard as he tried to imagine the reception awaiting him, he couldn't come up with a single likely scenario. His memories of the time with the Voss family were vivid and complete. He'd left the island soon after Natasha's death, unable to face her father or sister—unable to shoulder any more emotional fallout than his own. He wasn't proud of the way he'd left things. It was a unique shame that went far beyond losing the woman he'd loved more than anything he'd ever known at that time.

Reese squeezed his hand, and Cyrus blinked away the memory for perhaps the tenth time. His eyes were dark and rimmed with moisture. He'd long since given up hiding this pain and guilt from her. She knew every detail of his mission to infiltrate Voss's family compound. She knew it had been his one chance to reunite with a lost love from a past life and how it had ended in tragedy. People he trusted at the Coalition betrayed him. Natasha had paid the price with her life, and the world as he'd known it had changed forever. Cyrus had left the Coalition and tried to leave the remains of that world behind.

"You're sure there's a connection?" Reese asked. "There's no mistake?"

Cyrus shook his head and stared across the cabin at the empty couch. They sat on a matching sofa bolted with its back to the bulkhead. Three cabin windows were to their backs, the window shades drawn and dark. Hondo and Barnabe sat in fat, overstuffed recliners with their backs to the forward bulkhead twenty feet away. A narrow hall leading to the flight deck separated their seats. Barnabe lay back, snoring with noise-canceling headphones cupping his ears and a short stream of drool trickling from the corner of his mouth. Hondo turned the page on some mass-market paperback he'd pulled from his duffel shortly after takeoff.

The muffled whistle of air over the fuselage was audible. Reese nuzzled herself in tighter at his side and Cyrus smiled. At least he wouldn't be facing his demons alone. Still, it was awkward, taking his current love back to where he'd lost the first woman he'd loved. Stranger still to introduce her to Natasha's family.

This could go horribly wrong in a million ways, but it had to be done. It seemed the universe conspired against him, drawing disparate contacts from his past together. Could they help him deal with the problems of the present?

It all came back to the Halon. They still knew so little about them. A mysterious people who had sent a series of anonymous meteors to Earth. Whoever the Halon were, they appeared to know more about the world than we did, and the meteors seemed to be hints—study guides—coaxing us toward greater understanding.

But why?

If Tracy wasn't one of the Halon, she had a connection to them. They had photographic evidence showing how she'd participated in developing the teleportation technology over more than 80 years. In that time, she hadn't aged a day.

The Order of Origin preached an utter and complete understanding of the universe, immortality, and synergy with the world around us. They didn't believe in god or a higher power; there was no spirituality, at least not in the conventional sense. And now there were links between Tracy and the Order. Tracy...a trusted member of the team developing the revolutionary teleportation technology that would reshape the future of the human race.

Cyrus didn't like the way puzzle pieces were starting to line up. He was far from understanding how Tracy was related to the Order of Origin, but there was no denying a link. Now, there was a link between Tracy and Rutger Voss, a man from his past who was a veritable tangle of emotional barbed wire. Adding Barnabe to the mix further complicated matters. He was brash and egotistical, bringing his own headaches along for the ride. Regardless, they needed his help to locate whatever the nations of the world and the Order of Origin were searching space to find. And, even if they didn't need him, Barnabe was in the Order's crosshairs. He wouldn't last long without the protection only Cyrus could provide.

Reese squeezed his arm and pulled him from the cyclone of concerns flashing through his mind on an endless loop. "You're worried about seeing Voss again," she said. It wasn't a question. She knew him well enough to read his concern for that above all others. He didn't realize the full extent of his consternation until that moment, but she was right. Voss was the most immediate concern, and he was on edge.

"When did you last speak?" she asked.

The answer, of course, was the previous evening, but he knew what she meant. "It's been years," Cyrus said. He was surprised by the dry rasp of his voice and how it betrayed his deeper feelings. "Not since the morning after she died."

Reese watched him closely but was slow to speak. She was nestled close to his side, his arm wrapped tight in the warmth of hers. She'd dressed for travel with faded jeans and a long-sleeved flannel shirt he'd bought her for their place in the Colorado mountains. They sat close on the sofa, their hips touching. He could feel her body heat where her leg pressed against his. There was a chill in the cabin, the normal dry differential that occurs at altitude when the cold from the atmosphere is conducted through the fuselage wall to fight the environmental systems. Her presence felt good, and it wasn't just the warmth she provided.

"But he's welcoming you back?" Reese confirmed after a long, silent pause.

Cyrus nodded. "That's not even the part that surprises me. He's welcoming all of us—taking us all into his home."

She looked puzzled.

"Voss is...for lack of a better word, a recluse." Cyrus paused to consider the best way to describe Voss's manner. "He hasn't left the island in over a decade—Hasn't left the compound in years. He's kind-hearted but not fond of strangers. For him to readily welcome us into his stronghold is...concerning."

"Concerning?"

"I thought he would agree to it, given enough time," Cyrus admitted. "But he was welcoming. I didn't have to make the case I should have. Something's going on. It shouldn't have been that easy."

Reese stared at him momentarily, likely trying to interpret his concern. "Do you think Voss means us harm?"

Shaking his head, Cyrus smiled. "Never," he said with confidence. "No worry for that whatsoever. But the man I know would've gone deeper into his seclusion after what happened. He wouldn't have come out of his shell. Not without a damn good reason."

"What about the neural link you shared with him," Reese countered. "You said that was unique and telling. The kind of experience two people were never meant to share. Could that explain it?"

When the Coalition sent Cyrus to infiltrate Voss's compound, his objective was to gather information on a new technology Voss was developing. It was called Shadowlight. It was a revolutionary procedure designed for the treatment of memory-related illnesses such as Alzheimer's disease. Voss had developed a technology and drug cocktail that would allow him to capture human thoughts and memory to digital storage for later retrieval and review. Along the way, Cyrus had participated in one of Voss's experiments and Voss had experienced a massive download direct from Cyrus's mind. Though Voss had used the same procedure on other test subjects, the download he received from Cyrus had put him out of commission for the better part of a day. As a result of the process, Voss learned two important facts. First, Cyrus had a complicated romantic past with Natasha, Voss's oldest daughter. And second, for whatever reason, Cyrus's mind wasn't wired like everyone else. The data download Voss experienced was orders of magnitude more complex than any other test he'd worked with while using the prototype hardware. The experience had devastated him physically.

Despite all this, once the memory download was complete, Voss came to understand Cyrus in a way no one else ever could. They had shared thoughts, memories, and entire experiences on a tangible, visceral level. The download didn't just let Voss view Cyrus's memories; it allowed him to experience them.

Did that explain Voss's willingness to meet? It was possible, Cyrus reasoned. But it didn't explain the man's willingness to take all Cyrus's friends into his home. That home was a five-story office building that had been converted into a self-sustaining fortress. It had its own power, water, and security force. Voss lived and worked there and never left the grounds. For him to welcome strangers was entirely out of character—even if Cyrus vouched for them.

"It's possible," Cyrus said, but even his voice lacked conviction. "I'm just not sure."

"Whatever his reasons, we'll soon find out," Reese smiled.

She was right. The flight from Heathrow to Kapros would take less than two hours. They would begin their approach on the island before Cyrus was prepared.

―――――――――

The phone in Copilot Huff's breast pocket buzzed twice, then paused before buzzing quietly again. The alert didn't go unnoticed by Captain Morris. Huff had flown with the man for nearly ten years, and nothing happened in his cockpit without him knowing about it. Now that it was go time, Huff felt a moment of regret—like he might be getting himself involved in something he would live to regret.

"You're sure about this?" he said to Morris. "This is the point of no return."

Morris shot him a look that didn't offer the slightest doubt. His eyes moved back to the windscreen without offering a word in reply.

Huff swallowed hard and released himself from the safety belt. He climbed from the seat and knelt beside the closed storage locker at the rear of the cockpit. Releasing the cabinet's heavy latch, he pulled his flight bag out and placed it on the floor. It took only seconds to retrieve the pair of closed-loop rebreathers inside. He slipped his own under an arm before shoving the empty bag back into the locker and securing the door.

Huff passed the second face mask to Morris. The man slipped it over his head without comment. Marveling at the Captain's conviction, Huff wished he had the same clear conscience. The fact was they didn't know who had hired them, only that they had been well paid for what was about to happen. Neither had asked what would become of their passengers once the task was complete. Huff was afraid to know. It wasn't clear why the captain had remained silent on the issue. Despite his concerns, money had already changed hands. Huff sensed he wasn't dealing with people who would understand his change of heart.

Stepping to the cabin's rear wall, he paused for a deep breath. He slipped the breathing apparatus over his head and synched the retaining straps tight until he felt an airtight seal form around his face. A shallow metal box hung from the bulkhead beside the closed door leading to the passenger compartment. He opened the cabinet and turned the small valve inside. Closing his eyes, he placed a hand against the wall to steady a weakness in his knees. That feeling of regret wasn't getting any easier to stomach.

After reaching a count of 30 in his head, Huff turned back to the windscreen. The Captain sat at the controls, unfazed by what they were doing. He respected the man. In many ways looked up to him, now wondered how the man could be so cold. Their contact had promised that the gas was not lethal, but in his heart, he had doubts.

"I'm going to check on them," Huff said. His voice was muffled and flat from inside the mask.

"Negative," Morris said, speaking for the first time in almost half an hour. "We agreed there would be no contact with the passengers once we were in the air." His voice carried authority and a tone of finality.

Fully aware of the agreement, Huff could no longer abide by it. If their passengers were alive and well, then he would deliver them in good conscience. If they weren't…well…he didn't know what he would do. They had already crossed a perilous line.

Huff turned the release on the cabin door and felt a burst of air across his bare arms as the atmosphere from the passenger cabin flooded the cockpit. He stepped into the passenger compartment without pausing to consider his violation of the contract further.

Slumped bodies were scattered about. All four passengers had dropped where they had been the moment he'd flooded the compartment with the contents of the canister supplied by their contact. Three passengers had been safely buckled in their seats, but one had apparently disregarded the warning to fasten seat belts. The youngest one lay face up on the floor after having slid from his leather recliner.

Fighting the bile rising in the back of his throat, Huff knelt over the body on the floor. The boy looked dead. Huff's heart thundered, and his eyes began to blur. It was the beginning of a panic attack, he knew. Pressing his fingers into the flesh of the boy's neck, he held his breath and prayed for a pulse.

The boy's skin was still warm, but his eyes stared up at the ceiling, unblinking and fully dilated. Endless seconds passed, but Huff felt no sign of life. His vision darkened further as his heart rate increased. The panic attack had him fully in its grip—he couldn't breathe. He heard the rasp of his own airflow through the mask, and some part of his rational mind reasserted itself. The mask—he still wore the mask; it was the reason he couldn't breathe. He fought the urge to tear it from his face, knowing the consequences and struggling to control himself.

A wave of dizziness washed over Huff once more, and he teetered from his stooped position and fell to his knees. His vision cleared slightly, and he locked on the boy on the floor again. Reaching out, he made a second attempt at the boy's throat. This time he took greater care and placed two fingers against the jugular, just below the jaw. He was instantly rewarded by the strong rhythm of the boy's pulse.

Huff rocked back on his knees and sucked hard for oxygen. The surge of air through the filters of his mask hissed dramatically. When he blew the breath out again, he felt the seals of his mask strain from the pressure. His rational mind responded and warned him that breaking the mask's seal would be catastrophic.

Anxious to return to the flight deck, Huff made a quick circuit of the passengers and checked each for a pulse. He was more diligent in his first attempt with each. Whatever gas had been pumped into the compartment must have acted fast. There were no indications that the passengers were aware of what was happening. It was as if they had simply passed out where they sat, blissful in ignorance.

Returning to the cockpit, Huff secured the cabin door again and returned to his seat beside the pilot.

Morris stared at him for a moment, then shook his head. "You're going to get us in trouble," he said. "No contact. We agreed there would be no contact."

"Take it easy," Huff said. "I had to be sure they were still alive."

While the client had been very specific about the *no-contact* part of the arrangement, Huff couldn't see what harm his examination could cause. He hadn't even moved the boy who had fallen on the floor. Who would ever know he had violated that single point? Still, he could understand Morris's animosity. With the money they were being paid, they could each retire to the beach of their choice. The Captain's reluctance to mess up such a lucrative arrangement was reasonable. He just couldn't understand how his friend could live with any lingering doubts. He was glad he knew their passengers were alright.

Chapter 36 - Hidden Agenda

The Voss Compound, Isle of Kapros

Peter Krieg was the odd man out this week. Voss's compound was home to a 24-hour security force, but particular logistical concerns were shared across the team. One of those was dry cleaning. The entire team was outfitted with matching tailored three piece suits, quality duds as far as Krieg was concerned. He'd been with Voss for six years, and an Italian suit beat desert BDUs any day. Still, once a week, a single member of the team made the trip out and collected the dry cleaning for the entire outfit. Dropping off one set of clothes and picking up the set from last week took several hours round trip.

Krieg was on the return leg of the Laundry Run, as the team had come to call it. He pulled the Suburban to the gate outside the perimeter wall and shifted into Park. Two guards emerged from a service door beside the massive entrance gates and circled his vehicle. He buzzed his window down as one of them approached.

"Everything go alright?" the guard asked.

"Another exciting day on the town," Krieg deadpanned.

The laundry run was boring, but he secretly suspected everyone enjoyed the opportunity for time to themselves.

While Krieg spoke with the first guard, the second guard opened the rear of the SUV and began inspecting the cargo. Voss's security team dressed well, but they were simply well-trained soldiers. Many of their mannerisms spoke to this fact. The laundry run was a good example. The clothing was stowed in heavy-duty, impact-resistant transport containers. Some found it comical; Krieg found it practical. They could fit a lot of gear in the back of a single Chevy Suburban. In this instance, they were carting around $1800 suits like armaments.

Krieg heard the truck's rear door slam shut and glanced in the side mirror. He saw the second guard give his partner the thumbs up. Searching the truck before allowing it back on the grounds seemed overkill, but it was procedure. Understandable, even. The compound had seen some major action not too long ago. Krieg had missed the firefight; he'd been stationed at another of Voss's facilities at the time. He'd lost friends in the siege initiated by a rogue faction within their ranks.

The first guard stepped from Krieg's window and touched his ear. Krieg knew he was receiving a message from security control on the fifth floor. He looked closer at the dark sunglasses shading the man's field of view. Like the cameras mounted above the gate, they were linked to building security. It was procedure for the guard to engage any delivery driver in conversation while the vehicle was searched. A computer system on the fifth floor scanned the driver, searching his mannerisms and responses for biometric indicators suggesting any kind of hidden agenda. Thermal-sensitive cameras also checked waiting for vehicles for hidden passengers. Doctor Voss had all the best tech and the coolest toys. It was one of the reasons Krieg liked this job and had been with him for so long.

The guard said something into his radio and Krieg saw both men turn their attention to the street surrounding his truck and the gates. They took up a defensive posture, and several quiet seconds passed before the radio on the dashboard chirped.

"You're all clear, laundryman," a voice sounded from the radio. "Welcome home."

Shifting the transmission back into gear, Krieg kept his foot firmly on the brake. The gates began parting down the center as they swung open. As soon as the gap permitted it, he tapped the accelerator and eased the truck into the courtyard. Both guards followed him in, the men moving backward with their rifles in the ready position and their attention fixed on the street outside. Krieg knew they would remain on alert until the gates closed fully and latched shut.

Following the circular loop, Krieg passed under the portico at the main entrance and exited on a short spur on the opposite side. The brief stretch of pavement led to a massive steel louvered door that was retracting upward even as he approached. Behind the door was a broad winding ramp sloping down into halogen-lit gloom.

As soon as the Suburban cleared the overhead door, it closed behind him. Once he reached the bottom of the winding ramp, he met a second massive door. It was almost done retracting into the ceiling. He passed beneath it and entered the motor pool.

By the time he'd parked the truck, four security team members had arrived. They made short work of unloading the large boxy containers. They were all-purpose equipment carryalls, equally well-suited for shipping weapons or scientific equipment while protecting it from damage, so moving laundry inside the crates was simple. The boxes took two men to carry them due to their ungainly size and shape. Since they were dealing with laundry, weight wasn't an issue.

Krieg watched the last of the crates being toted from the room. He noted the sounds of the freight elevator in the distance. An added benefit of making the laundry run was that he didn't have to lug the bins or sort the garments. With more than two dozen men on staff, Krieg hated sorting clothes. He would have stayed in the military if he'd wanted to be a quartermaster.

Now alone in the motor pool, Krieg returned to the Suburban. He pulled open the driver-side door and flipped a switch to power the seat forward. Wedged between the seat and the door's support column was a small canvas bag about the size of a thermos.

Grabbing the bag, he closed the door and headed for the exit. Just beyond the door to the motor pool was a short hallway. The hall terminated immediately to his right, opening into a wide vestibule in front of the normal elevator and freight elevator. The corridor to the left was seldom used. The lights were off, and it was cloaked in complete darkness. Krieg turned left and moved into the inky black abyss.

Though the hall was dark, he knew exactly where he was going. He ran his fingertips along the wall for good measure. The smooth, poured concrete texture passed beneath his hand until he felt the raised edge of a door frame. Taking another step, he felt the cold steel of the door knob. He turned it and stepped into the next room.

Once the door was closed, it was safe to use the lights. He flipped the switch on the wall, and old halogen lights flickered and buzzed in their ballasts. Several large metal machines filled the back of the room. Until today, Krieg hadn't known any of their functions. They were responsible for distributing air through the complex, he'd been told. These units worked in conjunction with other units in the building, some located on the roof if he'd understood correctly. There was another room, higher in the building, with similar equipment, but that was a specialized air extraction system explicitly designed for Voss's lab. Now that he thought about it, he wasn't even sure where that hardware was located.

Kneeling at the base of the second of the three machines, Krieg flipped a pair of latches and removed a small aluminum panel. Behind it, he found three compact valves, each with its own small faucet-like nozzle. Pulling open the flap on the bag of the thermos-size container, he found a silver oblong compression tank. It was shaped like an oversized vitamin capsule, long and narrow with rounded ends. A valve at one end and a short section of rubber hose attached to it.

Krieg didn't waste time examining the hardware or the machine in question. His instructions had been explicit, and everything appeared just as he'd anticipated. The end of the rubber hose threaded easily over the end of the faucet. He released the valve on the container before twisting the dial on the machine open. There was a hiss as gas escaped the canister.

Only one step remained. Squatting closer to the floor, Krieg looked further into the machine. His instructor explained that a reset switch would be located near the valve. It needed to be toggled once the gas had been primed. But no matter how hard he looked, Krieg couldn't find any trace of the switch.

Laying flat on the floor, Krieg wished he'd brought a flashlight. Looking up into the small cubby of the machine was difficult because the light was poor. He took his time but still found no switch. It didn't make sense—his source had been explicit, and the instructions had been entirely accurate except for this single point.

Raising his hand to block the glare from the overhead light, Krieg paused and pushed his face to the edge of the access panel. He gave his eyes time to adjust to the dark conditions inside the small compartment. He had absolute faith in his instructions—he wasn't sure why, but he was confident. Blinking once…twice…three times, a vague shape appeared in the corner of the space. It was a shallow black wedge set against a black plastic panel, but it was a switch. A satisfied smile spread across his face as he flipped it. He counted to ten in his head and then added eleven and twelve to the count, just to be sure. Doing a good job was important to him—again, he wasn't entirely sure why.

Toggling the switch again, Krieg heard something large and mechanical click somewhere deep in the machine. There was a low rumble as a fan began to spool up. The sound grew until it became a massive whoosh of rushing air. Slipping the access panel back in place, he buckled the latches again into their closed positions.

Krieg headed back to the elevators. He pressed the call button for the passenger car and waited while it descended the shaft with a quiet rumble. There was a chime as the car arrived. The doors opened, and a warm rush of air touched Krieg's skin a second before his knees folded beneath him, and he toppled to the cold tile floor.

The stretch limo stopped at the wide gate. The surrounding city street was quiet, thanks to the early hour; it was almost 6:30 am. There was no pedestrian traffic, and they'd passed few cars on the short drive from the airfield. The gate was tall and made of heavy bands of steel. There was an almost imperceptible line down the center where the pair of massive doors would eventually separate to allow access. To the left of the formidable entry was a small human-sized service door made of polished metal. A complicated keypad was recessed in the wall beside it. Two cameras were mounted high above the door, pointing down at the entry at sharp angles. Leaning closer to the window, Cyrus saw a similar camera high over the gates. It was pointed at the gap in the sidewalk separating the street from the entrance.

If the gate and door could be referred to as formidable, the perimeter wall was impenetrable. It was twenty feet high, comprised of stone and concrete topped with neat, precisely spaced shiny silver razor wire coils. Cyrus knew what few others did: the wall was also exceedingly thick with a core of solid granite. It entirely surrounded the five acres belonging to Doctor Rutger Voss. Nearly the entire five-acre footprint was occupied by a massive five-story building faced with steel and glass. The top floors could be seen through the limo's sunroof, visible over the top of the wall. Rays of morning sun reflected off the glass facade. Every floor on the structure's face ended at the glass wall. Cyrus knew this offered an exceedingly impressive view of the city from the top floors.

Interestingly, a photosensitive treatment to the exterior surface made the effect one-way. No one outside the building could see inward. From where the car sat on the outside, the glass had a dull mirror finish that looked both high-tech and tastefully refined.

"This place is incredible," Reese said in a quiet voice. Her head was tipped back as she stared at the building.

Looking around the car, Cyrus was sure she was voicing the thoughts of everyone present. Even Barnabe, who seemed to work hard to keep anything from impressing him, was shifting anxiously in his seat. Hondo sat back on the leather upholstered bench and cast a look in Cyrus's direction. There was appreciation in his gaze, but something more. Cyrus suspected his old friend was thinking what it must be like to return here after all that had happened last time.

"Doctor Voss owns the entire building?" Reese asked.

"The building and the five-plus acres it sits on. The King sold it to him over twenty years ago when Voss moved his family here," Cyrus explained.

The Isle of Kapros was an independent nation ruled by a benevolent royal family with close ties to Voss and his family. King August Casper Borden II was godfather to Voss's two girls. The island itself was nearly an exact match for the big island of Hawaii, at least in raw acreage or square miles. On the other hand, their climates couldn't have been more different. Since Kapros was located not far off the west coast of Norway, even at the height of summer, the island never saw weather that would be considered tropical. But like Hawaii, the island had formed thanks to volcanic activity hundreds of millions of years ago. A number of rare ores were unique to Kapros, leading to the small nation's high economic status.

The service door beside the massive gates opened and a half-dozen men streamed through it. All dressed the same, wearing expensive black suits with thin matching ties. Their footwear was the only thing keeping them looking like a group of fit, well-dressed businessmen. Rather than being outfitted with thousand dollar John Lobb's, each man wore clean black tactical boots. Much more practical footwear, given that they toted automatic rifles and were each equipped with smart glasses and wireless earbuds.

The men formed up around the perimeter of the car. A man opened the door on the side of the limousine. He made a quick, if cursory, effort to examine the car's interior while another checked the driver's compartment. A moment later, the gates began to move. The doors split down the center, each tipping outward on unseen hinges and moving aggressively. When a gap was wide enough for the car, the driver accelerated quickly and powered through the opening. Cyrus saw a second limo follow them through the entrance, keeping only a few feet from their rear bumper. The second car carried their equipment and luggage. The gates were already closing before the second car was halfway through the breach. The security team was falling back through the fence gate along with the vehicles, every one of the men backpedaling while remaining watchful of the street.

Hondo observed all of this through their car's rear window. He'd commented on the cars being armored when they departed the airfield. Cyrus saw approval in his friend's assessment of the team's fieldwork. "Is there an active threat against Voss?" Hondo now asked.

Cyrus shook his head. "Not that I know of. This is SOP.

His old chief of security ran a tight ship. Apparently, the new guy is no slouch, either."

Upon Cyrus's last visit, Voss's security chief had been a burly Russian named Dargo. He'd worked for the Voss family forever. Actually, he had worked with Voss and Voss's late wife before Voss struck out on his own. Dargo had left Voss's employ shortly after what had transpired on Cyrus's mission here—Cyrus's final mission for the Coalition. After that, Dargo had resigned. He took his work too personally and couldn't remain after everything that had happened. Plus, Cyrus knew Dargo had distanced himself from Voss to exact retribution against those even tangentially responsible for those tragic events. Some of the people in question had been principles of a company Voss worked for twenty years earlier.

It was a complicated, painful mess. And for a time, Cyrus had been on Dargo's hit list. It wasn't until a year ago, when their paths crossed once more, that Dargo and Cyrus came to an understanding.

The first limo skirted the circular drive surrounding a massive ornate water fountain in the brief gap between the building and the perimeter wall. The car came to a stop beneath the wide steel-framed portico, shadowing a pair of wide sliding glass doors at the ground floor entrance.

The dour man standing at the curb had aged since Cyrus had last seen him. He stood about five foot six, and it appeared he'd lost a few pounds in recent years. Cyrus guessed his weight at one thirty-five, at most. He had a thin face with a mostly bald head; a fringe of gray remained, coving approximately two inches above his ears. He'd traded his customary white lab coat for a burgundy cardigan. A smile touched the corners of his lips and pushed back tiny wrinkles in the corners of his cheeks as the limo braked and stopped at the curb. Cyrus felt a wave of relief pass through his body at the sight of the smile.

The man beside Voss was tall and broad-shouldered. He

was dressed in the same dark suit that constituted a uniform for the entire security detail. Cyrus grinned at the sight of the man. With short dark hair and a strong jaw that had healed well after the abuse he'd suffered a while back. Seeing him was another relief. Cyrus hadn't been sure if Wagner would ever walk without a cane, let alone return to what appeared to be perfect health.

Glancing at Reese and Hondo, "Wait here a minute," Cyrus said quietly. For him, this was the moment of truth. Though he'd intended to make this visit a hundred times before, he'd always found an excuse to delay the trip. While he owed it to Voss to visit, he'd never been able to follow through and take the initiative. Now he was here, and it was because he needed help. He felt guilt for his extended absence, now compounded by the reason he'd come calling.

Slipping through the door on the driver's side of the car, Cyrus stood upright and felt his anxiety manifest as tightness across his back and down his legs. He could blame the discomfort on the short ride from the airfield, but he knew better. He looked across the glossy black finish on the limo's roof and met Voss's eyes.

Circling the rear of the car, Cyrus stepped onto the curb and approached the older man. He offered his hand and wanted to speak but was suddenly unsure what to say. Voss shook his hand but said nothing. He seemed equally unsure. Cyrus stared at Voss as Voss stared back at him. He could see the pain in the man's eyes and knew what it meant. He'd suffered in similar ways: endless nights of lost sleep, unending dreams, and no end to questions that could never be answered. They had shared a loss, but it had been different for Voss. While Cyrus had lost Natasha, the woman he loved, Voss had lost his daughter, the girl he had raised. What could he say to that?

Cyrus opened his mouth to speak, but the words disappeared from his lips before they ever became sound. He cast his eyes at the sidewalk and ground his teeth before trying again. Once more, his words were lost to the ether.

Voss, a shorter man, looked up at him and smiled. It was a tired, pained expression that spoke a thousand words. His eyes were brimmed with moisture. "It's alright," he said in a dry, quiet voice. "We understand each other completely." He stepped forward and threw his arms around Cyrus, pulling him into a crushing embrace.

Tears rolled from the corners of Cyrus's eyes, and he hugged the older man. He remained silent…he still didn't know what to say. He felt Voss tremble as he wept. Somehow, that seemed good enough.

After what might have been a minute or three, Voss released Cyrus and stepped back. The broad-shouldered man beside Voss wordlessly passed Voss a handkerchief.

Cyrus wiped at the corner of his eye and turned his attention to the man at Voss's side. "It's good to see you again, Mister Wagner," he said. "It looks like you've made a solid recovery."

"One hundred percent," Wagner said with a grin. He offered Cyrus a hearty shake of his meaty hand. "It's good to see you. It's been too long."

Cyrus nodded and glanced at Voss. "Far too long," he said. "I'm very sorry about that, sir."

Voss grinned. "Come now," he said in a good-natured grumble. "None of those formalities. There were none before—why should there be any now? You know I'll always think of you as family, don't you, my boy?"

"I'm thankful for that," Cyrus said. There was a heartfelt relief that was hard to express, so he just smiled. "Still, I should've come sooner."

Voss offered a slow, thoughtful shake of his head. "It's not an easy thing," he said. "We all deal with these things in our own way and in our own time. A lesson I've learned the hard way over many, many years, I'm afraid.

"Please, collect your friends and bring them inside. We

shall get you situated before getting down to business."

Cyrus looked back at the limo and felt the level of his anxiety finally ebb. He was normally very good under pressure. Until now, he hadn't understood just how much stress had accumulated before this visit. A stabbing pain radiated behind his eyes. He felt it suddenly but rationalized that it had been there for some time. Stress from returning to the island, he reasoned. But strangely, as the stress slipped to the background of his mind, the pain behind his eyes did not.

Chapter 37 - Readings are Erratic

Plains, Montana, United States

Verhoeven pushed through the set of double doors and into the lab. The overhead lights were turned down low, and the fifteen-degree drop in room temperature hit him like a slap. The circle of twelve pods was now fully occupied, his chill instantly forgotten as a look of satisfaction crossed his face.

"How are our guests getting along?" he asked the nearest technician. The man was one of three in long white lab coats who constantly moved around the wide circle of equipment.

"All readings are in the green," the technician said. "There were no problems launching the simulation, and their vitals are nominal."

With a nod of understanding, Verhoeven let the man continue his work. He moved closer to the pods. The room was mostly silent. A low rumble could be heard in the background as the ventilation system circulated fresh air and kept the lab at a precise sixty degrees.

The twelve pods were arranged in the same circular patterns as before, with the occupant's feet pointed at the center and their heads at the outer perimeter. A flat-screen monitor was now attached at the foot of each pod, displaying the vital statistics of each occupant. The same information was relayed to a central control console a few yards to Verhoeven's right.

The three closest pods drew Verhoeven's interest. Like the other occupants, they were still dressed in street clothes; only their footwear had been removed. Each form lay on a memory foam pad raised a few degrees higher at the head end. A sheer fabric mesh cap was pulled tight across the tops of each occupant's head. It was as fine as a woman's stocking, circling just above the brow line. The material was tucked back behind the ear before cupping the base of the skull and rounding the other side of the head. The skullcap was a weave of nanofilaments capable of sensing electrical activity deep within the brain. The cap was wirelessly linked to the computer system of each pod, and each pod was network into the same virtual environment.

Restraints were unnecessary inside the pods. Once a person entered the simulation, the computer became responsible for many bodily functions. Heart rate was slowed along with their metabolism; the subject's body went into a natural state of paralysis at the same time. All of this was accomplished without drugs. Once the computer and subject were linked, the computer had complete control of the subject's neurochemistry and could use it to regulate all natural functions. The slower metabolic rate helped with long-term immersion in the system. They could wait as long as 6 days before it became necessary to attach the subject to intravenous feeding.

The pods had taken a decade to develop, even with the advanced technical understanding of Verhoeven's people. A frustrating and clumsy experience for him since the process would have moved much more quickly with the benefit of Nyland's help. Verhoeven was reminded of Nyland's betrayal at every turn, it seemed. Never more than now, as they neared the Migration. No one knew more about this place than Nyland. Still, he'd been unwilling to see this world for what it was—a life pod for their people. He'd been too hung up on the original plan—content to watch his experiment and dead set on avoiding contamination from his people.

Progress has slowed painfully with Nyland's death. But the Migration was nearly at hand. So much time had been lost thanks to that betrayal. Millions of Tangury had been lost in those squandered years.

The years...

Time had once been such a foreign concept to him. An unexplainable parameter instituted by Nyland when he established this place. Here, it was ever-present and all-consuming. It had ruled everything he did since the moment he arrived here and Verhoeven could no longer recall a life without its relentless push.

Time. There was never enough of it. So many had died while they had laid the groundwork for the Migration.

Two pods stood separate from the rest. They were placed to the right of the cluster, connected to the others with thick black cables. The pair of machines stood upright. A tall young woman occupied one. Like everyone attached to the simulation, she wore the same thin skullcap. Unlike the others, a visor had been flipped down from the side of the headrest. It covered her forehead, eyes, and most of her nose. Light from the visor's display could be seen flickering across the pale skin of her face. While the simulation was monitored from the control console, she was directly attached to the neural network and a physical part of the simulation.

Verhoeven's eyes were drawn to the monitor standing at the foot of the nearest horizontal pod. Every pod had displayed a similar reading, except for this one. Ten small graphs filled the screen, but one was larger, occupying more of the screen due to its importance. The large graph showed wild shifts in a colorful waveform pattern. By comparison, the display on every other pod showed a single line that moved in slow, gentle arcs. The display here jolted and shifted constantly, with violent randomness and in three dimensions.

"This one's cortex and frontal lobe readings are erratic," Verhoeven said to no one in particular.

The lead technician was at his side in an instant. "Yes, sir," he said. "That one is Cooper, sir. Cyrus Cooper. We're running a diagnostic, but we're unsure what's happening. He has accepted the simulation without issue, but his readings are...irregular."

Verhoeven groused. He'd been told that everyone was within normal parameters. This wasn't the case. "What about his EEG?"

"Entirely," the technician responded without pause. "There is some deviation, but it's well within accepted ranges."

His eyes moving between Cyrus and the technical display, Verhoeven pondered the odd results. As long as his mind accepted the simulation, the unusual readings weren't an immediate concern. Still, the erratic readings were far from typical. He's never seen anything like them. Most likely a hardware malfunction. But moving him to another pod would be tricky. It couldn't be done until he was asleep inside the simulation.

"I want a full diagnostic report on this unit. Once everyone is accounted for, it's your number one priority." There was no way those inside the simulation would understand what was happening to them, but with the Migration drawing near, he couldn't tolerate any further delay.

"Has Barnabe made any progress locating the drone?" Verhoeven asked.

The question was directed at Fiona, who stood behind the control console. She shook her head. "He has dedicated significant computer resources to the effort," she said. "He thinks he's using a powerful computing cluster out of Zurich. I've piped his command input directly into our processing core. He doesn't know it, but he has ten times the processing power he believes. It should speed things along."

Satisfied, Verhoeven offered a curt nod. His concern was still focused on the abnormal readings coming from Cyrus Cooper. There was a chance, however remote, that the readings were accurate. But if that were true, Verhoeven had no idea what it might imply.

Rutger Voss occupied the pod to the left of Cyrus's while Reese Knoland was to the right. Hondo, the man named Wagner, and seven security team members made up the remainder of the pod cluster. The rest of Voss's security team was in a second pod array near the back of the room. Four pods on that assembly remained unoccupied.

Chapter 38 - The Dyson Cluster

The Voss Compound, Isle of Kapros

Cyrus entered Voss's office on the fourth floor and found it unoccupied except for Barnabe, who was set up on the massive oval conference table near the corner. He had his laptop attached to a pair of monitors and there were several large yellow legal pads on the table. Even from across the room, Cyrus could tell they were covered with a wild chicken scratch that was likely only legible to Barnabe.

A pile of spent Red Bull cans had already accumulated at the end of the table. The noxious substance seemed to fuel the kid's creativity. Cyrus figured, who was he to criticize? It was enough that Barnabe was quiet for a change. He hadn't had anything obnoxious to say in over an hour. It was a new record, as far as he could tell.

Barnabe had been in his own little world ever since Voss had arranged time for him on the famed Dyson Cluster. It was the world's top supercomputer, located in Zurich, Switzerland. Researchers could rent time on the system, using its cutting-edge parallel processing power to crunch massive amounts of data. Booking time on the system was normally complicated, with a waiting list over a year. Fortunately, Voss had called in a favor and moved them to the front of the line. It was a treat Barnabe wasn't willing to squander. He'd set right to work and hadn't come up for air since being handed the necessary login credentials.

Voss's hospitality was well-timed. Charlie Greene was supposed to schedule computing time for Barnabe, but reaching her had been a problem. Cyrus hadn't been able to get her on the phone since arriving at the compound. That fact was mildly concerning because the lapse in communication was entirely unlike her. She'd been head of Logistics while working for the Coalition. She knew precisely how crucial support was for field agents. And she should be safe. Clayton had complied with Cyrus's demand and put Charlie in a secure office at Coalition Command. Clayton seemed to be living up to his end of the deal, but Charlie's sudden lapse in communication suggested otherwise. If communication didn't resume soon, Cyrus decided he would utilize backchannels to confirm that she was alright and ensure his operation hadn't been compromised.

For the time being, he focused on the task at hand. Voss's office was expansive, if sparse, about forty feet wide and almost thirty deep. The side walls were covered by floor-to-ceiling bookcases stacked with every scientific and medical text Cyrus had heard of and even more that he hadn't. The conference table where Barnabe had set up camp was along the right wall, in the corner closest to the hallway door.

At the center of the rear wall sat Voss's desk. It was a wide, impressive, dark mahogany workspace that seemed almost abandoned given its contents. A closed laptop and a multi-line telephone were the only items on its polished surface. To look at the office, it was easy to assume Voss never spent time there. Exactly the opposite was true. Though the entire building was his home, the office and lab in the next room were his sanctuary. Unless things had changed since Cyrus knew him, he often spent more than twelve hours a day in this part of the building.

The wall behind the desk was unusual. From floor to ceiling, it was made entirely of glass. It was a pale shade of opaque white, but Cyrus knew that could change with the flip of a switch. He'd once seen Voss activate that switch and watched as the opaque surface transitioned into a fully transparent window overlooking the lab. A pair of double-wide automated sliding doors were located along the left side. They opened by triggering pneumatic actuators hidden in the door frame. The doors would part, each retracting into the wall on either side. Today the doors stood open, light spilling across the threshold from the lab beyond.

A guard was stationed beside the door. He nodded as Cyrus moved in his direction. The neutral but accepting greeting made Cyrus consider Voss's hospitality once more. He was impressed with how Voss had freely offered Cyrus's team access to the building—particularly his lab. Accessing that lab had once been an operational imperative handed down to Cyrus by the Coalition. Now, the entire team had the run of the building. It was interesting how things changed.

Moving through the doorway, Cyrus reached the tile floor of the main laboratory. It was easily twice the size of Voss's office. Counters were bolted to the walls, and a large island work area stood in the center of the floor. It was at least fifteen feet long and double the depth of the counters lining the walls. Like the other surfaces, it was topped in stainless steel and shined in the overhead light. There was a dogleg in the back right corner of the room where the space opened into another vast space outfitted with a massive stationary microscope—the largest centrifuge Cyrus had ever seen—and a dozen other pieces of high-tech equipment he couldn't identify. A wide steel door in one wall led to a substantial walk-in freezer. Cyrus recalled it from his last visit.

The overhead lights felt particularly unpleasant. Cyrus squinted his eyes against them briefly. They didn't appear to be brighter than usual, though there was no denying the stabbing pain he felt behind his eyes. The sensation wasn't new, he decided. It had been there for hours. In fact, the more he thought about it, a pressure or pain had started just before they had arrived at Voss's estate. He wrote it off as a migraine, but the way the discomfort continued to build was troubling.

Voss pushed a wheeled cart from somewhere around the corner and parked it beside Reese, who was sitting on a stool at the long island counter. They both looked up as he entered. "Any luck reaching your friend?" Voss asked with a hopeful smile.

Cyrus shook his head. "Not yet. But I'll keep trying." While he kept his concerns to himself, Reese met his eye. His worry wasn't lost on her.

Other than just checking in, Cyrus had been hoping for progress on Charlie's nationwide search of facial recognition archives. By now, she would have access to international networks and be sweeping them as well. It was only a matter of time before they turned up a lead on Tracy's location. However, that might be overly optimistic if Clayton wasn't giving Charlie the access he had promised.

Barnabe was using the Dyson Cluster to parse the images from the dark side of the moon. It was a slow, data-intensive search that was immensely more complicated because no one knew exactly what they were looking for or how it might be disguised. Intelligence sources were tight-lipped for a change. They knew the world's major nations were searching the skies for a small gravitational anomaly but nothing more. It was as if no one knew for sure what that meant. Maybe the Order of Origin hadn't provided additional information, Cyrus guessed. But if that were the case, why were limited and expensive resources dedicated to the unusual effort? Someone had to know something. In his experience, no bureaucracy could keep a secret.

While Barnabe was using the Dyson Cluster to parse the

data taken from the Chinese, he was running a parallel project and attempting to decipher the leather book. Cyrus didn't know what it represented, but the book—or book-like device—was important to the Order of Origin. If it was important to them, it was important to him. It was vital for him to understand the information it held. Barnabe insisted he now had the processing resources to attack both efforts simultaneously, so Cyrus had left him to it. The kid was a pain, but he clearly knew his stuff. That much had become clear after watching him work for even a short time.

Still, Cyrus felt like he was squandering resources. He was no good at waiting. He liked fieldwork because he was proactive. Sitting and waiting was hard for him. Patience was not his strong suit.

Voss must've noticed something in Cyrus's expression because he asked Reese if she needed anything and then moved from the table and guided Cyrus to a quiet corner of the lab.

"You've got something on your mind," Voss hedged.

Cyrus looked him in the eye, smiled, and nodded. "You've been very generous, seeing me on short notice and going out of your way to make room for my team. I appreciate that."

Voss smiled widely.

He decided it was time to put his cards on the table and explain what Voss had really become involved in. He owed him at least that much.

"I'm into something dangerous," Cyrus said. "Coming here for help was the last thing I wanted to do. I'm worried I might bring danger to your door."

Voss seemed to consider that for a moment. His eyes had a faraway look, and his mind seemed to drift for a time. Then his focus sharpened, and he nodded. He glanced over his shoulder to where Reese continued to work on whatever joint project had occupied their time.

"You're not with the Coalition anymore," Voss said when his eyes again found Cyrus.

Cyrus was surprised by the comment. It hadn't been a question. Voss was certain the Coalition was no longer a part of his life.

"Dargo was very clear on that," Voss said. "He checks in with me from time to time. He explained what happened last year when you took over as head of Meridian."

Cyrus felt a twinge deep in his gut. Dargo had shared information that wasn't his to trade. Misjudging a man like him was troubling, especially with information like that. It was a potentially perilous mistake.

Voss appeared to sense the concern. "No," he said suddenly. "It wasn't like that. I worked with Walter Meade, back once upon a time. It was some time ago, but we remained friends. We kept in touch until shortly before his passing. Dargo didn't speak out of turn when he shared what he knew. In fact, the subject only came up when I asked him to look into Walter's passing. Things I was hearing hinted that foul play might have been involved. Apparently, that was the case."

Reluctantly, Cyrus nodded.

"Only then did Dargo tell me what he knew," Voss explained. "And then, only after great effort on my part. I wish he had come to me sooner. Walter spoke of you often. Did you know that? If I'd known Dargo was pursuing you, I could've simplified your lives greatly."

Cyrus considered that for a moment. "Dargo had his own axe to grind. I'm not sure anything from you could've kept him from what needed to be done. He needed to come by his decisions in his own time."

The comment resulted in a grave look from Voss. He nodded. They both knew that things with Dargo could've turned out differently.

"I never blamed you for what happened," Voss said. "I hope you understand…Dargo believes that now as well."

Though they were a kindness, Voss's words were like a knife slipped between Cyrus's ribs. He fought his reluctance and kept Voss's eye. The best he could offer was a slight nod of appreciation.

"You've done right by Walter and his people," Voss said. "You should be proud of that. They're academics. They have no idea how many different ways the world would eat them alive."

The knife turned once more. His words were simple and carried no hidden meaning, but Cyrus knew Voss had more insight than most. In his time, he had suffered great loss.

In hopes of lifting the mood, Cyrus said, "I guess it's a small world. I shouldn't be surprised you knew Walter Meade."

"It's nice to meet Reese finally," Voss said. "After hearing Walter speak of her for so long…it's good to put a personality to the reputation. He held her in very high esteem. The daughter he never had, I would say."

That brought a smile from Cyrus. He'd never seen Meade and Reese together. Meade died before Reese had come into Cyrus's life, but he'd given the dynamic of that relationship considerable thought. Based on everything he'd heard from the group and the stories Reese had told, Meade truly had considered her a daughter. Hearing Voss voice the thought was greatly satisfying.

Voss watched Reese for a few long seconds. Cyrus looked more closely at her while she worked. She was still manipulating a small metal case. Turning it on the insulated anti-static mat, she laid the box at an angle and reached inside to insert a small metallic chip. Her hands moved across the outside of the strange device with comfortable ease, and her fingers moved through its wires with poise and confidence. She was in her element.

When he glanced back at Voss, Cyrus realized Voss was staring at him. There was a new glimmer in the older man's eyes that hadn't been there previously.

"She's sweet on you, you know," Voss said. His voice was low, as if he were expressing a secret; his tone had a hint of amusement.

Cyrus rocked on his stool, unsure what to say or how to say it.

"I see..." Voss grinned. "She's not the only one, then..." His head bobbed slowly, and Cyrus felt himself being studied. "Good for you, my boy. Good for you."

"Really?" It was a dumb question, but Cyrus didn't know what to say. The word had come out before he considered it.

Voss was watching Reese again. He seemed lost in thought for a few long moments, but Cyrus saw satisfaction in the man's gaze when he looked back. "Moving on isn't easy," Voss said. "I never managed it...but then I never let myself try."

Voss went quiet for almost a full minute before speaking again. He patted Cyrus on the knee and met his eye once more. "Moving on doesn't change the way things were. And it doesn't change what you and Natasha shared. It just means you go on living. That's a lesson I wish I'd learned twenty years ago. I'm proud of you."

Chapter 39 - Buffering

Plains, Montana, United States

Fiona Bell swiped her fingertip across the touchscreen of the wide glass control console. She slid a large waveform graph to the left of the screen and tapped a command into the touchscreen keyboard near the bottom edge of the display. A text-based terminal window opened on her right. She shifted it to the center of the screen and scaled it larger by 50%. Text spilled across the large window, scrolling upward at an unprecedented rate. Fiona's eyebrows arched in response to the flow of data.

"What the devil is that?" Verhoeven snapped. He stood over her shoulder, double-checking her every action. "What did you do? Why isn't the data buffering?"

Pursing her lips, Fiona fought the urge to push him away. She couldn't stand having someone standing over her shoulder. Foolish questions only made it worse. "It's buffering," she offered in a calm tone. It took considerable effort to state what should've been obvious. Verhoeven knew as much about these systems as she did.

"It can't be," he countered.

She glanced over her shoulder and offered a look to express her frustration. Taking a breath, she looked back at the console and set her hands in motion again. "That's the problem," she said. "The buffers are full. They aren't keeping up. Putting another operative in the system won't solve this."

Verhoeven was tapping rapidly on the tablet in his hands. She could hear his fingers striking the virtual keys and was certain she knew what he was doing. He would come to the same conclusion she had. Apparently, it would just take him a little longer.

"The buffers can't be full," Verhoeven said. "The processing core isn't even peaking at ten percent. There isn't a bottleneck. Put another Reader inside the system. Whatever is happening, we just need to push through it."

Fiona ground her teeth and kept her eyes focused on the console. Information continued to flood the dozen different windows she had open. She had a far better view of the system and knew Verhoeven was mistaken. Putting another operative inside the system wasn't going to help. Her instincts told her it might actually do more harm than good, but she knew Verhoeven wouldn't pay heed without quantitative data supporting the insight.

Still, she had to try.

"The system is running well within specifications," Fiona offered in a neutral tone. "Tessa just can't Read him."

"Nonsense," Verhoeven scoffed. "We knew this might happen. Once enough minds are linked to the environment, it becomes necessary to bond a redundant Reader. We expected this. I just didn't anticipate the system bogging down like this. I'll feel better when I can identify the bottleneck."

Verhoeven turned his attention to the two technicians who were standing by. "Get Heather prepped and online immediately," he ordered.

"It's not going to help," Fiona argued. "There's something different about Cyrus Cooper. His readings are just…*off*. It won't matter who we send in."

The diagnostic examination of Cooper's still wasn't finished. A complete system check was supposed to take exactly 39 minutes. It had been hours. That, in and of itself, might point toward an issue with the pod. But since the pod was a neural interface—a bridge between the user and the computer—it was possible, however unlikely, that the user was causing the problem. Not for the first time, Fiona wished Jasmine was on hand. She was their most skilled and experienced Reader. If anyone should be linked to the virtual environment, it was her. But she hadn't returned from Providence. Meeker reported some branch of law enforcement had arrested her, but if that were the case, they hadn't been able to identify the agency involved. Likely, it was whatever agency had been responsible for killing Javier Cruze and his team, though they knew precious little about that event either.

"We need to recover Jasmine," Fiona said, unable to restrain her frustration.

"I have someone working on that," Verhoeven said. "Kipling is looking into her location as we speak. I sent Meeker along as backup."

A chill went through Fiona at the mention of Meeker's name. She had never liked the man and she didn't trust him. For all they knew, he was responsible for the loss of Cruze's team—maybe even Jasmine's disappearance. He'd been deployed to Providence along with both other teams. Once more, she kept her thoughts about Meeker to herself. Verhoeven didn't like dissent within the Order, and he wasn't open-minded when it came to questioning the loyalty of its disciples.

At least Kipling had been put into play. By far, he was their strongest Pusher. That was, since the loss of William Waterford years earlier. This was war, Fiona reasoned. They needed to act like it. Verhoeven was committed, but he continued to underestimate the threats to the Order. Tracy Clark was still out there somewhere. Though she hadn't been sighted in almost a year, her goals had not changed. She intended to prevent the Migration, and the fact that she was missing only made her more dangerous.

A young woman in a skintight black unitard emerged from the darkness at the room's rear. Heather had short blond hair, small eyes, and a tall, thin frame. She was one of their elite Readers. Heather stopped short of the second vertical pod. A technician helped her slip the mesh skullcap over her head and adjust its position. The pod was tipped fully upright, and Heather stepped into it. Restraining straps were secured, and the pod was reclined thirty degrees. A moment later, a muted glow emanated beneath the woman's body as the electronics came online.

The pod's information flashed onto Fiona's screen and she entered the initiation codes. Heather's consciousness would take less than thirty seconds to enter the virtual environment. Like the Reader who was already online, she wouldn't appear in the simulation physically. Her mental abilities would allow the processing core to interface with those inside the environment. The Readers were an interface that the computer used to accurately depict the environment based on the cumulative knowledge of everyone inside it.

Eyeing the unusual readings coming from Cyrus Cooper, Fiona sat back in her chair and took a long breath. It wouldn't matter, she knew. The Readers weren't the problem. Cyrus Cooper was immune to their influence for reasons she didn't yet understand.

Chapter 40 - *Everyone Wanted Answers*

The Voss Compound, Isle of Kapros

They sat in a pair of overstuffed armchairs in the common area of the building's main floor. The space was vast and open, with a massive entertainment center along the back wall twenty feet to their left. Far to their right was a dining area with an enormous oak table surrounded by tall, high-backed chairs. Access to the elevator and a door leading to the emergency stairwell was at the extreme left of the room.

The room's most impressive feature was its front wall and towering ceiling. The roof soared five stories overhead with a crisscrossing pattern of industrial girders and ductwork that looked sleek and precise in their arrangement. The metal beams were finished in glossy black paint, and the ductwork was pristine silver that shined in the light. Sunlight poured into the space through the face of the building. The entire north wall was glass from the ground floor to the top of the fifth. The circle drive out front, the perimeter wall, and the city beyond the gates were visible in perfect detail. The air inside was warm with natural light, and everything on the ground floor was bathed in a radiant glow.

Each of the five floors above ended just short of the common area on the ground level. Every level ended at a balcony with a chrome and glass railing overlooking the ground floor and the city beyond. It was a truly unique piece of architecture, and Voss was proud of it.

When he first took over the building more than twenty years earlier, he had most of the structure gutted. He designed the entryway and the common area himself and had always felt great pride in the warmth his home offered. He knew how people described him—a recluse and a hermit who never left his home. They wouldn't have been so quick to criticize if they'd known the truth of his family history. In fact, the opinions of others had never mattered much to Rutger Voss. As long as he and his family were safe, he was content.

Voss watched Cyrus take a sip of cognac and marveled once more at how small his world was. He'd heard Walter Meade speak at length about the talented young man who had impressed him so thoroughly. Still, Voss had never pressed his friend for a name. He, more than most, had a great respect for privacy. It had made him content to discuss Meade's protege in the abstract. Knowing what he did now, the proximity of those relationships had truly blown his mind. He sipped his drink and smiled.

"Walter thought very highly of you," Voss said. "I hope you know that."

"He was a brilliant man," Cyrus said. "Unfortunately, I didn't know the full extent of his intelligence until he was gone. There is so much more I would like to have asked him."

Voss chuckled and nodded. He could relate to that sentiment.

"There's another matter we should discuss," Cyrus said. Voss could see tension creeping back into his posture along with the change in subject.

"You've opened your home to my team," Cyrus said again. "But you need to know something before Ashley Waterford arrives tomorrow."

Voss read the concern on his friend's face and leaned forward in his seat in response.

"I know that a great deal of your work is proprietary and secret," Cyrus went on. "You value your privacy. What I'm going to tell you might be difficult to explain..."

Voss's brows arched, and his eyes narrowed. "My word," he said in a whisper of a voice. "You know she's a Reader?"

Cyrus stared back at him, his jaw hanging slightly as if he didn't know what to say.

"You do," Voss muttered. A grin spread across his face. "You know what that means, don't you? *Reader*?"

Cyrus set his drink aside and folded his hands in his lap. He took a long look at Voss before speaking. "I do," he admitted. "To be honest, I'm surprised that you do."

Voss nodded, his smile slowly fading. "What do you know about Gertrude Waterford?" he asked.

"Eugenics," Cyrus said without pause. "Genetic manipulation and engineering...cutting edge and really horrific stuff. Vivisection, human experimentation, the list goes on."

The drink soured suddenly in his belly. Voss placed it on the end table and pushed it away. He was nodding with Cyrus's assessment. "That's not public knowledge," he said thoughtfully. "You must have some high-level intelligence sources."

Cyrus's face remained expressionless. Voss studied him for any hint of a reaction, but nothing was given away.

"Your old outfit, the Coalition," Voss said. "They were the ones who brought Gertrude in at the end?"

Cyrus's only response was to exhale a shallow puff of air.

Voss nodded. It explained things. "But you know about Ashley," he said, primarily to himself. "She wasn't part of any report, official or otherwise…"

Cyrus's eyes narrowed. An accusation, Voss was sure of it.

"It was you!" Voss concluded. "You were part of the operation that uncovered what Gertrude was doing. *My word!*"

Leaning forward from his chair, Cyrus placed his elbows on his knees and watched Voss through unblinking eyes. He said nothing for several long seconds. Voss felt the young man's eyes probing as if searching for understanding.

"You knew about Waterford's work," Cyrus concluded. "You were *friends?*"

Blowing out a gasp of stale air, Voss wheezed. "I thought we were, I can tell you that much," he said. "I knew of her work but *nothing* of the human experimentation. She was supposed to do genetic prototyping using computer models and test data. Everything was supposed to be assembled for virtual testing in her mainframe. I had no idea she'd moved on to human trials…not until sometime after her death."

Cyrus eyed him carefully. "How did you find out?"

Voss shrugged. "After she died, the FBI came to me. Actually, it was the FBI, Interpol, the FSB, you name it. Everyone wanted answers. It turned out that Gertrude had several facilities all over the world. She'd broken countless laws, and everyone wanted answers."

"And they came to you?"

A regretful nod was the best Voss could offer for a moment. "There are surprisingly few in the scientific community who deal in Gertrude's level of work. I was one of three called to consult while authorities sorted through her mess."

"But you know about Ashley," Cyrus said. "That wasn't part of *any* report. I made sure of it."

Voss smiled. The cold feeling that had gripped his heart when Gertrude Waterford's name came up began to thaw. A flash of warmth came with Cyrus's confirmation that he had kept Ashley free from the fallout now known as the *Waterford Initiative*. "You did it..." he said. "But why?"

"You first," Cyrus said. His tone was businesslike, almost cold. It seemed this was not a welcomed topic for him either.

"I worked with Gertrude, here and there, over the years. As I said, few of us understand the level of genetics she was dealing with."

"But you didn't know about the human experimentation?" Cyrus asked. He seemed dubious.

Voss shook his head. "Absolutely not. I would've turned her in myself—and she would've known that. I parted ways with Onyx Gander over a similar difference of opinions. I believe in pushing the boundaries of science, but not at the cost of human suffering. What she was doing was strictly outlawed, even without my overwhelming moral objections. You should know me better than that by now."

Cyrus nodded. "Her more advanced work seemed to be the result of recent experimentation. But you and I know that her research predated that by decades. She was messing with DNA for over twenty years before I entered the picture. She altered the chromosomes of her grandchildren before they ever left the womb."

In the blink of an eye, Voss suddenly understood the kind of choices Cyrus had really made in his lifetime. His decision to save Meade from a kidnapping attempt in the middle of a crowded city coffee shop, his choice to leave Ashley and William out of a report that would doom them to a life of study as human lab rats, and even his opting to leave law enforcement after what had happened to Natasha. At times, it must have been too much to bear.

"You saved their lives," Voss said. "William can rest in peace, and Ashley has moved on. She is quite happy now, thanks to you."

"You seem to share Meade's overinflated opinion of me," Cyrus said. "It sounds like you've heard from Ashley. When does she arrive?"

Voss smiled brighter. "She's here already. She arrived yesterday morning. Given travel times, I didn't expect you until tomorrow. Anna and Gretchen took her to Bergen for shopping. They'll be back this afternoon." He referred to Bergen, Norway, a relatively brief flight from Kapros. "The jet dropped them off yesterday before flying to collect you in London."

Voss took a moment. "Ashley and I have remained in touch since Gertrude's passing," he said. "Sorting through that mess is easier said than done. But Ashley is doing all she can, attempting to right Gertrude's wrongs. Gertrude developed an elaborate scanning apparatus. Did you know that? It's technology unlike anything I've heard of, and I keep myself apprised of the latest in those developments. Ashley shipped the machine here a few months after the lawyers finished their work. It's been incredibly useful to my work on Shadowlight."

Cyrus arched an eyebrow. "A big contraption? Looks like an MRI on steroids? A narrow bed that slides into an elaborate console eight or ten feet wide?"

"You've seen it?"

Cyrus nodded. "She kept it in the same room where she stored hundreds of failed genetic mutations. That sort of thing is impossible to forget."

Cyrus walked into Voss's lab to find Voss and Reese

huddled around a small metal box on the island counter in the center of the room. The box had been a mostly empty shell earlier in the afternoon. Now, it was filled with a myriad of small electronic components and delicate wire bundles. Whatever they were assembling was taking shape, much to Voss's interest. He seemed more excited about the project with each passing hour.

Voss's respect for Reese was obvious as well. Cyrus had yet to hear exactly what they were working on, but every time he passed through the room, one or both rattled on about one point or another. It was highly technical, whatever it was, and Cyrus didn't comprehend their discussion. For him, it was obvious that the two were communicating on some higher professional level. Admiration for Reese's expertise was evident in Voss's countenance, even at a glance.

"That won't work," Voss said. "We have to worry about a short. We need to disassemble the array to make the splice."

Whatever that meant, Reese didn't look happy about it. Cyrus watched her tap a fingernail on the cold metallic surface of the table. Their work area sat upon a thin rubberized mat, presumably some kind of insulator if they were worried about shorts. The inside of the metal chassis was filled with a rainbow of delicate wires.

"With the right tools, I can make the splice without causing a short," Reese said. Cyrus met her gaze and read the flash of an idea as it crossed her mind.

Voss surveyed the wide counter. It was covered with just about every instrument imaginable. They were working with circuitry and microcontrollers, Cyrus knew. It wasn't the scientist's area of expertise, but Reese excelled at this kind of work. She pushed off her stool and moved toward Cyrus.

"We don't have the right tool for that," Voss said. His eyes were still taking an inventory of the hardware present. "I'm not sure I have something non-conductive to make the delicate cut."

Reese stepped in close to Cyrus. She craned her head back and pecked his cheek just beside his ear. The move surprised Cyrus because they had decided to be careful with such displays around Voss. Discretion seemed respectful, at the very least.

The display of affection caught Cyrus off guard, tempered as it was. But when Reese stepped away, she pulled the pocket knife from where he normally kept it clipped to his hip pocket. He realized he'd misjudged her look of inspiration for one of mischief. She flashed him a wink and snapped open the 4-inch blade just before she sat back at the table.

Voss had caught the entire display. His eyes moved rapidly between Cyrus and Reese. Cyrus could see the wheels working in the older man's head, but his expression was unreadable. The moment should've made Cyrus far more uncomfortable than it had. He stared at Voss, but the image of the razor-sharp blade in Reese's hand was frozen in his mind. He struggled to process it.

"The blade won't work," Voss said. His voice seemed far away to Cyrus's ears. Time slowed as he watched Reese return to the table as if in slow motion. "The blade will still conduct enough power to fry the photosensitive transmitter."

"No," Reese said in a cheerful reply. "The blade is made of porcelain and razor sharp. There's no danger of a short. It's just a little on the large side for what we need."

Voss looked confused. "Porcelain? Not steel?"

It was clearly a question directed at Cyrus, but Cyrus didn't answer. His mind was still locked on the blade in Reese's hand. She was working the blade tip across a delicate strand of yellow wire.

What he saw didn't make any sense.

Reese chuckled and seemed flustered. "He always carries the knife," she said. "He forgets to leave it when he goes to the airport, and they always confiscate it. A friend gave him this one with a porcelain blade. It doesn't trigger the metal detectors. He doesn't get into trouble anymore."

Voss's furrowed brow was slow to settle. He locked eyes with Cyrus and offered a look that said *If you expect me to believe that...*

Voss knew Cyrus better than most. He wouldn't buy the story about needing a retractable porcelain dagger. But he smiled at Reese and nodded, unwilling to express his greater understanding. He seemed willing to accept her decision to cover for Cyrus and the knife. When the corners of his mouth turned up in the slight hint of a knowing smile, Cyrus decided that Voss found the dynamic amusing.

Cyrus took a breath and accepted the small reprieve. But that blade was a problem. There was no explanation for it, and its presence chilled Cyrus to the bone.

"Are you alright?" Voss asked.

Slowly slipping his mind back into gear, Cyrus nodded. His eyes moved around the room, observing everything as if he were seeing it for the first time. Nothing was amiss, but he couldn't shake the feeling now prickling at the base of his skull. He looked at the leather-bound book at the end of the counter and decided that any answers would likely come from it. The search for the satellite was still coming up dry.

The satellite...

Barnabe was still hard at work. His mountain of Red Bull had turned into an avalanche. One of the security guards had brought in a large trash can just to deal with building detritus. Cyrus had seen his share of geeks when they got in the zone, but he was worried Barnabe might suffer a stroke or a heart attack if he maintained his pace. Even more troubling, his search for the liberated lunar data had turned up nothing useful. He had located the remains of a crashed Soviet-era satellite, but it was obsolete technology dating to near the start of the space race. Clearly, the Russians had lost a bird sometime in the distant past. Either no one knew about it, or no one cared.

Cyrus pulled out a stool and sat at the counter's far end. Laying Barnabe's book out, he flipped to the first page. He was ten feet away from Reese's worked, so tuning out her quiet conversation with Voss came easy enough. She and Voss continued to poke around the inside of the small metal box and enter commands into the laptop that was now attached to it via a long, thin cable.

As far as Cyrus could tell, the book's first page was just like the rest. The paper was a little thicker than usual; it was a coarse parchment stock that had likely once had a rough texture. It had since smoothed somewhat with age and perhaps with use. A handwritten scrawl covered the sheet. The penmanship hinted at a precise, careful personality behind the words, while the words themselves were unintelligible. They meant nothing to him. Barnabe had already compared them to every known written language and found no match. As a result, he concluded that the book was written in some kind of code. It was a reasonable assumption, except Cyrus thought he recognized two words on the first page. If some cipher were used, that wouldn't have been possible.

Flipping to the next page, Cyrus scanned the surface of the paper. He noted the rough texture of the parchment and the way it seemed slightly yellowed. The ink had remained stark and black, creating an ideal contrast between the writing and the page beneath. It struck him as almost a perfect reading condition. Stark white paper covered with crisp black text seemed great for reading until you spent long hours staring at the page. Off-white paper stock, maybe even a light shade of yellow, was far more fitting. He learned these things in his own short publishing career.

What he saw made him wonder if the yellowing of the pages had happened by design rather than the passing of time.

Halfway through flipping to the next page, Cyrus stopped short. He moved back to the previous page and studied it once more. What he was seeing wasn't right. It didn't make sense. He flipped back again and confirmed that he was indeed on the book's first page. Satisfied, he flipped back to the second. Something had changed on page two—he was certain of it.

Slipping from the stool, Cyrus headed through the doorway and into Voss's office. Barnabe sat behind his computer, a can of Red Bull tipped back as he guzzled the contents. He smacked his lips and slapped the empty can on the table with a hollow clang. "I don't know why they make these things so small," he said. "They should put them in liter bottles if you ask me."

"You should save time and hook yourself up to an IV drip," Cyrus said with a grin.

Barnabe's eyes moved to the empty can, still clamped in his grip. For a second, it seemed he was considering the logistics of such a configuration. Then he smiled. "Very funny."

Cyrus held up the book. "You scanned this into your computer, didn't you?"

"Of course," he said with a roll of his eyes. "The computer can't interface with paper directly."

"Can you show me the scans?"

Barnabe glared at him. "Is it more important than this? I thought you were all about the lunar data?"

Cyrus's eyebrows arched, but he remained silent, glaring at him across the width of the conference table. Barnabe rolled his eyes again. "Fine."

Barnabe tapped several keys and Cyrus saw the cast of the

screen's display change as it reflected off Barnabe's pale flesh. Barnabe tapped his mouse button once and then pointed to the flat panel display mounted on the wall at the end of the table. It came to life, showing the first scan. The book had been lying open, face down on the scanning bed. Two pages were present; the left side was the blank inner cover of the book, while the right sheet was page one, covered entirely with handwritten text.

"Now what?" Barnabe asked.

Cyrus studied the screen. Every word matched what he'd seen in the book. Right down to the words he recognized earlier: *grannel* and *topel. Crucible* and *forge*, he thought, though he didn't know why he knew them.

"Bring up pages two and three," Cyrus said.

Barnabe clicked his mouse, and the screen changed. Cyrus stared at the screen, but Barnabe just watched him.

"What's the problem?" Barnabe grumbled. "Can I go back to work now?"

Cyrus flipped to the second and third pages of the book and passed the volume to Barnabe. "You can," he said, "if you can explain why some of the words on these pages *have changed.*"

"Very funny," Barnabe said. He accepted the book but glared at Cyrus. Seeing the seriousness in Cyrus's expression, he relented and looked at the book.

Cyrus watched while Barnabe studied page two. His eyes moved carefully down the page, examining it like a painting or a drawing since he couldn't interpret the words. Then, his eyes shifted to the computer screen in front of him. The laptop displayed the same content as the monitor bolted to the wall.

Barnabe's brows arched and met in the middle. His eyes shifted back to the contents of the book. "Incredible," he mumbled. "Unbe-freaking-leavable!"

Chapter 41 - Rejection

Plains, Montana, United States

Fiona watched Cyrus Cooper's telemetry. Information flashed across the central console, displaying real-time insight into what was happening inside the simulation. His readings were becoming increasingly erratic. Just as concerning, the diagnostic she was running on his pod had yet to be completed. Something was very wrong.

The swinging door banged against its stop as Verhoeven marched into the room. Thanks to his new host body, he moved with a healthy, youthful vigor. Fiona watched as his eyes swept across the array of twelve pods. He marched to the side of the unit containing Cyrus Cooper without hesitation. She knew what he was seeing. Cooper was covered in sweat, and all the readings on the display at the foot of his pod showed him well into the danger zone.

"He's getting worse," Verhoeven said as he moved to her side.

"The quality of his link is degrading," Fiona admitted. "Adding Heather to the simulation didn't help. It may have exacerbated the issue."

Thankfully, Verhoeven didn't argue. They both knew it was a gamble. They were in uncharted territory, working with barely tested equipment that functioned on principles that were in many ways foreign to the laws of their own world. The hardware was crude, but their standards and the biochemistry, though supposedly compatible, were still several generations short of ideal for their purposes.

"We need to put him into a new pod," Verhoeven said. "It's the only surefire solution."

Fiona didn't share his confidence. She'd been pouring over the data for hours, and while nothing was conclusive, she didn't think the hardware was the problem. Cooper was fighting the simulation. Out of everyone networked to the core, he was the only one mentally rejecting the neural interface with the pod. Though she couldn't be sure, the rejection seemed to accelerate once a second Reader had entered the system. The harder they pushed to access his mind, the harder his mind worked to reject their substitute reality.

Verhoeven wanted to pull Cooper out of the simulation to swap out his pod. The process would take five minutes, but there was no telling how his mind would react to the disruption. The system had been designed to allow for such events, but he wasn't currently interfaced with the system according to specifications. There were far too many unknowns.

"Considering how he's reacting to the simulation," Fiona said, "I'm not sure what will happen if we take him offline without the others."

"Based on what we've seen, he's the lynchpin for this group. Is he doing anything alone? Is he going anywhere by himself? If he's isolated when we take him offline, we minimize the disruption."

Fiona shrugged. "He's in the middle of everything. There's no predicting what he will do next or where he will go. If it was Barnabe or Wagner, no problem. If we have any clear opportunity, I think we need to wait until the middle of the night. Get him while he's sleeping."

Leaning over the console, Verhoeven examined the various feeds from Cyrus's pod. He grumbled under his breath. "That's not going to work. We can't wait that long."

"I agree," Fiona said. "It's not ideal, but we have to chance it now. We're about to witness an event. He will either suffer a stroke, or the system could crash altogether. I'm not sure which, but something is about to happen."

Since things had become increasingly tense with the reading coming from Cyrus's pod, more techs had been added to monitor those in the simulation. Four men in white lab coats were moving around the circular cluster, checking the displays attached to each pod constantly. Three additional techs monitored the secondary pod at the back of the room.

Waving the nearest technician to his side, Verhoeven said, "Prepare a replacement pod immediately. I want number seven replaced five minutes from now."

Fiona watched as the technician scurried off to arrange the hardware and prepare the interface for the modification. Her eyes moved back to pod seven and Cyrus Cooper. She couldn't place the cause of her concern, but something told her that the problem they were experiencing wasn't an issue with the hardware.

Chapter 42 - *I Don't Think the Book is a Book*

The Voss Compound, Isle of Kapros

Cyrus, Reese, and Hondo sat on one side of the long counter in Voss's lab. Doctor Voss and Barnabe sat on the opposite, facing them. Each was perched atop a tall stool and leaning over the polished stainless steel surface. The leather-bound book was placed in the middle of the table. Each had a digital tablet before them displaying the scans Barnabe had made in the back room of the book store in Providence, Rhode Island.

"I don't understand," Hondo said. "How could the contents of a page spontaneously change? Someone must have altered the digital files."

"No way!" Barnabe argued. "I did those scans. They haven't been tampered with."

Cyrus shook his head. "It's the simplest explanation, but Barnabe's right. We can be sure the files are original."

Voss looked perplexed. He continued staring at the book since Cyrus first explained the discovery. Now that the obvious explanations had been covered, he seemed intrigued. "How can you be sure?" he asked.

"Because I didn't discover the change by comparing the scans to the book itself," Cyrus said. "I was studying the book and noticed the contents were different. I was comparing the book to my memory. I only went back to the scans to double-check my suspicion."

The room went silent. Everyone was staring at the book or a copy of the scan on their tablet.

"But how is it possible?" Barnabe asked.

Reese was the first to speak. "My best guess? I don't think the book is a book."

Barnabe laughed. Hondo looked confused. Cyrus watched Voss more carefully. Voss studied the book for several long seconds. He pushed his tablet aside and reached out to feel the leather. He pulled the book across the table until it was in front of him. Tipping the cover open, he carefully leafed through the pages. He took time to experience the texture of each page. Finally, he closed the book and began examining the cover more thoroughly. "Amazing," he muttered, apparently to himself.

"Remember how it triggered the alarm on the platform," Reese said. "The signature was suggestive of a power source, though we couldn't find one. I don't think it's a book—at least not in the conventional sense."

Barnabe groused. "If it's not a book, what the hell is it?"

"Think of it as an ebook," Cyrus suggested. He understood what Reese was getting at. It made a great deal of sense, though the idea was astounding. "But rather than a single digital page, it has a hundred and fifty. The page's contents can change, just like the pages on an e-reader."

"What you're suggesting," Voss said, "is far more interesting. The contents of the second page have changed in small ways. It's as if the book was aware of your presence. How is that possible? Are you suggesting the device has some level of artificial intelligence?"

Barnabe made a face and chuckled derisively. Cyrus offered a shrug and a look that explained his uncertainty.

"Not necessarily," Reese countered. "The Halon made a substantial effort to teach us about quantum mechanics. What if the book works on quantum principles we simply don't yet understand? The contents of subsequent pages can only be deciphered once the previous page has been understood."

Barnabe burst out in a fit of laughter. "Preposterous!"

"Halon?" Voss asked. "What am I missing?"

Cyrus scowled. He needed to bring Voss up to speed on the Halon, but this wasn't the time. "That's a story for another time," he said. "For now, let's focus on the book. On the surface, I'll admit that the idea seems outlandish. But the idea would make for a nearly unbreakable level of encryption, sort of like a mutating cipher. The data would be changing on a page-by-page basis. Subsequent pages could only be read after those before them."

"It would be an incredible breakthrough in technology," Hondo offered. "Not so hard to believe when considering what you have in your hands. It's a book that appears to be made of paper, but that sure isn't paper. The contents of the pages are changing before your eyes. There's no disputing that."

Barnabe sat up straighter, crossed his arms over his chest and glared at everyone around the table. "You've got to be kidding," he offered impetuously. "Setting aside the fact that the necessary technology simply doesn't exist, you're all overlooking a fundamental principle of your own theory."

"Which is?" Voss asked in an even tone. He was genuinely curious.

Barnabe snorted, made a show of rolling his eyes, and

then finally got down to business. "Assuming the device operates similarly to the observation principles of quantum theory, the later pages wouldn't change unless someone understood what was written on the first page. I haven't cracked the code used on page one yet, so no one has a clue what is written on the first page."

Reese and Voss looked surprised. Apparently, Barnabe had made a valid point, Cyrus guessed. They were both looking at the book as if trying to divine some other rational explanation. Barnabe leaned back, cracked his knuckles, and grinned from ear to ear.

"You're saying someone would need to understand the first page's contents for the following pages to take on a readable form?" Cyrus asked.

Reese scrunched her nose, looked at him, and shrugged. She nodded slowly, apparently hating to concede Barnabe's point.

Cyrus looked to Voss, only to receive a similar, though less begrudging reaction. Voss hadn't had enough time to generate the same level of distaste for Barnabe. Cyrus was betting it wouldn't take the kind-hearted man much longer. Barnabe had a way with people.

"What if it was only a few words from the first page?" Cyrus asked. "Would that matter?"

Barnabe's grin drooped precipitously. Reese stared at Cyrus as if she wasn't sure she understood his question. Voss looked up from the book he'd been paging through. "You understood some of the words?" he asked.

Raising his hand, Cyrus waggled it in the air. "I'm not sure. Two words on the first page seemed familiar to me. I have the sense I've seen them somewhere before."

"You're wrong," Barnabe scoffed. "I've run the text against every known written language—even those considered long extinct. Whatever this is, it's entirely unknown."

Hondo raised a hand slightly. "I read somewhere that Tolkien invented entirely new languages when he wrote the Lord of the Rings. Just because the language isn't known, doesn't mean it isn't valid."

Cyrus grinned, and a sheepish expression appeared on his friend's face.

"Oh, shut up," Hondo grumbled. "Yes, I *read*. Don't even start with me."

Hondo never failed to add something unexpected to a conversation. This time, he'd outdone himself.

Reese seemed to regain her composure. Processing all of this seemed to throw her for a loop. "He's right. Factor in your eidetic memory...who knows why you recognize a few disparate words? You might have come across them at some point. They could be locked away in your memory. There could be more where that came from."

"I'm sorry," Barnabe interrupted. "Did you say eidetic memory? Is she kidding?"

Cyrus shook his head. Barnabe's expression shifted; he seemed to consider the conversation in a new light.

"Throw the Halon into the mix," Hondo added, "and who's to say it's not a real language? It could be their mother tongue, for all we know."

Cyrus saw Voss perk up at yet another mention of the Halon. He saw a different series of questions forming behind his friend's eyes. If he weren't careful, keeping the discussion on track would become a struggle.

"We need to find Tracy," Cyrus said. "She might be able to answer all of our questions."

Hondo pushed his chair back from the table. "You have things covered here. I'll check with Charlie and see if she's uncovered anything new."

The group fell into silence as they watched Hondo exit the room. Half the eyes were on the book sitting on the counter before Voss. The other half of the eyes rested on Cyrus. He knew the next step was about to fall back on him—he just didn't know what move to make.

"You really think you recognize words on the first page," Barnabe asked. "I mean, *for real?*"

Cyrus shrugged. "Two words. That's all. Only two out of whatever are there—maybe a hundred and fifty?"

Barnabe looked at Voss. "Do you mind?" he said and motioned to the book. Voss pushed the book in Barnabe's direction. Barnabe flipped to page one. "What words?"

"*Topel* and *grannel*," Cyrus said. "For some reason I'm pretty sure *topel* means forge and a *grannel* is a crucible."

"But that's not enough to help us," Reese countered. "Does anything else even seem familiar?"

"Nothing is ringing any bells," Cyrus said.

Barnabe was tapping his finger on the table in an idle manner while he examined page one. "It might be enough," he said in a quiet voice. "Two words out of 153. That's roughly one and a half percent. It's not enough for my algorithm to work with, but if we make some basic assumptions about the text, we might start to gain traction."

Voss seemed interested. "What sort of assumptions?"

"Well, in the English language, some words might commonly appear before words like forge or crucible. Words like *a* or *the*. One of the things my algorithm will do is experiment with common word combinations once we locate a promising string—in this case, translated words. If your suggestion is right, this isn't a cryptographic algorithm—it's a translation issue. We just need to create our own Rosetta Stone."

"You can do that from just two words?" Cyrus asked.

Barnabe looked unsure. One sign of this was how a respectful manner and civil responses had replaced his smugness. "Maybe," he said. "I think so. I've done more with less. I just need some time. But if you could find another word or two, it would certainly accelerate things. If you're right, once we unlock one page, each subsequent page will soon follow."

Reese, Voss, and Barnabe began to speak quietly amongst themselves. The three seemed to be attacking the book's contents with renewed vigor. Barnabe appeared to be finding a rhythm with the team. Cyrus hoped the kid would continue ingratiating himself, losing his abrasive attitude in the process.

The conversation regarding the book had surfaced a new concern for Cyrus—one no one had yet picked up on. If they'd guessed correctly and understood how the strange book functioned—he would call it a book until they knew otherwise—it indicated a connection to the Halon people. Since the Order of Origin had contracted Barnabe to decipher it, the book connected the Order to the Halon by the same logic.

Puzzle pieces were starting to connect, but the greater picture had yet to form. They still knew almost nothing of the Halon people or how the Order's motivations related to them.

Hondo walked back into the room. From the look on his face, Cyrus knew that he had news. Moving to the counter's far end, Cyrus slid onto a stool and sat beside him. They were well out of earshot of the others, still engaged in their hushed discussion.

"I still can't reach Charlie," Hondo said. "I'm officially worried."

Cyrus nodded; he was already concerned. Something was wrong. He'd felt that way ever since arriving on the island.

He couldn't trust Clayton to give him a straight answer, but maybe he could go direct to Luke Reid. Though Cyrus had never considered Reid a friend, they had a history. That history had its bumps, but Cyrus had helped Reid with some family issues a while back, and he was the kind of guy who believed in repaying a favor.

"Let me make some calls," Cyrus said.

Hondo looked relieved. "That would be great. We're stuck until the package arrives. I need to catch up with Wagner and arrange for delivery."

Cyrus nodded and watched Hondo head for the door. He sat back on the stool and rubbed the corners of his eyes with his thumb and forefinger. His headache wasn't letting up. It now felt like a pair of icepicks chiseling away behind his eyes. He took a deep breath and once more considered Hondo's comment. The *package* in question was a teleportation platform. They kept two platforms boxed up and warehoused at all times, ready to be shipped wherever required. One was en route via a courier service, due to arrive on the island tomorrow morning. Voss was willing to let them set it up in the subbasement. Cyrus would teleport back to the states and check on Charlie himself if worse came to worst. He just hoped he could get Reid to check on her sooner rather than later.

Chapter 43 - *Well Into the Danger Zone*

Plains, Montana, United States

The alarm blared in its piercing, chattering rhythm. Verhoeven shouldered a tech out of the way and pressed the hypo-spray injector against Cyrus Cooper's neck. The device puffed and hissed as the neuroinhibitor was shot directly into the bloodstream. Reaching his brain would take less than a second, but they were already well into the danger zone.

"His feet, now," Verhoeven snapped at the nearest tech.

The lab tech grappled Cyrus by the ankles, and together, they lifted him into the air. Another tech keyed the release sequence and worked to separate the faulty pod from the rest of the array. Yet another tech moved to assist Verhoeven and the other man. The third man supported Cyrus's midsection. The move came just in time. The frantic efforts of Verhoeven and his partner were clumsy, and the tech holding Cyrus's feet was fumbling to support his weight.

The defective pod was wheeled away from the circular array, and a new one was fitted. Verhoeven ground his teeth and wheezed to support the unconscious form in his arms.

He eyed Fiona at the perimeter of the circle. She stood at the control console, ready to reengage the simulation as soon as he gave the word.

"The pod is online," the disheveled tech sputtered as he stepped out of the way.

The man supporting Cyrus's midsection moved away, and Verhoeven guided himself and the remaining tech into position over the new pod. They lowered Cyrus onto the bed before making an awkward effort to position him appropriately. The free tech was already slipping the skull cap over the top of Cyrus's head and working it into the proper position. Verhoeven glared at the man. "Are we ready?"

The tech took another long moment to smooth wrinkles in the delicate mesh fabric of the cap before pulling it tight over the crown of Cyrus's head once more.

"Well?" Verhoeven snapped.

The lab tech stepped away from the pod, raising his hands as if the experience had scalded them. "Ready," he rasped.

Verhoeven pulled a second hypo-spray injector from the breast pocket of his white coat and flipped the protective cap away. He placed the smooth face of the injector against the side of Cyrus's neck and triggered the device. The device puffed and hissed, releasing a new cocktail into the bloodstream. Turning quickly, Verhoeven pointed a finger at Fiona. Her fingers tapped and swiped across the surface of the control console. Blue LED lights surrounding the perimeter of the new pod blinked to life and pulsed as the software was loaded and initiated. The buzz of the alarm silenced at last, and the room grew suddenly quiet. Only the whoosh of the overworked cooling system could be heard, and conditioned air was forced into the room through vents high overhead.

The three lab techs moved away from the pod and retreated to the edge of the dim bubble of light surrounding the twelve networked pods. Fiona chewed nervously on the corner of her lip as she studied the display.

Verhoeven moved to her side.

Three windows were arranged across the surface of the wide glass screen. Each showed a series of separate progress bars labeled with their functions. A larger progress bar was positioned at the bottom of the overall screen. It tracked the cumulative progression of the subroutines. Its movement was the focus of their attention. It was moving ponderously from left to right.

When the progress bar reached the 90% mark, its steady march stalled. Verhoeven leaned closer to the screen as if his proximity would somehow urge progress. From the corner of his eye, he saw Fiona's hands clamp into pale fists.

Neither of them breathed.

"This isn't normal," she said.

Verhoeven found himself at a loss for words. Moving Cooper while the simulation was active was a dangerous proposition. While the simulation allowed for it, conditions were not ideal. The issue they had seen earlier with the overloaded buffers meant that every second of downtime was potentially more problematic.

Still, the progress bar failed to move.

Fiona looked to Verhoeven, concern visible on her face. "It's never done this before."

They both looked at the pod containing Cyrus Cooper. The perimeter of his bed was aglow with blue LED lights that pulsed in a steady, slow rhythm. Those lights went dark all at once, missing their next rhythmic pulse. A beat passed, and still, they were dark. The lights flashed to life suddenly, this time lit solid red. An alarm sounded. A different blaring klaxon resonated from overhead. The dim bubble of white light illuminating the circular pod array shifted in tone and went red in the blink of an eye.

There came a gasp, audible even over the obnoxious siren—Verhoeven didn't know if it had come from him or Fiona. They both stared at the frozen display—nothing was updating. Fiona began tapping uselessly on the screen while six techs materialized from the surrounding darkness. They began examinations of the individual screens of each pod.

"What's happened?" Verhoeven said once he finally found his voice.

Fiona eyed the beds. She rounded the console and stopped beside number seven. Cyrus Cooper's pod was the only one displaying red along its perimeter. "The problem is here," she said.

"I can see that," Verhoeven yelled above the din. He moved to the pod one station to the left of Cyrus and studied the screen at its base. "I need to know if the entire simulation has crashed or is it just the control interface?"

A mechanical clattering drew both of their attention. One of the two Readers in the vertical pods to the right was convulsing, thrashing against the restraints so violently that the entire device was vibrating on the concrete floor. Inside the pod, Heather was shuddering from head to toe and smashing her skull against the supportive padding with crushing force.

A pair of lab techs were quick to react, but they were still ten feet away when Heather's head fell forward, and her body went limp. The nearest tech made it only a step closer when a torrent of blood burst from the front of her immobile head and splashed across the floor. The first tech stopped short, and the second wasn't fast enough. He hit the growing pool of blood and went sprawling onto his back. Verhoeven heard the man's head striking the floor, even above the klaxon.

Fiona stood immobile for long seconds; her eyes stuck on the gory mess. Her head turned in his direction, and Verhoeven saw the horrifying significance register in her mind. She seemed to process his logic in slow motion before breaking her trance. She moved quickly to the pod one station to the right of Cyrus and examined the screen. It's information continued to update at a steady pace. As far as she could tell, everything was as it should be.

"I don't understand," Fiona yelled over the chaos. "There are safety protocols and failsafes. This isn't possible!"

Verhoeven looked in her direction. Confusion was apparent on his face, even in the devilish red glare from the muted overhead lights. He didn't understand this any better than she did.

They moved simultaneously and converged once more on Cyrus's pod. The readout for his monitor had entirely flatlined. EEG and EKG were all reading zero, their graphs flat, red, and blinking. Fiona placed two fingers against Cyrus's jugular and seemed to shrink physically.

"He's alive," she said. "Solid pulse with a good rhythm."

Verhoeven shot a glance at the nearest lab tech. He had checked one pod and had just moved to the next. "What do you see?" he demanded.

The man looked like a deer caught in the headlights of an oncoming truck. "Fine," the man called in a squeak of a voice. "This one's vitals are stable. The simulation appears to be uninterrupted."

Verhoeven glanced at the next tech. "Same thing here, sir."

The next two techs confirmed the rest of the group was still alive. Verhoeven blew out an exasperated breath and considered the evidence. What they were experiencing was unprecedented. It seemed the core was still online and functioning, but pod seven and the control interface crashed simultaneously.

"Reboot the control system," Verhoeven ordered Fiona.

Her eyes moved to the three techs working on the secondary array at the back of the room. It was another circle of twelve pods that had just had its last three empty bays occupied. That pod was part of the same simulation. "Are you sure? The disruption could—"

"Just do it," Verhoeven snapped. He knelt beside pod seven and fumbled in the darkness. It took only a moment to locate the override switch. Verhoeven flipped aside the protective metal cap and slapped the large plastic button with the palm of his hand. The hum from pod seven went instantly silent. Three seconds later, three loud clicks sounded, and the pod began to hum once more as its electronic systems began to reinitialize.

Fiona was already following a similar procedure beneath the control console. He could see the glow from its display shifting sharply in the dim overhead light as it initialized.

"I need a status update as soon as you're back online," Verhoeven called over the earsplitting Klaxon. "And shut down that damned alarm!"

The alarm went quiet, but the overhead lights continued to pulse. Verhoeven moved to a position over Fiona's shoulder and watched the slow advance of the progress bars of the large display as it rebooted. He eyed the secondary pod array at the back of the room. The remaining three beds had been filled. One was occupied by Doctor Voss's daughter, Anna. Another held Ashley Waterford. Verhoeven looked down at Fiona, whose attention was focused on the monitor. She had met Ashley years earlier, in passing. He wondered if she recalled the encounter. The Order had worked extensively with Ashley's grandmother, Gertrude.

Progress bars moved slowly across the screen. Verhoeven eyed the display with a growing sense of suspicion. The system had never failed like this before. It had functioned strangely since they reinserted Cyrus Cooper into the simulation, but the system crashed moments after Ashley

Waterford was inserted into the virtual environment.

Surely a coincidence…but what if it wasn't?

Chapter 44 - How is that Heaven

The Voss Compound, Isle of Kapros

Cyrus walked into Voss's lab and found Reese and Voss once more at work on...well, he still wasn't sure exactly what they were constructing. But progress had been made. The small metal box was taking shape. Every time he saw it, the confined little device was packed with more wires and more tiny components. A small dish shape had been fixed to the top now. It looked like a shallow bowl...and, well, he thought it was the top. It could be the bottom for all he knew. Sooner or later, he would have to ask them what they were up to.

Wagner was sitting at a computer near the back wall of the lab. He was manipulating a spreadsheet and a charting application. The poor guy was in the process of scheduling shifts and distributing work details, Cyrus realized. He couldn't help wondering if the promotion had proven to be everything his friend hoped it would be. Wagner was sharp and tough. It was a shame to see him pushing paper. Still, a promotion was a promotion. As long as his friend was happy...

The glass wall separating Voss's office from the lab was now transparent. Cyrus could see Barnabe in the next room, still at the conference table and working on his computer. He was certainly making the most of his time on the server cluster. Unfortunately, still without anything to show for it.

Cyrus glanced at his watch and was surprised to see that it was 3:22. Hondo was supposed to make another attempt to contact Charlie in a quarter-hour. Perhaps equally concerning, neither of them had reached Luke Reid. Even calls to the Coalition Command's main switchboard were going unanswered. Something was very wrong.

Added to all of that, Cyrus had just about the worst headache he could recall. It had only grown worse over the last few hours. Light had become painful to his eyes, and he grew increasingly nauseous. He was glad to have Reese busy with Voss. So far, she had been too preoccupied to notice how out of sorts he'd been.

Standing ten feet inside the door of Voss's lab, Cyrus squinted against the overhead light. He watched Reese and Voss working at the counter and Wagner sitting at the computer near the far wall. The room around him seemed to tip sharply for a brief second. Cyrus added dizziness to his growing list of odd symptoms. He had tried to keep the discomfort to himself, but it was becoming serious. Maybe it was time to tell Voss what was happening. After all, the Doc had a fully stocked sick bay and substantial medical expertise.

Cyrus stepped forward, keeping his eyes locked on Reese, who was still seated at the counter in the center of the room. He watched her closely. Her lips moved as she said something to Voss. Voss's mouth moved in reply, but Cyrus heard nothing. It wasn't just their voices that were missing, he realized…he heard nothing at all. The world had gone entirely silent.

Looking down at his hand, he snapped his fingers and heard nothing. He repeated the process, this time snapping the fingers of both hands. Nothing.

"Ah, guys," he called to Reese and Voss. They were twenty feet away, but neither acknowledged him. He called to them a second time, this time more loudly...except he suddenly had no voice.

The room tipped and spun as another bout of dizziness swept over him. He spread his feet into a wide stance and fought to remain upright. That brought an idea. He stomped one foot, trying to slap the sole of his shoe against the floor. The gesture made no sound. No sound at all.

The pressure behind his eyes seized him suddenly. It was a crushing force smashing him from all directions. His ears popped. It felt like he'd just been submerged in two hundred feet of water...but he could still breathe. He tried to take a step forward but found he could not.

His vision began to darken, growing dim at the corners of his eyes. The room around him fell into total darkness in what felt like seconds. He could hear and see nothing, but the pressure against every inch of his body remained constant. Strangely, the stabbing pain behind his eyes began to lessen for the first time in what felt like forever.

Cyrus blinked hard, and his vision cleared. The crushing force, along with his dizziness and nausea, was gone in that instant. Even the headache was entirely gone. He was standing in exactly the same spot, ten feet inside the door of Voss's lab, with his feet spread in a wide, stable stance. His hands were clenched into half fists as if he had just snapped his fingers. He looked up at the long counter in the middle of the room when he heard Barnabe's voice.

"Yeah, but that's what I never understood about martyrdom," Barnabe said. "72 virgins? How is that heaven?" He took a bite of his apple and glanced at those seated around the table. "Give me a dozen girls who know what they're doing and are ready to rock. Heck, give me four smoking hot sluts—mine for all time—then I *might* be willing to blow myself to smithereens. *But virgins? No way."*

Everyone at the table stared at Barnabe. No one seemed to know what to say.

"I'm just saying," Barnabe grinned and took another bite of his apple.

As taken aback as everyone was by Barnabe's warped view of the world around him, they seemed even more surprised by Cyrus's appearance. Reese shot an errant look in his direction before doing a double take and then bolting from her chair.

"Cyrus," she called. "Where have you been? I've been worried sick."

All eyes were on him. Reese slipped into his arms, and he felt relief, both from her presence and from the sudden lack of stabbing pain from behind his eyes. It was like a night and day difference—he didn't know what had changed, but the pain had just disappeared.

Hondo slipped away from the table and moved in their direction. "Are you alright?" he asked, meeting Cyrus's eye. "You look like you've seen a ghost."

"I'm fine," Cyrus said, but his voice lacked confidence. "I'm just surprised that everyone is looking at me like this."

In truth, there was more to it. He was shocked by the presence of everyone in the room. In the blink of an eye, Wagner had disappeared. Conversely, Barnabe, Anna Voss, Gretchen Gamble, and Ashley Waterford had materialized out of thin air.

After studying the room for several seconds, Cyrus took Reese by the hand. He tipped his head toward the door before leading her out of the room. They crossed Voss's office and stepped out into the hallway before he stopped to look at her.

"What's wrong?" she asked. Concern was plainly visible

on her face.

"Where did they all come from?" Cyrus asked.

Reese scowled. She didn't understand. "Who?"

"Anna, Gretchen, and Ashley. Where did they come from?"

Reese only seemed more concerned. "We've been waiting for you. Where have you been? It's not like you to disappear without a word."

Cyrus was feeling more concerned by the second.

Disappear? What are you talking about?

He felt like he'd had a seizure or something—no...he was missing time. It would explain why everyone seemed to materialize out of thin air.

When he spoke, his voice was quiet. He wasn't sure he wanted to hear the answer. He sure didn't want to ask the question. "How long was I gone?"

Her brows furrowed at the odd question. "The last anyone saw you was late yesterday afternoon. What are you saying? You don't know?"

Slipping his phone from his hip pocket, Cyrus glanced at the display. 2:14 pm. The last time he'd looked at a clock, it had been just after 4 pm.

"What's going on?" Reese asked. She looked concerned. Cyrus couldn't blame her.

What's going on?

The question bounced around inside his head over and over again. Cyrus looked at Reese, but no answer came to mind. He looked at the blank, pale walls of the wide hallway and the glossy floor shine. Setting off slowly, he headed for the end of the corridor. Reese followed him onto the balcony overlooking the common room on the ground floor. The city's rooftops sprawled out in the distance beyond the glass face of the building. White billowing clouds hung high, and a small aircraft was visible in the distance. Movement could be seen on the city streets beyond the compound walls.

"Are you alright?" Reese asked.

Cyrus took a long look at her but didn't respond. His gaze moved on, sweeping across the interior of the five-story-high atrium and the contents of the first floor. He placed his hands on the rounded surface of the wide chrome railing and leaned over the open space.

"Cyrus, you're scaring me."

Cyrus stepped back from the rail and looked at the cold metallic surface. A damp smudge marked where his hand had been. The mark was disappearing as the cool surface of the railing equalized once more. He stared at the rail, reached out, and quickly rapped a knuckle against it. A hollow metallic resonant gong rang out from inside the metal tube.

Turning, Cyrus looked at Reese. Understanding written on his face. "Everything seems so real," he said.

Ashley Waterford looked out over the paved circular driveway and the large ornate water fountain. The compound's massive exterior wall marked the boundary of the courtyard beyond. She could feel the late afternoon sun radiating through the massive wall of glass as it bathed the entire ground floor of the compound. Doctor Voss's stronghold, she thought. It certainly was impressive. Though she'd heard her late grandmother speak of Voss and his family fortress many times, she had never seen it firsthand. And she never could have imagined the circumstances that would bring her here or the news she would deliver.

"What do you think of the place?" Cyrus asked.

The sound of his voice startled her. She'd been staring out the window for some time, lost in her thoughts. Turning on a heel, she smiled at the sight of him. "Gertrude often spoke of Doctor Voss," she said.

He nodded and approached slowly. Perhaps cautiously, she thought. His hands were in his pockets, and his eyes were roaming the empty room rather than focusing on her. It had been a long time since they'd met in person. They'd only spoken a couple of times in recent years. A lot had changed since their brief time together. Her thoughts flashed momentarily to Reese Knoland's smile and how she'd been so comfortable tucked in his embrace when Cyrus returned only a few short hours ago.

Yes, a lot had changed.

"I'm glad you could make it," Cyrus said. His gaze finally met hers, and she felt her heart race. A surprising experience since she had put their brief courtship firmly behind her. His proximity brought back a brief but vivid flood of memories and feelings. Some of them good, and some of them fairly horrifying. Suddenly, her grandmother's betrayal felt very close to the surface once more. She was less nostalgic about that, but it put things in perspective.

"You wanted to know more about my brother's involvement with the Order of Origin," Ashley said. Breaking his gaze, she turned back to the window and focused on the ground beyond the glass. "He wasn't the one you should be asking about. Gertrude had a lot more to do with the cult."

"Gertrude?" Cyrus muttered. Stepping up beside her, he looked out into the grounds. He tipped his head back, seeming to appreciate the warmth of the sunshine as well. "Evidence suggests that the Order killed Gertrude."

Ashley glanced at him. She appreciated the way he avoided referring to Gertrude as her grandmother. Even after years of processing that particular deception and betrayal, he seemed to appreciate how it could still be a sore subject. She glanced down at one of her closed fists and realized it might be obvious to someone like him.

Ashley smiled and squared with him. "Do you really think the cult killed her—or had her killed—and then left a card on her body?"

Cyrus grinned. "I'll admit, that part always seemed a bit on the nose to me. A literal calling card? It does seem unlikely."

"As you might've guessed, I've spent years untangling Gertrude's...*mess*." Even saying the words felt like acid dripping off her tongue. There weren't words to describe what she'd uncovered in the wake of the woman's death.

Cyrus arched a brow. "It's a good thing she left you the resources to do the digging."

Ashley nodded. The inheritance. At first, she'd been repulsed; the idea that any part of the crazy old woman's legacy could in any way taint her future was appalling. Then Ashley decided to put the money to good use. Cyrus's investigation of her grandmother had turned up a wealth of sensitive and potentially volatile information. When he closed the case, he turned the hard drive containing all of Gertrude Waterford's work over to Ashley and walked away. Though he'd never said as much, presumably, he didn't trust anyone with the sensitive information. Not even his own people. He left her the information, closed the case, and walked away.

It turned out that, though Ashley was not Gertrude's biological granddaughter, she had been legally adopted. As such, she was the old woman's next of kin. With Ashley's brother's recent passing, all of Gertrude's estate and wealth had passed to her. Since that day, Ashley had made it her mission to understand what Gertrude had really been up to, and why she had perpetrated the crimes she had.

"William was a pawn," Ashley said. "He didn't know

about Gertrude's work, and I'm certain he didn't fully understand the Order of Origin. William was different and seeking acceptance. He wanted to understand who and what he was. I think the Order preyed on that vulnerability."

"I don't think anyone fully understands what the order is all about," Cyrus said. "But William was special. And Gertrude didn't do right by him."

Ashley fell silent for a while. Gertrude had started as a physicist but changed specialties seemingly without reason. She moved into neurobiology, where she worked for decades before her death. It was only shortly before Gertrude was killed that Ashley learned the truth about herself and her brother. They'd been born in a lab, the results of Gertrude Waterford's genetic experimentation.

For Ashley, the revelation explained so much. It elucidated why she couldn't be near others without suffering intense discomfort and hearing voices that were not her own. It explained why she could hear the thoughts of others. For the first time, she understood what a Reader was. And since that day, digging deeper into Gertrude's work, she'd come to understand that there were others like herself out there. Others, like her late brother, could Push their will upon people and make them do what they saw fit. Gertrude had brought about these unnatural abilities through barbaric and horrible experiments in genetic manipulation.

"You're going after the Order of Origin?" she said. He watched her but didn't reply. He looked distracted. There was something unusual in his gaze. His focus seemed to move frequently between her and everything around them. Not so much that he wasn't paying attention—it was more like he was paying undue attention to everything around them.

It was odd.

"Radley Verhoeven has captured the scrutiny of world leaders," Ashley said. Her focus was now entirely on Cyrus as she tried to understand what was on his mind. Knowing him, there was more here than met the eye. "What did they find in Wyoming?"

"No one's saying," Cyrus offered with a shrug. "And we're talking about people who normally aren't good at keeping secrets, so it must be pretty important. Whatever it was, it must be damn convincing. It resulted in the Order being taken seriously on the world stage."

"That's what concerns me. As you know, I've been digging through Gertrude's database. It's taken me two years, but I finally found out who was bankrolling her work."

Cyrus looked interested. "She had a lot of patents in her name," he said. "I suspected she was paying for everything herself."

Ashley laughed. "That only proves you didn't get to know her. No, she had backers—one backer, really. Radley Verhoeven was footing the bill. It was very difficult to trace. The connections were buried under corporations, shell companies—a crazy number of international buffers were used, but all the money came from the Order of Origin."

The shock on Cyrus's face was unmistakable. "Verhoeven?" He shrugged. "I guess it's not hard to believe. What exactly was she doing for them?"

Shoving her hands into the hip pockets of her jeans, Ashley turned slowly in a half circle and contemplated the best way to answer the question. She paced slowly in front of the glass while she spoke. "Gertrude had facilities all over the world. Labs in over a dozen locations, several running experiments in parallel. It was a large-scale operation, all things considered. For the last fifteen years, everything she did focused on genetic manipulation in one way, shape, or form."

They had both seen the horror show Gertrude kept in her lab in North Carolina. Seeing the look on Cyrus's face, she knew he was picturing that lab, the wall covered with jars, and the hundreds of mutated specimens accumulated over time. There were more labs, each with similar horror shows on display. The old woman's willingness to pervert the natural order was horrifying.

"The abominations you saw in that lab mostly predated her recent work," Ashley clarified. "Modern technology and genetic mapping changed the way she operated. For the last decade, Gertrude was targeting and mapping specific genes, searching for the sequences and combinations necessary to achieve whatever goal she had in mind."

"Goal? Such as?"

"Apparently, she used me and William as a baseline," Ashley explained. "My ability as a Reader, and William's as a Pusher? She wanted to activate—for lack of a better word—those abilities in non-presenting specimens."

"And by specimens, you mean—"

"People," she grunted with a little more irritation than intended. "She tried to make others like us, if you can believe that. I was living my life in seclusion, thinking I was the only one with my disorder. The entire time, I thought my grandmother was helping to find a way to cure me. Really, she was trying to inflict my ability on others." The pain in her voice was impossible to hide.

Cyrus offered a sad nod of his head. He started to speak but stopped. She sensed there was something relevant there. Something more than a pleasantry. "What is it?" she asked.

"She did it, too," he said quietly. He looked her in the eyes. "Gertrude created more Readers. I ran into one earlier this week. The Order is using them to manipulate people."

Ashley huffed a frustrated breath and began pacing once more. She was confident that had been the case, but somehow, confirmation of the suspicion cemented the frustration. "If that's the case, there will be more freaks where they came from," she ranted. "Readers and Pushers were just the start for Gertrude. She moved on...got more creative, you might say."

Cyrus watched her. She saw concern in his eyes, but he didn't push her to continue. She appreciated the understanding.

"When I uncovered the hidden labs, I started digging deeper," Ashley said. "Everywhere I found a lab, I found death and destruction. Police reports of strange deaths, mysterious disappearances, mass graves of hideous bodies—every cliche in the book. Gertrude was experimenting with everything. I found records of experiments to accelerate healing and limb regeneration, increase intelligence and cognitive ability, modifications to increase muscle mass and bone density...the list goes on."

"It sounds like she was trying to re-engineer the human race," Cyrus said.

Ashley stopped pacing a glared at him. "That's exactly what it seems like. It was all a matter of mapping genes and experimenting with the way they interacted with each other. She was literally turning them on and off like switches and testing how they influenced each other. But it wasn't that easy. A given gene differs from one person to the next. So, the gene responsible for the color of my eyes could be entirely different from the next girl with the same eye color. Natural mutations made the work that much more difficult."

Cyrus raised a hand, motioning for her to slow down. "So you're saying it's not just a matter of turning the right sequence of genes on and off. They have to be the right genes with the right properties. The genes themselves are unique from one person to the next?"

Ashley offered a sad nod. "For Gertrude, it meant a whole

lot more trial and error. More invasive testing and untold human suffering. This wasn't the kind of thing she could do in a simulation. She did it all with test subjects. *Human test subjects.*"

The idea seemed to sicken Cyrus. He gnashed his teeth and stared at the floor. "So, the Reader I ran into in New England?"

"Gertrude had that pretty much dialed in, from what I can tell. It takes a host who is genetically predisposed, of course. But she developed a retrovirus cocktail to modify the gene sequence and bring about the mutation."

"Jesus," Cyrus mumbled.

"Something is interesting about the genes for Readers and Pushers," she said. "Gertrude never figured it out, but the roles are gender specific."

Cyrus looked confused.

"For whatever reason," Ashley explained, "only women can become Readers, and only men can become Pushers."

She watched his brows furrow as he tried to understand the significance.

"I know," she said with a shrug. "Apparently, it's just one of those things. From what I can tell, reconciling that twist drove Gert nuts. It's the one small point of amusement I've found in all this. Petty, but I'll take what I can get. The woman used me..." Her voice faded off, letting the implication hang in the air.

Cyrus was silent for almost two whole minutes. Ashley could see some heavy-duty processing going on behind his eyes. She just didn't know what he would make of everything she'd said.

"So you're saying the Order has other...*special members* I need to worry about?" he said at last. "Stronger, smarter, capable of God knows what?"

She shrugged. "Maybe. But Maybe not. From what I've uncovered, she was fixated on better understanding William and me. She wanted to make more like us. She found gene sequences that could result in different abilities in different people, but you have to remember that those genes also differed from one person to the next. Based on her records, she never moved into extended research on those other abilities."

He looked surprised at that. "Why not?"

Ashley shrugged again. "I've asked myself that question endlessly over the last few years. Trying to understand what motivated Gertrude is like trying to read tea leaves. But over time, I gained the sense that the people footing the bill had her looking for a specific genetic combination. I think she was trying to cultivate a specific gene sequence and accomplish a particular goal."

"What goal?"

With a shrug, Ashley said, "I have no idea."

Cyrus still seemed distracted.

"Level with me," she said. "Something's bugging you. Tell me what it is."

He seemed to take his time coming to a decision. His hands hung at his sides, folding and unfolding to and from fists. He turned and looked up at the series of balconies at the end of each floor overhead. No one was there. That must've been what he wanted because he stepped close to her and spoke quietly. "I want you to Read me," he said.

The request didn't make any sense. She'd never been able to Read him, and they both knew it. He was the only person she had ever met who had been entirely impossible to Read, so she simply didn't understand.

Do you think something has changed?

She started to say, "You know that won't—"

He shook his head and interrupted. "Just try. Please?"

There was concern written in his eyes. She could see it as plain as day but still didn't understand it. "Fine," she whispered, plucking the eighth-inch wide transparent circular patch from behind her left ear. She stuck its adhesive back against the sleeve of her shirt where it wouldn't contact her skin and took a calming breath.

She saw him staring at the tiny patch she'd just removed and realized he wasn't familiar with the technology. "It's a revision on Gertrude's neuro inhibitor," she explained, knowing he would recall how her grandmother had worn a similar patch to keep Ashley from Reading her. "Only in this case, the patch doesn't keep me from being Read. It helps me keep all the other voices out."

Cyrus was stunned. "You're kidding," he muttered. "Gertrude could've done that at any time? She wore the patch to keep you from reading her mind…but she could've given you one to keep everyone out of your head?"

A slow nod from Ashley. "She liked having me under her thumb. I stayed locked up in my apartment, hiding from the world for most of my life. She wasn't trying to help me. Everything she did was designed to control me."

"So this patch keeps you from Reading other people? She could've done that at any time?"

Ashley shrugged. "I made minor adjustments to her existing design and came up with this. It doesn't keep all the voices out, but it tempers them down so I can concentrate. On a normal day, I don't have any trouble at all."

"And if you take the patch off?"

"All the voices come flooding back."

Cyrus shook his head. He looked disgusted. "I'm sorry to ask this of you, but it's important. I need to know if anything has changed."

It was an interesting idea. It had been years since she'd last seen him. They had both changed in more ways than either of them probably realized. Would she be able to Read him?

Only one way to find out...

They stood face to face. Ashley closed her eyes. She reached out to him with her mind. There were voices all around her—she could hear almost a dozen speaking at once in the distance. It sounded like people at the far end of a wide room, with everyone talking simultaneously behind a closed closet door. The voices were indistinct, but they were there. She pushed them aside and listened for Cyrus. She knew the sound of his spoken voice and longed to hear the sound of his internal monologue. They had once meant a great deal to each other, and she wanted to know him in a way that only she could.

But there was no voice.

Ashley opened her eyes. Cyrus gazed back at her, and still she continued to focus. She could see thoughts behind his eyes...she could always do that. But there was no voice.

Nothing.

"I'm sorry," she said. The disappointment of her tone betrayed the secret desire she'd held that it might actually have worked. She felt her cheeks warm at the thought and hoped he didn't understand what she'd really meant. It was silly, she reasoned. His unreadability had initially been one of his most attractive traits.

Too much had changed. Their time had come and gone; there was no question about it.

Cyrus blinked hard and rubbed his temples with the pads of both thumbs.

"What is it?" she asked.

He smiled. "You're just helping me confirm a theory.

Now I need to figure out how to put it into practice."

Chapter 45 - Worried About Number Five

Plains, Montana, United States

The lab tech wheeled the cart down the long hall and onto the elevator. Milton Casper pressed the button for the lowest level and stepped back as the doors swept shut with an audible thud. The lift shuddered as it began to descend. The old contraption made him uneasy every time he used it; the buzz of the old bulbs overhead, the tired glow of the lights on the control panel marking each of the underground levels. None of it compared to the noise from the ancient cable system supporting the old steel car as it moved sluggishly through the shaft hundreds of feet underground.

The elevator car came to a jarring and abrupt stop, the bell dinging softly a half second before the doors began to slide into recesses on either side of the exit. Casper was in motion even before the doors had come to rest, pushing the wheeled cart through the opening as soon as there was room. The wheels glided silently across the concrete floor, and he moved swiftly through the wide corridor. Delivering the six canisters was the highlight of his shift because it meant he got to see Katherine. Her smile made braving the lift almost worthwhile.

Near the end of the corridor, Casper stopped the cart a few yards shy of the vault-like door in the concrete wall. It was twice as wide as a standard doorway, made of dense, shiny steel, and was over a foot thick. A rotary locking wheel occupied the center of the massive contraption, and a pair of hinges protruded along the rightmost edge of the frame. The pin in the center of each hinge was as big around as Casper's leg and 24 inches long.

He spun the massive locking wheel and heard a hiss as the airtight seal surrounding the door released. A gentle mechanical grumble passed through the wheel as it turned effortlessly, the slight tremble resulting from massive 8-inch thick pins retracting from the door's perimeter as part of an air-tight seal.

Pushing the heavy door back on the great hinges, Casper looked into the lab beyond the threshold. The room was about twenty feet wide and about twice as deep. A wide computer control console sat near the left wall, overlooking the stout torpedo shapes lined up along the right wall. Casper grabbed the first of the three cylinders from the top shelf of his cart. He took the handle on the end of it in his right hand and slid his left arm beneath the two-foot long, eighteen-inch wide chrome case to support its twenty-five pounds. The cylinder was rugged, but the small black box on the opposite end contained a fragile and easy to damage electronic interface.

Stepping carefully over the foot-tall lip of the door's frame, Casper entered the lab. The tall blond woman behind the computer console looked up and smiled. "Thank you for coming so quickly," she said. Her voice carried a trace of an English accent that mixed with her Indian tones in a way that Casper enjoyed. "You're just in time. Number five is ahead of schedule. His metabolism has hit a spurt, and he's consuming the cocktail at an accelerated rate."

Taking the cue, Casper passed the sixth pod and moved

to the fifth, which was placed parallel to it. He slid the chrome cylinder into a cradle on the small rack beside a matching cylinder. He turned the tube so its handle was parallel with the shelf and saw the light on the corner of the cradle turn green. Pressing backward gently, he felt the cradle glide backward on rails. There was a pop and a hiss. The light beside the cylinder went amber and then green, showing the new unit was online.

Turning around, he met Katherine's eyes. She smiled and nodded her appreciation. He felt his heart rate quicken at the sight. Fraternization within the Order was forbidden, but he saw mutual interest in her eyes. Those rules would change after the Migration, and he knew she was looking forward to that day. Certainly, they were both eagerly anticipating their involvement in the next stage of human evolution, but this was different. In recent months, he'd become more interested in what the Migration would mean for him personally. He knew Katherine was looking forward to the event for a similarly selfish reason.

"Should we be worried about number five?" Casper asked. Until then, he would try to keep himself focused and on task.

"Not according to Verhoeven," Katherine said. "It's likely they will all reach a similar point as the transition nears completion."

He was about to return to the cart for the next of the remaining five canisters, but her comment got him interested. Casper stepped to the side of pod number five. These six pods were all alike: eight-foot-long capsule shapes made of aluminum and an inch-thick acrylic polymer that looked and felt exactly like glass. An acrylic canopy made the entire top half of the pod, essentially a full length lid that hadn't opened since the occupants of each device had been inserted more than two months previous. Frost coated the edges of the transparent lid where it met with the aluminum housing that comprised the bed-like bottom portion rounded at either end. A thick cloud filled the space within, the inert form of a naked man lying on his back in the frigid space. Thick tubes ran into his legs and arms. His hair had been cut short before being inserted into the pod, and it hadn't grown noticeably over the last two months.

Each pod was attached to a bank of equipment on its right. The shelf containing the canister Casper delivered was just below chest height and had two positions. One slot held the feed currently supplying the pod, while the next was used to prime the upcoming supply. The two positions ensured the pod was never without a constant flow of nutrients and supplements vital to the men inside the pods.

"How long until they're ready?" Casper asked.

Excitement danced in Katherine's eyes. "Not long," she said.

She stepped beside him and gazed into the pod. The fog inside the enclosure drifted and circulated with some slow-moving random air current. Casper saw the man's chest rise and fall as he took slow, shallow breaths. He guessed the minor air circulation was due to his respiration.

Casper looked closer at the man, struggling to make out his form through the fog. It was Bauer, he realized. He recognized the man's features. Though indistinct, he was sure. His gaze shifted down the man's torso, and he struggled to glimpse the physicist through the mist. "Really? They're almost done with the regimen? It's hard to tell, but he looks no different than the last time I saw him."

Katherine cocked her head, glancing up from the glass with a toothy grin. "You and Bauer spent a lot of time in the buff, did you?"

Stammering, Casper's cheeks went pink. He shoved suddenly clammy hands into the pockets of his lab coat. "That's not—I mean, he's…"

She laughed and grabbed him by the elbow, towing him across the room to circle the computer console by the opposite wall. "You're too easy to tease," she laughed. "I know what you meant."

Casper watched as her fingers poked and dabbed at the glass of the large touch-screen display. She moved from screen to screen, finally stopping at the silhouette depiction of a man. A series of callouts faded into view, circling the silhouette with arrows pointing to different positions on the figure's anatomy. Katherine tapped from one callout to the next, its information filling the space beside the depiction and describing the feature in greater detail. She explained what he was seeing, saving him the trouble of reading.

"Muscle mass has increased by seventy-three percent on average," Katherine said after tapping on the figure's arm. "But you're right, Bauer doesn't look as different as you might expect. That's because the density of his muscle tissue has changed. On a cellular level, the muscle tissue is both denser and more efficient."

Casper couldn't hide his surprise.

"As you might expect," Katherine continued, "bone density, the composition of cartilage, ligaments, and tendons, as well as veins and arteries have adjusted to compensate." She tapped to the figure's leg and the depiction showed before and after examples of bone cross sections and ligament changes at a cellular level. "Similar changes have occurred in the lungs—" she tapped the screen again. "And the heart to allow greater oxygenation of the blood." A pair of animations came on screen. The left showed what was presumably normal blood flow, while an example on the right showed the augmented version: blood flowing faster, richer in color, likely containing increased oxygen levels, and who knew what else.

It was incredible but a little concerning at the same time. Stronger, faster, more powerful...the next stage in human evolution. But it was Bauer. He had always been sort of a dick. Why had Verhoeven chosen someone like him to be the first in this new line?

"What's wrong?" Katherine asked.

Casper believed in the Order. He had never found comfort in conventional religion, but the miracles of life on Earth convinced him there was something greater out there. Some extraordinary scheme behind all that we were and all that we had become as a race. Natural selection and evolution weren't enough to explain the miracle that was human life. Verhoeven's explanation of life on Earth, the Order of Origin, wasn't religion for him. It was the explanation he had been seeking. It made sense in a way that religion and evolution never could. The Order of Origin held the answers. It was only a matter of time before the truth was shared with the rest of the world.

"Why start with Bauer?" he said, finally giving up his reluctance to ask the question that bothered him most. "I understand we're an imperfect race and changes must be made...but if Verhoeven is going to fix us, why start with *Bauer*?"

Katherine met his eye. She gave a long, pointed look as if she were making a difficult decision. "Close the door," she said finally.

Casper's brows rose and pinched with concern. He glanced at the vault door, wide open to the hallway. Stepping back from the console, he moved slowly across the room, stepped over the foot-tall, foot-wide threshold, and grabbed the internal handle. The massive steel slab shifted easily on its hinges, and once more, the gap closed. With a spin of the locking wheel, he engaged the pressure seal. Whatever Katherine had to share, he anticipated the gravity of it as if something fundamental was about to change.

Back at her side, he followed her finger as she pointed at the console again. She tapped on the silhouette's head, and a small dialog box appeared in the center of the screen. It was asking for a security override code. "What's this about?" Casper asked.

Katherine didn't reply. She tapped a long, complicated password into the touchscreen keyboard, and the dialog prompt disappeared. A new arrow appeared, extending from the figure's head to a large callout containing a schematic illustration of a complicated computer chip.

"The procedure hasn't been perfected," Katherine explained, her voice no more than a whisper. "The physical modifications are entirely reliable—We can reproduce them every time. But something unexpected keeps happening in the brain. Portions become…unreliable…unpredictable. It's as if the brain is rebelling against changes happening throughout the body."

Casper nodded. "Motor control," he guessed. "The brain needs to adapt to these changes—recalibrate, essentially."

Shaking her head, Katherine's concern seemed to grow. "A likely assumption, but that hasn't been the case. The problems are entirely unrelated. Test subjects have, for lack of a better explanation, de-evolved."

"De-evolved? What does that mean?"

"Exactly what you might guess. They have become aggressive and animal-like—prone to violence…they quickly start to exhibit very primitive behaviors. It's as if their intelligence—their very humanity—is sucked away as part of the augmentation process."

Casper studied the concern on her face. She wasn't putting him on, and she certainly wasn't exaggerating. But it didn't make sense. The Tangury were responsible for putting life on Earth. They had birthed our entire universe. They shouldn't need to experiment to get these things right. His eyes moved to the illustration of the computer chip near the head of the figure on the display.

"What does this do?" he asked.

"It regulates motor skills and maintains baseline instincts."

"Baseline...what the hell does that mean?"

Katherine's lips pursed. "It means you should be glad it's Bauer in that pod and not you or me. When he comes out, he won't be himself anymore. He'll be an automaton. A biologically superior, neurologically absent human robot."

Stepping backward, Casper felt dizzy. He looked at the row of six pods aligned by the wall. This explained why there were only six, but he still didn't understand why Verhoeven was doing this in the first place.

"Why weren't we told about this?" he asked. Of all the questions passing through his mind, it seemed the least likely to cause him trouble. He trusted Katherine, but the walls had just started to close in on him. How could there be an explanation for what she was saying?

"It's the Migration," Katherine said. "Something has happened on their home world. They can't wait any longer—we're not evolving fast enough."

"So they're doing this to us?" he couldn't believe what he heard. "To what end? What's the point?"

"Of course not," Katherine said. "Bauer volunteered for this. He was a soldier before he joined the Order. He will be a soldier again when the procedure is complete."

"A soldier? With a supercharged body and no brain? How is that useful?"

Katherine placed to fingers on the screen, stretching the view of the computer chip and expanding it into greater detail. "You wouldn't believe what this chip can do."

Chapter 46 - He's Got an Addiction

The Voss Compound, Isle of Kapros

Cyrus eyed Barnabe as he walked through Voss's office with Ashley at his heels. Barnabe was one with this computer again, fingers flying across the keyboard and his gaze fixed on one of the two displays. He was a dog with a bone, Cyrus thought—tenacious when he had a task to accomplish. It was a shame he was such a pain in the ass the rest of the time.

They made it to the next-door lab without ever drawing Barnabe's attention.

The lights in Voss's lab were turned down low. Reese, Voss, Hondo, Anna, and Gretchen sat on stools arranged in a semi-circle around the counter in the center of the room. The small electronic device Reese and Doctor Voss had been working on was powered up. A vast, defused bubble of light was projected from the box, expanding to about five feet wide and hanging in midair. A video feed played in the field of light—a first-person view as if looking out from another person's eyes. A city street and a wide sidewalk along a towering stonework wall existed. Cyrus recognized it as the street outside Voss's facility. Everything they saw was displayed in shimmering three-dimensional detail.

"That's perfect, Mister Wagner," Voss said loudly. "Could you move in for a closeup of something? Anything that's handy?"

Cyrus saw the small speakerphone on the counter beside the box creating the projection and understood what was happening. They were seeing a live feed from outside the fence. The view shifted, tipping slightly left and right with Wagner's gait as he moved along the sidewalk. He crossed the street and stopped before a sandwich board standing upright on the walkway. It listed the cafe's lunch and drink specials.

"Remarkable," Voss muttered.

Wagner shifted left and right, pivoting around the upright display and studying it from each side. Murmurs of admiration escaped those present. Reese stared at the semi-translucent holographic display with bright eyes and a satisfied smile. She didn't offer a word.

She and Voss had been working on this device since their arrival at the compound. Cyrus had written it off as busy work, something to occupy both while they waited for Barnabe's efforts to bear fruit and distract from their struggle to reestablish contact with Charlie Greene. That busy work had turned out to be something extraordinary.

Cyrus was now sure he understood why they hadn't been able to contact Charlie. It was the same reason the ceramic knife he'd broken in Bangkok had mysteriously healed and returned to his possession. His raging headache had kept him from understanding what was happening sooner. Ironically, at the same time, it had been the first clue pointing to what was happening to them now.

Watching the video projection for a few extra moments, Cyrus didn't speak until he saw Reese's gaze fall on him. "That's incredible," Cyrus said with an approving smile.

"This is what you've been working on this entire time?"

She shrugged a bit bashfully.

Voss spun on his stool and slapped his leg with enthusiasm. He was grinning from ear to ear. "It's fantastic, isn't it?" he said. "I was explaining how Shadowlight worked and how we use the glasses to experience the downloads," he said. He referred to the memory recording technology he'd been developing and refining for several years. It was part of the mission that had first brought Cyrus to Voss's lab back in the day. The technology made it possible to record memories and experiences, but they could only be played back by downloading them into another person's mind. It was a problem because the experience was more invasive than Voss preferred.

"Reese had this idea," Voss went on. "A sort of middle ground to avoid the neurological trauma associated with repeated downloads. The three-dimensional aspect of the hologram gives us the same insight but doesn't include the emotional component."

Voss planned to use his technology to treat different types of neurological impairment, including Alzheimer's disease, as well as any number of mental and emotional disorders. His technology captured everything a user experienced: thoughts, emotions, and sensory feedback like touch and smell. In some situations, downloading experiences could be potentially dangerous, and filtering the massive amount of information had always been a problem.

"The 3D experience would have its own filter," Cyrus surmised. "Eliminating the emotional component?"

"Exactly!" Voss chuckled. "This type of interface would be far more practical for many applications. It's ingenious, really. Simply brilliant."

"It was your idea," Reese said. "We just needed to build the projector."

Voss looked at her with wide eyes. "Idea, yes. But the hardware doesn't exist. Nothing like this has been built. It's not just the projector—you designed a way to interface it with my existing hardware. This is a one-of-a-kind system. Surely you realize what you've done? It's incredible."

Reese smiled and shrugged. Cyrus knew what she was thinking. If only she could talk about the other things she'd built. Voss would be flabbergasted.

It was a shame she couldn't fully appreciate just how hard it was to impress a man like Voss, Cyrus mused.

He rubbed his temple, thinking about the sudden disappearance of his crushing migraine once more. This had to be the point of what was happening. Putting everyone in one place and letting them interact. If he was right, the headache would return. He didn't yet understand why it had dissipated, but as his eyes moved from face to face in the room, he felt confident he understood the situation. At the mental institution, Samuel Dabney had tried to warn him; Cyrus just hadn't expected something so elaborate.

Still, a little additional confirmation was required. The more he knew, the better his chances of solving their current problem.

He eyed the small patch still stuck to Ashley's sleeve. Though every minute without the patch was unpleasant and possibly even painful, Cyrus had asked her to leave it off for a short while. Finding everyone gathered in the lab had been a lucky break.

"What can you tell me?" he asked Ashley in a hushed tone.

Her eyes moved slowly around the room. "Doctor Voss is excited," she said. "But you don't need my ability to see that. The man's positively beaming. I can tell you this: he's interested in how this viewing technique will save people the experience he had with you. I'm not getting anything specific, but he's troubled by whatever happened during that test. Conflicted might be the best way to describe it."

"You might want to change the channel before you hear something more," Cyrus suggested.

The odd look Ashley gave wasn't lost on Reese. Their hushed words had drawn her attention, and she stepped closer with a quizzical expression.

"What else have you got?" Cyrus said, urging Ashley onward.

Her head turning, Ashley looked at Reese briefly before looking back to the room as a whole. "Hondo is worried about someone named Charlie," Ashley said. "He thinks she's been radio silent for far too long. He wants to get *the device* online ASAP so you can check on her. Do I want to know what the device is?"

Cyrus shook his head and waited for her to continue, so Ashley said, "Anna is glad you've returned to the island. She's worried you carry too much guilt for what happened the last time you were here."

Cyrus nodded. "I'm sorry to put you through this, but this helps."

Reese stared at Cyrus with unblinking eyes. Her lips moved with a silent display of words intended for his eyes only. She formed the words, *she's a Reader?*

"Guilty as charged," Ashley said. She turned to Reese and answered the question that had been silently mouthed to the back of her head. "He didn't tell you about me?" There was a prim smile on the corners of her lips.

Reese arched a brow and offered an accusing glance in Cyrus's direction. "He's good with secrets," she said. "But what's this about?"

"Confirming a suspicion," Cyrus said.

"That one," Ashley said in a sharp tone and motioned

vaguely in the direction of the doorway leading to Voss's office and referring to Barnabe, "is quite the perve, even for a teenager." She looked at Reese. "I'm sure you've caught him staring at your ass. Trust me, you don't want to know what he's thinking while doing it." She looked at Cyrus. "And seriously, someone needs to have a talk with the kid. I personally have no problem with collecting pornography, but he's got an addiction or something. He had to put a second drive in his laptop just to—" she shivered visibly.

"I don't want to think about it," she said. Holding the small patch up on the tip of her raised finger, she frowned. "I've had enough. Do you mind?"

Cyrus grinned. "Yeah," he muttered. "I'm sorry about that. That's more than enough. You gave me exactly what I needed. Thank you."

Reese looked concerned. "What's going on? What's wrong?"

Two simple questions without simple answers. Ashley had just finished placing the tiny patch behind her left ear. "Thanks again," he said. "That helped a lot. And...I'll talk with Barnabe." He failed to suppress a grin with the last part of the statement.

Slipping his hand over Reese's, he tipped his head toward the door and led her out of the room. They crossed Voss's office, this time drawing Barnabe's attention briefly away from his computer screen. Was he working or spending time with his porn collection, Cyrus wondered. Great. Now, he'd never get that concern out of his head.

They made it to the hallway. Cyrus guided Reese to the elevator and hit the call button. "What's going on," she insisted.

"I'm losing time," he said as the elevator doors opened. They stepped inside and tapped a button on the wall. The doors closed. "I told you I went to Chicago a couple of days ago, but I didn't have a chance to explain what happened. I met with a man who once worked with the Order of Origin. He was scrambled and incoherent a lot of the time, but when he was lucid, he was pretty sharp. Going back about twenty years, the Order funded his work. He was experimenting with ways to interface the human brain with digital technology."

She looked confused. "Twenty years ago? That's crazy. The technology would've been…"

He nodded. "Yeah. It was." The elevator chimed, and the doors opened. Cyrus led her out onto the balcony overlooking the ground floor. "The tech was incredibly crude, but I think the Order has been refining ever since. I'm fairly sure they've perfected it, actually."

Reese watched him carefully, her concern seeming to grow. "Perfected it? How?"

Pulling the knife from his pocket, Cyrus extended the five-inch dagger blade with a sudden click. He raised the blade to the light and turned it back and forth in the glare. He closed the blade and passed it over to her.

"This way," he said and headed down the wide hallway leading away from the balcony. "Back in the lab, did you notice anything unusual when Ashley tried to Read you?"

Reese followed him down the hall, tagging along like a confused puppy. "No," she said. "Nothing at all, now that you mention it. Should I have?"

"No," he confirmed. "No one seems to notice it. Readers seem to be able to pull the foremost thoughts from people's minds entirely without their knowledge. No one even knows it's happening. No one—except for me."

"Wait," she said, grabbing and stopping him by the arm. "You're saying you can tell when Ashley Reads you?"

He shook his head. "For reasons I don't fully understand, she can't Read me. None of them can. But when they try, I can sense it. It's like a pressure behind my eyes. The harder they try, the more it hurts. But they never get through—they never get into my head."

"Like the woman at the bookstore—Jasmine?"

He nodded. "She knew what everyone was thinking except for me. It's the only reason we made it out of there."

"Why you? What's different about you?"

He shrugged. "I wish I knew." Turning, he motioned for her to follow.

"Cyrus? Why is this important now?"

They rounded a corner and walked halfway down a long hall before stopping in front of a wide, closed door. "Because someone has been trying to Read me ever since we got here," he said.

Reese stared at him, clearly not understanding. "Since we arrived on the island? *Days ago?*"

"I was bombarded so intensely and for so long that I didn't realize what was happening. It was beyond any experience I've ever had, and I've encountered a couple of Readers over the years. The one doing this must have an ability that's off the charts. I thought my head was going to explode. It hurt so bad that I didn't recognize it for what it was."

She stared. "An attack?"

He grimaced and waggled his hand in the air. "That was my first thought. Someone was trying hard to break through. Then, I did the math and factored in what I knew. I considered what I learned from my trip to Chicago and Samuel Dabney's ant farms."

"Ant farms?"

Cyrus eyed the closed door in front of them. There were several matching doors scattered along the length of the long hallway. "What if you could create a virtual

428

environment that was a duplicate of the real world down to the smallest detail?"

Reese was silent as she considered the idea. "Alright. Assuming you have the processing power, I suppose it's possible. What's your point."

"What if you could create that simulated environment and then place people into it without them becoming aware?"

Her gaze darkened. "Why would you do that—and who could it it?"

"Maybe scientific observation, like ants in an ant farm. Only, in this case, you don't want the ants to know what's happening, so you put them in a farm that looks just like their ant hill out in the wild."

"Alright...but *why?*"

"It's a controlled environment. It makes the ants, or people, easier to study."

She shook her head. "The ploy wouldn't hold up for long. People in that situation would figure it out pretty quickly. You could never create a virtual reality that was convincing enough to withstand scrutiny for long."

Cyrus looked up and down the empty hallway and then back at her. "You're sure?" he said.

She laughed and shook her head. "A confident assumption. I'll give you points for creativity, but it's impractical."

"Are you saying the technology isn't ready yet?"

She considered the question. "No. I can think of ways that it might be possible, technologically speaking. At least feasible to create a plausible, realistic environment. But you're suggesting we're all in the same ant farm—in a *shared* environment. There's no way to trick us all for long."

"That's because we're tricking ourselves. What if you had a virtual environment and a Reader who was there to ensure that environment simulated every detail, right down to every known expectation?"

Reese was silent. He could see the wheels working behind her eyes as she processed the nuances of the concept.

"That environment would become stronger and more detailed as you added more people. The simulation would continue to learn from the people inside it through the Reader."

"Using the Reader as an interface to better adapt to the expectations of the people inside the simulation..." Reese said.

"Put everyone in an enclosed space, such as this compound, and you have an ideal scenario."

Her teeth ground as if she were literally chewing on the idea. "Seems *really* far-fetched."

"I broke my knife in Thailand," Cyrus said. "And I never replaced it. That porcelain blade isn't easy to come by. The simulation didn't know the blade was broken because it couldn't read me. But it could Read you; you expected me to have the knife in my pocket like I always do.

"You all maintain that I disappeared yesterday, even though I didn't. I literally blinked, and a day passed. I think that was some kind of glitch in the simulation. Like I said, I'm the only person who can't be Read. I'm the unknown quantity here. And I can use that to prove I'm right about everything." He placed his hand on the door beside them.

"How?" Reese asked. He could see she was becoming increasingly curious about what was on the other side of the door.

"Readers can only access whatever is foremost on someone's mind," Cyrus explained. "It's still unclear how, and we still don't fully understand why, but that's an established fact. If I'm right and we're in a simulation fed by information provided by a Reader, it would explain my crushing headache since arriving. It would also mean that this simulation only knows what the people in it have focused on since we arrived here."

She nodded, willing to acknowledge the idea, at least so far as the exercise was concerned.

"I'm willing to bet that no one has given any direct consideration to what's on the other side of this door, at least since we landed on the island yesterday. If that's the case, the simulation doesn't have a clue. The system can't let us through until it knows how to render the environment."

Reese looked like she wanted to argue the point but didn't know where to begin. Fair, but he sounded like a crazy person.

"I won't be able to open this door for the same reason I haven't been able to reach Charlie," Cyrus said. He tapped the display beside the pair of closed doors. The dark screen flashed to life. A numeric pad was displayed along with an enter and a reset key, just like every other bedroom on the floor.

"You know the code?" Reese asked.

He nodded and entered the sequence: 7 5 5 2 1 1. A dull buzzer sounded, and the number pad pulsed on the screen. A small message appeared above the numbers. Access Denied.

Reese shrugged. "It just means you don't have the right code. Maybe it's changed since the last time you were in there. What's in that room?"

Cyrus smiled. "It doesn't prove anything if I tell you want's on the other side of that door." He entered the code once more, taking great care and moving with slow precision: 7 5 5 2 1 1.

Another dull buzzing sound, and the screen pulsed. The

error message was displayed once more.

Reese shrugged but said nothing. *See?*

Cyrus pulled the phone from his pocket and tapped a number from memory. "Hey, it's me," he said and tapped the button to put the call on speaker. "I know this will be an odd question, but have you changed the access code for your sister's room?"

The line was silent for two long beats before Anna replied. "No..." she said. "There was no point. It's the same: 7 5 5 2 1 1. Why?"

Cyrus swallowed hard. He'd put Anna in an uncomfortable position and forced unpleasant memories on her from out of the blue. "I'm just feeling nostalgic," he said. "I'm sorry. I hope you don't mind."

"Not at all," she said. "I've been thinking about her a lot, too."

The line went dead.

Reese looked confused. "I'm not sure what that proved," she said. "Clearly, someone changed the code. Anna just isn't aware of it."

"That's not it," he said. "My headache has been back for the last twenty minutes. I just gave Anna a reason to think about her sister's room. If I'm right, the simulation now knows what's on the other side of this door."

Reese rolled her eyes. She still wasn't buying it. She stepped forward and entered the code into the keypad: 7 5 5 2 1 1. The doors swept open with a hiss, and the lights inside the room flickered to life.

Reese followed Cyrus back into the elevator. He hit the button for 5, the building's top floor. The doors slid shut, and the elevator went into motion with a subtle bump.

Cyrus had been right about the combination to Natasha's room. It didn't work, and then suddenly it had. But did that mean he was right about the simulation? Could they be walking around inside a three-dimensional, virtual environment? It felt authentic. She could smell the faint scent of disinfectant used to clean the inside of the elevator; she had eaten breakfast earlier that morning and still felt it sitting heavy in her gut.

It was all too fantastic. If the technology existed, wouldn't she have heard something about it by now? Of course not. Their teleportation technology was a closely guarded secret. It would be egotistical to think that other cutting-edge tech wasn't in use out there, classified and under-wraps. But could they have been inserted into a virtual environment without their knowledge? The idea that Cyrus might have lost his mind wasn't as chilling as the thought that he might actually be right.

The elevator chimed and the doors slid open. The couple walked onto the 5th-floor balcony. The sun was setting over the city beyond the building's glass facade, and no one was in the common area on the ground floor far below. "If you're right about this," Reese said, "who is doing this? Why would they do it?"

Cyrus seemed transfixed by the view of the city. The sun was low on the horizon, far off to the left, making the roofline of one building shadow the next in exaggerated ways. It was an interesting contrast in extreme light and dark. "It's an efficient means of interrogation," he said without pulling his attention away from the cityscape. "You put a bunch of high-value assets inside a simulation and then soak them for all their worth."

Leaning against the railing, Reese considered the idea. "The kicker is, we have no way of being sure."

He looked at her. She saw certainty in his eyes.

"There must be a way to quantify it," she said.

"My knife suddenly reconstituting itself isn't enough for you? Or how we were locked out of Natasha's room until I coaxed Anna into thinking about that room?"

Reese swallowed hard. It wasn't conclusive evidence of anything. There were alternative ways to explain each point. She was a scientist—her mind required incontrovertible proof.

"The headache is the big one," he went on. "It was unbearable for the longest time. Then it disappeared. I think something happened to the simulation. At the same time, my entire night went missing. It was like a computer glitch that jumped me to a point in time a day later. I can't explain where I was for the lost time—you can't either. You just know I was missing. But now I'm back, and that damned headache is spooling up again. Something's happening. I'm sure of it."

She wanted to write off his headache as nothing more than a migraine. If she didn't know him better, she would have. She would've been willing to write the rest of his ideas off as delusions, but they'd been through too much together.

"Tell me about this guy you met in Chicago," she said. "He worked on this kind of technology for the Order?"

Cyrus nodded but didn't elaborate. Of course not. If they were in a simulation, everything they said and did was being observed. He wouldn't divulge sensitive information under those conditions.

My God...

If he was right, every thought that had crossed her mind was now compromised. If someone was doing this to them, they knew what she knew. Some of their most closely guarded secrets were exposed. Their house in the Colorado mountains, their base in Australia—

Ah! I'm giving them even more to work with!

"If you're right, we have to stop this," she said. "But

how?"

Cyrus was leaning against the railing beside her. He looked her square in the eye. "I have an idea," he said in a voice barely above a whisper. "But it requires a leap of faith."

His expression was unreadable. Entirely serious—grave even. Then the corner of his mouth turned into the slightest of bemused smiles, and he said, "Wish me luck."

Cyrus flashed her a quick wink of his eye. Half a heartbeat later, he'd vaulted feet first over the 5th-floor railing and plummeted toward the unforgiving tile floor 80 feet below.

Feedback

Thank you for reading "Surviving Origin, Part 1." I hope you've had as much fun reading it as I've had writing it. If you did, you can show your support by posting a review with your online retailer. Those reviews make a big difference to new readers and are a definite aid when it comes to spreading the word about my work. Just a brief statement explaining what you enjoyed is all it takes.

Your time and effort are sincerely appreciated.

Thank you!

—Xander Weaver

Acknowledgments

Some believe that writing is a solitary endeavor, the result of a single author slaving over a keyboard until the story that needs telling has been told in its entirety, but this has never been the case for me. I do my best when receiving feedback and input from trusted friends and colleagues. I'm fortunate to have the friendship and support of some very talented people.

As in the past, I'm also fortunate to have a support team of fact-checkers, proofreaders, and subject matter experts who raise the quality of my work. For both their time and effort, I want to give special thanks to Terri and Wayne Manke. My generous beta readers include Dan Barbier, Rian Martin, and Becki Tapia Laurent. Jamie Dresser, in particular, championed this book from its roughest draft through to its final proof—truly a level of support that goes above and beyond. He read this manuscript more times than anyone, tenacious in his will to see it in print.

With friends and colleagues like these, the writing process is anything but solitary. I am not just fortunate, but deeply grateful to know the true meaning of "friendship."

The cover art for *Surviving Origin Part 1* and *Part 2* was thanks to the talented work of Paramita Bhattacharjee at https://www.creativeparamita.com.

Join My List

Newsletter:

Want to hear about the latest book release, contests, and giveaways?

Join the newsletter:

XanderWeaver.com/newsletter

About the Author

Thank you for reading *Surviving Origin*. This is the fifth book in the "Cyrus Cooper" series.

As is my way, this story is a mix of thriller, espionage, and science fiction. Like many authors, I am first a reader at heart. I write the genre of stories I *want* to read—that I *love* to read. I desire action, mystery, and suspense—I want to be thrilled! A book should make me think, even while taking me on a wild ride that sticks with me long after the tale is finished. Learning things along the way is a great deal of fun, but at the core of it all, I thrive on characters. Whether I love them or hate them, the greatest characters ever written are those that spark an emotional response that makes reading, and writing, fun.

If you would like to be notified of future book releases in advance, I welcome you to join my newsletter at: www.XanderWeaver.com. Rest assured, your personal information will never be sold or traded.

While I'm working on the next thrill ride, I frequently post updates to Facebook (Weaver.Books) and Twitter (@XanderWeaver). Please follow the progress and join in the fun!

Other Books

Cyrus Cooper Series:

Book One: Dangerous Minds

Book Two: Rogue Faction Part 1

Book Three: Rogue Faction Part 2

Book Four: Halon Seven

Book Six: Surviving Origin Part 2

Black Rock Series:

Black Rock: The Rising - Death Curse

For more information, please visit:

www.XanderWeaver.com

www.ingramcontent.com/pod-product-compliance
Lightning Source LLC
Chambersburg PA
CBHW030546020726
47494CB00005B/1499